Adulting

Praise for Four Women & The Appeal of Ebony Jones

"The characters may be fictional, but the problems are real and relevant in this period of #SurvivingRKelly and #BlackLivesMatter. The issues the women in this book face are not exclusive to Black communities but it does challenge the notion of people not taking the pain experienced by Black women to be serious."

— REWRITE London

"It's a sobering and chilling story . . . this book will make you see the world through the eyes of at least one of these black women — and it's a different world, indeed."

— *Creative Loafing Tampa*

"Williams . . . places her readers inside the very complex contemporary lives her characters lead: from reformed-ish parents to the intricacies of female friendships in the workplace. In this, it's also a deeply human commentary on race, policing and justice in America."

— *Folio Weekly*

"Williams exhibits her ambitious nature by the subject matter she chose to tackle in her debut novel, which includes domestic violence, sexual abuse, bigotry, and the abuse of power."

— Cultural Council of Greater Jacksonville

Also By Nikesha Elise Williams

Four Women
The Appeal of Ebony Jones
Love Never Fails

TED Talks

Pregnancy is Inconvenient — TEDxFSU (March 2018)
Representation Matters — TEDxFSCJ (April 2018)

Adulting

Nikesha Elise Williams

Copyright © 2019 by Nikesha Elise Williams

Library of Congress Cataloging-In-Publication Data

Williams, Nikesha Elise.
        Adulting/Nikesha Elise Williams

        ISBN 978-1-7335848-2-1

To all the women, in all my group chats, that hold me up, hold me down, pray, prophesy, lay hands, and then some . . . this is for you.

Contents

Part 1

A Housewarming, A Wedding, and a Baby Shower

Then the Lord answered me and said:
> "Write the vision
> And make it plain on tablets,
> That he may run who reads it."
> — Habakkuk 2:2 (NKJV)

1.

#TylersTietheKnot

Rushing. I'm always rushing. That's because I'm always running late. Even at work where my life is ruled by the clock, I'm still not in place, on set, exactly when I'm supposed to be. It's not that I set out to be late on purpose. It's not even that I'm trying to be trendy by being casually late, so as to not seem so thirsty that I'm the first one to arrive. And I for damn sure am not out here trying to perpetuate the stereotype of CPT. Even my coworkers, the white ones especially, think it's okay to say that to me if I walk in the conference room late.

"Oh, Naomi, you're on CP time today, aren't you?"

How about no. First of all, stop clocking me. Secondly, do you realize that stands for colored people? Like, just because you don't call me a nigger doesn't mean it's okay if you call me colored—even if it is in an acronym. That's off limits for you too. Reappropriation. Reclamation. All of that. But then if I say that out loud it's going to be a problem.

"Why are you bringing race into this?"

"We were just joking."

"Naomi, why are you so sensitive?"

It would be a problem. And heaven forbid I try to use any of my real-life experiences in this world on the show. The show may be called "Naomi Tonight," but it's less and less about me and more and more about ratings, and viewers, and everybody else's opinion except mine. Hell, my associate producer damn near has more say over the show than I do, and it's my name and face all over the TV. It might say executive producer in my contract, but they for damn sure don't treat me like one. Probably because of what happened with Dawn. She ran circles around them, did what she wanted to do, and when she was ready, she bounced out to Atlanta to live her best life with her name, her show, and everything else still intact. For the few months I worked with her, all I have to show for it is this damn Post-It note she gave me. And she had the nerve to have it matted and framed.

Red ink on yellow paper. "Know yourself. Know your enemies."

I said, "Thank you," because what else was I supposed to say? Question the great Dawn Anthony. Nah. Doubt it. She's got that Oprah anointing. At this point, I'm just trying to get my post R. Kelly interview Gayle on. So, I took the Post-It note with the cryptic message and put it on the desk in my cubicle. Then when they gave me my own show, I put it in my office. The office that used to be hers. And now that I've bought this house, it's one of the few things I've unpacked. I brought it home from work last night and set it on the floor in the middle of what will eventually be my vision room.

And that's why I'm late. I was trying to unpack some more of my house before the housewarming tomorrow. But as my life usually goes, I'm overbooked, overextended, and I have too much to do and not enough time. If this ain't the busiest weekend, I don't know what is. Today it's Lexington's wedding and tomorrow it's Tarren's baby shower, and then my housewarming. All social events where coworkers will be present. That's why I'm standing in the bathroom trying to decide whether or not to keep the conversation short and wear my wig, or let them see these sister locs I had installed three weeks ago, because hell, I wasn't doing anything else with my natural hair. Might as well loc it up.

There are more than one hundred tinily, single-strand twisted, honey brown and blond locs of hair framing my face in a fluffy bob. I took them out of the cornrows I had in to make sure my wig fit securely without too many lumps and bumps, and now they're fluffy and crinkly and giving me complete life in this mirror. In any mirror really. Not that there are many in the townhouse. At least not yet. Just the ones in the bathrooms, though I only ever look in the one in my room; because well, it's mine. It's all mine, and even that feels weird. Every room, every bathroom, every inch, nook and cranny is all mine, including this master suite. Honestly, this en suite in my bedroom is what sold the house for me. Big mirror with sky lights, makeup lights, and natural light from the window overlooking the pond and the community park . . . and don't let me add my ring light. It gets brighter and is more high definition in here than anything the invisible man could have siphoned off using incandescents. When I walked in this bathroom for the first time two months ago and hit all the lights, the sun was just right, and it was enough for me to say, "Sold," even though the house is a strong fifty-thousand dollars over my budget. But a girl's got to be comfortable, right?

Right.

I told my mother that on the phone last month when I finally got my closing date. The supposedly wonderful and understanding psychotherapist that she is, didn't see it that way. Her only words of wisdom, support, encouragement, whatever you want to call it, were, "You better find another job to help you pay for that house so you don't go broke, fall into foreclosure, file bankruptcy, and ruin your credit."

"I'm trying to keep up with the Joneses," I said before she could say it to me.

"I know, you are. I don't know why you didn't get a condo."

"Because I wanted a house," I answered her.

"But you can't afford it."

"And if I stay on the phone with you, I won't be able to afford my phone bill."

I resisted the urge to hang up the phone on her then. So much for the trained counselor who's nurtured people back from the brink of suicide. All I get is her cold shoulder and condemnation.

My daddy, on the other hand, he loved the place when he saw it on FaceTime. His only concern was who was going to cut the grass in my yard. I didn't know when he asked me last night and I still don't know now. I don't even have time to think about it. I need to leave so I don't miss Lexington's walk down the aisle. I know her wedding isn't starting on time, because no wedding I've ever been to ever has; but that doesn't mean I need to be an hour late because I'm playing in the mirror.

Locs, lashes, red lips, dark brown brows. That's about as much as they're getting out of me today. I don't need a bunch of cake on my face if I'm not on TV. Phones on cameras have gotten better, but they ain't that good. I just hope nobody trips out about my hair. Or this outfit. At its core it's a simple wrap dress, only in African print. Orange, red, blue, black, and white weaved and woven together to cinch this waist, fit this frame, skim these hips, float off this booty, and make my skin complexion pop.

I call it the caramel-colored struggle.

I'm not so dark that I can throw on any color and just bask in the glory of melanated radiance. And I'm not so light that I'm forced strictly into bright colors, with deep pigment so that I'm not washed out. This middle brown, between raw honey and a cinnamon stick, is a little tricky. Too many earth tones and I'm washed out. Too many reds and oranges, and I'm washed out. Pinks and purples, and sunflower yellows are usually my thing, but this dress has just enough breakup in the orange that I can wear it and not have it wear me.

Now, where are my shoes? Hopefully the pumps I want are at the top of the box in the closet and not the bottom. It doesn't matter. It's easier to dump them, out on the floor anyway since they will ultimately end up on the shoe rack I bought from Ikea. One thing the Swedes know for sure is how to organize a closet. And make a good meatball. I really didn't think Ikea would make that big a difference in Jacksonville; but the Ikea effect is real. I'm a believer. I can never go in there and just leave out with the one thing I went in for. It's worse than Target. But at least I'm saving money.

I told that to my mom too, but of course, she didn't see it that way.

"Why would you spend money on something you know you're going to have to buy again?" She asked me last night on the phone. "You know that stuff is cheap and doesn't last."

I laid on the floor in my closet, rolling my eyes at the phone that laid face up beside me so all she could see was the ceiling and not my face, as I tried to brush off her criticizing question, as if it didn't bother me.

When I was ready, and tired of hearing her breathe and wait for my answer, I picked up the phone and finally said, "Yeah, but I don't plan on having many visitors to break up what I bought, so I plan on it lasting a while."

"It's still a waste of money."

That was the last negative comment I could take. I got off the phone. That's why I call my parents separately. They may live in the same house, but that doesn't mean I have to talk to them at the same time when they each have their own cell phones. I call my mom and she criticizes. I call my daddy and he compliments. That's why I saved him for last. And that's why I don't plan on moving back to New Orleans no time soon. Aside from the fact my whole family lives there and thought it was okay to show up when I was shooting a story because they saw where I was from my Twitter feed, I just needed something different and away from my mom.

Jacksonville has been good to me. Started off reporting and I got my own show just a few months later. Boyce wasn't paying me lip service in my interview when he said he planned to put my name and my face on a billboard within my first year. He even said I could break my contract if that didn't happen. Big talk from a news director. I thought he was playing, or just trying to negotiate me with perks so I didn't ask for more money, more vacation days, and more all-expenses-paid conferences. But he knew Dawn wasn't staying when he brought me in to shadow her. Now here I am four years later with everything I negotiated for, and I still don't think it's enough. Not with this new house anyway.

There are my shoes.

Blue, patent leather, chunky gold spikes on the heel. The hair is fluffy, my face demure, the dress bold, and the heels fierce. I will definitely make a statement when I walk in. Which is the point. There's no ring on my finger and no baby on my hip. In fact, I'm only wearing studs to this wedding, and chunky wooden bracelets, so that the men know they can feel free to dress me in diamonds. It may sound superficial, but you have to speak what you want into existence, right?

Right.

Now where are my keys?

I think I left them downstairs on the island in the kitchen. It's the only surface I didn't clutter with bags, and boxes of stuff. Mostly because I don't have a lot of kitchen stuff. I can cook, I just don't. For what? It's just me. It's just as easy to eat out as it is to buy the same amount in groceries. After being behind a computer, and then on set all day, the last thing I want to do when I come home is stand behind a stove and wait to eat, when there's all manner of deliciousness down a few blocks and around a few corners.

Bartram Park has every fast food restaurant I could want, every cuisine I could imagine, a grocery store, if I ever do get in the mood to cook, a liquor store I frequent weekly, and the convenience of being five minutes away. It's the reason I moved here; even if it is a good thirty sometimes forty minutes from the station, depending upon how many people have wrecked on I-95. But it's so worth it. As soon as I cross the bridge and I hit the highway heading home, it's like everything: all the death, the destruction, the gore, the blood, the guts, the negativity, the policies, I leave it all behind in the building dedicated to telling the truth, giving the facts, and the occasional viral video, even if noone ever asked for it.

That's my job. Read the words on the screen. Cultivate the conversation. Curate the water cooler quips. Inform the community.

Today, I will be doing none of that. Today, I will just be Naomi. Not Nine News Now anchor Naomi Grace. Not daughter, cousin, sister, Naomi Jean. Just Naomi. A solo guest at the wedding of Lexington Holcomb and Derrick Tyler. She didn't even bother to offer me a plus one on the invitation, because she knew good and well I didn't need it. I'm just happy to see her get married. At least someone is getting loved on around here. Hopefully, it won't take me too long to get to the venue. St. Augustine isn't that far, but on a Saturday night, 95 is unpredictable.

As long as I get to see them say their vows to each other, I'm good. That's the best part of any wedding to me; when the bride and groom start talking to one another like the rest of us aren't listening, witnessing their love and commitment to each other. At every wedding I've been to, I love hearing what the groom says the most. The brides are always expected to cry and be emotional and use poetry and pretty words to express their undying love for their partner, lover, and best friend. Blah, blah, blah. It's sweet, but it's expected. I wait for when it's the groom's turn to speak. Some grooms forget how to use their mouths and formulate words because they've never seen the woman they've asked to be their wife, look so good. It's amazing what a white dress can do. And then some grooms come prepared with stories, anecdotes, and poems of their own, so they don't get tongue tied. Those are my favorites. It's in those moments that you can really see how much the two people love each other. I prefer it to when people just repeat the standard vows from the priest or pastor or use the text from the Bible. I mean, Jesus and the prophets said good stuff, but being original doesn't hurt.

I hope Derrick is original.

We really don't know much about him except, he's the reason Lexington can't go to Cuba with Jennifer, Diedre, and I on Monday. But hey, life happens. She met him and was apparently swept off her feet to go from dating to engaged to married in a matter of nine months. And I know she's not pregnant as little as she is. Ain't no shotgun weddings around here. I just hope I'm not too late.

"Where can I park?" I ask myself as I drive around looking for a spot.

Thank God for the valet's directing people into this little dirt and gravel lot, off in the cut. Trying to find street parking here is horrible. I know all the old, tight roads are what make St. Augustine, St. Augustine, the nation's oldest city, but that doesn't mean it can't add some modern influences and upgrades to make visiting here something I'd want to do again.

"Ok, Naomi, don't break your ankles trying to get to the door."

That's the only thing about heels and old cities. They don't go together. Especially in this gravel lot. The gravel, the grass, the cobble stones, none of that is made for striding in stilettos, trying to show off these legs and these thighs and this booty. That's the only reason we women go through this torture of jamming our feet into pointy-toed soles, six inches off the ground. It's all in the name of men, because as soon as I sit down, I'm going to slip the backs of these pumps off of my heels, slide my toes back and let them breathe.

"Ooh, this venue is cute. Come through River House with the fancy four-tiered fountain and the white column facade for the entry way."

I know Lexington's parents broke the bank for this place. It looks expensive with these oversized mahogany doors, and they have the nerve to have a "D" and "L" in golden letters hanging from the black iron bars of the door. I hope the inside is as exquisitely and visually enticing as the outside. I've been to some weddings where only the outer decor is pretty, and then the inside, the carpet smells waterlogged and moldy, the paint is peeling, and the food is dry, bland, and nasty. Here's to hoping tonight won't be like that.

Music is the first thing I hear walking inside the door, and then I smell an assortment of potpourri. The interior is as beautiful as the exterior, with thick, brown and tan paisley print carpet that is so freshly vacuumed, I can still see the lines. The white paint of the crown moldings glow beneath the dimmed, yellow lighting. I follow the signs that read "Tyler Wedding" in a large calligraphy script, to the back patio of the building. The sound of a violin and a harp gets louder as I go until I'm on the covered back patio, looking out at rows of seated guests facing the river of a wedding already in progress.

The flower girl is walking down the aisle throwing red, white, and pink rose petals on top of the white runner covering the slate gray, stone pavers on the ground. Amid the crowd of guests I see Jennifer and Diedre, and the empty seat I assume they were holding for me. As much as I want to take my seat beside them, I know better than to try to sneak in now. If my face doesn't bring unwanted attention my way, this outfit surely will. None of what I have on blends in with the bridesmaids or the groomsmen who are walking down the aisle arm in arm. The men are in tuxes and the ladies are in pea green, ankle length dresses with layer upon layer of chiffon, floating atop what appears to be a satin skirt. A high, thigh slit up the left leg adds a hint of sexiness to the crew that is supposed to act as an accessory to the bride.

I watch Jennifer pat her bra-strap length twist out as Diedre cranes her arms to snap pictures toward where the bridal party is making their way down the aisle. They have been my rock since I first moved here. Jennifer is my producer. She was an associate producer on Dawn's show but got promoted when Dawn took Kelly, the former producer of the eight o'clock hour, with her to Atlanta. That's how you know you have pull as an anchor, when the network just makes a spot for your own producer like they don't already have qualified people working there. Diedre came along about two years ago. First as an intern, because she was still in school. After she graduated, Boyce gave her the title of Associate Producer, which is what she had been all along, but as an intern, he didn't have to put her on the payroll. Lexington was hired before Diedre as a morning reporter, but she was soon moved to the evening shift when they saw she was a waste of talent in the morning, when there's nothing but shootings and car crashes to cover.

The three of them have helped me get through many a day since I started. Diedre reminds me to not be so cynically ambivalent by way of her sheer youthfulness, while Jennifer keeps me in check and from becoming too safe. She always pushes me to keep my edge and tell the stories I want to tell, even though that rarely happens. And Lexington, my dear, sweet, getting ready to walk down the aisle at any moment Lexington, she knows what it is to live this life in front of the camera. This life where people think they know you but they don't, they have access to you, so you can never really be yourself unless you're out of the country; and sometimes not even then, because the News On app makes every local small, medium, or large size market anchor available to be watched, reviewed, and critiqued, with a tap and a swipe.

It's going to suck that she can't go to Cuba with us Monday, but I guess a honeymoon is a good excuse.

The crowd stands up to the opening chords of "Here Comes the Bride" like trained dogs. Guests on both sides of the aisle face the center and turn their heads my way, as they wait to see Lexington come from the center doors that open onto the patio where I'm standing. Try as I might to go unnoticed, it never works out in my favor. I see Jennifer and Diedre smirking at me as they watch and wait for Lexington to walk out. I would shrink to make myself small and take some of this unwanted attention away from me, but that defeats the purpose of me wearing this dress and leaving my wig at home.

All eyes turn to Lexington as she comes out of the doorway. Almost all eyes. I see Boyce staring at me in wonder and confusion. It's the wide-eyed, deer-in-headlights look white people get when they see something they recognize, but they know something is different. His eyes bulge as he tries to place what is different about me while trying not to get caught staring. I look at him staring at me until he can feel the heat from my gaze. His jowly face immediately flushes red from his chin to the top of his half-bald head. He runs his hands over his dome, down his bulbous stomach stressing every inch of the elastic in his suspenders, before shoving them into his pockets. He turns his gaze little by little, so as to not be so obvious that he knows he's been caught looking at me too long.

I give him a break and turn my gaze toward Lexington. She is breathtaking in her white Amsale gown. When she first described it to me, I admit, I couldn't see it. We were standing in the newsroom after my show as she was writing her story for the eleven o'clock newscast, when I asked her how the wedding planning was going.

"I found a dress," she squealed, turning away from the computer screen at her desk in a shared quad of cubicles.

"What does it look like?" I asked, indulging her excitement.

"It's like a strapless tuxedo on top, and Cinderella underneath," she said.

I smiled and nodded because my imagination could not do the work for me.

"Let me pull it up for you," Lexington insisted, quickly opening and closing windows on her computer screen to get to the Internet.

"No," I said. "Don't worry about it. I'll see it on your big day."

She tried over and over again to show it to me, but I declined. Wedding dresses have never really been my thing.

Weddings either. But since I'm at that stage in life when all of my friends and acquaintances are getting married and having babies, I put on a face like I do any other day of the week, and play pretend in their fairytale. The only part that's bearable, that makes the whole ordeal worth my time, are the vows. I'm indifferent to weddings, but I'm still a sucker for a good love story.

Today I don't have to play very hard. If at all. Lexington is bespoke. Even Derrick is speechless. He stares at her unveiled face in the gown that is both deeply feminine and structurally masculine. The plunging sweetheart neckline gives him peeping access to what's beneath the corseted bodice. A bow falls away from one of her hips, a brooch sparkles on the other, and the asymmetrical cut of the top skirt gives her every angle of any model to ever walk a runway. Her lotioned, cocoa skin is luminescent beneath the fading sunlight and the glow of the gown.

I stay standing on the porch well after everyone has sat back down. In my bare feet, and on my tip toes, I force my senses to work overtime so that I see and hear everything. Lexington and Derrick are front and center beneath the white, lattice archway. Four bridesmaids and four groomsmen trail away from them like the sides of an equilateral triangle. The Matanzas river sparkles behind them. It's a marked difference from the dirty, brackish brown water of the St. Johns Jacksonville is known for. When it sparkles blue, it is only a reflection of the sky.

"The bride and groom have prepared their own vows for one another," the celebrant says.

Lexington and Derrick have a woman performing their wedding. Hazel skin and silver hair dressed in a cream robe. Her voice is rich and harmonious, like a woman who got tired of singing solos in the choir and longed for her own pulpit to preach from. She hands the microphone to Lexington first. Ever the reporter, she takes it naturally and goes into a spiel about her love for her Love with the ease of an adlibbed live shot. She doesn't flinch, stumble or cry. She is poised and rehearsed, like she's been standing in front of her mirror memorizing her words and running her lines for this moment, when she knows multiple cameras will be on her to capture the declaration of her undying commitment.

This should go on her resume tape.

"And, Derrick, it is your turn," the grandmotherly celebrant says.

He takes the microphone from her, and looks from her to the audience before speaking.

"Man, I wish she didn't do so good giving her vows," he says.

Me and the rest of the crowd chuckle with knowing laughter. Derrick waits until it passes before continuing.

He says, "But that's, Lexy. Always prepared. Always ready. Always doing good. Even when we met, she was just trying to do good. As a first responder that's usually my job. As a firefighter the whole point of my job is to do good, and at the very least, stop the bad from getting worse. We usually see people like Lexy, the media, as sycophantic, feckless, emotionless vampires, but not Lexy. I don't know if she's told y'all, but we met at the scene of a house fire. Instead of coming up to me with her camera already rolling in my face, she approached me by herself. She didn't have her phone out, or a note pad, or a pen or anything. She just walked up and said, "Excuse me," and asked me if everyone inside was okay. My first thought was, "Wow, this girl really cares." The house was empty, so I told her, "Yeah," and kept heading back to the truck. The next thing I know, she was standing beside me offering me a bottle of water. The rest of the night while the guys doused the few lingering hot spots, I watched her work. I watched how she approached neighbors, and eventually the family. It was the same way she approached me, no pretense, and without the camera. Lexington Janice Holcomb, that's what I love about you. You lead with your heart. Your big, loving heart that just wants to make sure everyone, and everything, is okay. And from the day we met, that's all I've wanted to do for you. To make sure that you're better than okay. That you're better than good; and as your husband, I promise to do that every day of our lives. I can't wait for you to be my wife."

Applause resounds across the outdoor patio space. My hands clap incessantly, and my tears flow freely. I can see why Lexington didn't tell us much about him after they met. I wouldn't want anyone to know anything about him, either, if he was my man. I hope he came in a box set with a twin or cousin or even a young uncle, because they don't make them like him anymore.

This is the reason I come to weddings. The vows of the groom, when they say their own, they never disappoint. I hope my husband, if I ever get a husband, is as in love with me as Derrick is with Lexington. Or even as in love as my daddy is with my mama, because I know she can grate a last nerve.

Most people come to weddings to see the kiss; and if it's a black wedding, to see who lands first after jumping the broom. Legend has it that whoever lands first runs the relationship, but people, black people especially, make up a saying about anything. Eye twitches, hands itching, there's a saying for some of the most benign and innocuous things, right down to the kiss at weddings, even though it's the vows that show the true character of the couple and the staying power of the relationship. I can tell that if ever Lexington gets tired of married life, or feels like she's growing apart, Derrick will be the one to grow closer. From his vows, I don't see divorce in his future; and for that matter, hers either.

"You may now kiss the bride," the celebrant says.

I look down at the white painted, wood patio as I shove my feet back into my shoes. I don't know why people at weddings get off on gawking at other people kiss. That's a private moment that we shouldn't be privy to, but are because of tradition. I don't need to see all that. Whether they peck or tongue each other down, before God and a few of his creations, is not my business.

"I present to you, Mr. and Mrs. Derrick Tyler."

Derrick and Lexington walk down the aisle as their guests file out from their seats to meet them in front of the patio. I walk down the steps and take my time pressing through the crowd of congratulatory family members, friends, and coworkers.

"Congratulations," I say, squeezing her shoulder once I reach the front of the dispersing crowd.

"Thank you, thank you, thank you," she squeals, reaching out her arms.

"You're welcome. Your dress is gorgeous."

"You see it now?"

"Well, obviously."

"Why were you sitting up there?" Lexington asks.

"I got here right as your niece was walking out with the flowers and I didn't want to interrupt the procession."

"Oh, okay," Lexington says. "You were the first thing I saw, but I couldn't say anything to you. Um, ma'am, these locs are gorgeous."

"Thank you."

"When did you do this?"

"Almost a month ago."

"Has Boyce seen you?"

"When everyone turned to look at you, he saw me. So, did everyone else, but he definitely saw me."

"Has he said anything to you yet?"

"Not yet."

"Well, here he comes," Lexington says. "I'm going to greet the other guests. You better see if Jennifer and Diedre can save you."

Lexington stalks off to another area of the property, leaving Derrick behind. I extend my hand and say, "I'm Naomi."

"Nice to meet you, Naomi." We shake.

"Congratulations to you. I'm happy for you guys."

"Thank you. Now where's my wife?"

Derrick walks from the bottom of the steps toward the river where Lexington stands taking pictures along the concrete, and iron-gated dock that drifts off into the water.

"He is so sprung," Jennifer says.

I turn around to face her and Diedre. Jennifer's burgundy sheath dress hugs her little frame, emphasizing her tiny waist. Mascara, eyeliner and lipstick the same color as her dress, is the only makeup she has on her clear, licorice-colored skin.

"I think it's cute," I say. "He loves her. Every woman deserves that."

"I'm sorry, Jennifer," Diedre says. "Who is this imposter and what has she done with our friend Naomi."

"Ha, ha, ha," I say, rolling my eyes.

"I thought you hated weddings," Diedre says.

"I never said I hated weddings. I just said they weren't my thing."

"That's the nice way of saying you hate weddings."

"Whatever?"

"Why didn't you come sit with us?" Jennifer asks.

"Got here too late."

"I thought you weren't coming, until I turned around and saw you back here looking like the embodiment of Serengeti couture."

"Thank you," I say through laughter. "Let's get a drink. The bar is open."

I usher Jennifer and Diedre with me toward the bar on the patio where I sat. Our timing is just a step ahead of Boyce, who is still trying to get to me through the throngs of people who stop and make conversation at any and every point in his path, frustrating his mission to inevitably question me about my hair, and whether he needs to remind me that my image, in all of its wigged fakeness, belongs to the station.

"So, are you guys packed?" I ask Jennifer and Diedre, watching Boyce from the corner of my eye.

"I'm trying to narrow down my outfit choices so they all fit in the one carryon bag," Jennifer says.

"Same," Diedre says. "Picking just two pairs of shoes to wear day and night for the five days is going to be difficult."

"What about you?" Jennifer asks.

"I will pack when I find my suitcase," I answer.

"That's right, you moved this week," Diedre says. "I can't wait to see your place tomorrow."

"Me either. When I sent out the invitations for the housewarming, I thought I would have closed and been in the house for at least a week by now."

"I told you don't send out those invitations until after you closed," Jennifer says. "But you don't listen."

"I'm sorry, Diedre, do you hear that?"

"Hear what?"

"That incessant drone of Miss Know It All over here," I say, nodding toward Jennifer. "She must think I asked for her opinion about when to have my housewarming."

"Don't get bitchy because you know I'm right."

"I swear you're worse than my mother. You just love to rub noses in shit."

Jennifer says, "I know you meant that as an insult. But I'll take it as a compliment. I love your mother."

"That's because you don't know her."

"Malibu and pineapple, please," Diedre says, reaching the front of the bar line. "Naomi, do you need help unpacking before tomorrow?"

"Yes."

"I'll help you. Just tell me what time and send me the address."

"Tomorrow morning before Tarren's baby shower. The address is on your invitation."

"Jack and coke," Jennifer says to the bartender.

I don't ask for her help and she doesn't offer. That's fine with me. I love Jennifer. She's a good producer. And most of the time she's a good friend, but she's set in her ways. When she feels like something is rushed, or isn't being done right, or isn't following her chosen course of advice, she becomes obstinate and self-righteous. I don't need her sanctimonious attitude funking up my space with her bad vibes, while I'm trying to set a specific mood and atmosphere for what I want to come home to. I don't really know how to Feng Shui, but I'm gonna damn sure try to get it as close to energetically balanced as possible.

I'd rather have Diedre anyway. She's young and gullible. She's still got a naiveté about life that you don't find in people at or on the other side of thirty. She's barely twenty-five. She's down to live her best life, even if that means it's on credit, or vicariously through others. She hasn't yet gotten to the place where she's questioning herself, her life, her passion or her purpose. She's at a point now where she's just trying to establish a consistent enough routine so that she's not fired or doesn't become delinquent on bills. Her burdenless buoyancy is evident in everything about her, from her jet-black hair with the midnight blue highlights to her halter-neck, liquid legging jumpsuit, paired with a black waist cape that billows out into a train with different shades of blue printed on the inner side of the material. Even her makeup is fun with blue eyeliner instead of black, and a smoky eye in red, instead of muted off-black, silver and gray. She is a nubile ingenue on the cusp of figuring out this life thing is what you make it, and whom you make it with. Her help will be refreshing.

"Ma'am, what can I get for you?" The bartender asks.

"Bourbon neat," I say. "Knob Creek if you have it."

"That's a drink that'll put hair on your chest."

I purse my lips in a subdued smile, but don't turn around. It is Boyce. Directly behind me, baiting me to turn around with his subtle sexism. I wait for my drink using my periphery to see Jennifer and Diedre more than an arm's distance away, huddled together, sipping from straws, waiting to see what might go down between the anchor with the new hair, and the head manager in charge who makes decisions by numbers, studies, and surveys, even if it is against his personal wishes.

"Will that be all for you?" The bartender asks me.

"No," I say. "I'd like a few cherries, please. Three on a toothpick would be great, thanks."

The brown-faced bartender bobs up and down behind the bar searching for plastic gloves. I watch him as he moves, dabbing sweat from his brow with the back of his long-sleeved arm. I can see the perspiring water beads on his scalp through his strands of short and spiky, jet black hair. I imagine the sweat on his body is equivalent to what is beading on the top of Boyce's head as he matches my recalcitrance with his own silent insolence, waiting for me to turn around so he can tell me, in his way, that my hair is not appropriate for being on air.

"Is this all for you, ma'am?" The bartender asks as he slides the third cherry on the toothpick.

"Yes. Thank you, Javier." I say, reading the name tag pinned to the left corner of his uniform.

"Have a good day ma'am."

"I will.

"Mr. Butler," I say, finally turning to look at Boyce, "the bar is all yours."

"Rum and coke," Boyce barks at the bartender without looking at him. "I almost didn't recognize you," he says, staring at me from head to toe. "You look so different."

"Just call me a chameleon."

"And your hair . . . What did you do?"

"I know. I look like a real black girl now. Have a good one. I'm going to go inside and find my table."

I ignore his blushing red face and the agape, oblong shapes Jennifer and Diedre have contorted their mouths into. I sip my drink and breeze by all the mingling guests until I get inside the doorway to the ballroom where dinner will be served, toasts will be made, and drinking and dancing will be done. Jennifer and Diedre catch up to me as I sign the guest book. I can feel their eyes burning through my wrap dress, but I take my time adding embellishments and flourishes to my name that I haven't done since I first learned to write in cursive in third grade.

"Shall we find our table?" I ask turning around.

"Are we not going to talk about how you just gave me all the life by shading the hell out of Boyce?" Diedre asks.

"That wasn't shade. It's true. I do look like a real black girl now. Now people don't have to squint and wonder what I am when they look at me. They can see these nappy roots and know."

"Only if they see you off air," Jennifer says. "Otherwise, they're going to see your blonde wig and keep on guessing that you're something exotic."

"That's not my problem."

"We're at table ten," Diedre says, looking at the seating chart next to the guest book. "Everybody from the station is too."

"Including Boyce?"

"Yes, ma'am."

"Then I'm going to go."

"Why, you just got here?" Jennifer asks.

"Because I don't want to spend the rest of my evening with him staring at me, trying to ask rude questions without being rude."

"I thought we were all going to try to catch the bouquet together," Diedre says.

"You still can. I'm going home."

"So much for having husbands next year," Diedre says.

"I learned that tale about bouquets and husbands was a lie about eight weddings ago, but you have fun. Don't let me stop you from dreaming."

"And just like that, you're out?" Jennifer asks.

"I've learned not to arrive too soon or stay too late. It's always good to leave right before you wear out your welcome."

"Okay, Diva. I'll remember that tomorrow at your housewarming," Jennifer says.

"As you should."

I set my empty drink on the white linen table cloth at the space I won't be occupying, pull out the toothpick of cherries, and walk out of the ballroom. I wave at Jennifer and Diedre and make my way back outside on the patio. Lexington, Derrick, and the wedding party are still taking pictures. I move toward them ignoring Boyce, who's sitting in a chair on the patio with his drink propped on his belly.

I don't know what it is about weddings, but they always seem to inspire deep introspection. I'm glad for the excuse to escape. As much as I don't want to spend my time sitting in the vicinity of Boyce and coworkers talking about my hair, and work, and news related topics, I also don't want to spend my time drinking away my thoughts about the lack of husband material anywhere in my orbit. I don't want to be coaxed into thinking about Aaron who had me believing one thing, while he was doing another. I don't want to watch Lexington and Derrick move around as if they are the only two people in the room, make their rounds so as not to be rude to guests, and then find each other with a look, a glance, a head nod, or a wrinkle of their nose. I don't want to sit and be reminded of what I don't have, and what may or may not be on my horizon. I may never get married. I may never have children. I don't even know if I want those things. But at weddings, even people like me, secure and assured in who I am, hear insecurity as loud as a ringing bell about what life milestones we didn't prioritize properly.

Ugh. Lexington is beautiful.

"Hey, pretty lady," I say, walking up to stand by the photographer.

"Hey Naomi. Wassup."

"I just wanted to tell you that I'm getting ready to leave."

"So soon?"

"Yeah," I say, trying to evoke my own disappointment, "I have a lot to do in the house before the housewarming tomorrow."

"That's right," Lexington says. Her disappointment in my absence is more believable than my lie. "Well, I'm sorry to miss it, but I hope everything goes well," she says.

"Don't worry about it. You'll be on your honeymoon, having hot sex, with a man who adores you. You can always come by when you get back."

"I'll hold you to it."

"Sorry to hold you guys up," I say, backing away from the photographer and the wedding party.

They wave their goodbyes and I wave mine, as I walk away from the river and through the venue. I pass some of the workers as they carry cardboard cutouts of Facebook and Instagram photo booth posts with the suggested hashtags for the wedding already written on the boards. #Tylerstietheknot and #DelexWedding are how Derrick and Lexington are choosing to archive their love for all their friends and followers who were not invited. I rush through the front doors with the gold-plated initials draped over them and pick up my pace as I cross over stone pavers, grass, cobble stones, and gravel to get to my car.

2.

In My Feelings

I don't know what it is, but I've always liked the drive home from a place, more than I've ever liked the drive going somewhere. For one, the drive going always seems like it takes forever compared to going home. And since I'm usually running late, the first drive is more stressful. Now I can take my time, relax, listen to the radio, and think about nothing.

Who am I kidding? I wish I could think about nothing. I wish I could think about anything except for Aaron. He's reporting now at NNC. The same station Dawn went to. We were supposed to be a power couple. Taking over New Orleans together. Moving together. Our contracts were synced, our end date was set, and then his agent got him an interview at the mother of cable news and he couldn't say "no," or even, "My girlfriend's really good, can you get her an interview too?" He made no suggestions in my favor. Didn't even tell me about the interview. All he said was, "I got a job." Six months before our contracts expired and he had a job, while I barely had interviews lined up.

"Where?" I asked him.

"NNC," he said.

He didn't stutter. He didn't stumble. He didn't blink or shrink away from telling me. In the living room on his side of his French Quarter adjacent double shotgun, I could see that this job was his way out. Our relationship had plateaued, and he was bored, restless, and wanted out. NNC was his escape route. That was four years ago and the shit still makes me mad. I'm not mad at him for following his career. I'm not even mad he didn't tell me he wanted to break up, and used the job and the distance to do it for him. I've dated other people. Even came close to love, it's just now I have to try. That's why I'm mad. The fact I have to try for love; that shit sucks. Now I have to allow my representative to guide the relationship and not me, because if it doesn't work out, I can't have people throwing salt on my name. At this stage in my life and career, my name is all I have.

My name, and my house.

It's weird saying that. My house. Even with all the street lights and porch lights on in the neighborhood, it's still pretty dark on my block. I appreciate being able to see the moon and the stars, even if it's just for a moment since I'm parking in the garage. The neighbors don't need to know my comings and goings, especially not once they figure out who I am. Hopefully, this hair will keep them confused. At least for a little while.

Home sweet home. Or rather boxes sweet boxes. I might as well unpack. I think I'll start on my vision room first. That should help get Aaron off of my mind. Manifest my future and forget about my past.

It's the first room to the right at the top of the stairs. Since I don't need three bedrooms, I knew when I bought the house I would use one of them for an office space of sorts; not that I do any work at home, but it's the adult thing to have. My mother asked me when I bought the house if I had a designated prayer closet. I laughed because even she doesn't have one of those in her house. But I liked the idea, and since I have the space, I have not just a room for prayer but one to make my dreams come true. Like the inner sanctum of

Aladdin's cave when he found his lamp, this is my room to put my wants into the world and give God anything I can't do myself. Like for starters, take away these thoughts of Aaron so I don't block myself from whatever fine six-foot, chocolate Adam you're sending my way.

I start with everything that needs to be hung on the wall. Three large portraits. Maya. Oprah. Michelle. Together they are mom. Not my mom, but the three I'm always learning something from. Their images will go on the main wall of the room. The one I share with the townhouse on the other side. Beneath them will be my own personal Holy Grail. All eleven thousand, seven-hundred and twenty-four words of the 2011 *The Atlantic*, magnum opus, "All the Single Ladies."

The first time I read the article was right after I met and began dating Aaron. I thought the writer was exaggerating, even though she had solid evidence and statistics to argue her point. After Aaron and I broke up, I reread the article in the midst of my grief that wouldn't let me cry, or eat, or binge bad TV. Instead, I read those nearly twelve thousand words with a new revelation. "If it's hard in these streets for white girls, and they're the standard, then it's a drought out here for anybody darker than alabaster." That day I copied and pasted the article into a blank document on my computer and printed it, and out came twenty typed pages of the most revelatory thing I had read in my life. It became my bible as I moved from New Orleans to Jacksonville, and now from my Riverside apartment to my Bartram townhouse. I didn't have it framed in the apartment, because I didn't have the wall space. Sixteen hundred dollars for a one-bedroom apartment at seven hundred square feet was a lot more than I wanted to pay, but it was worth it. To me anyway. My mother thought it was too much, and I'd be broke then too. Now in the townhouse, my mortgage is only a little higher than my rent, but it's all mine, and these words are going on the wall.

My actual vision boards will go on the back wall of the room. Three large, elementary school display boards hold my vision for love, career and money, and health and faith.

Most people use one board to illustrate the vision for their lives in magazine cutouts, but my dreams are bigger than one quadrant. Instead, I have them broken into three. Framed and matted because if I have a framed and matted Post-It note, everything else should match accordingly.

Other than that, only my five-rung ladder, book shelves are against the walls. Two book end my vision boards, and a third is on the wall shared with the stairwell. That set of shelves holds my "must reads" and "read again" books. Books that my M.O.M. would approve of. Next to that is a small white wooden table. I saw it at the flea market on Beach Boulevard one day while I was walking around bored, before my shift, and picked it up. It looks like it's from a little girl's life-sized tea set, or doll table, but I'm going to use it as an altar. Some purple fabric, a little stone pot of water, a few crystals, a bundle of sage, and my "Precious Moments" Bible I got when I was confirmed, and just like that, Jesus is in the building.

The last thing to add in here is my yoga mat. Not that I actually do yoga, but Five Below had a mat, towel, block, and elastic band for about twenty bucks all together. I have a whole yoga starter kit if, and when, I ever decide to twist myself together in the name of rest and relaxation. Most likely though, I'm going to sit on it while I pretend to meditate. I haven't been successful at that either, but it doesn't require much effort. Just sit on the floor, clear my mind, and forget about Aaron.

He would've loved this house. Filling it with stuff, cooking in it. Hell, we could've even played hide and go freak in here. But this is how it's supposed to be. He's doing his thing in Atlanta; I'm doing mine in Jacksonville. He's on television on a loop, and I have a house, with a vision room, that's done.

Where is my phone?

Right on the stairs where I left it from following my own unwritten house rules. No phone, and no one other than Naomi in the vision room.

I see a group photo I am absent from. The happy couple smile from the center while Jennifer stands beside Lexington, and Diedre beside Derrick. I text back a quick "cute," turn the phone on airplane mode, and walk to my bedroom where I toss it on my unmade bed. It lands face down. I shut out the memories of the party I left as I take my dress off and toss it into the closet. In bra and panties, I move around the second floor organizing what's mine, trying not to edit out Lexington's face in the photo for my own, and putting in Aaron as Derrick.

I work, hanging curtains, folding towels and sheets, fluffing pillows, hiding some toiletries, and displaying others. I work, organizing the second floor, resisting the urge to run to my phone, open my messages, and stare at the picture I'm not in, zooming in on Lexington, trying to find her imperfections to make myself feel better. I refuse to let my inner comments section come to life. I work until all that's left to do is vacuum.

Back in my vision room, I stare at M.O.M. in the darkness. Sitting on my towel-covered yoga mat, the women with smooth brown faces, and varying lines of age, watch over me with wisdom as I brood. My head is against the wall beneath this year's vision for my life. Only three months into the year and already I don't see it happening. One wedding halfway attended and I'm already second-guessing the headless groom taped beside a mirror, so that when I see him, I see me, too, as the bride.

This is why weddings are not my thing. Unless you're the bride, you always end up feeling some kind of way about your life, after the vows are said, the kisses have been kissed, and the bouquets and garters have been thrown. I hate that feeling. After the first wedding Aaron and I attended together, we ended up getting into an argument. That was probably the beginning of the end for us. He was too afraid to say it, and I ignored it and didn't act on my own intuition. Yet here we are. Broken up, hundreds of miles apart, several sets of lovers between us, and I'm sitting alone in a room orchestrated and decorated for vision, and all I can see are the pictures I'm not in, in the places not meant for me.

3.

Baby on Board

"Naomi, why didn't you call me?" Diedre asks as I walk into the multipurpose room of the subdivision in a neighborhood, just three miles from my front door.

"I did a lot last night, since I left the wedding early. Where can I put this?"

"The gift table is up front by where the chair for Tarren is setup." Diedre points.

I follow her finger to the table covered in pink, yellow, and blue tissue paper. Sparkly confetti baby bottles are all over the table. The centerpiece is a four-tiered diaper cake. I set my oversized bag down and sign the guest register.

"Where's Jennifer?" I ask once I get back to Diedre.

"Over there in the corner," Diedre says. "We saved you a seat."

"Thank you," I say.

I follow her along the doorway to the table in the corner where Jennifer is seated.

"Hey, hey, hey," I say.

She opens her arms out to me in a hug and pulls me in close.

Whispering in my ear she says, "Boyce told me to tell you that he loves the new changes you've made with your look, but to tone it down, because he's not ready to shoot new promos."

I pull back from her and glare. She reads the annoyed disbelief in my eyes and matches it with a look of her own before shrugging her shoulders. I know Boyce made his feelings on my hair known to both her and Diedre, if not the entire table, after I left. I also know Diedre handed off the job of telling me to Jennifer. It makes sense. She hasn't learned how to handle uncomfortable work situations yet. It's obvious in our post meetings when she makes a mistake and I have to correct her. Her mistake or not, it's my face that's the mug for her error. Friend or not, work is work, business is business, and my name and image is what people come after when lawsuits are filed, and heads are expected to roll if facts become alternative to the truth.

"What else did Boyce say after I left?" I ask sitting down.

"Nothing really," Diedre says. "At least nothing else about you."

"Good. I like it when people keep my name out their mouth when I'm not present. Where is Tarren?" I ask, looking around the room.

"You know she's been on bed rest," Jennifer says. "They're probably trying to get her together so she doesn't hurt herself or go into early labor."

"I forgot. I know she's been recording those videos of her journey for the mom blog section of the website; I forgot that she hasn't actually been at work reporting."

"I don't see how you could forget," Diedre says. "That's all Lexington has been talking about the last few weeks. She seemed to know more about Tarren's pregnancy than her own wedding."

"Well, that's what happens when you marry the girl's brother," Jennifer says.

"I guess," I say.

"Is that why they did the wedding and baby shower the same weekend?" Diedre asks.

"Probably." I shrug. "Everybody they needed was already coming for one reason, might as well make it two."

"Then, Naomi, what's your excuse?"

Jennifer's accusation hits me and I'm not sure if it's supposed to.

"What do you mean?"

"I mean . . ." She clears her throat. "What's your excuse for adding your housewarming the same weekend we're already jam-packed with stuff to do? You know you could've waited until we came back from Cuba. Or I don't know, next month after you've had a chance to move in, instead of rushing to get a place together and you're still figuring out how to get around in the dark."

"I guess I didn't want to feel left out of the big life events, so I slid my invitation right on in there."

I roll my eyes. It would be like Jennifer to have judgement for me about my housewarming and not Lexington or Tarren. Life happens. Friends plan events on the same days, depending on their own family situations, and real friends try to show up to all of them, even if there's a conflict in the schedule.

I mean, none of us even realized Tarren and Derrick were related until a month ago when we saw our invitations and realized Tarren's parents' names were the same as Derrick's parents' names from the wedding invitation. That's how much Lexington kept her relationship under wraps. None of us could ask Tarren because she was already on bed rest with her twins.

Forty and pregnant with twins. I cannot even imagine it. But that's the beauty of sperm donors and invitro, I guess. Two popsicle babies for the price of one. When I asked Tarren what made her want to have twins this late in life, she looked at me with the most serious, stone-faced, reporting at a murder scene face she could give me, and asked me right back, "Why not?"

I said to her, "But, Tarren, you're forty. You're not married. You're not going to have any help. And by the time they go to college, you'll be damn near sixty."

I was in the newsroom hours after my show was already over. I had been in my office logging sound and writing a package for a couple sweeps specials that would eventually air during my show, when I saw Tarren sitting at her desk. She was sitting there rubbing her growing belly through the stretchy fabric of her ruched teal dress.

She looked at me and said, "I don't know if I'll ever have a husband or get married. But I don't have to wait on those things to have the babies I've always wanted."

I nodded and watched her as she made figure eights over and around her navel.

She continued, "There are two things I've always wanted in my life. To be on TV and to have twins. I've been on TV in one way or another since I started sideline reporting in college, because that's all there was. I've traveled all across the country and even around the world, for work. It's been fun. The network thing never happened for me, like it did for Dawn. The anchor thing never happened for me because Boyce says he can't stand to lose me in the field."

I looked at her straight in the eye to see if that was her truth. I knew when I was promoted she had asked for the anchor job first. I knew she filled in for Dawn and thought, naturally, she would get the job because she had been at the station longer than I had damn near been in the business. That didn't work out in her favor, and we've never talked about it. In fact, when I got the job, she got me a bouquet of white orchids and handed them to me, personally, in the middle of the newsroom. At the time, I thought she was just giving them to me for show. To prove to Boyce and maybe even to herself, that she was okay with the idea of being passed over twice. That like Ann Curry, she needed to know her role and be content with where she was, never aiming higher, just relaxing against her own glass ceiling.

Tarren said to me then, "I like what I do; I like the life I've made for myself here. I make good money, and I'm tired of spending it on shoes and makeup. I'm not an animal person, but I've always wanted kids. I was an only child and I always wished I had a sibling. What my parents didn't give me, I will give my own children, unconditional love and attention, and a nanny when momma's gotta work."

"Sounds like you've got it all figured out," I said. "Have a good night."

I walked away from Tarren with a sadness I couldn't explain. Even when I watch the videos she posts on the station website, I can't help but feel sad. She's pimping out her pregnancy to stay relevant as a reporter, even though she's not reporting. Meanwhile, she's settling for the best she can make of her life at this stage in the game. I guess my mom wasn't lying when she said my generation is the first one to put ambition, career goals, and by virtue, ourselves, before anything and everyone else.

I know she meant it then as an insult, or at the very least, a way to get me to stop being so selfish. I didn't take it that way. I took it as a compliment. If my generation is the first one to realize that time is finite, and we have a limited amount to do everything life possibly has to offer, then we're the first generation to prioritize what is wholly important to us, over what parents, grandparents, and generations of history have said should be important. That's probably the only empowering thing my mother has ever said to me, and she doesn't even know it.

"Ooh, look. Here she comes," Diedre says.

"Her hair is gorgeous," Jennifer says.

She looks like she's about to pop. "Those babies will be here before she knows it," I say.

Who I assume to be Tarren's dad, rolls her into the baby shower room in a wheelchair. Tarren's hair hangs down the back of her chair, and to where her nipples would be if she were naked. Her sandy brown hair is long, thick, and full, thanks in part to the pre-natal vitamins she's taking. She smiles and waves at everyone as she's pushed to the center of the room beside the gift table. I watch as her mother and father come together to help her out of the wheel chair and into the decorative throne that's set up for her. An entourage of other family members fill in the empty tables in the room. I spot Lexington's mother among the crowd and smile. The two families have been joined for a day and they're already supporting each other.

I watch as Tarren's dad fusses over her, making sure she is comfortable, that she's not in any pain, and that he doesn't need to put her back in the wheel chair and roll her away.

"Daddy. Daddy. I'm fine," Tarren says, swatting at him.

He fluffs the cushion of the stool beneath her sandaled feet and then ducks out of the way.

"I want to thank everybody for coming this afternoon," Tarren says. "This won't be your traditional baby shower, because I can neither stand up nor play any games. So, feel free to eat, drink—non-alcoholic beverages of course—and be merry on me."

The room claps and people shout epithets about her looks, as others disperse to the snack table where silver trays of food, stay warmed by silver cans of cooking fuel.

"This may be the best baby shower I've ever been to," Jennifer says.

"I was kinda looking forward to playing Pin the Bottle on the Baby, or Guess the Poop, or something," Diedre says.

"I'm sure you'll have plenty of games to play at Naomi's housewarming."

"We'll see about that," I say. "I'mma say hey to Tarren."

I watch Tarren's eyes dart back and forth around the room at everything and everyone, making sure they're having a good time. She sees me and her eyes smile before her face does. I appreciate the familiarity. Even though she didn't get the job she wanted, I like the fact she didn't shun me afterward, either. Her gesture of congratulations proved to really be from her heart and not from calculating motives.

"You look good," I say approaching her.

"Naomi, don't lie to me. You and I both know I look like a pink bottle of Pepto-Bismol."

"Your jumpsuit is cute. Very seventies inspired."

"It's the only thing in the thrift store that would fit. I refused to buy a real outfit that I'm only going to wear once. I've been living these last few months in T-shirts and sweatpants sans elastic."

"But your videos always look good," I say.

"That's because the effort I don't put into myself from the neck down, is the effort that goes into beating this face and trying to hide these bags. I'm so tired. All I want to do is go to sleep."

"You better get your rest now, because you know good and well, you won't get it until these babies come."

"I don't even count on it then. I expect to be sleep deprived for at least the next six to eight months. I toss and turn all night because I can't get comfortable, no matter how many pillows I put around me. The most comfortable place for me to be is my daddy's recliner. I made him bring it to my house after I fell asleep in it one day."

"Well, this part will be over soon, and then you can get to the fun stuff. Raising babies."

"I know. I've ordered all their stuff on Amazon. Having this baby shower was pointless, since the only thing I can do from home and halfway have fun is surf the net and shop."

"Your credit card got some extra miles on it this month, huh?"

"Extra doesn't even tell half the story. How about they upgraded me to a whole different card and expanded my credit line, the way I've been shopping."

"Be careful," I say.

"You don't have to tell me twice. How's the new house?"

I shrug my shoulders. "It's nice. It feels weird though."

"I know the feeling. You probably envisioned yourself buying your house with someone and not by yourself."

"It's not that. I can't really say I ever had a plan for what my life would ever look like when it comes to men. I know I want one around, but that hasn't stopped how I operate about what's right for me."

Tarren nods. I can sense that what I say is a hard lesson she learned she had to accept for what it was. A decision that may have prompted her to decide on invitro fertilization and a sperm donor long before she ever made her very private plan public.

"It just feels like I'm putting roots down," I say, filling the silence between us.

"Never thought it would be someplace like Jacksonville?" she asks.

"I don't know. New Orleans in and of itself is a small town. Kind of. But the personality of the city and by and large, us as its people, are bigger than life."

"So why not go back home?"

"Because I've been a Nola girl my whole life. When I left it was to go somewhere new, do my time and keep on moving, and four years later . . . I . . ."

"You feel stagnant?"

"Yes and no. Just trying to figure my life out, that's all."

"Let me tell you a secret," Tarren says, motioning her hand for me to lower my head. "You never figure anything out. Every time you think you know everything there is to know, life throws another curved fastball straight for your face."

"Thanks for the vote of confidence."

"Anytime," Tarren says.

I wave away from her and make my way toward the line where Jennifer and Diedre are waiting. I walk up beside them and wait as they heap piles of food on their plates. Hot and spicy, fried chicken wings from Publix, red beans and rice catered from Copelands, and finger sandwiches courtesy of Jimmy Johns.

"You're not eating?" Diedre asks, biting off a piece of a wing.

"I'll wait. I still have to pick up the platters for this evening."

"You better have plenty of food and plenty of alcohol," Diedre says.

"Why? Seems like you're stuffing your face right now."

"And I'm going to stuff my face again at your house."

"That's right. You're still an associate producer, meaning, they pay you shit for a salary."

"Exactly," Diedre says. "And you're the new face of the station which means, you got money to spare."

"Whatever. I just bought a house. I'm broke."

"You not that broke if you just bought a house," Jennifer says.

"I didn't realize you went from being my producer to my financial adviser. Count your own coins, ma'am."

"I'm just saying," Jennifer said.

"As am I."

"Wait, Naomi. Where are you going?" Diedre asks as I walk toward the door.

"I told you I have to pick up the food, and I still have some straightening up to do. I'll see y'all in an hour or so."

"Nearing the point of wearing out your welcome?" Jennifer asks.

"Something like that," I say.

I wave at Tarren to say goodbye, surprised at our apparent closeness. If I'm looking and thinking about my future, it could very much look like hers. A soon to be single mother of twins, working a safe job that I'm good at, but is no longer important to me; only there for the check and the benefits. The thought makes me wrinkle my nose and suck teeth.

4.

Home Sweet Home

Outside, the warming air greets me. I look around at this part of suburbia, at all the newly built, single-detached homes for young families, and wonder what Tarren's neighbors think about the pregnant spinster who's spent more time pushing a microphone in front of people's faces, than she's ever spent pushing a stroller, or changing diapers, or doing anything that didn't involve her immediate needs first.

I look around at the women walking or running behind fancy strollers with bicycle wheels, or on their own with wireless headphones either in or over their ears, and I see what my own life has become. My neighborhood of townhomes is not unlike this one. The winding paths will serve as my track where I will complete my own runs in the name of fitting into all of my clothes and the ones that come monthly, so I'm never seen in the same thing twice on air.

My mother says that expense is a frivolous one, but for me it will be a necessity until it's not. Meaning, until something in my house breaks and the bill is as big as a year's worth of renting the runway, I will continue having fresh fits every day of the week I say, "I'm Naomi Grace, and you're watching Naomi Tonight."

The parking lot is crowded when I pull into the complex housing the Publix, a Kohl's, and a bunch of other stores and restaurants, along with a doctor's office, a daycare center, and three banks. And that's just on this side of the boulevard. On the other side is even more. There's enough stuff this way that my Saturday morning errands are all spent within a five-mile radius.

Inside the grocery store I go right to the bakery beside the deli from the hot food section. A woman behind the counter is making sandwiches.

"Pickup for Grace," I say.

"One moment ma'am," the woman in the green work smock, khakis, and a hair net, says.

She finishes arranging the sandwiches and then puts a plastic cover over the platter and sets it on the glass top, covering her display of fresh ingredients that can go in any sub.

"Just finished up, Ms. Grace. Let me grab the rest of your order."

"Take your time," I say.

I watch her as she opens a warmer and pulls out a rotisserie chicken and the box of wings, like the ones Tarren had at her baby shower. Then she opens a refrigerator and pulls out two platters, one of assorted cheeses, crackers and cold cuts, the other of fresh cut fruit. The last thing she pulls out is four, gallon jugs, all of them containing sweet tea.

"Ms. Grace, are you going to need help getting this to the front to check out?" she asks, noticing I don't have a basket.

"Yes. Please," I say.

"I'll get someone to help you. Just hold on right there."

As if I'm going anywhere. I try to dismiss my sudden bitchiness as soon as it appears, knowing that even though I look different, people still know who I am. Once again, my representative must be on display. Especially in this neighborhood. These are the type of people to call or email the news station with messages that say "Naomi Grace Rude" in the subject line. Messages written in all caps and using more than a dozen exclamation points to express a point from "Joe Blow in Bartram," or "Misty in Mandarin."

I plaster my fake smile across my face to at least look pleasant until the woman comes back with another worker, pushing a cart.

She says to me, "You know, you have the same name as the news lady on channel nine. I thought it was her we were preparing the platters for, but then you walked in. You favor her a little bit, you know."

"You don't say."

I smile at the woman and walk off toward the cash register with the other worker pushing the cart behind me.

Maybe one day when Boyce is off, I'll actually anchor in my locs, and she'll be able to tell all her coworkers she really did prepare my food.

I walk into the line for ten items or less and wait for my cart to catch up with me. By the time it does, the customer in front of me has figured out her pin number and cashed out.

"Will this be all for you today, ma'am?" the cashier asks.

"Yes. Thank you."

She rings up the platters, the chicken, and the gallon jugs as she hums to herself. She is an older woman, with a perfect silver roller bang to go with her tightly pulled back French roll. I watch her hum and work and wonder about her story. I wonder why she is still working when her hands show she is at least in her sixties. I wonder if she's working in the grocery store because she has to, or if she wants to because she was bored in retirement. I watch her and wonder where she lives. On what side of the river does she call home. In what neighborhood is her abode, and whether or not it is safe. Does she go to sleep to the sound of gunshots or crickets? Does she wake up to find the windows of her car smashed in, or is it stolen completely?

"Your total is $68.72," she says.

I insert my card into the machine and follow the prompts to pay. When I'm done she smiles at me. I smile at her as she hands me my receipt. For a moment her skin touches mine and I feel her warmth.

She says, "I like you better with the locs. That other hair makes you look too fake, too plastic."

"Thank you," I say as I load the food and drinks into my cart.

I push away from the woman as she rings up the next customer, still feeling her warmth, appreciative of her compliment, and wondering about her story. The longer I work in the business, the more I wonder about the people who don't make the news. When I was a child, I used to make up stories about anybody I came across. I would give them homes, jobs, husbands, wives, children, or the lack there of. Now that I tell stories for a living about the lengths people go when they lose their jobs, or husbands, and children, and everything else in between, I've settled on wonder. I stop myself from imagining exactly what could be and instead, remain in wonder at the probability of multiple possibilities. It is safer to wonder many outcomes compared to only one.

Even in my own life, with my three visions hanging on the back wall of what is supposed to be a bedroom, I have left myself room to become all three, instead of sticking to just one. I have given myself room for love, money, and a bomb career, because I learned a long time ago an "and" is a lot better than picking between an "or."

The drive back to my townhouse is quick and without scenic stimulation. There are office parks, apartments, and subdivisions, on one side of the street or the other, until I get to the massive entrance for my neighborhood. The neighborhood that is so large there is an elementary school inside the columns that officially welcome residents and their visitors to Bartram Springs. I turn down one winding street and then another, until I'm in the section of the subdivision for townhouses. As I near my door, I see more and more cars waiting and people standing on my lawn.

Jennifer and Diedre are waiting with their boyfriends. I see Owen Major, another of the reporters from work, and a few other people who call the station their second home. There are some faces I don't recognize. Most likely plus one's of those I do know, and then there are the neighbors on either side of me. One family I share a wall with, and the other a patch of grass. They all wait outside my door, in my driveway, or loitering about the yard as I pull in.

I roll down the window and say, "Y'all make me feel like I'm late to my own party."

"You are," Jennifer says, shaking her head.

"I thought you guys were still at the baby shower," I say cutting the engine.

"By the time everyone finished eating, Tarren thanked people again for coming, opened one or two cards, and then said she was tired and going back home," Diedre explains. "So we left and came straight here."

"I see. Well, help me get this stuff out the car."

Diedre, Jennifer, Owen, and their dates walk over to the car and grab trays and jugs from the backseat. They follow behind me as I walk to the front door and turn the lock.

"Welcome to the House of Grace," I say, flipping on the light switch inside the main entrance. "You guys, can put the stuff down on the counter in the kitchen."

"Naomi, this is cute," Diedre says.

"Thank you," I say. "Feel free to look around. I'll do a tour later."

Everything in the townhouse is staged and ready to be shown off. It probably looks more like an open house than it does a home that's being lived in. Which is the reason I wanted to have the housewarming soon after closing instead of weeks or months later. I wanted to show off the house in its very best condition, before my laziness kicked in, and guests got to see me living with dishes in the sink, clothes thrown into piles, and shoes kicked off just inside the door.

I busy myself in the kitchen, watching as friends and acquaintances take the open opportunity to be nosy and stare at the pictures on the wall, examine the condition of the furniture, and guess the size of the television.

"Naomi, do you think you have enough mirrors in this place?" Owen asks.

"I wanted to make sure I could see myself at any and every angle before I leave the house, so I can never be caught at a bad one at work?"

"Okay," he exaggerates.

"You're so damn vain," Jennifer says.

"Just like the dude Carly Simon was singing about," I say. "The song is definitely about me."

"What song?" Diedre asks.

I laugh. Jennifer rolls her eyes.

"Hey, Siri, play "You're So Vain," I say to my phone.

The opening rumbles of the seventies track begin to play, followed by the intentional strumming of a guitar and the loud chords of an accompanying piano. I can see my neighbors that share a wall with me, Diane and Jeff Golden, bobbing their heads as Carly begins to sing about the man who walked into a party.

"Am I supposed to know this song?" Diedre asks. "Sounds like it came out way before I was even thought of."

"What year were you born?" Owen asks.

"Nineteen ninety-three." Diedre answers.

"Oh my God," he says, slapping his hand over his face. "I was graduating high school in '93."

"I was eight," I say.

"You guys just stop talking to me," Owen says.

He walks dramatically to the canary yellow sofa, falls into it, and then slides down to the carpet. He lays there between the sofa and the red-stained, wooden coffee table and sings the words to the famous chorus at the top of his lungs. Diane and Jeff sing along with him as do Carol and Avery, my neighbors in the townhouse on the other side of me. I watch Jennifer sing to the boyfriend she's been dating off and on for the last year, as Diedre talks to the guy she met on a dating app three months ago. I set out the trays of food, watching the couples have their own private conversations in their twosomes.

"This is really nice, Naomi," Owen says, coming up behind me.

He stares out at the room of couples. His wistful look is similar to my own and I wonder if he plays the wonder game; if he's giving everyone a specific life made up from his own imagination and the stories he's told over the course of his career.

He says, "I like that sign you have over the couch."

He nods toward the wooden panel I had made by one of the artisans at the weekly market in Riverside. It reads "Yaaasss" in curly, arching letters over an arc.

I say, "It's the way I plan to live my life. Saying "yaaasss" to everything that's coming my way."

"Must be nice," Owen says.

"It is. You should try it."

"I would be talking that same game if I was going to Cuba tomorrow, too. But we can't all be as fabulous as you."

"I'm not the only one going."

"Yeah, but you're the only one that matters."

"That was mean!" I yell, slapping his arm.

"I kid. I kid," he says, grabbing a sandwich and sauntering out of the kitchen.

"Y'all, come eat this food," I yell over the music that has manifested a playlist of its own. "I'm going out of the country and none of this can stay in my refrigerator while I'm gone. Well, the chicken can, but everything else, y'all, need to eat."

"Yes, ma'am," Jeff says.

"Dinner on Naomi. Alright," Avery says, slapping Jeff's hand.

I watch and wonder as Carol, Diane, Jennifer, and Diedre fix plates for the men, even if they got to the refreshment counter first. I watch traditional gender roles reveal themselves in the assorted crowd and wonder if there will ever be a time when men and women break the molds we've been indoctrinated with and live authentic lives that are true to who we wake up to be, and not what we've been groomed into since birth.

That's why you're single. You know that, right?

Maybe that is why I'm single. Relationships take conforming, and after trying and failing with Aaron, I refuse to do it again.

"Why do you look so serious?" Octavius, Jennifer's boyfriend, asks me. "Everytime I see you, you always look so serious. So mean."

"Sorry," I say smiling, trying to mask my own thoughts. "Just thinking about stuff. Nothing important."

"It's cool," he says. "It's your party. You can look serious if you want to."

He walks into a corner with Jennifer against the wall that leads to the patio outside. I haven't bought patio furniture yet, so I left the blinds drawn. And I still haven't figured out who is going to cut my grass, or weed eat, or do any of the other outside maintenance I never learned how to do.

I guess I'll look for a yard man when I get back.

Part 2

Work-Life Balance

"What is work without worry?
What is life without love?
What is balance but another way to best the scale?"
— Nikesha Elise Williams

5.

Girls Trip

Hot. Humid. Muggy. Sticky. Those are the only words to describe Havana. We lay on the foldable chairs on Santa Maria Beach beneath the canopy of an umbrella. Three brown girls toasted enough by five days in the sun. It is our last day in Cuba before we have to travel back to Florida. It has been five days of food, culture, and trying our hardest not to stare at the men, women, and children who look like our aunties, uncles, and cousins, only this set of relatives speak Spanish. It makes the popular meme that floats around any time there is a rift in the diaspora and inevitably argued on Black Twitter, all the more true; the only difference between them and us is a boat stop.

On this stop we have eaten our weight in beans and rice, ropa vieja, and every seafood imaginable and available from the Malecón. Now resting on the ocean front ninety miles from Florida, all I can think about is how much I don't want to go back. How much I don't want to return to a place where I have to always be on. This getaway has been as much fun, rest and relaxation, as it has been eye opening.

On our first day in the Cuban Capitol we explored the city in a shiny old car. Our guide and his driver chauffeured us around in an original 1958 Fairlane 500, pointing out the sites central to the Cuban Revolution as well as how the mafia took over the island, contributed to the economy, and plotted plans for American black market domination while sipping Cuba Libré's, and spending time with an endless supply of prostitutes. We drove around the city being told about the different influences in architecture; one distinctly American, the other distinctly Russian. Everywhere we turned there were images of Fidel and Che. Castro and Guevara. Of their history, it appeared the Cubans were proud, defiant even, and completely, diametrically opposed to the tint from the American stain spent on their story, and weaved into textbooks that only tell tales of war from the perspective of the dominating, conquering, hegemonic force, or their attempt to be so.

We rode around with our eyes wide and our phones constantly in front of our faces as we snapped picture after picture of the monuments to progress and a new way of living that was stopped before they could even begin, because the neighboring country to the north had a tantrum. The tour was the first step in the undoing of our belief of the lessons we'd learned. This part of history is also more murky than clear, and deserving of more than three pages dedicated in a high school textbook, or the optional elective offered at some universities for those seeking deeper understanding of Latin or Caribbean history.

Over drinks and plates of assorted fish and vegetables where even the garnishes were edible, we spoke in feverish English with our guide, trying to peel back the layers of what we'd seen and articulate it in a way that wasn't in complete dissonance with what we had been taught. Inside a house that was turned into a restaurant, we discussed what was not easily accessible or even Googleable.

"All we here about in America is about the famine, and the ration system," Jennifer said as she cleaned the last grains of food from her plate. "Nobody ever talks about why it was necessary."

"We were a new country with very little international support," our guide Elena said. "We had to rely on ourselves for everything we had so the ration was necessary. And as the world went through recessions, ours were more like depressions."

"You know what they say?" I asked, looking at Jennifer.

"When the United States gets a cold the rest of the world gets the flu," she said, finishing my thought.

"That means we had pneumonia," Elena said to us, picking up on the joke.

"Cuba and everyone that wasn't white," Diedre said.

"No, white people felt it too," I said. "I don't know how many packages we ran, how many headlines I saw, how many front-page photos that were printed in full color that showed every Tom, Dick, and Harry with the boo-boo face."

"When white folks start losing their money, they start to lose their shit," Diedre said.

"The suicide rate even went up. Among men especially."

"That's extreme."

"Now imagine how you felt during that time, and multiply it by ten, and you may begin to understand what Cuba has felt for years," Elena said to us.

She had been sitting at the head of the table, listening to us intently. Her long brown hair was pulled back in a low ponytail. Strands of it were stuck with sweat to her shoulders, cheeks, and around her collarbone. She was shapely and thin at the same time. Her eyes were shaped like almonds with the corners pressing in toward her nose. Even though we had been in the heat for most of the day, her makeup had not completely sweated off. The glittery, iridescent shimmer on her eyes still twinkled in the dim light. Her heavy black eyeliner and mascara gave a brooding quality to her playful pupils. Residue from the crimson red stain she smeared on her lips had faded to a shade of pink, thanks to the bottles of water we'd swallowed.

Elena Álvarez met us at the airport with a cardboard sign with our name on it. She ushered us through hawkers trying to get us to jump into their taxi instead of the one she had waiting. At our Airbnb she waited while we changed, and was a bottomless source of information as we rode in our old car, walked around historic hotels, and took the same picture over and over again until it was perfect to post. She was as thoughtful about her answers to our questions at dinner as she was the next day outside of the Museo de Historico de Guanabacoa, or as Diedre began calling it, the Black Museum.

"There's one in every major city, state, and country from here to New Zealand," she said.

We paid inside the lobby for a guided tour and to take pictures of the exhibits because photographic evidence is unmatched when compared to three shoddy, sometimes alcohol confused, memories.

We walked from room to room in the museum that was more a monument to religion than anything else. The first set of rooms on the tour were all about Santeria. Among the mannequin embodiments of Orishas and a Babalawo, were elements of Christianity. A crucifix was prominent among the masks, and pots, a staff and feathers. In another room, dedicated to a secret society that was both religious and social, spiritual and the catalyst to keep old culture alive, was an oil painting of what looked like an African priest, blessing the new recruits into the society of the masked spirits. Despite the passage of lives from the dirt they were stolen from, to the dirt they were forced to work, this old forgotten edifice memorialized more than just the history of bondage. Through religion and ancestor worship, secret societies considered cults, and extravagant costumes used to mask identities, as much as they were used to embody others, was an honored journey of triumph and struggle instead of just a trek on a trail through sorrowful turns of tears and tragedies. The museum neither began nor ended with life on a Cuban sugar plantation where men who lived to forty were considered elderly. The museum, humble in its outward appearance, told stories in its few rooms that traversed centuries of time that began and ended with the enduring power of custom, tradition, and religion.

Elena said to us as we were leaving, "I always tell my American tourists that we have more in common between us, Cuba and the United States, than we have differences."

"A fucked-up history because of slavery," Diedre said. "Yeah, you're right, we do have a lot in common."

"I don't think she meant it that way," I said.

"Maybe not, but you know it's true."

Elena looked on as we three brown American girls in loose booty shorts, with floral designs, crop tops, and leather, hard-soled flip-flops processed the vibrant imagery from the museum. A museum that reminded us of the so-called "Blacksonian" at home. The National Museum of African-American History and Culture on the national mall that took the outward headdress, a three-tiered crown of a Yoruba man or woman, prince or princess, and turned it into a bronze building amongst white marble statues.

Five days of art, culture, walking, touring, and eating has become our crash course in Cuba, and the reason we are laid up on the beach looking out toward the water, not yet ready to go home.

"Oh, look," I say. "Lunch is coming."

We ordered plates of white fish, white rice, and mango salsa from two men who apparently work the beach. They bring us food piled on three real plates, along with real silverware. We take them and say "gracias" as we rearrange ourselves, our magazines, and our bags to make room to eat.

I chop my fish with my fork and watch them as they go and wonder about their story. They walk away from us in their board shorts and white T-shirts with the sleeves torn off, kicking up sand with their feet. I wonder which part of Havana they live in. How many family members live in their home? Is it multi-generational as Elena explained, and if not, did they opt for the house instead of owning a car? I watch them and wonder if they live here, by the beach, or do they travel all this way for work.

"Why do you keep staring at them?" Diedre asks, commanding my attention.

"I wasn't staring," I say, quickly shoveling food into my mouth.

"Yes, you were," Jennifer says. "You stare at everybody. I just got used to it."

"Well, tell me something else about myself I don't know," I say.

"How can you not know you're staring at someone?" Diedre asks. "Like, you're looking so hard it's like your eyes are trying to print their X-rays."

"Y'all don't just look at people and wonder about them sometime?" I ask. "Wonder about where they've been, what they've been through, what they've seen, what's brought them to the point that they are standing in front of you in your space, or interacting with you?"

"I thought this trip was supposed to be fun, but every time we end up in deep conversations," Diedre says.

"We've had fun," Jennifer says. "You forgot we danced on the tables at the bar last night?"

"Okay, that was fun," Diedre says. "But I need more of that and less of this existential stuff Naomi's been on."

"I just like looking at people and wondering about what stories they have to tell," I say.

"Is that why you got into news?" Jennifer asks.

"Probably. I really just always wanted to be on TV, and this seemed to be the easiest way to do it. No talent required."

"What you do takes talent," Jennifer says.

"Perhaps," I say. "What do you want to do for our last night in Havana, ladies?"

"I want to go to a club like the one in *Dirty Dancing Havana Nights* and dance and kiss strangers," Diedre says.

"And what about Internet Bae?" I ask.

"What he doesn't know won't hurt him," Diedre says.

"Sounds like y'all broke up?" Jennifer says.

"How?" I ask. "We've only been gone five days. They were just hugged up on my couch on Sunday. I thought I was going to have to get that thing scotchgaurded the way you two were booed up. It was like you were trying to become one person or something."

"Tell her," Jennifer says.

"Tell me what?" I ask.

"After we left, we got into it about something stupid," Diedre says.

"How stupid?" I ask.

"As we were leaving, he asked me if I would rather own my own house like you, or move in with someone else," Diedre says. She sets her plate down to the side.

"And you said?"

"I said I'd rather own my own place, because that way, I can never be kicked out if I'm living with someone else."

"So, what's the problem?" I ask.

"Wait for it," Jennifer says.

Diedre continues, "He said that means I had trust issues, if I couldn't ever see myself living with someone."

"He got all of that from you answering a hypothetical question about your preferred living situation?"

"Yup," Jennifer says.

"Then I guess I have major trust issues," I say, shrugging my shoulders.

I reposition my plate on my lap and plow through my food as Jennifer and Diedre further dissect the conversation that led to the demise of her relationship.

"Trust issues," Diedre says emphatically. "How can I have trust issues with someone I barely even know. We haven't established a plane for trust, let alone have issues with it."

"How old was he again?" Jennifer asks.

"Thirty-two," Diedre says.

"He's at an age where he's trying to find out if he's ready to settle down, and with who. He seems like he's just testing the waters on the idea of long-term commitment himself, and this was an excuse to let himself off the hook. Don't take it personally."

"Men should come with warning signs," Diedre says.

"Like on a prescription bottle?" Jennifer asks.

"Exactly. Right on the back of their shirts it should have directions on how to use, and the potential side effects."

"Ooh," Jennifer says, putting her empty plate on the sand. She stands up and begins talking with her hands. "Like it should say, this man is only good on Monday, Wednesday, Friday, and every other Sunday."

"Unless the month has five Sunday's, in which case, he will only be good on two out of the three," Diedre adds.

"Yes," Jennifer says. "Ideal conditions for this man are in the afternoon on lunch dates when everyone else is working and, therefore, no one who is important to him will see you with him."

Diedre adds, "And the side-effects are, running when confronted with a decision that involves putting someone else before himself. Fighting if his manhood or masculinity is ever tested . . ."

"And violent tendencies if you say anything bad about his mother, grandmother, or the coven of women who raised him," Jennifer finishes.

"You can't forget about the warning," I say, fueling their fire.

"Yes," Jennifer says. "Warning, this man may leave you dickmatized, with trust issues, feeling insecure, questioning your sense of self, your value, and your worth."

Diedre says, "If you develop any of these symptoms, please put the man back, no matter how pleasing the peen, or the promises to do better. Seek immediate help twice weekly for the first six months from a licensed therapist."

"Y'all are sick," I say laughing.

"You know it's true," Jennifer says, sitting back down on her beach chair. "You're still in recovery from your last relationship."

"I'm over it, him, and you," I say standing up. "I'm getting in the water."

"You see she's running away, right?" Jennifer says to Diedre.

"Whatever," I mutter.

I slow jog across the white sand toward the two-tone blue of the water. It is lukewarm when it hits my ankles. I walk until I am knee-deep, and then throw the rest of me under. The saltwater tingles as it hits my scalp. I open my eyes and look at the strands of my locs as they float in front of my face and along the sides of my cheeks.

Still in recovery.

I can't argue and say they're wrong. I can't lie and say after Aaron every other man has made me skittish, less confident in my ability to succeed at coupledom. Even the janitor at the station isn't impressed by me. Yeah, he's married, at least that's what the ring on his finger says, but he could at least play along a little bit when I flirt with him. I mean, he won't even clean my office if I'm in there, and that's when he's actually on shift and doesn't send other workers.

I'm not so much in recovery as I am on a sabbatical. A four-year sabbatical. There have been dates here and there, but mostly it's been dry as hell, or dudes just looking to see if I would give them the time of day and my real phone number, instead of my office line, where the voicemail is not setup.

I come up from beneath the water to see Jennifer and Diedre walking toward me. I shake my head, thinking about the warning labels for men.

Men aren't the only ones who need warning labels.

I know I need a sign. It would say: Best after 8 p.m. and before noon. At the most optimal when complimented and praised. Can be passive-aggressive. Side-effects may make you feel crowded and cramped or insignificant, depending upon the state of the woman. Warning if you feel any of these symptoms you should probably either try to get closer or run away fast, because at any moment, the woman could self-destruct.

"The water is nice," Diedre says, reaching where I am.

"Makes me wish I had learned to swim," Jennifer says, holding tightly to her arms across her bare stomach.

"You still can," I say. "They have adult swim classes all over Jacksonville."

"I'm not trying to be in a swim class with a bunch of young moms who are teaching their six-month-old's the basic water survival skills."

"Then I guess you're not trying to stay too long in this water, either?" I ask.

"Damn right," she says. "We came down here to get you. Elena came back wanting to know what time we wanted dinner tonight."

"Where are we going?" I ask.

"Like you would know," Jennifer says.

"Point taken," I say. "Eight-thirty is good. I'm going to need a nap after this sun and this water."

"You've barely been in the water," Diedre says.

"And, your point," I say. "I'm still going to need a nap."

"Why . . . yes, yes, of course, your majesty," Diedre says.

She splashes water at me and then swims away. I swim after her as Jennifer walks away from us, back toward the sandy bank and up to our chairs beneath a tree. I catch Diedre's foot and pull the rest of her to me. She wriggles away, swims, and comes up a few feet away from me holding her crocheted, Rasta-colored bikini top, with both hands over her boobs.

"Girl, you're going to make me flash all of Havana," Diedre says.

"A little peep show ain't never hurt nobody," I say.

"Then let them peep at you not me," she says, retying the top around her neck.

"These boobs are meant to be appreciated in clothes," I say.

"As are mine."

"Well, someone else is appreciating them too," I say, nodding my head toward a group of men walking down the beach.

"Oh shit, Naomi! You didn't tell me the United Nations of Fuckably Fine were coming down here."

"I just noticed them," I say, keeping my gaze toward her while looking at them from the corner of my eyes.

"Don't do that staring thing you do," Diedre says.

"I'm not."

"But you are. You don't need to imagine everyone's story."

"Too late," I say. "One of them is walking over here. Come here."

Diedre walks backwards to me in the knee-deep water, holding the neck and back ties for her bikini. I move her hands from her back and knot the strings as the man approaches. He's under six feet and the complexion of bark. Long, thick locs like cord jump ropes hang just past his shoulders, but the line across his forehead is fresh. He is without facial hair and his arms are covered in tattoos from his shoulders to just past where his bicep should be. He is lanky, appearing taller than he actually is. There is no definition in his arms, or his bare chest, just a smattering of hair across his undeveloped pecks, and beneath his navel.

"Good afternoon," he says.

The clear American accent and the depth of his voice surprises me. I pop Diedre's shoulder to get her to speak as I tie and retie the strings behind her neck, while I duck my face into her blue and black hair that's curled up due to the water.

"Hi," she says, mustering the words through a forced laugh.

"And hello to you, too," he says to me specifically.

I lift my hands from her shoulders and wave. He waves one hand as well, as I dive beneath the water trying not to wonder where in the states, he's from. I swim until the blues in the water begin to change and I'm in the dark of the open ocean that has the power to consume. When I surface, I see the lanky stranger with the ropes for hair has rejoined his friends in the water, squinting distance away. I swim to catch up with Diedre, who is walking toward the shore.

"Oh, now you want to come see about me," she says as I reach her legs.

"You told me not to do my staring thing. I can't stare at someone I don't see."

"Yeah, yeah, whatever. He asked about you."

"And what did you tell him?" I ask as we walk up the sandy bank together.

"I told him if he wanted to know about you, he needed to ask you himself."

"And what did he say?"

"He called me the gatekeeper and walked away."

We trudge up the sand. I focus on Jennifer's former twist out that has turned into a full 'fro, thanks to the one hundred percent humidity of the Cuban air. She pulls at tufts of hair to round it out and shape it. I focus on her in her brown bikini that nearly blends in with the color of her skin to keep from looking to my left, down the beach and toward the men, who all wear invisible labels listing their uses, warnings, and possible side-effect symptoms.

"Y'all ready?" Jennifer asks as we reach her.

"I am," I say quickly.

"Who was the guy who approached you in the water?"

"Diedre?" I say.

"I don't know," she says. "I didn't ask his name and he didn't give it. He wanted to talk to Naomi, but she ran away."

"I didn't run," I defend.

"Okay you swam," Diedre says.

"Why didn't you stay to talk to them?" Jennifer asks.

"Because my name ain't Stella and vacation boos aren't real. Besides, I'm not the one who wants to kiss up on strangers," I say, knocking Diedre's shoulders.

"Cuban strangers," she says. "Not American strangers."

"He was American?" Jennifer asks.

"Yeah," I say.

"Well, that just made things a lot more interesting," she says, sitting up rigidly straight.

"Uh-uh," I say. "I know that look in your eye. We gotta go. Elena's standing right over there waiting for us. Let's go."

I grab my large, floppy straw hat that hides my face and shove it on my head as I gather up my towel, oversized beach bag, and flip-flops. I leave Diedre and Jennifer behind, kicking across the warm sand in my bare feet until I reach the sidewalk and stand beside Elena.

"Are you all ready?" She asks me in the crisp English of someone trying to impress a native speaker of their command of the language, that is not their own.

"I am," I say. "Just waiting on them."

I drop my flip-flops to the ground and turn them over with my feet until they are right side up. Inside my bag I dig around for my water bottle. I pop the top and use it to clean off my sandy feet, so I don't get the interior of the cab dirty. One thing I noticed, whether we've been in the cab with Elena's chosen driver, or if we were in the old cars, is that all of them have been spotless. Inside and outside. The paint gleams as if from daily applications of wax, and the insides have a seemingly permanent scent of new car smell. Even the heavy gas and oil in the old cars eventually subsided to reveal a fresh scent never found in a Christmas tree shaped air freshener back home.

"Do mine too," Diedre says, knocking her foot with mine.

"Use your own water," I say, knocking her foot away.

"But I want to drink mine," Diedre says.

"And who says I don't want to drink the rest of mine," I say.

"Naomi, you barely got more than a swig in that bottle," Jennifer says. "You might as well use it to clean our feet."

"My name ain't Jesus and this ain't the last supper. You're going to need to put a "please" on that before I waste the rest of my good water on you two heifers."

"Pleeeeeaaaasssseeeee," they drawl with their heads smashed together like begging children.

I roll my eyes and empty the last of my water over our sandy feet. I look toward Elena and she's laughing at us, amused by our friendly tension and shady playfulness. We follow her to the curb of the sidewalk where the taxi awaits. There is no beach walkover or access point built on top of mountainous dunes meant to protect homes and buildings from the power of the ocean like there are at home. Here, there is the shore and the land without a divider between them. A lifestyle of either complete harmony, or foolish and unnecessary danger when you think about hurricane season.

We load up into the van cab and drive away from the seaside beach community. With my head against the tinted window I ignore Jennifer and Diedre chattering about dinner, work, and the quad of men who made the beach their squatting spot as we were leaving. I ignore their conversation as they play their own version of the wonder game. They wonder where the men were from and how long they've been in Cuba. If they were wrapping up their vacation or just getting started. They tried to run the probability of whether they'd see them again, perhaps at the airport tomorrow, if they were on the last leg of their vacation like we were.

"Unless they took a cruise," Jennifer says. "And then they'll be going back to the port."

Diedre says, "They were a long way from the port to be on a cruise."

I ignore their chatter as it turns away from the men and toward what they plan to wear for our last night in Cuba. Instead, I try to clear my mind. I try to reach that state of empty mindfulness my meditation apps and mixtape say I should achieve at least once a day. The least I can do for myself when it comes to my own self-care. But empty thoughts don't come, and my mind wanders back to the beach, back to the quad of men, to the lanky stranger with the ropes for hair, and I wonder what his warning label says. I wonder if he comes with damage and baggage. I wonder who hurt him and how it may have affected him. Was it his family or a previous lover? I wonder about the things people don't readily talk about. The secrets even people in relationships are reluctant to reveal to the man or woman they consider their life partner. I wonder about what his inner thoughts may have been as he watched me swim away, loaded down by my own invisible warning sign that I keep taped to the inside of my skin so that my flaws aren't easily seen, and used against me as weapons in a verbal war.

I wonder about the Andre 3000 wannabe, and if he decided to approach Diedre and I because he realized we were American, or if his boys put him up to it. I wonder about him because I didn't take the opportunity to speak to him. I didn't seize the chance to get his name or tell him mine. I only know that he called Diedre "the gatekeeper" and he asked about me.

You're still in recovery from your last relationship.

Jennifer's sharp assessment of my single life interrupts my wonders of the man with the precise edge, despite the new growth gathered at each root of the ropes of his hair. Her critique of my current relational condition makes me question her motives. Does she want to see me with someone because she thinks it will make me happy?

Does she think I'm incapable of being happy alone? Or does she just want me to be with someone because she is?

Why are people in relationships always trying to rush their friends back into the game? How long is too long to be single?

I let the questions roll around my mind as we arrive in front of our vacation rental. Elena says she will be back for us at 7:45 to go with us to our final Cuban dinner. I nod my head okay as I walk past her into the beautiful home, in the unassuming neighborhood. All around us are stone buildings in various levels of decay and disrepair. The area in any other country would be labeled with a historical landmark and marked as must-see ruins. Here, the houses with the rocks falling from the roofs, and the cracks in the stone façade, are the homes of the citizens who don't get HGTV, let alone care about the latest craze in renovations. I take the long hallway in our five-bedroom, five bath rental to my room at the back of the house. I close and lock my door, and then turn on my air conditioning unit. My body is damp and sticky from the ocean and the humidity. There is sand in places it shouldn't be and moisture where I should be dry.

Stripping out of my clothes, I kick them into a pile in the corner before going into the bathroom. The fixtures inside our rental are surprisingly upscale, considering the economic state of the people around us. But that has been the one lesson I've learned since we first landed. Exteriors typically don't match interiors. The outsides of buildings, neighborhoods, places, even the people, rarely align with what is on the inside. I step into the marble and glass shower, turn the chrome handle, and stand under the water as it changes from cold to warm to hot.

Under the running head I douse my whole body. From my sister locs down to the pink painted pinky toenails on my feet, I let the power of the water run over my skin, withering and weathering the dirt and grime away from my body until it is no more. It is under the water I find the empty state of mind I had been looking for amongst my boy crazy coworkers. Under the shower, listening to the sound of cascading water, I find the empty stillness of peace as I look down at my own body.

Thirty-four years old and not a stretch mark to be dually ashamed and proud of. I look at my empty womb and unblemished skin and wonder what life would be like if Aaron and I had worked out. I see his face and I shake my head. Just like that, my peace is rattled. My stillness is gone. The state of emptiness I had at long last hoped I achieved, is filled with a face I don't want to remember, a name I can't forget, a lie of a life I can't unlive. They say time heals all wounds, but I think it's the opposite, time reveals all wounds.

Four years after fleeing a dead relationship and the only city I've ever call homed, I'm still as Jennifer says, in recovery. Just like Cuban architecture that was once pressure washed, freshly painted and pristine, but has now deteriorated due to lack of care and upkeep, I see in me what I see in the buildings in the neighborhood that I'm staying in; what could be and what used to be beyond the crumbling, molding mortar, and my broken heart.

The scrub of the loofah on my body helps me forget, or at the very least, think of something else. Now it is the feeling of the porous sponge scraping away dead skin and more from my body. The deliberate sting of the soap in my eyes. The water dripping from the tips of my locs and my scalp over my body, as I turn off the water and step out of the shower. I open one eye to grab a towel to wrap around my hair. I move around naked, my bare feet feeling the grains of sand I tracked into my room from our day at the beach. Dirty clothes in one corner, my bag with my money, passport, magazines, and phone are in the other. I go through it, grab the phone and turn on music. A sultry voice of a twenty-something singer with guts and soul come through the speakers and set the mood of my brooding, as I look through the wardrobe for the only thing left for me to wear, besides my travel sweats.

The red and royal blue color block, cutout dress is something I would never wear at home. Too risqué, too revealing, too many questions would have to be answered if I were to be caught by somebody else's camera wearing a dress with the belly and thighs cut out of it and my caramel skin showing through. Here, in Cuba, where nobody knows my name, my face, or what I do for a living, the dress is acceptable, and the pictures we take will only be from the neck up. Thank God for selfie-culture.

I yank the dress from the hanger and lay it across the queen-sized bed as I walk my nakedness back into the bathroom. Lotion, moisturizer, conditioner. I groom my body until my skin is soft, my hair is moisturized, and my face glows.

"Naomi, you ready?" Diedre asks from outside my door.

"I'm getting there," I say.

"Well, hurry up. Elena is here. She says we don't want to miss our reservation."

"I'm coming," I yell.

I turn off the light in the bathroom and quickly pull on the dress. With it as tight as it is, I can get away with wearing it without a bra or underwear. My a-cups are supported by the spandex as is my posterior. My body is as much my job as is my face and my voice, and it is well taken care of.

I step into my shoes. The same blue heels with spikes on the pumps I wore to Lexington's wedding, and then unlock and open the door.

"Well, damn," Diedre says, taking me in. "Don't you look thottish."

"Thank you," I say grinning. "You look like a schoolmarm."

"I was going for sexy librarian," she says adjusting her outfit.

In a long, balloon sleeved, white off-the-shoulder crop top and high waist, wide legged white pants with splits from the mid-thigh, to the genie ankle cuff of her pants, she is just as naked as I, only the billowy fabric of her outfit disguises her provocative garb. She's re-wet her hair and the curls of her blue and black weave are moisturized and fresh, against her olive brown skin. We walk to meet Jennifer, who is waiting in the solarium at the front of the house with Elena. Her big afro from the beach is pulled into a large, fluffy bun showing off her chiseled cheek bones, long tear drop earrings, and chunky coconut necklace she bought from one of the hawkers who walked the sand selling their wares. She, too, is clothed in little, wearing tiny high waist denim shorts that allow the bottoms of her booty cheeks to peak through, and a black tank top with the infamous Rolling Stones's lips, teeth, and tongue emblazoned across the chest.

"I can see your nipples," I say as we reach her.

"And I can see yours," she says to me.

"I think we may need security," Elena says to us with a crooked smile.

"We'll be fine," I say. "We just plan to enjoy our last night of anonymity with a little wardrobe debauchery."

"Okay," she says with an extended drawl that sounds more American than Cuban. "Follow me."

We walk behind her jeans, T-shirt, sneakers, and sticky hair ponytail teetering on our stilts of choice, trying not to fall or flash the neighborhood of nosies who have made a point of hanging on their porches or just outside their front doors, any time a taxi pulls up in front of ours. I wave to a few as I climb into the cool cab. Elena slides the door shut behind us and we take off down the street into the evening traffic.

"I guess we all had the same idea tonight?" Diedre asks."

"And what's that?" I ask.

"Naked or bust," she says.

"It's hot here," Jennifer says. "I can't imagine what it would feel like if we came in the middle of July or August. It's only March, and already the heat and the humidity are on hell."

"True," Diedre says. "I don't know how they do it down here and not everybody has AC. That's probably why everybody is so in shape. They sweat off everything they eat."

"Don't forget all the damn walking," Jennifer says.

"I'm surprised more people don't just walk around looking like us wearing little or nothing."

"That's because airy, white clothes breathe better," Elena says from beside me.

"Like me?" Diedre asks.

"Something like that," Elena says.

"So, I take it no one here really likes body con or spandex?" I ask.

"No," Elena answers quickly.

"She told you," Jennifer says.

"Whatever," I say. "I like my dress. I like that no one else will see me in this dress except you three and people who don't know me. And when I get back home, I will put it in the back of my closet with the rest of my *Rainbow* acquired, vacation, freakum dresses, until they are needed for another occasion."

"And what occasion is that?" Jennifer asks.

"Don't you worry about that," I say, cutting my eyes at Jennifer.

"The same occasion you probably pull out them shorts for when Octavius comes over," Diedre says to her.

"He doesn't need shorts," Jennifer says with her own sly smile.

"Oh, so you just greet him at the door ass naked?" Diedre asks.

"Sometimes," she says. "It depends on whether he deserves it."

"And what, pray tell, makes Jennifer's deserving list?" I ask. "You know you can be a cantankerous bitch when you want to be."

"I know," Jennifer says. "He's so patient and that's always deserving. And I still get the win."

"How is that?" Diedre asks.

"Because he gives great head," Jennifer says.

"And I'm done," Diedre says immediately.

"What?" Jennifer says. "You asked."

"And now I'm not."

"Well, I am," I say. "He gives great head, but what's on his warning label?"

"Ooooh . . ." Jennifer says, bringing one finger to her lips.

"Hold that thought," Elena says to us. "We're here."

She opens the sliding door to the van and leads us into the brick faced storefront of the restaurant. We follow behind her and the hostess up a set of winding iron stairs until we reach the turf covered rooftop over-looking Old Havana, as the sun begins to set on the island. At a long table overlooking the edge of the building to the pavement below, we take pictures and selfies, posed and candid, modelesque and silly, some to post and some to savor between each other. It is not until drinks have been ordered, appetizers served and removed, and steaming plates of fried fish, white rice, and stewed black beans have been placed before us, do we get back to the conversation from the cab.

"Don't think you got out of answering," I say to Jennifer as she pulls a piece of fried snapper away from the bone.

She looks at me with her eyebrows raised as she rushes her fork into her mouth.

"What's Octavius's warning label say?"

She chews, slowly pushing the disintegrating fish from side to side in her mouth, as she pretends to mull the question to delay her answer.

"Okay how about this," Diedre suggests. "We know he gives great head. Which is the most important characteristic. And we know he's patient with your moody ass."

"We know he makes bomb ass lunches for you, because you stay with a tupperware dish that has the whole newsroom thinking we ordered from somewhere fancy, and it's just your home cooked meals," I say.

"Hell, yeah," Diedre adds. "Soooo . . ."

"So is he perfect?" I finish.

"Hell, no," Jennifer says fast behind a swift swallow.

"Damn, girl, why'd you say it like that?" Diedre asks.

"Because nobody is perfect. Not me. Not you two. And for damn sure not Octavius."

"Then what's on his warning label?"

"He's junky. He's messy. He cooks great but he hates to wash the dishes. He squeezes the toothpaste from the middle instead of the bottom. He shaves his hair and cuts his toenails over the tub without washing it out."

"Girl, those are all things that can be fixed," Diedre says.

"True," Jennifer says. "But that doesn't mean I'm the one who wants to fix them. I blame his momma. I'm so tired of these single mothers who treat their son's like kings and allow them to occupy space in this world like they're Prince Hakeem. The royal penis is not clean, and neither are your clothes, your drawls, or your stank-ass apartment."

"Well, I guess you can add junky and messy to the warning label," I say. "This man will make you think your middle name is maid, or that his name is Your Majesty. He expects you to clean up after him because he was too busy being babied instead of raised, that he is inept when it comes to household chores. This seeming innocuous rift will cause you great grief when you come home and find he's self-pleased himself all over your sheets and didn't change them, expecting you to either do so or sleep in the jizz."

"That's just nasty," Diedre says.

"Same," Elena says. "Eso es muy asqueroso," she says in Spanish.

"Side-effects of grown ass baby men include rapid aging," Diedre begins.

"Sudden migraines," I say.

"And loss of hair either from stress induced alopecia or trichotillomania," Jennifer says.

I say, "If you experience any of these symptoms, please return said man to his mother with explicit instructions that he should not be allowed to roam the streets as a fully functioning adult, until he is able to fully function as an adult."

"He's not that bad," Jennifer says.

She laughs and chuckles at our jokes in her jest.

"She's headmatized," Diedre says.

I see Jennifer roll her eyes and then avert them back to her food. A cloud of emotion covers her face and I can tell our jokes hit a little too close to home and that she, too, was trying to be patient. She told us willingly about his messiness, but it may be a foil for something else entirely. A metaphor for some other quality she wishes Octavius had an abundance of, but does not.

I ask, "Is he kind to you?"

"Yes," Jennifer says.

"Does he treat you right?"

"Yes."

"Then ignore us."

I give her an out to return to contentment about her relationship, but I know it is not enough. I know our japes and jovial jabs at her expense have bubbled up a specific set of feelings and emotions she was trying not to focus on, while on vacation. I know that because it is what we do when we are on vacation. We convince ourselves we are getting some much-needed rest, relaxation, self-care, and rejuvenation time, when in reality, we are running from the problems that don't need a passport to cross borders and greet us at our rental doorstep, or on the rooftop of a restaurant.

In our ignorance of the direction of the conversation, Diedre and I have acted as mirrors for the glaring issues in Jennifer's relationship, she didn't want to admit to herself that she's seen. It's like when my mother told me, after only meeting Aaron a few times, that she didn't like him.

"Naomi, he's going to break your heart," she said to me. "He doesn't want you, nor does he need you."

"You don't even know him," I said, trying to defend my still budding relationship.

"I don't need to know him," she said. "I've known men like him. You're a placeholder for the real woman he wants to be with. You're close, but you're not his ideal. He's going to leave you."

I never forgot the words that she said to me three months after we had first started dating, twenty-one months before our break-up, and nearly six years ago from the moment I am in with Jennifer and Diedre now. I know this moment, this vacation of male derision and levity, she will not forget. The moment a small disagreement goes left into a full-blown argument over what she thinks is a suggestion, one borne out of frustration but coated in sugar, and he takes as a critique; she will remember this conversation. She will remember that she was the one to voice concern about his junkiness, his lack of perfection, and that we pounced on it and made him into a grown ass baby man, impotent of adult characteristics, reduced down to the dexterity of his tongue, and simplified as someone who has gotten older but never grown up. She will remember. As I watch her face swallow food she no longer enjoys because we've soured the taste in her belly, I am reminded of how I felt when my mother's prescient words rang true and I was scouting for jobs alone instead of as one half of an engaged power couple to be.

In the beginning darkness of the Havana night, and the cooling of the humid heat, forks scrape plates, throats swallow sangria, and teeth chew food. We three are quiet as we finish our meal. Pulsing, instrumental music from a hidden DJ sets an atmosphere for a Saturday night in the city, instead of our trio of the love-deficient, the recently uncoupled, and the holding on for change who will go back to their beautiful house, and sulk in their beautiful rooms, until the sun rises to whisk us back to the land of failed dreams and insecure opportunities.

"Are you girls looking forward to going back home?" Elena asks us after the waitress brings out the final check.

"No," Diedre says quickly. "I need the life where I can be on vacation forever."

"I don't mind going home," I say. "I'm just not sure I'm ready to go back to work."

"But you're not coming back to work until Wednesday," Jennifer says.

"I know. I need a day to recover from traveling, and a day to get my locs tightened and braided down, and my wig cleaned, so Boyce doesn't lose his shit, since he's seen what my hair really looks like."

"I still can't believe you did it," Diedre says.

"I don't see why not."

"Because you're on air. You have to maintain basically the same look you came into the business with, when you first got in."

"And as long as I look as such on TV, what I do personally does not and should not matter," I say.

"So are you going to wear your wig twenty-four seven in Jacksonville, so that people don't see you running errands on the weekends one way, but then on TV another."

"Nope. I'm going to live my life. People will see me how they see me. They'll figure it out or they won't."

"I still can't believe you did it," Diedre says.

Jennifer says, "In this day and age, with all the Black and Latin, and other people in the business, managers should know by now that everybody's hair doesn't come out the scalp, blonde and bone straight. This is not *Mad Men, Mary Tyler Moore,* or *Murphy Brown.*"

"The old one or the reboot?" I ask.

"Take your pick," Jennifer says. "Either way, my point is, the world looks a lot more like Naomi, than it does any woman on any one of those shows."

"The world may for real look like us, but that doesn't mean people want to see that behind an anchor desk," Diedre says. "Just like the rest of media, be it news or entertainment, people want to see the best representation of themselves, not always the out there and eccentric."

"I'm eccentric because I loc'd my hair?" I ask.

"If people only wanted to see the best representation of themselves on TV, we'd still be watching *Leave It to Beaver* or some shit like that," Jennifer says. "People like mess. People like trash. People like raw. That's why reality shows exist and thrive, that's even why *This Is Us* is so damn popular. They look like a well to-do, melting pot America, nice TV family, but they got issues too."

"That show should really be called *Randall and Beth and Them,*" Diedre says.

"Not even," I say. "I could do without Randall. It should just be *Beth and Them.*"

"Don't do Randall like that," Jennifer says.

"He's another mama's boy, grown ass baby man, too," Diedre says.

I suck my teeth because I feel the sting just as much as Jennifer does. Maybe even more since I've been known to take shit personally. I push back from the table and stand up. Pulling the hem of my dress down, I wait for Jennifer, Diedre, and Elena to follow.

"Are you all ready?" she asks us.

"Yes," I say. "We have early flights in the morning."

Elena shuffles in front of Jennifer and I and leads us out. We wave to the woman who served as our waitress and the patrons who were sitting around us. Gripping both banisters, we carefully teeter down the three flights of winding iron stairs back to the ground level. Outside of the courtyard, our faithful taxi driver is waiting for us in the van.

I say, "Randall is okay, but Kevin could have died from an opioid overdose after he hurt his leg in that movie he was filming."

"Don't do Kevin like that," Diedre says. "That's my blue-eyed baby."

"First of all, his eyes aren't even blue," Jennifer says. "Secondly, why? His story is so white-boy, woe is me privilege. And now he wants to be woke because he's got a black girlfriend."

"Not anymore," Diedre says.

"Either way," Jennifer says. "I can't."

"And this is what makes it a great show," I say.

"Because we're all talking about it?" Jennifer says.

"Exactly," Diedre says.

"People talk about a lot of things," Jennifer says. "That doesn't mean they're good. Or bad," she adds. "It just means people talk."

"Everybody talked about that trash-ass Aaliyah movie," Diedre says.

"Okay, see, here's the thing with biopics about musicians," I begin. "If you don't get the rights to the music from the family, then you probably shouldn't do the movie."

"Unless of course you find you a Deborah Cox to re-sing all the Whitney songs to make your movie work like Angela Bassett did," Jennifer says.

"That part," I say.

I put a finite period on the conversation that doubled as Jennifer's defense of Octavius against our opinions. Silence fills the van until, at last, Elena's perfect English breaks the void.

"Ladies, we're here," she says as we pull up in front of our temporary home for the last time.

She opens the sliding door for us and waits as we file out. We exchange hugs, and thank you's, keep in touches, and promises to return and see her again. We give her a decided on tip for being so gracious and kind and patient with us as we traversed her city, and kept her away from her family, and then once again she disappears with the taxi down the street, away from the foreigners and the eyes of the watching neighbors.

Inside the cool house from leaving our air conditioning units on and the doors open, we file to our individual rooms and change. I strip out of the tight, cutout dress and pace naked in the room as I make piles to eventually transfer to my suitcase.

Five days is not enough for vacation.

I look around my room at the tiny suitcase that could fit twin toddlers and think Diedre could be on to something, when it comes to working a job where vacationing is a career. I could push time shares on luxurious islands, or run a travel agency, or a travel blog, or something that doesn't require me to put the world on my back, and then try to escape it without looking up the Homeland Security reports to find the latest threats for the area. That's how I vacation, armed with information about what could happen to me, and the address of the American Embassy written down just in case, just in case happens. I sigh as someone knocks on my door.

"I'm going out to the patio to smoke."

The voice belongs to Jennifer. She bought a pack of the infamous Cohiba Cuban cigars from a massive shopping complex, flea market, swap meet type place, under the guise of bringing them back for Octavius. I bought a half dozen packs for myself because wine and cigars are how I wind down my nights when it's been one of those days in the newsroom, when the news is breaking, the tensions are high, the tempers are flaring, and the empty, peaceful, stillness, that already eludes me, becomes a foreign entity. I find one of my cigar boxes, run my fingernail through the cellophane wrapping, and open it, pulling out one of the pre-cut fatties. I grab my robe from the edge of the headboard post and loosely tie it around my naked body and head to the back patio of the house.

Jennifer is slouched on one of the cushions of the patio chair with the cigar between her fingers and smoke coming from her lips. Diedre is opposite her, lighting up one of the thin Romeo & Juliet cigars she bought. I take a seat at the tip of our triangle and grab the lighter in front of Jennifer and light my desire. Smoke fills my mouth and I hold it until I can't breathe, and then exhale it in one long smoky breath.

"So, Diedre, what were Internet bae's warning signs before the sudden breakup?" Jennifer asks.

"I don't know," she says. "We didn't date long enough for me to see. I'll find out when I get back, I guess."

"Well, you already know one of his issues," I say after a puff.

"What's that?" Diedre asks.

"He's insecure with a woman having her own or more than him."

"I guess," Diedre says, puffing her cigar.

"And what about you, Miss Thing?" Jennifer asks.

"What about me," I say.

"What were Aaron's warning signs that have left you so jilted, you can't date anybody for more than three weeks and keep a cuddy-buddy in the cue."

"Wow, that was harsh," I say.

"The truth hurts, Babes," Jennifer says.

I sigh and puff my cigar before answering. I know she is reacting to the tear down we did of Octavius earlier. She is asking us the same questions we asked her, because to find what makes us hurt, makes her think she will feel better. She doesn't know the same hurt she feels for herself I feel for her and for myself, as well. She doesn't know that her words on the beach, "You're still in recovery from your last relationship" broke me down just as much as Diedre's "grown ass baby-man" comment broke her down. I leave them waiting and puff my cigar before saying the words that were said to me about the warning signs and the side effects that I didn't see.

I say, "I was a placeholder for the real woman he wanted to be with. I was close to what he wanted, but I wasn't it. I wasn't his one. I wasn't his ideal, and so we broke up."

"So, he was supposed to be your one, huh?" Jennifer asks.

Her eyes hang low, and her long, sinewy limbs are stretched on the paved ground in front of her as she brings the cigar back from her mouth. In black boy shorts and a cut up white T-shirt, she looks like a new-aged Hanes model on break from a commercial shoot.

"Was he the one, Naomi?" Diedre asks.

I look at her in her satin romper and bonnet. Her eager eyes ask out of both genuine curiosity of my own life and for what her own future may hold. Her eyes jump from me to Jennifer, the woman who's wrestling with jilting her own self out of a good physical love that may leave her empty in more ways than one.

I answer them honestly. "I don't know," I say. "I don't even know if I believe in that. The one. Is there any just one right person for all nearly eight billion people on the planet?"

"The answer to that is "no" since women outnumber men," Diedre says.

"Not necessarily," Jennifer says. "With LGBT etcetera, plus, etcetera, plus, I think there's someone for everybody."

"Etcetera plus?" I ask.

"You know they got damn near every letter of the alphabet under the rainbow. I can't keep up, so I just say etcetera plus, so I don't offend anybody."

"What did you lace your cigar with?"

"I wish I had something to lace this cigar with so I can take my ass to sleep."

"Mmhmm."

"Don't change the subject," Diedre says. "Why do you or don't you believe in the one?"

"Because I think it's bullshit," I say.

"Did you think that when you thought you and Aaron were supposedly making moves together?" Jennifer asks.

"That's what I get for telling you my business." I snicker.

"Yeah, it is," Jennifer says. "You know you bought into believing in the one, just like rest of us who grew up on fairytales and castles. You know you want to have it all."

"Hell, nah," I rebuke quickly. "Some girls, or women rather, want marriage, kids, career, the whole bit. I just want to live my life, travel, and eat well."

"That just sounds like the new lie you're telling yourself," Jennifer says.

"Sure does," Diedre adds. "You didn't even mention sex."

"Yeah, well, I'd like to be booked, busy, and unbothered in that area too."

"Exactly. You want it all too."

"No. Wanting it all is what got Joan in trouble. I'm not trying to end up like her waiting on a ring forever and when I get it, it's not what it's cracked up to be."

"You still mad there wasn't a *Girlfriend's* reunion, huh?" Jennifer asks.

"Hell, yeah," I say.

"You need to get over that. Other people have it all."

"Like who?"

"Girl Melanie from *The Game*."

"Oh, please," I say. "She only got it all after Derwin lied, cheated, had a baby by somebody else, and then got mad at her for doing the same thing, almost."

"Okay," Jennifer says. "Olivia Pope."

"Don't nobody want Fitz ass. And we don't even know if they ended up together, or if she became President. She leaves the White House with bundles, but then on the portrait she's got a full natural. I needed one more season for explanation and clarification."

"Okay, Oprah," Jennifer says.

"She's not married. She lost her baby, and she can always give her girls back."

"Then I won't even say Beyoncé," Diedre says.

"Lemonade," I say.

"You're making my head hurt with all this truth," Jennifer says. "Do like Kendrick say: Bitch, don't kill my vibe."

"That's why we need medical marijuana cards," I say. "It takes the edge off. I'd get me a cute little hookah and be right."

"Too bad they piss test at work," Diedre says.

"I didn't even know," Jennifer says.

"Why do you think the background check takes so damn long," I say.

"Gotcha," she says, bringing the roach of her cigar to her lips one last time before stubbing it out.

"The more you know," Diedre says.

"Thank you, walking PSA. Now I do. I'm going to bed."

I stub out the end of my half-smoked cigar in the ashtray on the patio table and then take it back with me to my room. Behind my closed and locked doors, I organize my piles inside my suitcase until all that's left out are my underwear for the morning, my sweats, socks, and sneakers. I move my bags by the door, turn off the lamp light on the nightstand, and lay across the bed, sticky, sweaty and naked, in my open robe, beneath the fan with the air conditioning blowing to cool my body.

You're still in recovery from your last relationship.

You know you want to have it all.
That sounds like the new lie you're telling yourself.
You're a placeholder.

The words of our last conversation lull me into a tormented sleep. The voices of Diedre, Jennifer, and my mother alternate until I stop seeing them in my dreams and I wake up naked and alone in a black room against a black sky, in what I imagine to be the final shade of a lonely death.

The heaviness of my mood stays with me through our last breakfast of fresh mango and guava. I know I am barely present in the taxi to the airport. Jennifer and Diedre chatter beside me while I lay my head against the window, staring outside at the passing streets. At the airport, through customs, I still hear the voices.

You're a placeholder.
You're still in recovery from your last relationship.

I hate to admit it, but the shit stings.

"This is a full flight aboard Southwest fifty-four eleven to Fort Lauderdale," the flight attendant says as we schlep with our bags onto the plane, looking for an empty row.

"Look right there," Diedre says, tapping me on my shoulder. "Behind those guys. We can sit there."

Jennifer guides us to the empty row Diedre pointed out at the back of the plane. We shuffle there to claim our seats before anyone else does. Jennifer says "Excuse us" to the men as we bump by them into the tighter space that will be our row. With my luggage bag pushed into the overhead compartment, I slide into the window seat with my purse, pull down the shade, and lean my head against it with my eyes closed. The flight attendants' instructions become background noise, as do the conversations, irritable traveling arguments, and discussions of all the news we missed from Jennifer, and Diedre beside me.

"Ladies and gentleman, this is our final boarding group," the flight attendant says. "If you do not have the seat you desire, that means you're sitting in the middle."

"Hey, look, it's the gatekeeper and the fish," a male voice says from the row in front of us.

"Ow," I say, rubbing my shoulder and opening my eyes to glare at Diedre, who elbowed me.

"She speaks," the voice says.

"I do," I say.

"She did," he says.

In front of me is the brown skinned, lanky man from the beach. The man with ropes for hair, and tattoos on half of his upper arms. Today he is clothed. His black, graphic tee nearly hides all of his tattoos. I can only see the ends peeking out of the bottom hem of his sleeves.

"Hi, I'm Kiyan," he says extending his hand.

We shake. "That's an interesting name," I say.

"My moms named me Kiyan because I'm hot like pepper," he says with a satisfied grin.

"Hmm. Is your middle name corny like flakes?" I ask.

"The fish has jokes," he says. "Are you guys finished in Lauderdale or going somewhere else?"

"Is this your way of trying to find out where we live?" I ask.

"We're going to Jacksonville," Diedre says.

"Huh, the gatekeeper had a little slip. So are we," Kiyan says, gesturing to himself and his friends.

"My name's Diedre," she says.

"One down, two to go," Kiyan says.

Jennifer tips her hand in the air, "I'm Jennifer."

"Two down, one to go," Kiyan says. "Just waiting for the fish."

"I don't appreciate being called an animal," I say indignantly.

"I wouldn't call you an animal if I knew your name."

"Surely, there are other things you can think of to call a woman when you don't know her name that are not also the names of animals."

"There are other things I could call you, but I would run the risk of offending you by being overly familiar, too casual, or too old, archaic, and formal."

"And so, you think your continued use of "fish" is appropriate."

"You're still talking to me," he says smiling.

I notice the singular dimple in his cheek, the cleft in his chin, and the bushiness of his eyebrows set against the crisp edge of his hairline.

"Naomi," I say, extending my hand. "My name is Naomi."

"Kiyan Fontaine English," he says taking my hand.

I feel the burning stares from Diedre and Jennifer. They are watching me to see if I will stick with Naomi and give Kiyan more of my cold shoulder, or open up. His eyes hold the same question theirs do. How far will I be willing to play?

Fuck it.

"Naomi Jean Grace," I say.

6.

Bills, Bills, Bills

"So how was your trip," Dominique asks me as she runs her fingers through my locs.

I rest my head and neck into her capable hands and sigh from beneath my navel as she begins to massage my scalp. Next to an orgasm, getting my head rubbed by strong, nimble fingers, is one of the best experiences in the world. I even put it before my favorite meal. Head rubs are an act of love, and the way Dominique's hands feel against the coverings of my head, I would think I was her only client and our relationship was more than a friendly business transaction.

"It was good," I say through a yawn. "Exactly what I needed. What I need more of."

"So, you would recommend going?" she asks.

"Every day of the week I'm alive. Cuba owes me nothing."

"And how does your hair feel?"

"Itchy and dirty," I say. "I rinsed it under some water while I was down there, but I didn't put my hands in it because I didn't want to mess up any of the locs or cause them to unravel."

"You ready for a shampoo?" she asks me.

"Girl, yes. This is about to feel better than a shower after a good sweaty workout. Wash me!"

"Come on to the back."

She pulls me out of my scalp massage induced trance and walks from her front corner work space into the rest of the shop she owns along 103rd Street on Jacksonville's Westside. Her shop, D's Divine Natural Hair Care Salon and Weave Emporium, is in a strip mall sandwiched between blocks of liquor stores, convenience stores, and Internet cafes.

I follow her onto the open tile floor of the salon past the unoccupied stations for the three other stylists in the shop, to the back area where there are two wash bowls and four massive overhead drying units. I sit down in the booty worn leather chair and lay my head back into the neck rest of the sink. She throws a towel and cape around me and starts the water. Sighing with anticipation of the professional washing that's coming, I wait for the water and tea tree shampoo to begin their magic to cleanse and clear out my sebaceous glands.

"So, what were the people like?" Dominique asks me as she scratches my wet head.

"They were just like us," I say. "There are rich Cubans and poor Cubans, and there are black Cubans and white Cubans. Even our guide said that to us. Elena, she was like 'Our countries have more in common than most people think.' She didn't lie either."

"I don't know," Dominique says as she rinses the shampoo. "It just seems so isolated. No Internet, no real way to get in touch with people in case something happens. Doesn't seem safe to me. If something's going down, I need my people to know how to get to me," she says.

"It's not that isolated," I defend. "It's just like anywhere else you go out of the country. You adapt to what they have and call home when you can."

"That's easy for you to say," Dominique says, working the conditioner through my locs. "You don't have a baby-daddy, a husband, or any badass kids running around wondering, talking about, 'Mama, where you at.'"

"All the more reason it seems like you need to go somewhere where people can't and don't know how to find you. Help you get your peace back."

"Chile, please," she says, sitting me up in the chair. "I won't have peace for another fifteen years. That's when Taylor graduates from high school. When she's gone, and hopefully to a college a ways away from me, then I can talk to you about peace."

"Seems like it's too far away to wait that long for peace of mind," I say.

"Spoken like a true woman who only has to care about herself."

"If you say so."

"You'll go crazy for your kids . . . the right man, too," Dominique says more to herself than to me. "C'mon under the dryer to let this deep conditioner set, and then we'll rinse you and see what you're working with."

I follow Dominique just steps away to the bay of dryers and sit in the one she has up and warming for me. She secures the head of the dryer over my plastic cap covered locs and walks away from me. I watch her as she goes. In light denim jeggings, worn Converse, and two layers of colorful tank tops plus bra, Dominique walks away, her hips swinging all on their own from birthing two children without thought of a snap-back plan. The dimples of cellulite and fat show through the stretchy, thin jean material of her pants. Long, black box braids hang to the rise of her behind. They sway across the span of her back as she goes, her face buried in her phone. I watch her until she disappears into her own work space, where I left my wig she still has to clean and curl.

When I first moved here from New Orleans, I found myself lost on the Westside after a day of exploring the city's dozens of communities and micro-neighborhoods. It was my plan to use my weekends off to drive all of Jacksonville, the largest city by land mass in the United States, until I knew it as well as I knew the West Bank from Uptown, Downtown from the Treme, the ninth from Carrollton, and the Garden District from the Bywater. Somehow, I made a few wrong turns and ended up on Timuquana Road, that took me from Ortega to smack in the middle of the Westside. I crossed under the viaduct at 295 that would have taken me back to my apartment, to explore this side of the city that I happened upon by accident.

It was overwhelmingly busy and overwhelmingly black. The type of neighborhood where everybody is moving and everybody is rushing because nobody has time to waste; not the dope boys, not the corner car salesmen, not the fast-food workers, or gas station barbecue hawkers. I drove until the busyness and the blackness of the main thoroughfare began to shift and I ended up facing a golf course subdivision on my left, and a sign pointing toward a new subdivision being built on my right. I drove until I ran into too much construction, and a confused curved street, and made a U-turn. It was on my drive back down, when I was stopped for a light near the Waffle House, that I looked over and saw the big purple sign and the long name for the hair salon. I maneuvered my way into the far-left lane, made another U-turn at the light and drove into the parking lot for the salon. I've been coming over here ever since, for whatever I needed done to my head.

When Dominique first started laying her hands in my head, she had only one child, and was newly pregnant with the second. I came in, got a touch up on my relaxer, and then a full sew-in and went about my day. That lasted for the first six months of our friend-client relationship, until she informed me that since I was wearing a full weave anyway, she might as well transition me to natural. I agreed, so long as she planned to keep up the maintenance on all the different textures as my hair grew out. She did, and when she went on her own scheduled maternity leave after delivering her daughter, she still made time for me even though I was at her house, instead of her salon, and she did my hair while I fed and rocked her baby girl to sleep in my arms, and answered all the "Why" questions her toddler son could think of.

She said to me then as I sat in her kitchen, "You're not around children much, are you?"

"What makes you say that?" I asked.

"Because you have the patience of Job, answering all of Treon's questions. I would have been told him to get out my face and go play with his toys."

"He's cute," I said, defending my indulgence in his childish curiosity.

"He's annoying is what he is," Dominique said.

Sitting sideways on one of her high-backed, plastic covered kitchen chairs, she washed, detangled, and cornrowed my hair as I cooed at baby Taylor, sleeping milk drunk in my arms. She has been doing my hair as her life has changed from single mother of one, to married mother of three; her children, plus a bonus daughter from her husband. As her life has changed, I have been her constant and consistent client, driving thirty to forty minutes away from the place I call home to make sure my edges are laid, my length is flourishing, and nobody who can tell a wig from a weave, from a natural head of hair, is clowning me in the comments on a video posted by the TV station. Her life has changed and mine, for the most part, has stayed the same. No husband. No kids. Just a job, a promotion, a new house, and different hairstyles.

I roll my eyes at my own contemplation of the stagnation of my life and pick up one of the old magazines. They're scattered across a purple cushioned bench that serves as a middle table of sorts, for clients sitting under the dryer. The cover story is on an unshirted male actor with burnished bronze skin, six-pack abs, sultry bedroom eyes, and a face that's softer than a mean mug but still not quite a smile. The male version of the Tyra Banks "smize." While he is yummy, he is not what catches my eye. Instead, it is the smaller headline at the bottom right corner of the magazine. The place most people don't usually notice, because their thumb is covering the words, as they hold and stare at the magazine with the eye candy on the cover, considering whether or not the story inside is worth their coin. Looking down at the discarded magazine, the bottom corner story is what intrigues me. "How to Turn Around Your Relationship Woes: Our pros weigh in."

I pick up the magazine, find the table of contents, and thumb to the page with the article. Pictured on the pages are what are supposed to be feuding couples. There's a man and a woman standing with their backs turned, another of a man and woman sleeping in a white-sheeted bed with a noticeable gap between them in what's supposed to be the snuggle zone, and then there's a third picture showing a man and a woman walking away from each other.

I read the three main pages of the article plus the continuation on a fourth page in the back of the magazine. Despite the promise of expert opinion, there was nothing new any of the so-called experts were quoted as saying. The advice, for the most part, was have more sex. If not that generic catch all, then the suggestion to leave outside problems at the door. I swear, I'mma start buying men's magazines to see if they're told this same garbage, or if their experts actually advise them to be acquiescent at times in their relationships. From where I'm sitting it seems the onus is always on the women.

"C'mon, let's rinse you out," Dominique says standing over me.

I quickly close the magazine over my thumb to hold my place as I make my way back to the sink bowl.

She says, "So what else is new, Ms. World Traveler?"

"Nothing much," I say. "Everything is everything."

"You didn't go to Cuba and find you a good vacation boo? A week is a good long time to have an adventure no one else will remember in English but you."

"Nah, it wasn't like that," I say. "It was a girls trip."

"Then you all should've been on the prowl then."

I imagine her smirking face even though my eyes are closed as she rinses the conditioner from my locs. Chubby cheeks, full lips, and a pug-like nose, her face is cute and child-like no matter the amount of makeup she puts on.

I say, "Well one of the girls has a boyfriend, and the other one doesn't know if she's broken up or not."

"And what was your excuse?" She asks as she sits me up. "C'mon, let's go to my chair."

"Who needs the drama of a long distance, international, bi-lingual relationship. I don't speak Spanish, and even if I did, what would be the point."

"I didn't say start up a relationship. I said have a fling. Oh, oh, oh, is the same in every language," she says faking a moan.

"I'm good."

"Are you sure?" she asks. "You got your nose buried so deep in the relationship advice column, you didn't even hear me talking to you about how you want me to curl this wig."

"I was under the dryer."

"It wasn't that loud."

"Wait, you washed it already?"

"Girl, that wig has been washed and dried. I walked back and forth past you two or three times, trying to talk to you, asking you questions, and you never looked my way once."

"I didn't hear you."

"I know. Did you learn anything from the magazine?" She asks, drying my locs with an old T-shirt, and then a micro-fiber towel.

"These people don't know anything more than the rest of us. The only thing the title of relationship expert means, is that they have tried and failed at a lot of relationships, and now they've finally gotten one right, they can talk about all the dirt they did before reaching the relationship promised land."

"It works for Steve Harvey," Dominique says.

"Who's on his third marriage," I say. "The people who are the real experts don't write books. They live their lives and die."

"That's harsh."

"It's true."

"So, what do you think about the *Black Love* show on Oprah's channel?"

"It's good. But it's also another lesson in how much shit you're going to have to put up with. All those couples have gone through something, they just decided to stick it out and go through it together. It just lets you know on front street that men and women, we're always going to put up with each other's shit, we just have to decide which man or woman is worth it."

"Now look who sounds like Steve Harvey," she says.

"Whatever. Tell me it's not true, married lady?"

Dominique doesn't answer. She doesn't negate my hypothesis, my theory that all relationships have a certain "shit-taking" threshold. I'm sure hers does, as did mine with Aaron, as does Jennifer's with Octavius, as does my mother's with my daddy. She keeps her thoughts on my approximation or over-simplification of coupledom to herself as her fingers fly through my scalp, greasing my parts with Jamaican Black Castor Oil.

"You did good," she says, lifting various pieces of hair. "None of them unraveled or need to be retwisted."

"Good," I say.

"I'mma braid you down so you can fit under this wig; and then the next time you come we'll do a tightening."

"Okay," I say.

Dominique works quietly as she braids my hair. There is no TV in the shop to break up the quiet drone of background noise. I add to the sounds of traffic outside, the hum of the plugged-in appliances, and the sizzle of the curling iron stove, with my turns of the magazine pages. I flip away from the relationship advice column, thumbing through pages, staring at the pictures, reading some of the captions, and ignoring the articles. I give up on the mag altogether as Dominique turns and twists my head, braiding the locs around my ears. She is the only hairstylist I know who begins cornrows in the middle of the head and works out instead of just going from right to left.

"All done," she says. "I just have to curl this wig and you will be good to go. Do you want it flipped in our out?"

"You can flip it in and curl it under," I say.

I get up from her chair and sit on a small wooden stool in a corner beside a full-length mirror in her work space. I watch her as she focuses on curling each section she pulls out. Her hands click and turn the Marcel irons with expert skill. Sweat beads on her forehead and drips down her nose from the heat of the stove, the iron, and the entrapped heat of the hair. This is the reason she wears two tank tops. A hot pink one over her signature purple. Her arms are strong and cut from turning the irons for most of her teenaged and adult life. It is the most in shape thing about her. I watch her and wonder what made her decide to go into the hair business. I wonder if it's because it's something she really wanted to do, or something she became good at out of necessity of her birthright. I wonder if she was one of the girls who did hair during her lunch period in middle school and high school, making extra cash providing a service, most teens wanted but couldn't afford to get at a regular shop. I wonder if this is her love or just an easy way to make money.

"I told you I bought a house, right?" I say as I watch her.

"No, you didn't," she says. "When did you do that?"

"I closed and moved in right before I left."

"When is your housewarming going to be?"

"Girl, I had it already. I closed Thursday morning the week before I left. Moved everything in and put everything up for the housewarming Sunday."

"That was fast. Did you decorate and stuff?"

"I used the stuff I had in my apartment, and I had gotten some extra items from Hobby Lobby here and there. I didn't mean to have it that fast. The closing got pushed back a few times, but I'd already had a date set for the party, so I kept it."

"Why am I not surprised?" Dominique asks looking up at me with a knowing smirk.

"What do you mean?"

"How do you plan a housewarming party before you officially have a house?"

"It's called goal setting," I say. "I gave my realtor a deadline and a goal and she met it."

"Barely," Dominique says.

"A met goal is still a met goal, even if it is one minute 'til midnight."

"So where is it?" she asks.

"It's a townhouse in Bartram. The neighborhood is huge, but you have to know me to get to me, the way they have our little section of the subdivision tucked away."

"That's nice," she says, spraying the curls of the wig with oil and spritz so they shine and don't move.

"Yeah. Nice and expensive," I say.

I grab my purse from the floor beside the stool and dig for my wallet. Inside are five crisp twenties I transferred from my credit card to my checking account, and took out of the ATM just for this moment.

"Here you go," I say.

She tucks the twenties inside her bra without asking if I need change, and then grabs a broom from the corner near where she stands, and starts sweeping. There isn't much hair on the ground. Just a few strands from the natural shedding of the wig.

She says, "So you bought a big, pretty house, and it's just you?"

"Yes, ma'am," I say.

Dominique shakes her head. "I don't know if I'd a been able to do it. A house. That's like something you do with somebody."

"That's an old-fashioned way of thinking."

"Perhaps."

"I don't know," I say, trying to soften my judgement, "I was tired of renting. It made no sense to pay what I was paying in rent when I could have much more space for the same price, if not a little more."

"So, is it worth it?" she asks me.

"I'm about to find out," I say.

"It's so permanent," she says.

"Not really. Houses can be sold."

"But don't you get lonely?"

"Let me ask you this, are you lonely when you're in your house by yourself?"

"Hell, nah," Dominique says quickly. "If I can ever get the house to myself without them screaming kids, it's like the best present no one has ever thought to give me. That's when I get some of that fancy-ass peace you be talking about."

"Then same here. It's not lonely. It's just mine. I'll see you later."

She lifts the wig from the mannequin head and hands it to me. "I'll see you in a few weeks," she says.

Outside of the shop, I get into my car and maneuver my way across six lanes of traffic into the far-right lane that will let me jump back on 295 and go home. Home. The place my mother assumes is a money pit, my daddy believes will be hard to maintain, and Dominique thinks is lonely because I bought a house by myself. It may be all of those things, it may be none of those things, but what they don't get is that all of those things that my house is, or represents to them, is still all mine.

Who cares if it's a money pit? It's now my money pit. Right there with my Rent The Runway bill that just came for my on air clothes and the one hundred dollars I gave Dominique; courtesy of the bank. Maybe doctor mom was right. I should get another job; put my master's degree, that I'm still paying for to work, teaching or something, because clearly my prayers into my wallet aren't working.

I look at my bank statements and say, "Money will come," the way I used to look in the mirror at my hair and say, "You will grow," when Dominique chopped it after the natural texture got to what she thought was long enough to live on its own. I guess I get that from doctor mom. She used to walk around our house, and out in the back yard where she had a little garden, talking to the plants saying, "You will sprout." Now I talk to everything. Even the bills I rebuke.

I should have negotiated a ratings bonus in my contract, or a higher percentage increase for every year I stay with the show. I've been underpaid and undervalued since I got in the business. A fact my mother, as per her usual, was always happy to remind me about.

"Why would you accept a job making less than fifteen dollars an hour after six years of school?" She asked me after I told her I got a job at home.

I said, "Because that's better than taking a job for eight-fifty an hour in some Podunk town where I'd have to pay for rent and everything else. At least this way, I'm saving money."

We've never seen eye to eye when it comes to my life. She went to Xavier; I went to Dillard. She works for herself, I work for the proverbial man in an industry under attack by the Internet and the President. She wanted a husband and children, and a small home fit for the four of us, and I have none of those things.

"Naomi, by your age I had all the finer trappings of life and none of the headaches you have by going out there and chasing your dreams," she said to me right after I told her I found the townhouse.

I don't know what she wants from me. If the children are supposed to do better than the parents, then I thought she'd be happy that I'm doing something I actually love, and doing it well enough and on my own. But like Dominique and even Jennifer and Diedre, they can only see what I don't have.

I have a roof over my head, gas, and groceries. Who cares if I don't have a pot to piss in or a window to throw it out of, or a flat iron to halfway straighten my hair, and some place to shake it? What's mine is mine, what I have is what I have, and what I don't have is what I don't have. If I'm not concerned or complaining, no one else should be either. We're all out here trying to live our best lives and be great, as long as the God of the universe is willing. I'm not a child. I don't need someone constantly at my side reassuring me that what I'm doing is right. Though it would be nice if my guardian angel manifested themselves and was at my side day and night, anytime I needed a reassuring word for my soul.

Don't you get lonely?

Dominique's last question about my choices returns to me. Am I lonely? I can't say that I don't want someone to share my life with, but I know I'm not putting my life on hold while I'm waiting and looking. I'm breathing, I'm living—hell, I'm learning how to better, balance my budget and my time, and prioritize who and what gets my attention, so I don't fulfill my mother's prophecy and go broke, fall into foreclosure, file bankruptcy, and ruin my credit.

But you just paid for your hair on credit.

"Who asked you?" I say out loud to the inner voice that likes to remind me when I'm wrong.

I get out of my car and close the garage. I wait for the door to fully close shut, and then another moment to make sure I don't see or hear any other movements and noises, before I open the door to go inside. In my kitchen I look around my space, thankful and grateful it is just me. I don't have anyone to please and no one's pleasure to make or maintain. I open the refrigerator and stare inside. What stares back at me is the lonely box of Publix wings from the party. I pull back one of the flaps and see two cold and soggy fried chicken wings. I close the door, exit the kitchen and head upstairs. I open the door to the vision room but don't go in. Instead, I head for my bedroom, awash in navy blue, gray, and white. My semi-nautical theme is apparent from the comforter, pillows, and curtains. There's no better way to sleep than to the sound of the rain or on a boat, so I tried to bring the darkness of the water into the room, but even that presence doesn't comfort me. I walk through the bathroom into my closet and turn on the light. My eyes sweep across my clothes and shoes on shelves and racks, and the portable rack for my monthly rents.

"It's mine. Even if it's just for this moment, it's mine."

My own words comfort me. The sound of my own voice calms me. I am my own peace. Or as my mother still says, "You just like to hear yourself talk." In my closet, surrounded by my things, tangible things I can see, I reassure myself into security with my own wisdom, "It's all mine, even if it's just for a moment," and ignore my inner voice that says *if it's just for a moment it's not really yours.*

7.

Give 'Em More Grace

"Barbecue Becky.

Permit Patty.

Corner store Caroline.

Golf cart Gail

And now Neighborhood Watch Wanda.

When we come back on "Naomi Tonight" we'll see if we can give the latest Pollyanna, who thought it was okay to be out peeping and call the police, a little bit of grace.

That's next on "Naomi Tonight" only on Nine News Now."

My mic clicks in the studio to let me know that we are in the commercial break.

"You're going to get us in trouble out there," Jennifer says through my earpiece.

"How is that?" I ask.

"You know we didn't write that," she says. "I'm sure Boyce is on his way up here to glare at us and watch the end of the show play out."

"Then I guess I'll have to give him something to see," I say. "How does my wig look? Is it to bumpy and high in the top?"

"A little bit," Diedre says coming into my ear. "Pat it down in the back and maybe slide it a little, and you should be just fine."

"If you can braid down your locs, why don't you just get a sew in?" Jennifer asks.

"Because I never thought of it until you just said something. I'll have to ask Dominique the next time I go in."

"Don't do a sew-in," Diedre says. "That defeats the purpose of the locs if you're never going to wear them out."

"A lot of the things I do defeat the purpose of my initial intent," I say. "Asking doesn't mean I'm waiting for the needle and thread to be run through my head, it's just asking."

"One minute," John the floor director yells.

"Thank you," I say.

I pull out my pressed powder compact I keep on the cart beneath the desk and pop it open. Bringing the mirror close to my face, I move my mouth from side to side to check for cracks or wrinkles in my makeup. I doused my face with setting spray before we went on air to make sure everything held up for the hour, but I like to check during commercial breaks just in case, so viewers don't catch me on their screens slipping.

If it's not about the content of the show, it's about my looks. Those are the two categories viewers send in emails regarding me the most. When I first got here there was a swift wave of backlash. Emails with subject lines in all caps that said, "WHERE IS DAWN?" Or "Why Can't She Talk." After viewers realized Dawn was on another channel, I then started getting more and more emails about my voice. Too high-pitched, too much of an accent, too much Louisiana, New Orleans specifically. Even my best code-switch wasn't enough to placate the men and women who complained, while sounding like their dipped snuff was permanently lodged inside their mouths. So much for strength being in differences and not similarities.

Now that I've been here four years, worked with a vocal coach, drink dark liquor straight, and smoke half a cigar once a month, there are no more emails about my voice. Now it's either about the content of the show or how I look. Their emails are the reason I run when I'm not being chased, rent the clothes I'm wearing, have a subscription box for bras, a DSW Visa card, and I spend a small fortune in Sephora at least once a month. People are mean and words hurt worse than sticks and stones.

"Standby, Naomi," John says, raising his large hands into the air to count backward from ten.

His fingers make a fist and the open rolls for my "Give 'Em More Grace" segment. I run my tongue over my teeth to remove any possible lipstick that's there and slide the compact back under the desk. The mic clicks.

"Tonight in "Give 'Em More Grace" we take a look at the story of the woman who's been dubbed "Neighborhood Watch Wanda." The woman's real name is Patricia Knapland," I say as the camera cuts away from me to the video that accompanies the story I'm reading live.

"Knapland, who is white, is accused of calling the police on a group of African-American children in her neighborhood. The children range in age from seven to ten. The oldest were a ten-year-old boy and a nine-year-old girl. They were dressed in bathing suits and playing with a sprinkler and a slip-n-slide they had set up in their yard with their own water hose. Knapland says she told the children to stay off of her grass and to make sure their sprinkler did not oversaturate her cacti, she recently planted in her yard. She says the children did not listen, she did not see a car in their driveway that would have let her know their parents were home, and so with no other recourse, she called the police."

My mic clicks as the sound of the 911 call takes over in the studio. The editors built the audio from the call under a graphic with the woman's face they pulled from a confirmed picture from her Facebook page. The text of the call animates word by word.

"Nine one one, what's your emergency?"

"Hi, I'd like to report a group of children who are vandalizing the neighborhood and my property right now."

I zone out on the nine one one call I've heard more than a dozen times. Instead, I focus on the woman. She looks like all the rest who have been dragged online and shamed by television and radio outlets across the country, and around the world, for being foolish and calling the police on people for participating in the most mundane and innocuous activities in their lives. She is pale, her thin lips are pursed together until they disappear, her eyebrows are scrunched together illustrating the level of her vexation, and her cheeks are pink with either anger or rosacea. And this was the photo she posted of herself. Not a screen grab from a clip of the video showing her on the phone with 911, because like a coward, she made the call in private from behind her closed front door.

The mic clicks.

"Let's just take a moment," I say, leaning forward on the desk as the camera zooms in closer on my face. "Not only did Patricia Knapland call the police, but she called the police and lied. She said there were children vandalizing her neighborhood and her property. They were not. They were playing. We know that because there is video of them playing from a neighbor's surveillance camera. She said in the call she didn't know how many children were out there, maybe ten. That was another lie. There were four. Two girls and two boys. Siblings and their cousins. But here's the part that gets me. When the dispatcher asked for a description of the suspects . . . and I'll let go for a moment, that the dispatcher called these children suspects . . . but when the dispatcher asks for a description, Knapland for once is honest and says they're all African-American, under five feet, and wearing bathing suits. Now I'm not the Nine News Now crime analyst, but what my common sense tells me is that maybe the dispatcher should have stopped and asked Knapland more follow-up questions instead of dispatching units. Instead, this is what happened."

My mic clicks and the sound and video roll from cell phone video Knapland recorded live to her social media page from her window with the caption, "getting what they deserve."

"Oh look, the police are finally here to get these kids off my lawn."

This is the first time I'm seeing the video of the encounter between the children and the police since we decided to run this story tonight. I didn't want to watch it beforehand so I could have a natural reaction to the exchange. It chills me. To hear the woman's happy, sing-song voice as she watches four children, who were enjoying a day in the sun, even though their neighborhood pool was probably still too cold for a proper swim, approached by the police and begin to cry in fear when they realize they are being questioned, is infuriating. I watch the video play out. The children cry tears as they "Yes, sir," and "No, sir" their way through the initial questions in high-pitched voices until two adult women come outside to see what is happening.

Watching the video, I am thankful the women aren't fat. I am thankful the women are not in housecoats, or sweatpants, but wearing business casual. I am thankful they have their hair done, instead of coming outside in bonnets, turbans and do-rags. I am thankful the women start with "Excuse me, officer, is there a problem?" with minimal detectable attitude. I am thankful they do not represent the stereotypes or the caricatures they could have been compared to if they were all those things I am thankful they are not; and then I am ashamed I'm so thankful. I'm ashamed of my gratitude for their accommodation to assimilate and be less of themselves.

"Officer, if the neighbor had a problem with my children or my niece and nephew, she should have come and rung my doorbell," one of the women says in the video.

"I didn't know she was home," Knapland says to her own recording camera.

I watch the video and the audio jumble and shake until Knapland is outside her front door, her own camera still rolling on what she caused, as she says, "I didn't know you were home. I thought the kids were alone, your car was not in the driveway."

The mother of one set of siblings says toward Knapland's camera, "I have a garage. Just because you don't see my car, does not mean I'm not home. If you had a question or a problem you could have asked them, or been a real woman and come rung the doorbell and asked me."

"Well, I told them to get off my lawn with their game, and to make sure the water doesn't touch my plants."

"Ma'am, you called us about some plants," the officer says in the video.

"Yes," Knapland says. "They're vandalizing my property. I spent eighty dollars on those cacti, not to mention the money I spent on the new mulch and soil I had to get to plant them. If they get too wet from that water hose they'll die and that is vandalism, and they're still trespassing."

"They're kids," the woman yells.

"I'm sure they were just playing," the officer says. "You do realize it's illegal to call 911 for a non-emergency."

"But vandalism and trespassing are crimes," Knapland insists. "You deal with criminals, so I thought you all would deal with this."

The video and the audio to the exchange ends. I see myself on camera, I look in the prompter, and the only direction there is says "natural reaction" bolded, underlined, and starred, since that is what I said I wanted to give.

"The . . . The . . ." I stumble. I swallow. I start over. "The name of this segment is "Give 'Em More Grace," but I have to admit, I'm feeling less than gracious right now."

I swallow and nod to acknowledge John's hands that show me there are two minutes left in the show.

"Patricia Knapland like so many other people who have been maligned for this behavior before her, was and is still wrong. She has since posted an apology for her actions on her Facebook page."

I wait for the prompter to roll to the script before speaking.

"She says in part quote: 'It was never my intention to cause harm or great distress to my neighbors or their children. I was so caught up in my new outdoor accoutrements being killed, before it had a chance to grow, that I overreacted when the children didn't heed my warnings to be mindful of the lawn. I hope they and their parents may one day forgive me and don't have any hard feelings toward me.'"

The prompter rolls past the statement to more direction for my natural reaction.

I say, "Why Patricia Knapland thought social media was the proper forum in which to incriminate and indict these children is beyond me, but it is neither my place to do the same to her."

I blow air through my nose.

"I have more advice for Knapland and her ilk than anything else. My advice is that you mind your business. Calling the police on pigmented people has real consequences in this country. Sometimes deadly consequences. Unless you see them with a bomb, mind your business. And yes, I said bomb, not gun. If you see a bomb, then by all means see something, say something. Otherwise guns are legal, fireworks are legal, sleeping is legal, barbecuing is legal, coaching your kid from the sideline of a soccer game—even if it breaks the rules of the game—is legal, brushing up against someone with a loaded book bag—while maybe not desirable, because . . . personal space—is legal, and playing with a slip-n-slide and a water sprinkler to cool off from the heat is also legal. Patricia Knapland, my grace for you is to not tell you where you can go, I will not say you are racist, or ignorant, instead, my grace for you is to simply, and politely suggest, that you mind your business."

I exhale another breath as John's hands make the sign for thirty seconds left in the newscast.

I hear Jennifer counting down in my ear as I say, "If you have a comment about tonight's grace recipient, I'd like to hear from you. Follow me online at Naomi Grace everywhere, and of course, follow the Nine News Now pages. And if you have a suggestion on someone you think needs more grace, then by all means send me an email, and maybe your suggestion will be featured on "Give 'Em More Grace." I'm Naomi Grace, thank you for watching "Naomi Tonight," on Nine News Now. Linden and Hillary will be back for Nine News Now at eleven."

The mic clicks. I yank it off as I yell, "That was dumb. She really got that mad over some plants that she called the police?"

"I told you to watch the video," Jennifer says in my ear.

"Fucking ridiculous," I mutter. "Is Boyce up there?"

"No, he left after the 911 call."

"Good," I say. "I don't even think I can deal with him right now. Let's shoot these promos so we can go. Y'all still up for drinks tonight, right?"

"It's your first night off since you got promoted to this show," Diedre says. "Hell yeah we're still up for drinks."

"Naomi, are you ready?" John asks.

"Yes, John. Thank you."

He holds up his hands and says, "In three, two, one, cue."

I fly through the three promos for Wednesday night's show. I read the words, add inflection when necessary, and try to make minimal stumbles. I'm excited to go out after work, instead of having to go home because it's midnight and everything else is closed. For the last three and a half years, since I was first promoted to the eight o'clock show, I also anchored the early evenings, and the late-night newscasts. The gig Dawn picked up late into her contract that just rolled over to me. I was on air all the time with none of the extra benefits, perks, or raises, that come with being the official face of the station. I did all the main newscasts with the exception of the mornings, and had my own show, and not the quarter million dollar salary that comes with it. My agent said I was working too much, doctor mom said I was working too much, even my daddy said I was working too much. I was happy to just be working, but as my mother said, "Slavery is illegal, sweetie. If they plan to work you like a Hebrew slave, they need to pay you like your name is George Soros."

"We're clear," John says.

"Thanks, guys," I say to the crew. "John, tell your wife I said 'Hi,' and kiss that new baby for me."

"Will do," he says while rolling cable, and shutting down the studio until the next newscast. "She says 'Thank you for the clothes you got Charley. We really appreciate it.'"

"No problem," I say.

I walk out of the studio and head toward my office. I see Jennifer and Diedre are already at their desks at the back of the newsroom. Normally, they come into my office for a brief post meeting to talk about the show, but I guess we can do that over drinks. They don't look my way. I see why as I walk into my office. Boyce is sitting in my chair, with his feet on my desk, and doesn't move when I walk in. Instead of sitting in one of the cloth covered chairs for guests and visitors, I stand at the door.

I will not be subjugated in my office. I don't care if he is the news director.

"Boyce, I'm surprised to see you here," I say, trying my best to keep my voice nonplussed and nonchalant.

"The latest Pollyanna who thought it was okay to be out peeping and call the police," he says.

He takes his time enunciating the words I said on the fly. His hands are entwined together and resting atop his bulging stomach. Brown suspenders are pushed to the sides of his waist, and nearly off of his shoulders to make room for his belly. The brown freckles on his pinkish face are prominent, along with the dew drops of sweat on his half-bald head. Even though the newsroom is as cold as an ice box, he perspires profusely. It shows in the sweat stains beneath the arms of his now-wrinkled white shirt that's buttoned up to the collar, squeezing the gullet of his neck.

"I will not say you are racist; I will not say you are ignorant," Boyce says. "You do realize that by you saying you won't say something you are saying it any way."

"I don't," I say.

"It's a dog whistle, Naomi. You're familiar with that term, right?"

Now that was racist.

I don't answer. I wait for him to make his point, get out of my chair, and leave my office.

"I was on my way out of the door when the tease for the last segment came on. I was in a good mood. We had good, distinguishing coverage all day, all over the market, and then you called a woman who'd already been given one undesirable nickname, Pollyanna. Then you further maligned this woman, insinuating that she was racist, and ignorant, and urged people everywhere to only see something, say something if they're sure someone has a bomb."

"And," I say.

"And you can't fucking say that shit on TV. We report the news. We don't give our opinion of the news. I told you your "Give 'Em More Grace" segment was getting out of hand. I told you to not make our station your personal soap box. You're not listening. You want to be a commentator go start a blog, or a podcast, or see if you can get a job at one of the networks in New York. Don't do that shit here."

"If you don't want me to comment, then don't give me a show where it's my job to make comments. If you don't want me to have an opinion, don't give me a show where it's my job to take a story, report it, dissect it, and give my opinion in the name of cross talk and chitchat. If you don't want me to do what you hired me to do, then let me go."

"That can be arranged," Boyce says, swinging his feet to the floor.

"Don't threaten me," I say. "Either let me go or let me do my job. You said when you promoted me to the show that we weren't always going to agree, but that I'm supposed to push back to fight for the integrity and the autonomy of the show. Now, were you telling the truth, or were you just feeding me lip-service because you needed to name an anchor and didn't want to spend the money on a national search, for someone who would come here and do everything, every show, for half the money and none of the power?"

"Naomi, you get what you negotiate. But this conversation is not a negotiation. Our content as a station, as a company, as a brand, and on each and every one of our newscasts, must be straight down the middle. Tell the story, bring in your expert, and keep it moving. You want to give the subjects of the stories more grace, do it anonymously; and hope I never find out about it. Starting tomorrow night, there will be no more giving of grace. Do the news. That's it."

Boyce pushes his body upright using the adjustable arms of the mesh office chair as leverage. The reclining back of the chair rocks back and forth as it is relieved from his weight. He walks around the front of the desk, past the chairs he should have sat in, and through the door. I squeeze myself against the frame to make sure none of our parts brush against each other. When he is gone, I slam my door shut. The noise reverberates in the nearly empty newsroom.

This is bullshit.

My chair is warm as I sit in it. I want to put my head on my desk but I know there are people watching me. I feel the eyes of my coworkers. Linden Beale, the main male anchor who was my co-anchor until today, and Hillary Kim, the new anchor who was hired to do the evening and the late shows, when I refused in my last contract review.

Naomi, you get what you negotiate.

His flippant remark about my less than thrilled attitude with my salary, my position, and status in this newsroom stung, but I can't let him know that. I can't let any of them know that.

I wonder what they offered Hillary.

The first Asian-American main female anchor in the market. She is a cross between a young Connie Chung and Lisa Ling. Her face is long and oval shaped, her nose thin, and the false lashes on her eyes make her stand out on camera. Her hair is bleached blonde, long and layered, probably thanks to the help of beauty supply store bundles. Thin and trendily dressed, she is the latest obsession of viewer emails from what I can tell. She's only been on air for a day and a half and the vitriol inside the messages in my inbox are pure hate. There are some good comments and questions, but for every one of those there are ten spiteful ones.

I'm not supposed to have access to this part of the email. I wasn't put on the "news-all" email list when I first started, but I asked our IT guy to change my settings so I could see what the managers see. It's one thing to be ignorant because you simply don't know, it's another to choose not to know and to be okay with your ignorance. Everything that's said about me, or that is happening in this community or being discussed in closed door meetings without me I want to know, if it is possible. Newsrooms are gossip mines and information always leaks. Before I come in tomorrow, everyone will know my "Give 'Em More Grace" segment is canceled. Before I come in tomorrow, everyone in the building will know about Boyce's late-night visitation to my office. My office is a fish bowl, and just like people can observe what's going on within, I can see what's going on outside of it.

Jennifer and Diedre wait at their desks talking to the eleven o'clock producer, Linden and Hillary. I know they are waiting for me, but I also know they are talking about me. I watch them over the top of my laptop as I pretend to do wrap up work of which I have none, because we haven't had a post meeting. Boyce had a post meeting.

Tired of being the subject of the conversation and not being able to defend myself, I close my laptop, get out of my chair, and walk toward the door. Before I open it, I check in the long mirror I mounted to the wall. When this was Dawn's office, she only had a TV in the corner, the bookshelves with her degrees, Emmys, and a few books, and a coat stand. Now I've added mirrors and pictures to the décor, since there are no awards preceding my name. My parents are behind me, my degrees between them, and pictures of Jennifer, Diedre, and I from the last company Christmas party hold center court on the shelf. The mosaic tile framed, full length mirror was a late addition to the office, but my best one yet.

I adjust the flip of the long, feathered bang on my wig and play with strands that have muddied the part. The wig is dark brown, the color of my natural hair. I stare at myself in the hair that is not my own and wonder if I should add some color.

It would be nice to change it up.

I leave the wig alone, adjust the lay of my peacock printed pencil skirt, and open a second button on my jade blouse. I didn't bring a jacket, so I hit the light in the office, open the door, and walk out into the newsroom. I hear the whispers stop as I walk toward the back of the room where Jennifer and Diedre are waiting. Hillary and Linden walk away from the pod for producers and back to their desks on the other side of the newsroom.

"Y'all ready?" I ask walking up to them.

"Just waiting on you," Jennifer says.

"You could have told me, he was waiting for me in my office," I say.

"We didn't know where he went," Jennifer says.

"He didn't even say anything when he walked into the control room," Diedre says. "He just stood there for the whole commercial break, watched you intro the segment, and left. I thought he was going home."

We walk the long hallway out of the newsroom, past the sales offices, and to the back door that will let us out into the employee parking lot. One of the men from the cleaning crew is in the hallway. Noise canceling headphones cover his ears. The vacuum is leaned against his chest, and his phone is in his hand as we pass him.

"Goodnight, Mosiah," I say.

"Goodnight, ladies," he says without looking up at us.

We turn the corner and quickly walk out the door. Jennifer and Diedre burst out laughing as soon as we're outside.

"What is so funny?" I ask.

"You know he doesn't like you, right?" Diedre says.

"I don't like him either. All I said was goodnight."

"You know that man is married," Jennifer says. "Has been ever since he started working here."

"I saw the ring on his finger," I say.

"It's real," Jennifer says. "Unlike the one you wear."

"I got it, I got it. The man is married in real life and not just for TV. I'm not trying to push up on him. All I said was goodnight."

"Whatever," Jennifer says.

"Where are we going?" Diedre asks.

"Let's go to The Cookbook in Springfield. The food is good and they have wine."

"Bet," Jennifer says.

"I'm down," Diedre adds.

"Y'all can follow me," I say.

I unlock my car door with the key fob and get in. Aside from my townhouse, my car has always been one of my happy places. My red three series BMW was my first major purchase. I bought it after I made full-time weekend anchor in New Orleans after three years of reporting. Before then, I'd been driving my 1998 Nissan Sentra I got when I first learned how to drive. Though my beamer is not as new as it used to be, it is all mine. Especially since I finished paying off the car note.

I back out of the space and drive to the gate. Diedre and Jennifer are behind me. Once the gate opens, I lead the way away from the station and the developed corner of downtown to the historic neighborhood just to the north. We drive away from the sports complexes, the arena, and one of the local breweries, down Bay Street passing the Maxwell House warehouse. I take the scenic route through downtown, passing the police headquarters and the jail, high rises, storefront bars and restaurants, until we get caught at the light in front of the new steakhouse at the foot of the Main Street Bridge. The restaurant where I will be attending another event in two days.

I wait until the light changes and then continue to the next light at Laura Street, where I make a right. I drive in the light evening traffic filled with workers, passing the Main Library, city hall, Hemming Park, and First Baptist, until I leave downtown and get into an area that is more residential. The houses are large, either brick faced, or with paneling, the porches wrap around, and the neighborhoods are quaint and quiet. In a way it reminds me of home. It reminds of St. Charles Street. I drive slowly through the neighborhoods gawking at the houses, wondering who lives inside. When I first moved here, I was told to be careful on this side of town. Even though it was considered Springfield, and historically preserved, it was still part of the Northside. I was told don't come down these old rugged streets, that have been neglected and overlooked, alone at night. Being told what not to do, made the area my first visit after I moved into my apartment, and I've been coming back ever since. I drive until I get to Eighth Street and then make a left. Two blocks down and one right turn, and we have arrived.

We park in the empty grass lot and get out. On this stretch of Pearl Street there are several small storefronts. Auntie Peaches, the black-owned apothecary is one reason I will forever drive to Springfield, and The Cookbook Restaurant is the other.

Inside the restaurant the evening's menu is written on a chalkboard, the R&B is noticeable from the speakers, and the conversation from table to table is lively.

"Will it be just the three of you tonight?" the male hostess asks us at the door.

"Yes, please," I say. "Can we have one of the booths along the wall, please?"

"Yes, ma'am, right this way."

We follow his lead to the booth about three back from the front door, and with a good eye line toward the kitchen and preparation table.

"Would what you like to drink?" he asks us.

"I'll start with water, please," Diedre says.

"Me too," Jennifer says.

"And for you, ma'am?" he asks me.

"Water, and can you bring us a bottle of Rosé, please?"

"Yes, ma'am. I'll be right back."

"I never would have known this was over here," Jennifer says. "And I've lived here all my life."

"That says more about you than it does about me," I say.

"Okay," she says nodding her head. "Feeling a little shady this evening, aren't we?"

"Call it what you want," I say.

I drum my fingers on the table for the lack of anything else better to do. There is no water to sip, and no wine yet to guzzle. I look up at the art and knickknacks mounted on the wall. Beside abstract prints, there are bicycles, oversized utensils, and other odds and ends.

"Are you happy to be off?" Diedre asks me.

I turn to her and nod. I want to answer, to speak, but the conversation with Boyce and the atmosphere of the newsroom before I left, has soured my tongue. I want to ask them, why they didn't let me know Boyce was waiting for me in my office before I got there, but I don't know. I don't know if he confronted them when they came downstairs out of the control room, or if they didn't think I deserved a heads up coming off the set.

I sigh hearing his voice.

You get what you negotiate.

Do the news.

"So, what did Boyce want?" Jennifer asks as the waiter arrives with the water.

"Thank you," I say.

"You're welcome, and I'll be right back with your wine," he says. "Do you need one glass or three?"

"Three," I say.

I wait until he leaves the table. I look at Jennifer. No makeup, perfect twist out, and serious eyes. Her question could be both that of a friend and a colleague, but I'm not sure which.

I say, "He canceled the "Give 'Em More Grace" segment is canceled starting with tomorrow night's show.

"Why?" Diedre asks.

She is the opposite of Jennifer at work. Jennifer wears jeans and T-shirts and flats daily. If she's cold, she'll add a blazer or hoodie, depending on her mood. Diedre, on the other hand is fully dressed as if she, too, is on air. Today her little black dress pulls double duty going from day to evening. The top of the short-sleeved dress is sheer, and shows off the opaque, sweetheart cut for the bust of the dress. A leather choker is secure around her throat, and her blue-black hair is pulled back in a low ponytail. Her question is as naive as her wardrobe.

"Because he didn't like it," I say. "Because it went too far. Because, he thinks I called homegirl ignorant and a racist and he doesn't want to rock the boat."

"So, what are you going to do?" Diedre asks.

"I'm going to do my job," I say. "The segment is canceled; we'll do a story there and have our expert stick around to comment on it instead of me."

"Can we still put the same kind of fun stories there?"

"You're a producer. Can you?"

"I guess."

"Dawn would've never let him do that to her," Jennifer says.

"Let's not forget "me too" was started by a black woman at least a decade before it was trending," I say.

"Yeah, well I'm not her. She had her way of doing things, and I have mine. I told him to fire me, he told me the segment was canceled."

"So, are you going to quit?" she asks.

"If I quit every time somebody in this business pissed me off, I would have flunked my high school print journalism class. It's score one for Boyce, but I have some other moves."

"Here's your wine, ladies," a different waiter says to us as he sets the bottle and three glasses in front of us. "Are you all ready to order?"

"I'm not hungry, but you guys go ahead," I say.

I wait until Diedre and Jennifer have decided between baked chicken or fried fish, and an assortment of southern sides. I love the restaurant, the atmosphere, and cuisine, but after Cuba, I need to eat only salads for the next week. That's why I wore this skirt and blouse, because the dresses from my rented rack all felt too snug by at least two inches.

"So what are your other moves?" Diedre asks as the waiter walks away.

"I don't know yet." I say.

"That's fucked up," she says. "The best segment of the show canceled because he can't deal with the truth."

I smile as Diedre takes up the soapbox Boyce says I started. I see a smirk cross Jennifer's face as well. We both appreciate seeing our younger selves in the new producer who hasn't yet been hardened by cynicism, and defaults to sarcasm as a method of coping.

"I swear," Diedre says, "We need our own 'me too,' movement."

"Yes," Jennifer agrees. "You could start it on Twitter."

"Where all great social justice movements begin," I say.

"Yeah," Diedre says. "I could tweet something like: Say me too if you are black and have been falsely accused of something by white people who don't know how to mind their business."

"You know the feminists would have your neck for coopting their movement and using it to fight racism," Jennifer says.

"Every good thing is stolen or borrowed," Diedre says. "Just like music, dancing, hair styles . . ."

". . . Body features, people." I say.

"Exactly," Diedre says. "I'm sure they won't mind me saying "me too" to fight another civil justice cause."

"Good luck with that," Jennifer says.

In the small restaurant on the border between the hood and the historic, our conversation adds to the mellifluous cacophony of other discussions being had in the restaurant. I look around at the other tables and see mostly faces like ours, people like us, and relax into my corner of the booth. I resist the urge to remove my wig and become totally at home amongst the room full of strangers.

Next time I wash these twists, I'll plait them in two, instead of all these cornrows.

"So, what are you guys doing once you get home?" I ask.

"Octavius is coming over," Jennifer says.

"I may call Jacob," Diedre says.

"Is that the app boy?" Jennifer asks.

"Yeah," she says. "He texted me."

"What did he say?" I ask.

"He apologized for being weird after your party. He says he doesn't have a problem with strong women, who want their own stuff."

"He's whack," Jennifer says.

I nod and pick up my wine glass. I take a long sip, listening to bits and pieces of other people's conversations that I can decipher. The man behind us is on the phone talking about the cost of insurance for some procedure he didn't mention. A woman at a table across from us eats while on FaceTime with someone I can't see.

I watch her and wonder her story. I wonder if she's on a long-distance date that she will later charge him for through Venmo or Cash App. I wonder if it's not a date, then maybe she's talking to a son in the military, or a husband at home whom she left to get a moment to herself, or a client for a business she runs.

"Earth to Naomi," Diedre says, snapping her fingers in front of my face.

"What," I say, sipping from my glass again.

"You were doing it again."

"Doing what?"

"Staring at people you don't know like you were caught up by that demon spirit from *The Ring* or *The Grudge*."

"I was just thinking," I say.

"About what?" Jennifer asks.

"About that woman, eating dinner on FaceTime."

"Why?" Diedre asks.

"Because it's what I do."

"Well, we want to know, what are you going to do when you leave here?"

"I'm going to go home and enjoy my house," I say.

"That's lame."

I shrug my shoulders, "Then I guess I'm lame. I don't have an Octavius or a Jacob to go home to. It's me, my couch, and Hulu Live."

"We need to set you up," Diedre says.

I'm already paying someone to do that. "I don't need a matchmaker," I say.

"Okay, let's pretend you do," Jennifer says. "What kind of guy do you want? What's your list?"

"I don't have a list."

"Every girl has a list," Diedre says. "Even girls who say they don't have a list, have a list."

"Tall, dark and handsome," I say to dead the conversation.

"Oh, Naomi, please," Jennifer says, picking up her glass of wine. She sips before continuing, "Be real. Idris Elba and Morris Chestnut are every woman's man prototype. Now be more realistic. Something more tangible."

"You mean attainable?" I ask, raising an eyebrow.

"Yes," Jennifer says. "Attainable."

"Now that's a fucked-up thing to say. So, you want me to settle?"

"No. I said be reasonable," Jennifer counters.

"My ideal man is unreasonable, unattainable and I need to lower my standards. Don't you think we hear that bullshit, don't-be-so-ambitious logic enough in every other area of our lives, that we don't need to bring it into romance?"

"Don't start caping for women's socio-economic, and political equality now, like you're some kind of super hero. We're talking about your love life or lack thereof. We're drinking and playing a game. Answer the damn question."

"I did. Tall, dark and handsome is my type."

"How?" Diedre asks. "Wasn't Aaron white?"

"No. He was very light skinned," I say.

"Questionable," Diedre says.

"Fake Shaun King, Jesse Williams looking ass," Jennifer says.

"There's no doubt he probably had more white blood in him than anything else, but the one drop rule counts, and it was definitely in effect if he let his hair grow past a week," I say.

I sigh thinking about Aaron. His name is never far from my consciousness. His memory is never too far to be summoned. It doesn't help that I can look up at any given moment in the newsroom and see his face during one of his segments on NNC from any one of the TV's hanging from an apparatus above the assignment desk octagon. Eight television monitors and the one that faces my office is on NNC. I asked one of the assignment managers to change the order of the channels so I could see what was on MSNBC or FOX. That lasted about a day, and then it went right back to NNC in my face all day, all the time.

Maybe that's why I've never gotten over the breakup. Even though I have the physical distance between us, I don't have the emotional distance. He's always there. He's always around. He's always on, always a reminder that we're not together; we're not living our dreams together. That he's moved on without me, to network, and I'm still in local television trying to keep a dying industry alive with straight newscasts, designed as magazine style infotainment shows.

Don't the rules of breaking up say no contact with an ex for the first six months to a year, after the relationship ends. Somebody needs to write an addendum to that rule for people in any industry with an iota of visibility. Aaron and I might not have contact with each other, but I have involuntary contact with him daily. He's the reason I don't have cable now. I don't need him, his energy, what he represents in my house. WiFi and a Fire Stick, that's my window to the outside world, sans Aaron Moore.

"So besides tall, dark, and handsome," Jennifer says, "what else do you require in a man?"

"I told you, I don't have a type," I insist.

"So, you mean a high school drop-out, with five kids by four baby-mamas, no credit, and a passion to take his mixtape game to another level is your ideal candidate if he's six-seven and bow-legged with a low fade?" Jennifer asks.

"If he's bow-legged and packing the way M'baku looked like he was packing in that leather skirt, sitting with his legs open on his ice throne, then Bitch, Wakanda Forever," I say crossing my arms in the cinematic salute.

Diedre cackles and Jennifer joins her. I eventually break my straight face and join the laughter. The sound draws attention to our table as heads turn toward us. We laugh even louder. Taking sips of wine doesn't help as we try not to snort the Rosé all over the table.

"He was fine though," Diedre says.

"Beyond fine," I say.

"The trapping type of fine," Jennifer says.

"That's just trifling," I say.

"Call it what you want, but if you do it right you know you got him for at least eighteen years, more if you fuck around and have ladder babies."

"And I'm done," Diedre says. "Check, please," she yells aloud in the restaurant holding up her hand.

"How are you calling for the check and our food hasn't even come out yet?" Jennifer asks.

"Then they better hurry up," she says.

"He's coming right now," I say, looking toward the kitchen.

The waiter moves quickly in his black and white striped apron, balancing the platter that holds the two plates for Jennifer and Diedre. He sets each one down in front of them and disappears quickly.

"This looks good," Diedre says excitedly.

"Naomi, you sure you don't want some?" Jennifer asks.

"I'm good," I say. "Everybody can't eat everything like you and not gain a pound."

"Chile, the struggle is real. I've been eating collard greens and cornbread all my life trying to grow an ass, and don't nothing work."

"You know you can go buy one, right?" Diedre asks between bites of her baked chicken.

"I'm not trying to put fix-a-flat and concrete in my booty from these corner-hustling booty injector pros."

"I meant going to a real plastic surgeon," Diedre says.

"I'm good," Jennifer says. "After that exposé on the doctor in Atlanta who was dancing during people's surgeries and making YouTube videos, I'll stick with being founder, CEO, and chairwoman of the itty-bitty booty committee."

"I thought it was the itty-bitty titty committee?" I say.

"Yeah, well, these boobs are small too," she says, taking a big bite of fried fish and macaroni and cheese.

"But I'm sure Octavius loves it, and that's all that matters."

"He better," Jennifer says.

"So what does Naomi love?" Diedre asks.

"Are we back on this," I ask. "I love me. Is that good enough for you?"

"And you love fine men, even if they are basic," Jennifer says. "Just general admission, no VIP."

"I know I don't like you right now, I know that much," I say.

"You don't have to like me. I don't want to fuck you."

"Ugh, you get on my damn nerves."

I sigh, sip the last of the wine from my glass, and refill it with the last swallow from the bottle.

She's always pushing people. Trying to be their mirror and show them their ugly selves. I don't need a mirror Jennifer. I have enough. Trust me. I just bought another one for my vision room.

"I'm going to go," I say.

"See, Jennifer," Diedre says slapping her arm. "You've pissed her off and made her leave."

"No one's making me leave," I say after draining the last of my wine. "My drink is finished, I didn't eat, and I've got to get enough sleep so I don't look like some dark-circled hag in the morning. I'll see y'all later."

"Bye," Diedre says.

I wave goodbye and walk out of the restaurant into the cool evening air.

"You love basic men," I mumble, mocking Jennifer's words about what my dating preferences are.

There's nothing basic about me. Not the way I look, not my car, not my house, not even my personality. I'm not basic and the person who dates me can't be basic, either.

I unlock my car and get in, knowing my anger is steeping and rising. That is why I left. I didn't want to argue with a friend, even if she sometimes has a fucked-up perspective on things. I roll the windows down as I pull onto Pearl Street, and then turn on Eighth. It is a straight shot home once I hit 95. I ride with the music from the radio low and my thoughts loud.

What kind of man do I want?

Hell, the better question is what kind of man do I need?

I'm not of the belief that women don't need a man, a significant other, a person to do life with. We all need companionship. We were created that way. It's just that until we get it, we learn how to do everything ourselves. But in one of my mother's greatest moments of advice, she said, "Just because you know how to do, and take care of everything in your life by yourself, doesn't mean you should have to." That's the best thing she's ever told me. In fact, that's one of the quotes on my vision board for love. Right under the title and above the mirror, and the headless groom is her quote.

I don't have to do everything, even though I can.

I don't like making the man list. I don't like writing down the characteristics that need to be checked off before I say "yes" or "no" to a first date, a third date, a handshake, a hug, a kiss, or sex. When it's right, I'll know. The closest I'll get to the list of listing everything from patient, smart, and kind, to tall, dark, and handsome is my vision board, and even it is an abstraction. I'm sure my mother would say it represents the fact that I don't know what I want in my life, but I disagree. Keeping parts of the vision for my life abstract leaves me open to change, and flexible to life's unpredictable nature. I have an outline and I will live out the details and the fine print. Degrees, number of children or not, number of marriages or not, family issues, health issues, looks, and quality characteristics will all reveal themselves and work themselves out the way they are supposed to, when they are supposed to. I don't need a list to recite or put on the altar to make sure God and Osun see my prayers.

I just wish people stopped asking me about my love life. When I start dating, I will tell you. Until then, mind your business.

Getting my house has never been a better idea than it is right in this moment. Driving up, I'm okay knowing there isn't anyone or anything else here to greet me but the mail. That, and the mirror I ordered from Amazon. It's just like the one hanging on my wall in my office at work. I decided I needed another one for the vision room when I realized I closed the door and I couldn't see myself. The room may be focused on my inner work, but I can't pretend like the outside doesn't matter. Just because I look in, doesn't mean I want to lose sight of what is already being put out, nor do I want to miss the changes my navel-gazing produces, for the better, in my outward appearance and demeanor. My mother thinks my obsession with mirrors is purely vain. It's easier to agree, like I did with Owen at the party, then it is to explain why I feel compelled to confront the woman in the mirror, like we don't go together every day of my life.

Inside, I take the mirror that arrived, and I leaned against the wall at the bottom of the stairway before I went to work, up to the second floor. I lean it against the open door to the vision room until I change out of my work clothes and wig, and put on my robe. In the kitchen is where

I stored my little do-it-yourself tool kit. All I need is a hammer and a hook. I find the items I need and take them upstairs. Closing the door to the vision room, I work with the eyes of the wise women watching over me. The first lady, the mogul, and the literary pioneer. The lawyer, the news anchor, and the show girl. The rape victim, the pregnant teen, and the girl from the Southside. They all knew and know, every part of who they are on the inside and the outside. I hang the mirror as a reminder that I want the same level of clarity. I want the same level of love for me, before anyone else I happen to be fucking. If I had a list that would be the only thing on it, love me like I love me.

8.

It Goes Down in the DMs

There are thirty messages on my phone when I wake up in the morning. A text from Jennifer and Diedre from last night in our group chat, wondering if I made it home safely. I text back quickly, "I'm alive." The other messages are in my apps. Eight from Twitter and the other twenty from Instagram. I open the 'gram, go into my inbox, and start looking through the direct messages. Most of them are the same. A clip of me from last night's show talking about Neighborhood Watch Wanda was picked up by a late-night comedian on one of the networks. Most of the messages are from people I don't know. People who don't watch local news but will watch a comedian satire or drag the local news. Some of the messages are mean, some of them are supportive. Those I save for whenever I'm feeling some kind of way, I don't feel gratitude, and the vision for my life seems more like a joke than a tangible dream. On those days, the saved messages in my various inboxes give me the instant gratification I need to remind me that I'm the shit.

The last message surprises me. It was sent at seven-thirty in the morning. It's not praise, it's not criticism, rather a question:

So you're the news lady, huh?

I look at the account for the sender. The username is Fountain of Fontaine.

"Who the hell is this?"

I go to the feed and scroll until I find a full-face picture instead of memes, videos featuring a bunch of people, and posts of painted bodies done in full color on canvas. I click on the face picture and immediately remember; the ropes for hair, the fresh line up, the one dimple and the cleft in his chin.

"Hello, Kiyan."

I go back to my messages and respond:

I'm the news lady

Let's see where this goes.

I close the apps on my phone and get out of bed to start my new morning routine. Bathroom, brush teeth, wash and moisturize face, and then it's down to my vision room for the best part of my day. I haven't gotten to the point yet where I start my day without first checking my phone, but so far, in the few days I've been back home, I've been consistent in setting aside time without my phone glued to my hand, to come into my vision room.

I open the door to my sacred space and close it quietly behind me. Though no one else is in the house with me, I keep my actions reverent of the atmosphere I'm trying to create. Inside, I dip my hand in the pot of water on the altar and then make the sign of the cross, as I walk over to my series of vision boards.

In front of love, I look myself in the mirror attached to the board and say, "Just because I *can* do everything, doesn't mean I have to. You are love. You are loved. I love you."

I affirm myself with my words, activating myself to stir my spirit, and create within me that which I took the time to cut out, paste, and have embodied around me. I acknowledge myself before I acknowledge the headless groom or anything else on the board. I look me in the eye and give love to myself the way I expect someone else to, the way I would love someone else who is not me.

Eye to eye with myself, I say, "I am a good wife. I am the best he's ever had. I am loved. I am safe. I am protected. I am covered. I am his. He is mine. He is safe. He is protected. He is covered. He is loved. We are love."

I sidestep over to the career and money board, look at myself in the mirror decorated with actual dollar bills and gold dollar coins, and say, "Purpose over everything. Greater is coming. More money is coming. Network is coming. I am a boss."

I repeat my last affirmation for career and money until I create my own echo in the room, until I'm sure God is as awake as I am, and He's paying attention and putting His priority into my part of the Earth.

"I am a boss."

I repeat the self-aggrandizing phrase until it doesn't feel silly, until the braggadocios affirmation doesn't sound comical to my own ears, coming out of my mouth while I look at my eyes with the sleep recently washed out of them, in the mirror.

"I am a boss."

I say the four word sentence of encouragement until it propels me to believe for the future everything I have taped and stapled to the board: a full bank account with the decimal point moved two spaces to the right, and the comma two spaces to the left. Also, on the board are pictures of a shiny glass and chrome desk, in a remodeled newsroom with the cityscapes of the northeast for backgrounds, either Central Park, or the Capitol building.

"I am a boss."

I repeat the words until I convince the critical inner me that is always ready with a gauntlet instead of grace, that I have conquered my own fears, doubts, and anxieties that threaten to cripple me in stagnation and leave me dormant, lazy, lethargic, and without the necessary fight it takes to reach my own dreams. I don't move and I don't stop repeating until the fight in my voice, matches the fight in my heart and body, and has completely silenced the woman who should have stopped believing in herself four years ago.

In front of health and faith there is no mirror to look at, no eye contact with myself to make. Instead, there is an arrow pointing down from an image of a cathedral that reminds me to look down. I look down at where my belly-button is beneath the fabric of my pajamas and give time to myself to navel gaze. I close my eyes, place my hands against the wall, and balance my weight between the ends of my limbs, look inward and say the first words that come to my lips.

"I'm okay. I'm breathing. I can hear my heart beating. Life is moving through me and for that, I am grateful. Air, breath, and water give me the key ingredients to live. I am healthy. I am wealthy. I am strong. I am okay. I am."

Standing up straight, I open my eyes and release the wall. Turning to the closed door, and the new mirror I hung on the back of it, I stand atop my yoga mat and look at all of me. I look at me and try not to focus on the clutter. Focusing on the image of myself, in all of my raw, unpolished, unvarnished, unfinished-ness, I say, "I love you," and mean it.

The sun is getting high in the sky by the time I finish my mantras. I know it is closing in on ten o'clock, but I don't rush myself to finish. I don't rush myself to get ready to go to work and report the news. Instead, I sit on my yoga mat, lean my head against the wall and search for emptiness. I search for stillness. I search for peace until what I get is a thought and a plan to reclaim my stifled and muffled voice.

Be straight down the middle. Tell the story, bring in your expert, and keep it moving.

Boyce's voice comes barreling through my thoughts along with a conjuring of his face. I don't let my mind runaway from what my subconscious is thinking of. I focus on it and lean in to it, knowing it has come back to me in this moment, in this space, under the watchful eyes of my M.O.M. and God.

There will be no more giving of grace. Do the news. That's it.

"So let's make it news," I say to myself out loud.

Looking in the mirror I see the resolute will of my plan holding steadfast. I stand up and say, "Thank you," open the door and take the hallway back to my bedroom. My face up phone is alive and alight with messages. Direct messages from username Fountain of Fontaine catch my eye first. I open the picture sharing app and go to my inbox.

You've gone viral

I type back:

It happens

I close the messages and check the time—10:08. I move quickly to make my bed and catch up on what I've missed. I scroll through alerts from our station app and competition—the New York Times and Huffington Post, The Daily Mail and The Guardian, CNN and BBC. With a visual snapshot of what's going on locally, nationally, and internationally, I switch to a podcast that will give me a 30-minute breakdown of the biggest news stories that may have not ended up as a push alert on my phone, as I stand in the closet and get dressed.

Another member of the President's administration is under investigation.

The solemn voices of the podcasters begin to tell me the latest scandal surrounding the current occupant of the White House as I pull a navy knit skirt and hot pink blouse, from my wardrobe instead of my rack of rented wares.

In the latest casualty of the "me too" movement, the system of workplace sexual harassment and reporting is under fire in industries across the country as employers, CEOs, and higher-ups, try to understand why whispers and rumors never reached them before now.

"They knew," I say aloud as I pull pink suede pumps from my shoe rack. I keep the ensemble simple, carrying my shoes with me as I move back into the bathroom and turn on all the lights, to do a base layer of makeup.

"They don't call it the worst kept secret in Hollywood, or everywhere else, if the people didn't know."

I moisturize, apply sunscreen and foundation, as I react aloud to the report.

"It's just like Jerry Sandusky and Penn State; Larry Nassar and USA Gymnastics. All of 'em. They knew and acted like they didn't because everybody was winning and making money at the expense of somebody else."

I sigh my anger as I start the last step in my process: putting on my wig. Using a toothbrush, I brush down the baby hairs that don't stay tight in the cornrows of my locs. Once they're set with edge control, I velcro my wig grip around my head and set my hair hat in place.

Next, we go to a story out of Florida that's making the rounds on the Internet this morning. A woman nick-named Neighborhood Watch Wanda was eviscerated by a local evening anchor. Take a listen.

I hear my own voice come through the speaker of my phone as I hit the lights in the bathroom and walk down the stairs with my shoes in my hand. I shake my head at myself as I hear the tone of my voice in the clip, not calling the woman racist or ignorant.

"Mama, I made it," I say aloud.

They end the clip after my advice to the woman to mind her business and move into the next segment.

Cancel culture is costing another popular brand big business. Cosmetics company, "Daughter of the Diaspora" is facing backlash from its core group of customers, for creating a product they've called "Mel-Sun Shea."

"They should've known better," I say as I shove my feet into my shoes.

The product is described as melanin in a bottle. The breakthrough organic, natural, and gluten free cream is designed to help fair-skinned people naturally enhance, deepen, and darken the pigment of their skin without the use of harmful UV rays, or chemicals used in typical spray tans. The CEO of the company says "Mel-Sun Shea," which is short for Melanin, Sun, and Shea Butter, is a product that is not just for what has been assumed to be a white-audience. Kelly Cummers said quote, "Mel-Sun Shea" is meant to help people all across the diaspora have the healthy complexion they want in a natural way. We are still the company we have always been, but we will continue to grow and expand. We hear you and we are not ignoring you; we will never ignore you, but we will not stop growing and putting out products that are absent from the marketplace.

"It's the opposite of bleaching cream in a bottle," I say as I lock my door and get into my car. "It gives everybody the opportunity to have their own *Black Like Me* moment. It's blackface in a bottle."

The podcast ends as I open the garage door and back out of my driveway and into the street. The time on the dash says 10:50.

Ooh, I have time to stop and get some breakfast.

In the car I switch to the podcast from the local NPR station and replay the morning's episode. I have forgone listening to it live due to my new morning routine in the vision room. I inundate myself with news at all levels and in varying degrees of seriousness as I leave my subdivision and drive through the main thoroughfare of the neighborhood, until I pass the fire station and office park, and am facing a myriad of choices for sustenance.

Despite the line for Starbucks, I add my vehicle to the drive-through and wait my turn to order.

Just when you thought Neighborhood Watch Wanda was going to disappear into obscurity, her story, and her actions were rekindled and fanned into flames by Nine News Now anchor Naomi Grace.

"Can I have a grandé latte with skim milk and a buttered and toasted croissant," I say when prompted at the ordering window.

I listen to my voice as it comes through my car speakers in the drive-through. I listen to another local journalist critique the segment as I pay for my food, receive my order, and drive off. I drive away from the suburban sprawl of the Southside into downtown, as callers into the show discuss why they agree or disagree with me. I listen to the opinions of others as they attack me for being liberal, progressive, a reverse racist, fake news, and a half-wit who doesn't know the difference between a comma and a semi-colon, journalism or sensationalism.

The segment finally ends twenty-five minutes after it began, as I come down the ramp from the Main Street bridge.

Next up on Weekday Roundup with Julia Gillé, a new report shows the Jacksonville Sheriff's Office hasn't closed a deadly police shooting case since 2016. Officer's declined to comment on the report, but say the holdup is not coming from their agency.

"If they didn't investigate themselves, they wouldn't have this problem," I say, talking back to the car radio.

. . . JSO investigates itself when a shooting involves one of their own officers. They have declined the suggestion to bring in help from the Florida Department of Law Enforcement, and have them investigate the police shooting cases.

"Even if FDLE did come in, it's only for appearances."

I sit in my car, sipping my latte until the segment is finished. Inundated with news, triggered by story after story, overstimulated by my consumption of truth and facts from other trustworthy agencies, I come back to my plan hatched in my vision room of how I will answer questions about "Give 'Em More Grace" being canceled.

"I won't," I say opening the car door.

"I will do the news and I will go home."

My phone buzzes in my hand as I stride across the parking lot into the back entrance of the building. Fountain of Fontaine has messaged me again.

> How many people know your middle name is Jean?
>> How many people know your middle name is Fontaine?

His animated typing ellipses appear immediately followed by another response.

> Everyone who follows me on Instagram, only they don't know that they know it.
>> Good for you.
>> Shouldn't you be working?
> Today I make my own schedule.
>> What do you do?
> Art.
>> What do you do with art?
> I teach, I draw, I paint, I give classes.
>> Like a paint and sip?
> Something a little more adult and maybe a little too risqué for you.

I pull the phone down away from my face as I read his last line. *Too risqué for me. You don't even know me.* I say as much in my next message.

> You don't even know me.
>> I know enough.

Again, I take another wide-eyed phone drawn away from face look at the screen, as I consume his bravado. I'm thankful for the text conversation and his free time which allowed me to walk into the newsroom, directly into my office, and close my door without noticing the stares, the whispers, or even the waves. I close the door, sit at my desk, and turn my back to the fish bowl of glass doors, so all my coworkers see is the back of the mesh chair and the top of my wigged head.

> So tell me what you know.
>> I know there are two of you inside that one body.
>> The fish with the locs I met on vacation, and the lady who tells the news.
> No, I'm pretty sure we're the same person.
>> That's because you don't even know you

Who the hell does he think he is?

And you do?
I didn't say that.
I'm asking.
I would like to.
Was that your play the whole time?
What play?
Asking for my number.
I haven't asked for it yet.
Good.
And why is that?
Because I'm not sure you deserve it.

I hold the phone and wait for a witty response, or a sarcastic one, or an enlightened one, but nothing comes through. Not even bubbling ellipses to show me he's typing.

And just like that, you're not worth it.

I set the phone to the side of my desk and flip open my laptop. I open the program we use to produce our show and open the rundown Jennifer and Diedre are already working in. I see the final segment is templated for news. I type the name of the segment and the message "Come see me," on the six empty lines.

He wants me to do the news and that's it. Let's talk about Cancel Culture.

I watch through my fish bowl and wait for Jennifer and Diedre to see my message. I wait for them to mention it to each other before looking up to acknowledge me. They stride quickly from their pods toward my office. Today Diedre's blue highlights are purple, and Jennifer's long twist out is pulled up into a high-top knot. They wear an assortment of colored pants and graphic tees.

I say as they walk in, "Was today message T-shirt day and I missed the memo?"

"We didn't plan this," Diedre says.

Across Jennifer's chest are the words "Dope Chick." They make a halo around the black woman character on her shirt who sports a colorful headwrap, and looks side-eyeingly above her sunglasses. Diedre's shirt is a little more subtle. A T-shirt from an old stadium tour that says "Boycott Beyoncé."

"So, Cancel Culture?" Jennifer asks raising an eyebrow.

"Yes," I say. "It's news."

"It is, but what's your angle?"

"Me," I say.

"So, I guess this is your other move?" Diedre asks.

I say, "I thought of it this morning, while I was meditating."

"You do that?" Jennifer asks with raised brows.

Why did she ask it like that?

"I try to. I'm only a few days into the practice."

"What do you need from us for the segment?" Diedre asks.

"I'll write it," I say. "I just need you to pull the video and have the editors cut it. And find us a social media expert we can talk to. Someone from Edward Waters College who will be able to relate."

"You mean somebody black?" Jennifer asks.

"I didn't say that, but it wouldn't hurt."

"Let's do it," Diedre says excitedly.

"We'll see how this plays out on air," Jennifer says standing up.

I pick up my phone as it buzzes with messages.
Fountain of Fontaine:

But do you?
Do you deserve to give yourself permission to get to know somebody who clearly intrigues you?

He is bold. Talking like he knows me.

"Why are you blushing?" Jennifer asks.

"What are you talking about?" I ask, setting the phone down on the desk.

Jennifer swipes my phone before I can stop her and reads the messages still on the screen face.

"Diedre, you need to see this," she says.

They both read the two messages on the screen, and I'm thankful they don't recognize the name of who they're from.

"So that's why you didn't speak to us when you came in," Diedre says. "Too busy caking with your own Internet Bae."

"Hmmm," Jennifer says, putting the phone back down. "So, Naomi, are you the pot or the kettle today?"

"I'm not a hypocrite," I say, grabbing my phone before they can take it again. "I never said anything bad about Diedre's app Bae?"

"You never said anything good, either," Diedre says.

"That's because I don't care."

"Well, damn, tell me how you really feel."

"I didn't mean it like that. I care about you. But you just met the guy a few months ago, I just met him last week. I don't have a stake in whatever y'all's relationship is."

"Okay," Diedre says.

"Thank you," I say. "Now, can you go find me a social media expert and let me write?"

"You see how we just get dismissed?" Jennifer says to Diedre leading the way out of my office.

"And close my door, too, please."

"I'm not," Jennifer says.

Heifer.

Diedre closes the door as she passes through. I watch the two of them slink back to their desks. It isn't until I'm sure they're no longer looking at me, that I pick up my phone, turn my back to the door, and prepare to answer the message.

I conjure the face of Kiyan Fontaine English. I see him as he was on the beach; shorter than I prefer, thin, and lanky.

The body of an artist, apparently.

Despite his statuesque shortcomings, he was as confident and curious then, as he was when he recognized us on the plane, as he is now sliding through my DMs.

I respond to his message with a personal challenge of my own:

> I deserve a lot of things, but there are very few willing to give them without any expectations in return.

I close the app, shutter the face of the phone, and turn back around to my desk. I am face to face with Jennifer staring hard at me from her desk, straight through the outer glass walls of my office. I roll my eyes, ignore her, and wake up my computer screen, ready to write the scripts for the last segment of the show.

The phone buzzes:

> Everyone wants reciprocity.

I reply:

> Okay, Lauryn Hill
> I thought it was better to give than receive.
> Depends on the situation.
> And what would that be?
> Depends.
> I take it that you can't be more specific.
> I can.
> I'm waiting.
> Let me take you out tomorrow, and then I'll be as specific as you need me to be.
> Here you go again shooting your shot.
> Here you go not answering and deflecting.
> I have a prior commitment for another event tomorrow.
> Then Friday?
> We'll see.

Again, I close the app, shutter the face of the phone, and turn back around to my desk. Diving into the rundown I write two scripts and mark them with my initials to let Jennifer and Diedre know they're done. I resist the urge to give into the addicting feel of talking to a stranger, I know is interested. I steady my mind and focus my brain on the less involved tasks of my day. I clear my emails, respond to some, send others. The time passes as I scroll through webpages on my computer. Some news related, most not. With the door closed and the volume at a medium level, I listen to Internet experts give their take on love and relationships; broken ones, bad ones, abusive ones, stagnant ones, interracial ones, same-sex ones, open ones. I let the playlist of the videos play out until the time tells me the news is on.

I turn on the TV in the corner of my office and listen as Hillary and Linden list the top eight reasons to hate the city I live in. Every day, every show, the first eight stories are usually always ones that make me remember the worst in the world, and think that is the norm. I watch the scenes change from crime scene to crime scene, neighborhood to neighborhood, mug shot to mug shot, brokenhearted family members, scared neighbors, and nonchalant police officers, one after another.

"You busy?" Boyce asks, knocking and opening my door at the same time.

Does it matter if I was since you just barged into my office?

"Just watching the shows."

"So, what are you doing tonight instead of your segment?" He asks.

"The news."

"I know that. What's the story?"

It's in the rundown. Read it.

"The sudden shift toward a social media culture of intolerance, aimed at corporations who make public missteps in their messaging and branding."

"What's your angle?"

"Daughters of the Diaspora."

"Is that the company everyone's been talking about for that ad?"

"Yes."

"I don't see the problem. It's just a little suntan lotion. We could all stand to color up."

I nod at Boyce as he satisfies himself with my answer. He pushes his body off of my door he held open with his weight, and leaves as quickly as he came. The door lock clangs behind him and shakes the outer glass walls of the office. I see Diedre and Jennifer looking at me. I shake my head, shrug my shoulders, and turn back to the news. I watch it for the full two hours, until Hillary and Linden have told all the stories of bad news, perpetrators, predators, and the occasional puppy, and they retire from the anchor desk until they have to do it again at eleven.

It's seven o'clock and I've done little to nothing all day, besides sit in my office and waste time on the Internet. Aside from writing the last segment of the show, my day has been a flood of solicited advice in an area I'm relearning how to activate within myself, beyond the physical need of my desire. For that I have Matt. A corporate attorney I met two years ago while he was in town on a business trip for a London-based company, he provided in-house counsel for. Based between their London, New York, and new Jacksonville office, I've seen him a few of the times he's come into town, when I'm in the mood and our schedules allow. He provides maintenance without question, for built up tension without interrogation, and an outlet for my subdued rage without questioning the source. The mutually beneficial situation-ship has worked until now. Until someone willing and available walked into my inbox without fluff, flourish, or pretense, asking questions and making observations like he's known me all my life.

Or maybe he's been waiting for me all of his life.

Who am I kidding?

This ain't no Lifetime movie.

I resist the urge to unlock my phone and scroll through the unlocked account for the man behind the Fountain of Fontaine. I do my makeup instead. At my desk, in the mirror of my black leather caboodle, the adult version of the teal and green plastic contraption I had as a child, I apply more foundation to reduce the shine of the oil in my skin, and then add color. Eyeshadow, blush, contour, highlighter, bronzer, liquid eyeliner, mascara, lashes. By the time I finish, I look like the TV version of myself.

I know there are two of you inside that one body. The fish with the locs and the lady that tells the news.

Kiyan's words come back to me as I stare at my reflection. I apply a plum, matte lipstick and close the kit. Jennifer and Diedre are no longer sitting at their desks. I'm sure they're on set waiting for me. I get up from my desk and check my full reflection in the mirror. I see the woman I'm supposed to be. The woman I portray myself to be, and no signs of the woman I am beneath the wig, clothes and high end cosmetics. The woman in the mirror in the vision room has light brown spotted freckles, acne scars, and freedom. The woman I look at in the mirror is inhibited.

Maybe he knows something about me, I don't know about myself.

I smirk at my own thought, straighten my collar, and open the door.

"Let's do the news."

***

"You ready?" Jennifer asks me in my ear.

"For what?" I say.

"For this segment?"

"I wrote it. I'm ready."

"Thirty seconds," John says from the floor.

"Did Boyce read it?" Jennifer asks.

"Doubt it, since he didn't complain about the intro."

"So why was he in your office?" Diedre asks, coming into the conversation.

"To make sure I had news in the last segment."

"In ten, nine, eight . . ." John says doing the countdown.

I look into the camera that will open on me, and wait until my cue before I speak.

"Welcome back to Naomi Tonight. This is normally the part of the show where we do a segment we like to call, 'Give 'Em More Grace.' But that segment has been canceled effective immediately. From this day forward, we will use this segment of the show for our typical news and interview format. The subject tonight is Cancel Culture. Take a look."

My voiced over package rolls as I narrate the story about Daughters of the Diaspora being the latest company to face backlash for an ill received message. In the package, I weave in other brands that have been "canceled" on social media for one wrong or another, as well as celebrities who've been maligned for past or present misdeeds. The package ends with a clip of me from last night's show. A freeze-frame of me mid-story, and then a red stamp comes down across my face and says "canceled."

"Joining me now is Doctor Chinedu Juliard from Edward Waters College. The professor in the Communications Department is here to discuss with us the implications of cancel culture in today's society. Doctor Juliard, for those who don't know, what is cancel culture?"

"Cancel culture is exactly what its name suggests," he says. "It's when the collective culture of people, cancels a person, place or thing."

"How does that affect said persons, places or things?" I ask.

"Well," he begins, "it's relative."

I watch John give time cues from the corner of my eye as Doctor Juliard explains how canceling can affect a corporation's bottom line, if people follow through on the social media suggested boycott of a company or its product.

He says, "More often than not, cancel culture is a public rebuke and shaming of a brand, or company, or public figure, for their actions. It is quick, it is mean-spirited, and it is the illustration of mob-mentality at its finest."

"Would you go so far as to say it's a high-tech lynching? If I may invoke the words of Clarence Thomas."

"I wouldn't go that far," Doctor Juliard cautions. "What I will say is that if left unchecked, "cancel culture" creates an environment where differing opinions are not allowed to coexist in a way that leads to greater discourse."

"So, take me for example," I say. "After last night's segment on the woman dubbed Neighborhood Watch Wanda, I have, in a way, been canceled. Does that bother you?"

"I can't say that it bothers me, because I don't know the intent behind the cancellation. But if it is what I think it is, then, yes, it does bother me."

"Thank you so much, Doctor Juliard for joining us on Naomi Tonight. Hillary and Linden will be back for Nine News Now at eleven."

"Clear, Naomi." John yells.

"You're lucky Boyce already left," Jennifer says.

"I wouldn't care if he didn't," I say.

"Doctor Juliard, thank you for coming," I say. "Let me walk you out."

"Anytime."

"I'll be back to shoot the promos," I say to John.

I hop down off of my chair and lead the way out of the studio, through the newsroom, and toward the lobby doors.

"That's an interesting segment you chose to have on tonight," Doctor Juliard says.

"I thought it was appropriate," I say.

"Well, make sure you don't poke the bear," he says. "We want to keep seeing you, even if it is different from what you want."

"I'll take that into consideration," I say. "Goodnight."

"Goodnight."

I watch as Doctor Juliard leaves out of the swinging doors of the lobby and crosses the parking lot to his car. In a brown tweed suit, and his salt and pepper hair picked out into a half-inch 'fro, I recognize in him the generational gap between us. The gap in mindsets that says it's just good enough to be at the table, without recognizing that we can build and own our own damn table.

Make sure you don't poke the bear.

For as progressive as some people posture themselves to be, they still have that same enslaved, submission mentality.

I sigh to myself as I walk back to the set. I am both satisfied and dissatisfied with the segment, because there is no next. I didn't win anything but the last word, for now. In the newsroom, I stop in my office where I left my phone. I grab it off of my desk and walk with it toward the studio. Sometimes I like to have it with me on set, sometimes I keep it in my office. It feels weird to not always have it in my hands, but I find when it is not near me, I am more focused. Today I needed to be more focused instead of reacting to messages that come in real-time from viewers who know they can easily access me, in any number of ways. I illuminate the screen face and there are messages from every outlet in all my inboxes. I scroll until I see the one I'm looking for.

He is there.

Fountain of Fontaine:

You did it again.

I reply.

Thanks for watching.

His response is immediate.

What about Friday?
	I said we'll see.
Where are you going tomorrow?

Once again, his cut through the bullshit personality confronts me and I feel exposed by his words. He is real. He is persistent. He is not going away.

Especially not if you keep entertaining him.

I roll my eyes at the inner me showing up to tell me to either put up or shut up. I illuminate the screen and his message is in front of me.

I hold out a little longer.

Why do you want to know?
	Dodging and deflecting again?
I am not.

I know it's a lie as I tap type with my thumbs.

He responds.

Then where are you going?
	Chophouse.

9.

The Dating Game

Cowford Chophouse is dim and moody when I walk through the front doors of the more than a century old, recently renovated bank building. A sign posted by the elevator tells me the event I'm in attendance for is being held on the rooftop. I press the button and wait to be whisked away to the bar and seating area in full view of the St. Johns River, the Main Street Bridge, and the rest of the flat skyline waiting to be filled in with hotels, high rises, and skyscrapers.

If I knew we were going to be on the rooftop, I would have brought my blazer.

I step out of the golden elevator onto the partially covered patio, and immediately feel the chill bumps rise on my skin. My arms, chest, and back are exposed in the wide-legged, calf-length jumpsuit that's a cross between rose gold and bronze. The velvet material has a deep V cut in the front and back. A bow tied string runs across the tops of my shoulders, and the tassel ends hang down to my mid-back, tickling my skin. The bell shaped short-sleeves are more an affectation of the design than anything useful. Though created out of velvet, the jumpsuit is anything but warm; especially with the evening breeze entering my body from both V cuts and a peek-a-boo slit beneath the closure of the V, so that my breasts never make it to wardrobe malfunction level exposure.

On set I wore a black blazer that I kept buttoned, so no one would see the depth of the cut in my clothes. Now, out of work, away from Boyce, Jennifer, Diedre, and everyone else who wanted to know why I was leaving so quickly, I stand on the rooftop overlooking downtown, at night and I feel exposed. I'm more than an hour late for the mixer among the Single, Ethnic, and Not Taken, a group I was convinced into joining by the persistent founder who follows me on Twitter, Facebook and Instagram, who responded to me one day when I lamented for my followers that I wish I'd had a date. Matt was gone and I was lonely and in need of something that didn't come with batteries.

I let Twitter into my business, and among the DMs from men offering their services and women understanding my singleness, was Margo Westscott. Her message was simple — "If you're really looking for a date, and maybe more than something fleeting during cuffing season, then come to one of my events." I recognized her name from a business card Dawn left behind in the desk drawer when she left. I programmed her information into my work phone with all the other sources and interview contacts she gave me, but never followed up. With her in my inbox I didn't have to. Included in the message was a link to her website that looked more like a wedding planning service, with the number of bridal shots featured on the home page, than it did a dating service. I liked her offer because it didn't require me to set up a profile, fill out a long questionnaire of my likes and dislikes, or to swipe left or right. She said right on her website that she didn't believe in computer algorithms to love. Her philosophy was simple, she provided a venue the men and the women, and after that, she allowed nature's chemistry, to take its course. The only paperwork involved was a background check she ran with basic information through public records.

I see her standing at the opposite end of the bar from where I am, with an older couple. A woman with curly hair pulled into a messy bun, and a tall, dark-skinned man with full lips and deep waves. I can hear bits and pieces of their conversation as I approach them."

"We decided to take dating seriously after all we've been through," says the woman with the curly bun.

"I'm so glad you did," Margo says. "Dating is so much easier than divorce."

"I told her that, but you know your friend is stubborn," the man says.

"As if you don't have any flaws, sir," Margo says.

"Oh, I see how it is," he says. "You two always like to gang up on me."

"Nobody's ganging up on you," the woman says. "She's just pointing out that neither one of us is perfect."

"Aww, Baby, you're so sweet," he says. "I'm going to get me another drink, you want anything?"

"Club soda with lime, please," she says.

He kisses her hairline in the space above her ear before he walks away.

That's sweet.

"Good evening," I say, getting closer to Margo and the other woman.

"Well, hello," Margo says singing her 'O's. "Naomi, correct?"

"Yes, ma'am," I say.

"I'm so glad you made it."

"Thank you for inviting me."

"This is a really good friend of mine, Dr. Edwards, and that man who just left is her husband, Nathan."

"Jonelle," the woman says, extending her hand.

"Naomi," I say.

"Jonelle and Nathan were my very first clients," Margo gushes. "They've been married almost twenty years now. Their success has taken SENT to levels in the matchmaking business I never imagined."

Weren't they just talking about divorce?

Margo walks me toward a corner of the rooftop, from under the cover of the patio, where there are a few groups of people mingling. As we go she tells me about what she calls the epic romance of Jonelle and Nathan, two people she knew individually, she thought would be good together. She tells me about their meeting at her behest, their quick courtship, pregnancy, and life together as they built their family, while they were still building themselves. She gives me the Disneyfied version of their lives ending with, "Tyler's off in college now and they also have a daughter who's about to turn ten."

"That's nice," I say.

I don't ask what the conversation prior to me introducing myself was about and she doesn't offer. I look around the rooftop at the "guy walks into a bar" atmosphere that she's created, and I know she has a vested interest in the success of her friend's marriage as much as they do, maybe even more. All around us are well dressed, professional, men and women, with drinks in their hands, the crispest command of speech in the tone of their accents, and none of their personality showing in the clothes they, too, wore to transition from day to evening. Some ties have been removed, top buttons loosened, blazers taken off, but I know this is not a room of the unattached and free. All around me are men and women with an agenda. Not necessarily marriage, but an agenda, nonetheless.

Like you don't have one.

My critic checks my ego as I try to relax in the rooftop pit of my peers. I look over at Margo, who's telling me who is who around me, what they do, and where they work. Though her business is matchmaking, I notice her left hand is empty and bare.

What kind of match maker lives without a permanent love connection for herself? Maybe this is a scam just like everything else. Another time suck that yields no results.

I look over at Margo as she talks. She is short and I'm not tall. She is smaller than petite, barely adult height, but what she lacks in stature she makes up for in body. She is shapely and developed, large bust, large behind, wide hips. She wears a simple green cocktail dress with an A-line skirt and thin black belt that defines her waist and smooths out what rises, rounds, and curves with age. A brunette wig is cut into a severe stacked bob with a long bang. She is old, yet trying to be trendy at the same time.

I interrupt her diatribe about the benefits of this setting and say, "This is nice."

"Thank you," she says. "Oh, I almost forgot. There's someone here looking for you."

"For me?"

"You're the only Naomi on the list of confirmed attendees, and the only Naomi Grace from TV."

"Did he leave his name?" I ask.

"He didn't. He just said you'd find him by the fountain. Whatever that means. I didn't see him leave, so I guess he's still here."

"Thank you," I say.

"Enjoy your evening. I'll send a survey in the morning. It's completely anonymous, so please give your honest feedback of what you think about the mixer and how we can make it better."

I nod as Margo walks away. I wait until she's found another group of the well-heeled and socially mobile to sidle up to, before I look toward the corner of the rooftop with the clearest view of Friendship Fountain. Standing slightly behind a group of men and women is the man with ropes for hair, and the unassuming face of an adolescent boy. Only his clothing gives him his age. Instead of swim trunks, or travel sweats, he wears fitted navy slacks, a thin gray hoodie, and a pea green jacket with the sleeves scrunched to his elbows. I look at him until he looks up at me. He smiles, easily, and raises the tumbler glass in his hand.

I smile back and I wonder:
Why is he here?

Because you told him where you would be.

I didn't tell him what time.

It's not hard to find out about events with every business from here to Timbuktu advertising and inviting folks on Facebook.

I argue with myself as I make my way away from the known stranger from my Instagram inbox, toward the bar. Underneath the patio the heat lamps are on providing warmth as the chill of the night sets in.

"May I help you, ma'am?" The bartender asks before I even get to her.

"Bourbon neat," I say.

She makes the drink from a bottle of my favorite brand, places a thin straw inside, and pushes it toward me.

"Thank you," I say.

I turn around and I see he is no longer standing where he was. The space he occupied for however long before I arrived, is empty. I walk around the patio no longer interested in participating in the scene I signed up for. I was hesitant when I first agreed to attend, excited when I got out of the car, and wary on my way up in the elevator. Seeing everyone in their Thursday's best with their representatives in full command of all surface conversations, I am suddenly overwhelmed by the pretense I was late to arrive to.

You can always go home and surf the Firestick.

I take a sip from my drink, walk to an empty set of facing love seats, and sit down.

"You don't pay attention to your surroundings, do you?"

"I didn't know I had to in this environment."

"You should always be aware of your surroundings. You never know who may come up behind you when you least expect it."

"You mean like you?" I ask as he sits down on the love seat facing me.

"Perhaps," he says.

I nod and sip my drink.

He's different.

"Good to see you again, Naomi."

"Likewise, Kiyan."

"What are you drinking?" he asks.

"Knob Creek," I say.

"Hennessy," he says holding up his glass.

It is his turn to sip his drink while I drink in his face. The lighting on the patio is minimal and does nothing against the black of the night. If not for the coloring of our clothes most of the brown skinned people scattered about the rooftop would disappear into the evening.

"What are you doing here?" I ask.

"I came to see the fish in the flesh."

I roll my eyes resenting his characterization of me from our first meeting.

I was in the ocean and wanted to swim.

"So, is this kind of thing your scene?" he asks.

"What do you mean? My scene?"

"This meet your mate in five minutes or less thing," he says, gesturing with one hand across the patio.

"This isn't speed dating," I say.

"It might as well be. The women are cliqued up four deep and the guys hunt in packs from clique to clique to see if anyone will bite their bait."

"That's a very Animal Planet version of what this is."

"We're all animals," he says. "At the basest sense of our essence, we're all animals."

So, he's a metaphysical mack. Game is still game.

"So, are you a scientist, too, in addition to being an artist?" I ask.

"Science was never really my thing. School in general was never really my thing."

"But you went to school, right?"

I thought you didn't have a list.

He needs to at least have a degree. A certificate of something from somewhere.

Again, I argue with myself while Kiyan leaves the conversation open. He is unhurried, unrehearsed, and unbothered. I try to still my body with resolute anticipation, not letting him see that he might excite me in any sudden movements. I don't cross or recross my legs, I don't shake my ankle across my knee, I don't tap the caps of my six-inch heels against the ground. Looking down into my drink, and then over the rim of my glass at him, I wait for him to either answer the question, or make a declaration, an observation about me, most people, men or women, friend or lover, don't take the time to notice.

"I was actually very good at school," he says after an inordinate amount of time has passed. "I just knew it wasn't for me. I went because I had to. I passed because my mother threatened me with an extension cord."

"And how far through did you pass?" I ask.

"Ask the question you really want to ask."

"Excuse me."

"You're being nice and euphemistic like I'm one of your interview guests or something. There's no camera rolling around you, and no one but me to get at you in your comments section if I don't like what you say. So ask the question you really want to ask."

Damn he's even more forward in person.

He said be blunt. So be blunt.

"Did you go to college?" I ask.

"Does it matter?"

What the hell kind of answer is that. Of course, it matters.

"Of course, it matters." I say.

"Why?" He challenges.

"Because I want to know if you will be a waste of my time or not?"

"And you can determine whether I will be worth getting to know by which letters I have behind my name?"

"I didn't say that."

"In a way you did."

"Don't worry about it," I say standing up.

This was cute over text messages. Now it's just trivial.

I drain my glass and sit it on the table. "Have a good night," I say walking away.

"Wow, you walk away because I questioned the motive behind your question?" He asks, keeping in step with me.

"No," I say. "I'm walking away because I have to get up in the morning and go to work. I can't just art my days away. I have a real job."

"I have a real job too," he says.

"Good for you. Goodnight."

I press the button for the elevator and wait in silence. I stare straight ahead at the golden doors and wait for them to open. I don't look at him with wonder and curiosity. I wait, trying to maintain my stance and my stare. I keep my representative in control and allow the real Naomi to be frustrated and pissed, in a tucked away corner of my body I know I can't tap into right now.

"You know when you're mad, you hold your jaw tight to the left side like you're biting the inside of your cheek."

"I didn't know that," I say. "Thanks for the information."

The elevator dings to announce its arrival. I step forward as the doors open and get on. He is in step with me.

This is what I get for opening my big mouth and telling him where I would be tonight. I should have left him unanswered with the rest of the flyby fuck boys just looking to see if I run my own page, and whether or not I'll respond to their inquiry.

"I see running away from uncomfortable situations is your default self-defense mechanism," he says after the doors closed.

"I'm glad you think you know me well enough to make all these unsolicited observations about me as a person, but no one asked you."

"Ah." He begins to laugh. It is smooth and surprisingly sexy, the sound of his chuckles. "The fish fights back."

"I'm not a fish. You don't have me hooked. I'm not taking the bait. Now you have a good night."

Why am I mad. This was supposed to be fun. This was supposed to be exciting. He made it way too serious, way too fast.

You don't even know me.

"Have breakfast with me."

"Now why would I do that?" I ask, as the elevator opens into the lobby on the first floor.

"Because you're curious."

You don't even know me.

But you are curious.
That doesn't mean he needs to know that.

"See, I can see you thinking about it," he says as I war with myself. "You want to come."

"I'll pass."

"Come to breakfast with me."

"I just told you no."

"Come to breakfast with me," he says again.

I leave him in the lobby and exit the front doors of the restaurant onto Bay Street. I found a meter a block up and around the corner on Laura and Forsyth. I walk down the street with him walking beside me. Neither of us is talking.

"Kiyan, it was nice meeting you officially tonight, but I'm going to my car, and I'm going home. I don't know you, and you're following me. I have Mace on my keys and a taser in my purse."

"Wow, you think I'm trying to do something to you?"

"I don't know what your intentions are."

"My intention was to make sure you got to your car safely because it's dark outside, we're downtown, and you're alone."

"I'm single. I go a lot of places alone in the dark."

"And this is why chivalry is dead," he says.

"Oh, please," I say. "Don't start bashing the independent woman thing. I'm living my life."

"And I'm living mine, and I'm trying to convince you to go to breakfast with me."

"Why? So, we can do more of this cat and mouse thing? I'm not interested."

"I would take your "no" if I thought you were telling the truth."

"Haven't you been told that no means no?"

"I didn't know I needed consent to ask you a question."

"I've already given you an answer."

"And I'm asking again."

"No, is a complete sentence."

I reach in my purse and chirp the lock on my car door as I get to it. Kiyan doesn't fall back. I move my finger over the button to spray the hot pepper, if necessary, as I reach my door.

"Come to breakfast with me, Naomi?"

The latest iteration of his request is different. The quality of his voice is different. It is exasperated and slightly desperate. Gone is the bold, discerning, and intuitive bravado of the Fountain of Fontaine, the man on the beach, or the one who moments ago told me to be more aware of my surroundings. Now he is just a man. A man taking risk after risk of being turned down by the same woman he insists to persistently ask out on a date. I take my finger off of the nozzle of the pepper spray and open my door.

Just say yes.

I ignore my thought and ask, "Why?"

"Because we can have a real conversation without all of this," he says, waving his hand between us.

"And what's all of this?"

"You all done up, being someone you're not. Me looking like this. We're pretending just like everybody else up on that roof. How many of those people will actually find what they're looking for. A fraction if that. A fraction of that may get married. And we already know the divorce rate is fifty percent."

He's not wrong.

I resist the urge to agree with a nod of my head, even though Jonelle, Nathan, and Margo's intense and earnest faces before I approached them, rush back to me with the force of a tsunami induced flood.

Dating is so much easier than divorce.

That's what Margo told the couple she built her business off of. She was wrong. All three of them were wrong. Dating is hard. The whole thing is hard. Dating. Marriage. Divorce. No matter what stage of a relationship you're in, the beginning, the coast and plateau, or the break-up, it's all hard.

I sigh. "Where do you want to go, Kiyan?"

"Maple Street. San Marco," he says.

"Time?"

"Eight a.m."

"I don't wake up until nine, nine-thirty."

"Then I guess you're going to have to get up earlier then."

Who in the hell does he think he is? That's what I get for giving in. I should have made him sweat a little more. I guess I still can if I don't show up in the morning.

"Good night, Kiyan," I say, getting completely in my car and closing the door.

I don't wait for him to confirm the time, place, or even my presence. I start the engine and drive away. Down Forsyth, a right at Main, straight ahead up and over the bridge onto I-95 south, heading home. I ride home with the windows cracked and the radio low. I hear the rush of the wind and only the downbeats of the music.

Who the hell does he think he is?

It is the only thought I have about the man named Kiyan who calls himself the Fountain of Fontaine.

Fountain full of shit is more like it. Overconfident. Thinks he knows everything. Can't answer questions to save his life, fountain full of shit. I'm sure he's running game just like every other dude on that rooftop, only his version comes off as clairvoyant, like he's got love sight or something. One breakfast, no bullshit, and we'll be done.

And this is why people say don't bring sand to the beach.

Sighs and headshakes are all I have for myself as I park in my garage. It is all I can do as I retire in my bedroom, take off my clothes, wig, and makeup, and scrub my face and body. Sighs and headshakes. I scold myself for giving in; at the same time, I congratulate myself for giving in. In the shower, in the mirror, in my prayers, laying in my bed waiting for sleep to chase me down and tackle me, I war with myself over the levels of stupidity of what I agreed to.

Is it a one, or is it a ten?

I don't know.

You know who would know, my mother?

Too bad I'm not calling her to find out.

I'm good on all that drama.

I'd rather be confused alone than confused on the phone with her, and criticized.

I take my phone off of the charging pad on the nightstand to set the alarm to an earlier time. I see I have two messages from the Fountain of Fontaine.

They are instructions:

8 a.m.

No makeup. Don't wear your wig.
I want to meet Naomi Jean.

He's got a lot of damn nerve. A lot of damn nerve.

10.

Breakfast at Maple Street

I arrive in San Marco at eight-ten and spend five minutes hunting for a parking space in the quaint square filled with local businesses. I am late intentionally and unintentionally. My alarm went off at six-thirty, but I didn't get out of bed until seven. I completed my morning routine, then hunted in my closet for something to wear to work. That outfit, shoes, wig, and makeup bag are in a garment bag, hanging up on a hook in the backseat of my car. I came as requested. I have arrived as I am. No makeup. No wig. That's part of the reason I was late. I started to come to breakfast in one of my satin-lined beanies, since my locs are still in cornrows, but my pride, and the mirror, mostly the mirror— wouldn't let me leave the house. All I could hear was my mother's voice yelling at me in her way, "Girl, you look like who did it and why?"

In the mirror in the living room next to the TV I stood, taking down each one of my expertly intertwined cornrows. My hair is my only embellishment as I walk into Maple Street Biscuit Company; the local café with the cult-like following. Gray sweatpants, my Dillard Blue Devil hoodie, and a lion's mane for hair. Kiyan is surprised when he sees me. Pleasantly. I can tell by the look in his eye. I try to keep my smile to myself.

I guess I dress down nicely.

"You made it," he says.

"You insisted."

"But you're late."

"I can leave," I say.

"Okay attitude. Chill. I won't get on your case this morning."

"You don't know me well enough to start getting on my case. Did anybody ever tell you that reading people you don't know is rude?"

"You have now," he says. "Anything else you want to get off of your chest."

"I'm good. For now," I say.

We order biscuits, topped with fried deliciousness and doused in various sauces, before giving the cashier our answer to their question of the day. The answer which will be the name they call when our order is ready.

"If your name was a color what would it be?" the cashier asks.

"Red," I say.

"Blue," he says.

Kiyan pays for the two breakfast meals and drinks, and then we make our way to the back corner of the restaurant. I sit in the booth with my head leaning against a wall, and he takes the chair in front of me.

"Why red?" he asks.

"It fits," I say. "Love, fire, passion, desire, destruction. All of that's red. All of that's me."

"You're destructive?"

"Depends on who you ask."

"Don't do that. Don't do that now."

"Don't do what?"

"Open up one minute and then clam up the next."

I do what I want to do.

"Why blue?" I ask.

"So, you're not going to answer my question?"

"Nope. Why blue?" I repeat.

"It's mellow. It's calm. It's tranquil. It's also love and peace, and everything good in the world. The ocean, the sky."

"So, you're just a Zen type of dude who likes to rile everybody else up?"

"Do I rile you up?"

I ignore the innuendo in his voice and roll my eyes hard right. He chuckles. It is the the same easy laughter from last night. The same melodious sound that was sensuous and sexy the first time I heard it. Like mothers who smile the first time they hear their new babies laugh, I can't help but smile at the sound that is a symphony to my ears. The notes of his tenor are light and mellifluous.

This might be worth the lack of sleep.

"Red!"

I stand up to get my order.

"Sit down. I got you."

It is a command and I obey. I watch Kiyan walk to the counter to grab my plate as one of the workers yells out blue. In black, loose leg running tights, and a tight sports tee with vented gray patches on his back and elbows, his easy gait moves through the moderately packed restaurant with an astounding sense of self-awareness. His rope locs are drawn up into a man bun. He comes back with two trays of food, steam still rising from the plates.

I cross myself, mumble a prayer, and dive into the first real breakfast I've had in days. Cut. Bite. Cut. Bite. We eat in an easy silence that is surprisingly comfortable. I watch the muscles in his face work as he chews. His expressions range from pensive to playful as he eats. I enjoy the boyishness of his face compared to the deeply masculine candor of his conversation.

"Why breakfast?" I ask.

"What do you mean?" He asks looking at me.

"I mean, most first meetings, first dates, are over dinner, maybe lunch. Why breakfast?"

"So, you consider this a date?"

"Why do you always question me about the words I use when I ask you something?"

"Always? We've only spoken twice."

"The DMs count too," I say.

"Because I want to be clear in the conversation. I don't want to assume, and I don't want you to assume. Words matter."

"Okay, and?"

"And do you consider this a date?" he asks.

"Sure," I say. "Why breakfast?"

He doesn't press me to explain why my voice went up when I said sure. He picks up his fork and knife, cuts through his sauce covered fried-chicken biscuit, and eats.

He says, "Where I'm from, going to breakfast is a thing. Breakfast dates are a thing. Dinner is nice, and lunch doesn't mean anything, but breakfast is big. If a person is willing to spend the first hours of their day with you, when they haven't settled back into the people they've made themselves into for the world's ease and convenience . . . If someone is willing to give you that raw, up out the bed spirit . . . that says a lot."

"Okay. So where are you from, and what does this mean?" I say, waving my hand between the two of us.

"I'm originally from Chicago."

"Oh, cool. I'm going up there in a few months for a conference."

"If you need a tour guide let me know," he offers.

"We're not there yet and you haven't answered the second part of my question."

"What was it again?"

"What does this . . . us having breakfast together, mean?"

"This means you're willing to take a chance on me."

There he is back to thinking he knows me.

"Hmm. How did you get to Jacksonville from Chicago?"

"Life," he says.

"Be more specific."

"I went to SCAD for painting . . ."

"So you did go to college."

"I didn't say I finished."

"Did you finish?"

"Does it matter. You're here. We're eating."

"It doesn't matter, but I want to know."

"Why?"

"Because I do."

"Yes. I finished," Kiyan says. "Would you feel differently if I didn't?"

"I don't know what I feel right now. We're talking."

"Yes. And you're thinking."

"Aren't we always?" I say. "Researchers say we think up to eighty-thousand thoughts a day."

"Don't you sound like the news lady. I didn't ask her to breakfast."

You can't separate one from the other.

"I'm not two people. My job is my job. I am who I am."

"And I want to know the part I don't see on TV."

I sigh and resist the urge to roll my eyes. He is challenging without giving very much of himself. He is getting to know me, without me getting a peak into who he is. But then again, I'm at an unfair advantage. With much of my life televised or documented, if not by a professional camera, but my own, it is easy to know me and challenge me, because I am out and about and in the public.

Maybe that's why Aaron and I didn't work out in the end. We never stopped being our public selves when we were in private. I didn't let my guard down, and he for damn sure didn't either. We were always the job.

Cut. Bite. Chew. I shake away the unintended thought of Aaron and try to get back into the groove of the conversation we were having, until Kiyan pushed me to check my own motives and intentions for every word I say and every question I ask.

"What makes you cheat?" I ask.

"Whoa," he says dropping his fork. "Where'd that come from?"

"We've already established that we're on our first date, and I'm willing to take a chance on you. So let's cut the cutesy first date questions and get right to the nitty gritty. What makes you cheat?"

"Ass, access, and opportunity."

Damn that was honest.

"That was honest," I say.

"My turn. What makes you lie?"

"Judgement. If I feel like I'm going to be condemned for being me, I lie and I hide."

He nods his head and I can see his mind working. His dimple has disappeared, and the cleft in his chin is twisted as he thinks. His eyebrows have formed one as he turns over my answer and words to decide where we go from here.

"When was your last relationship?" he asks.

"Define relationship," I say.

"Hmmm," he says with a register of surprise.

"You asked for Naomi Jean," I say. "Here I am."

I ignore the last quarter of my foodie breakfast sandwich on my plate, as I wait to see in what direction he takes the conversation. I already know one of his weaknesses and he knows one of mine. He also now knows I have different categories of relationships. Most men want the women their involved with to pretend their pasts never happened. The gap between his answers, his raised voice "hmmm," and the phrasing of his next question will show how evolved he is, or isn't; it will reveal where he falls on the spectrum of the Madonna-whore complex. I wait in the ease of his quiet, studying his face, waiting to see if he's really worth my time, or if this breakfast is a one-off detour with sand I should have left on a Cuban beach.

"When was your last relationship where there was mutual emotional support, compassion and respect?"

Well, damn.

"I don't know if I've ever had one of those," I say.

"When was the last time you thought you had one of those?" he asks.

"Four, almost five years ago."

"And your last purely physical relationship."

"It's ongoing," I say cutting my eyes.

"What does that mean?" he asks.

He didn't flinch.

Nowhere in his body does it register that I just told him that I'm in a relationship only for the sex and nothing else. His face is still soft, warm, and inviting. I can't even tell if he's thinking at all or just waiting for me to answer.

I say, "It's long distance. Never set in stone. It's always spur of the moment whenever we're both around and we both have time."

"So basically, a tune-up."

"It's more frequent than a tune-up. More like an oil change."

He nods his head in understanding of my situation-ship with Matt. The Matt I haven't felt in months or heard from in weeks. The Matt I only hear from a week before his impending visit, with an emailed itinerary, and a "I can't wait to see you, Beautiful," typed in the closing of the greeting.

"What about you?" I ask.

"What do you mean?"

"When was your last relationship when you felt emotionally supported, and provided that for your partner?"

"Last year."

He moves fast.

"What happened?"

"It stopped being emotionally supportive. Felt more like a business transaction than love. A checked box rather than fire and desire."

"You like the red too," I say.

"Don't we all? I've just learned we can't stay in the red too long. It's too hot. Too dramatic. Too needy. We have to mellow out at some point."

"You think I'm dramatic and needy?"

"I didn't say that," he defends.

"I know," I say, trying to soften my tone. "I'm asking."

"I don't know if you are or not. Dramatic probably. Needy, I'm not sure. You did threaten to Mace me last night, so maybe you're one and not the other."

"I'll take that as a compliment."

"Receive it as you will."

I nod and feel the smile spreading across my face.

This is a good date. A damn good date.

I look down at my plate as I feel myself blushing. I know he sees it, since my color can't hide it. He is thoughtful and introspective, curious and prying, but respectful. We've covered more ground in the forty-five minutes we've been sitting across from each other than most couples cover in the first few years of dating. In breaking the first bread of the day together, in clothing just a step above pajamas, he has met Naomi Jean, and I have been introduced to Kiyan Fontaine.

And you thought he was full of shit.

He still might be, but right now I don't care.

My breakfast is unfinished, my hair is loose, and my eyes are tired, but sitting across from this man, who is nothing like the tall, dark, and handsome specimen I proclaimed I wanted over drinks with Jennifer and Diedre, I don't care. He has seen me blush at his behest and I don't care.

It feels good to be seen.

"When was your last sexual only relationship?" I ask, finishing out the couplet of questions he began.

"At least six months ago," he says.

"What happened to ass, access, and opportunity?"

"The stars haven't aligned."

"Don't think they're about to align over me."

"Would it be wrong if they did?"

The question on his tongue is forward and innocent. It is just a question, but it is more than just a question. And just like that, the timbre of the conversation has changed. The vibration of the frequency around us has changed. We have moved beyond the nitty-gritty into the murky area of stimulation and sexual tension; the palpable energies that always exist between men and women who are interested in being more than just friends.

I push back from the table and stand up.

"Is the fish on the run?"

"I'm going to the restroom," I say.

I retreat from the table and try not to run as I get away. Inside the stall of the bathroom I relieve my bladder. I see the verbal stimulation of our conversation, and the affects it's had on my body, and my panty liner, and I regret not bringing my purse in out of the car.

This is the best first date I've had in years and I didn't have to do anything extra, besides show up looking a step better than busted.

Back in the dining area, Kiyan is waiting for me by the door. His unfinished sandwich sits across from mine; our appetites are full more from the conversation than the food. I stride to where he is with butterflies in my stomach and excitement tingling across my body.

He says, "I wasn't sure if you were going to sneak out of the back or come back up to the front."

"Ha, ha, ha," I mock. "There's no back exit for customers."

"That doesn't mean you couldn't have found a way."

"Did I shake your little pride?" I ask.

He nods. "A little bit. A little bit."

We walk out of the doors of the restaurant into the warming morning air. Many of the store fronts around us aren't yet open. San Marco square is barely alive with the typically heavy foot traffic found in the afternoons and on weekends. The fountain roars and a few homeless people sleep on its slabs, but other than them, we are basically alone in front of the southern fried cafe.

"This was nice," I say looking at him.

"I'm glad you enjoyed our first date."

"I did."

"So, does that means there will be a second?"

"Possibly," I say. "Possibly."

"Does that possibly also mean you will give me another way to contact you besides your DMs, and at matchmaking events disguised as rooftop bar parties."

"Are you asking for my number again?"

"I am," he says.

Two words and the conversation shifts again. He is no longer expectant and playful. He is serious. He wants access, opportunity, and maybe even some ass. I smile to myself and wonder. I wonder if he will be as candid on the next date as he was today. I wonder if he will be as open with me in a month as he was today.

The question is, will you be as open and candid with him as he was with you?

I don't shush my inner critic. She is right. I am right. He is right about me. Running is easy. Avoidance is easy.

Being a fish is easy. I don't swim in a school and I don't mate for life.

Or do I?

"Give me your phone," I say.

He hands me the device out of his back pocket and unlocks the screen. I add myself to his contacts, send myself a message, and then hand it back to him. I walk across the street toward my car as he scrolls to find my math.

"I don't see your name," he says yelling after me.

"You will," I say.

He doesn't chase me down like he did the night before. I'm glad he read the moment right. Sitting in my driver's seat, I fish my purse from the floor of the car underneath the passenger's seat, and take out my phone. I open the message I sent to myself and dial the number. He answers on the second ring.

"You're funny," he says.

"I thought you'd like that."

"I do," he says. "I do."

I imagine him nodding. The singular deep-set dimple in his cheek on full display, I can see him pleased with me.

He says, "When can we do this again?"

"Whenever you like," I say. "After tonight, it's the weekend."

"That it is," he says. "Are you the same over dinner as you are over breakfast?"

"I don't know," I say. "There's only one way to find out."

"Dinner it is," he says. "I'll figure something out and let you know later."

"Sounds like a plan to me. Will you have any special instructions for me this time or can I come how I want to?"

"Do what you feel will make the stars align," he says.

He ends the call without a goodbye, but I'm not miffed. I left my number in his phone under that moniker:

Stars Align. Every time he calls or texts, he will send his hope, his wish, his prayer for whatever he wants from me through the universe, beaming off of satellites until the signal gets to me. Then just maybe, just maybe, the balls of energy light years away will come together between the two of us like the three-starred belt of one of the closest constellations.

11.

Netflix and Chill

"You want to go out for drinks tonight?" Jennifer asks, stepping into my office.

"Can't," I say, grabbing my purse out of the bottom drawer of my file cabinet, beneath my desk.

"That's the third time you've canceled on us," Jennifer says, "what's gotten into you?"

"Nothing."

I haven't told either Jennifer or Diedre about reconnecting with Kiyan at the SENT mixer, or our breakfast date. In the last month and a half, I've managed to leave work as soon as I finish shooting the promos for the next day. I take notes in an email during the show to send out as soon as John says, "clear," which leads to a thread I can jump in and out of at my leisure. That suffices as my post instead of having an actual meeting that takes up more of my time.

It's been thrilling to have something to look forward to after work, and sometimes before work, besides ordering from Postmates and calling it cooking dinner, and binging another show that went straight to streaming. He's introduced me to his art world, shown me his studio at CoRK, allowed me to sit in on his classes at both the University of North Florida, and at an elementary school in Arlington. The only thing I haven't seen are the private classes he conducts from his studio. The ones he said would be too risqué for me. The ones he said he would decide whether or not I'd be able to come to. Despite his openness in everything else, it is the one thing he has protected.

He said a few weeks ago, "I want to keep this for myself and from you until I know that it's right."

"That sounds selfish," I said.

"It is," he said. "I'm being selfish with myself and establishing a boundary. Everyone has them. Including you."

"Whatever," I said rolling my eyes.

"Your boundary is why I've never been on the second floor in your house, right?"

Right.

"You're right," I grumbled, not wanting to agree with him.

I respected the way he was open about what he was ready for and what he wasn't. There was no pressure between either of us to do anything. In a way it is refreshing, and, in a way, it makes me wonder if we are friends, more than friends, or working toward being more than friends. We haven't had a relationship talk, a "what is this" talk, a "what are we doing" conversation, and I'm not sure I want to. I'm not sure I want to define what it is we're doing, when what we're doing is what feels right. Another reason I haven't bothered to tell Jennifer or Diedre where I've been going after work and why I keep canceling on them. And tonight, is not the night to explain. After weeks of waiting, I'm finally going to his evening class that is invite only, through an email list, from people who have expressed interest in his body of work, artistic openness, and a willingness to grow.

"You're hiding something," Jennifer says to me, still standing in the doorway.

"I'm not hiding anything," I say checking myself in the mirror.

"Yes, you are," she says. "The way you've been running out of here, emailing post notes, and always in your phone, you're hiding something, and I know what it is."

"Is that right?" I say, removing my wig, wig grip, and silk stocking cap.

"Yes," she says. "You've been getting some and haven't even told us who the new Boo is. I can tell. You've been coming in here, locs flowing, only putting on your wig when you're about to go on air. You're doing stuff not just to piss Boyce off. You're changing. The only thing that makes women change like that, is a dick attached to a man who halfway knows what he's doing."

I cut my eyes at her. "You should strive for better in your life," I say.

Looking at my reflection in the mirror I commence to unraveling the twisted halo I wear to make sure my hair hat doesn't look lumpy or bumpy on TV. I run my fingers through each twist, letting my locs fall where they wish, delaying an answer to Jennifer's inaccurate observation. She waits in the doorway watching me pay meticulous attention to my reflection.

"What's going on in here?"

The voice belongs to Diedre. I don't turn to acknowledge her. Just nod my head and continue looking at myself in the mirror, until I have finished unraveling and fluffing the locs.

"Naomi's canceling on us, again," Jennifer says.

"Okay," Diedre says. "More wine for us. There's only two glasses in a bottle anyway. We be stretchin' it trying to make it into three."

"It's only two glasses if you've got those *Scandal* sized glasses from Crate & Barrel," Jennifer says.

"Or the knock offs from the dollar store," Diedre says.

"Ain't nobody drinking wine out of those plastic glasses from the dollar store. What I look like with a twelve-dollar bottle of red, and a cup that barely passed the warehouse inspection?"

"You look like just what you are. Bougie on a budget."

"If you ladies are done, I'm going to go," I say.

"Where the hell are you going?" Diedre asks.

"Out," I say.

"I told you she's been getting laid," Jennifer says. "She just won't say it. Coming in here hella different."

"Hella different," Diedre echoes. "Skin is glowing and what not."

"I use a vitamin C serum," I say.

"I don't care what you use," Jennifer says. "The only thing that makes you glow like that is peen or pregnancy."

"Or both," Diedre says.

"For your information, I'm not pregnant, and at the moment we're not having sex. So get out of my business and I will see you tomorrow."

"For somebody not having sex, you're hella sprung," Jennifer says.

"Maybe she's just happy," Diedre says.

"Thank you, Diedre," I say. "Jenn, you should try it."

"I'm happy," she says. "But I'm not walking around like the floor is made of clouds and the birds are singing in the trees like I'm Cinderella or somebody."

"That was Snow White," I say.

"No, it wasn't," Diedre says. "It was Sleeping Beauty."

"It was one of 'em," I say. "Except Princess Tiana. She didn't get birds and forest friends. Baby had to go to work making them beignets."

"Either way," Jennifer interjects, "you're still walking around happy and glowing, and since you said you're not having sex, I'm still right. It's because of a man."

"I believe you were trying to fix me up and find out my list a month or so ago," I say. "Now that I've found someone without your help, attitude, or input, you feel some kind of way?"

"Duh!" Diedre says. "We want to know."

"Give up the goods," Jennifer says.

"You already know who he is," I say. "Can I go now? You're going to make me late."

I push past Jennifer and Diedre in the doorway and make my way toward the back of the newsroom, down the long halls, and to the back door of the employee parking lot. Their heels are a couple paces behind me, but they catch up quickly. Right as I'm walking out the door, Jennifer grabs the push bar and shuts it again.

"Uh-uh, heifer. You don't get to say we already know who he is and then dip."

"You're a dog with a bone," I say. "You should've been a reporter. Or at least a police officer, with all these damn questions."

"And you're not slick," Jennifer says. "Who is he? We know you're not talking about maintenance man Matt. He's never been this available."

"No, I'm not talking about Matt."

"So who is it?"

"It's the guy she was texting the day you took her phone," Diedre says.

"Ding, ding, ding," I say. "Diedre is correct for three hundred points."

"But we still don't know anything about him," Jennifer says.

"Yes, you do," I say. "Diedre met him before I did."

"Not the boy from the beach," Diedre says.

I don't say anything. I use both my hands to push the door open and step out into the evening. It is still warm as our spring makes the quick transition to summer well before the rest of the country, or the calendar says so. I leave Jennifer and Diedre with their hands on their jean clad hips to guesstimate and speculate about my relationship, or the lack thereof, amongst themselves.

They can figure it out or not figure it out. I'm going to live my life.

I'm sure I will have a hundred messages from them in our group thread about when Kiyan and I met for real, why I didn't tell them, and why I've been holding out.

I put my phone on vibrate and do not disturb as I get in my car. I don't want their thoughts disrupting my vibe as I head to his studio; but even the music in the car, can't drown out Jennifer's voice.

The only thing that makes women change like that, is a dick attached to a man who halfway knows what he's doing.

The only thing that makes you glow like that is peen or pregnancy.

It's always amazed me how women ascribe their happiness in terms of men. My mother would tell her patients to find their happiness on their own terms, but let her get into it with my daddy and she's walking around the house like a sad sack of potatoes until they eventually worked it out, whether he was at fault or not. Even when she was right in a situation or argument, she was the one who ended up sad, hurt, on her phone with her friends, and in her feelings like the world was about to end. Now here I am, and my friends are doing the same thing to me. Like I can't be happy just being me, by myself.

Men never do this type of shit to each other.

My brother is good with, or without a woman on his arm, in or out of a relationship. Nobody walks around asking him if he's okay after a breakup. The world doesn't stop for him when he has a broken heart. But for women it's always assumed we're ruled by our emotions. We assume it about each other. It's the reason the "I don't mess with other females" syndrome exists. We can't see ourselves outside of the male gaze, and that's why I didn't tell them about Kiyan.

As soon as I introduce a man into the conversation, the picture, my sphere of orbit, my atmosphere, it becomes about us and not about me. I'm still an individual. I'm still a person. I still have needs, and wants, and everything else built inside of me outside of him. I'm getting to know him, and he's getting to know me, and while that adds to my happiness, it's not the only contributing factor. But they don't get that.

Nobody gets it.

Women get the wrap for being too emotional and men, not emotional enough. Women are supposed to be all wrapped up in their man and their family, and men in their jobs and their money.

"This shit is a mind fuck," I say as I drive down Phyllis Street, searching for a place to park.

I pull into the lot of an art gallery named for what it is and the color of paint on its exterior walls, and park in the gravel amongst half a dozen other cars. The street is dark and quiet. Though it is Riverside, the unlit area still makes me nervous. I hurry across the street to the warehouse where Kiyan has his space. The colorful graffiti art on the outside of the building makes it look as if it is abandoned, as if this area was left for ruin and decay when the last of the industrial era left the city for the tech booms and busts, in a similar climate a coast away. When Kiyan first brought me to his studio space, I walked around with my arms crossed tight across my chest.

He said, "Relax. Looks can be deceiving. Like you."

"What the hell is that supposed to mean?" I asked.

"Nobody's going to mug you. You're safe. Loosen up."

When he brought me inside, I was amazed to see the paintings and drawings on the walls, the collective of artists working alongside each other, but on completely different projects. The network of warehouses forms a kind of "We Work" space for artists. Tonight, is my first time seeing his space in use. When I've come by before, he stopped working. I have not been privy to his creative process until now, and even this experience will be limited since he's leading a class, and not working out the ideas in his own mind on the canvas or paper, or whatever medium he chooses to use for his creations.

Inside the warehouse I walk to his specific space, slide open a barn door, and am astonished by what I see. Eight people paint canvases set on easels. The subjects of their work are live, naked, models who are posed together. I look from the models to the paintings. Each person's work reveals various body parts of the human subjects, serving as their muse. I hear Kiyan's voice before I see him.

"Every shape we could ever name is somewhere in the human body. The curves, the lines, circles, squares, triangles, and much more can be found in the body. It is the ultimate work of art."

I look to my right and there he is standing against a wall, observing the class as they paint. He is in paint-splattered tan cargo pants, and a tattered green T-shirt. He motions toward me with his hand. I go to him as he speaks again.

"Don't just paint the body parts you see to make a replica of the people in front of you," he says. "Give them a story. Illustrate how they feel with your colors and your brushstrokes. Give them anger or joy, give them rage, or make them recluses. Use the raw materials in front of you to create your own masterpiece."

"This is different," I whisper when I reach him.

"Are you uncomfortable?"

"I wouldn't say uncomfortable, so much as I would say, unprepared."

"I'd agree," he says. "You're not really dressed for painting."

I look down at my two-tone jumpsuit. The top of it is stark white with a halter like collar that buttons down the back of my neck. From my belted waist flow the wide-legged black pants of the one piece. On my feet are red patent leather pumps. The pop of color I know is there, even if no one else sees it on air.

"It's a work night," I say.

"You managed to change your hair," he says.

He gently wraps his hand around me, brings me close to him, and kisses the top of my scalp. His lips in my locs send tingles down my spine as he guides the class again.

"So, I saw this woman when I was on vacation a while ago and I couldn't stop staring at her, he says walking away from me. "Watching her swim in the ocean as if it were her natural habitat was captivating to me. I had to know her, to know her story, and at the very least her name, even when she wanted nothing to do with me. In the same way, capture the story of the models with your brush and your stroke. What do you want to know about them that they don't want to tell you? Take that information and put it on the canvas."

I watch Kiyan pace the room, slightly dragging his feet as he goes, as he guides the class through the art of painting by encouraging them to trust their instincts and not get hung up on perfection. He talks them away from the egregious and obvious of focusing on exposed body parts, and emboldens them to see the overall beauty and power in the body, and use that as a means to convey something beyond the surface nudity.

From where I stand, against one of the black painted walls, I can see all manner of shapes, colors, and sizes used to depict the models who lay in front of the class. Some people have chosen to stick with the color pattern of the actual brown-skinned people, while others have streaks of red, and sky blue mixed in with the various hues of brown. Against the wall, I watch Kiyan talk his students into the appreciation of the parts of us that are usually only seen by one other person and in the dark.

He says, "When you leave here tonight, I want you to go home, look at yourself in the mirror, and see the same power and beauty and story in your own body, that you've created here in this environment. Make your own mind and the thoughts you tell yourself about yourself, as safe and free from judgement as this space you're in right now. Thank you, everyone."

The class claps as Kiyan grabs robes for the models who volunteered their bodies for the project. I wait against the wall and watch as people pack away their portraits. Light conversation returns to the room. It's as if the students have come out of a trance Kiyan held them in, by the sheer sound of his voice. The students talk about what they have to do when they leave, about what they hope the traffic conditions are, how relaxed they feel after class, why this is better than yoga, therapy, or a massage. I listen to the bits and pieces of conversation until, one by one, the students file out, and Kiyan and I are alone in his space.

He walks around the work stations picking up the dirty cups of paint water the students used to clean their brushes and switch colors. I step off the wall and help, collecting water cups and brushes. I follow Kiyan out of the sliding barn doors into a common area where there is a little kitchenette set up. There, we dump the water and he begins rinsing and cleaning the brushes with a bottle of Dawn dishwashing liquid.

"What did you think?" He asks as I dry off the brushes.

"It was different," I say.

"Was it too much?"

"No," I say. "Not the way you teach."

"What do you mean?"

"I mean, you said it was risqué but it wasn't. It wasn't especially sexy. Sensuous maybe, but there was nothing dirty attached to it. It was about seeing the beauty of the body as it is and painting a story around that."

"You listened."

"I did."

What did he mean by that.

His comment makes me wonder how many other women he's brought to this sacred space. I wonder if they came and only focused on the nakedness of the subjects, or if they saw the vulnerability of what was happening. Did they make jokes about what was displayed, or did they treat the models, the students, the teacher, and the environment with the reverence it deserves.

"What's on your mind?" he asks, breaking my thoughts.

"What you said. Why did you seem surprised that I listened?"

"Because it's easy to get zoned out in the imagery and not hear direction. Whichever sense is stimulated the most, the signals from the others become drowned out."

"I see."

"C'mon," he says.

Holding damp paint brushes, I follow Kiyan, who holds an armful of clay mugs, back toward his space inside the barn doors. He resets the stations with cups. I follow behind him placing the two brushes in the cup for each station; one skinny, one fat.

He says, "It's like when you eat something really good. Like a mango."

"Okay."

"If the mango is just right, not too soft and not too hard, not too sweet, and not too bitter, and juicy, all of your focus goes into enjoying that mango. Your taste senses are overloaded that you don't hear the noise of your smacking or recognize the stickiness of your skin from juice running down the sides of your mouth and fingers. You don't smell the citrus of the fruit or see anything else in front of you, because you're so concentrated on the taste of the fruit."

"And what does that have to do with painting nudes?" I ask.

"Some people can get so overwhelmed by seeing a naked body that all they can focus on is what's in front of them and they don't hear the guided instruction to see beyond the models and to express on the canvas what's already inside of them."

"So, the goal of coming to this class is to reveal more about yourself that you may not know until you see it in the body of someone else that you painted."

"There is no goal," he says. "At least not for me. Everybody gets something different out of it, I just provide the space, and the atmosphere for everyone else to get what they need to."

"And how did you get into this?" I ask.

"What do you mean?"

"Just what I said. How did you get into being the facilitator for nude painting classes that pass themselves off as being some high-brow existential experience in search of the inner self?"

"You mean, was I always this deep or was I just trying to make some money and see some booty?"

"You said it, not me."

He laughs. He pulls his thick locs out of his face and laughs that beautiful sound that sounds like a song.

"It started as an idea from one of my boys to make money. He was like, "Girls love that paint and sip shit. You should do that."

"Figures," I say rolling my eyes. "So where did the naked model part come in?"

"That was my idea. Every artist is out here doing paint and sips. They even got them for kids. I thought if I made mine adult only, and invite only, I'd get more interest. People love being apart of exclusive shit."

"So how did it turn from a "booty and money" project into something you really care about?"

"How do you know it's still not just about the booty and the money?"

"Because I've been asking you for six weeks to let me come, and this is the first time you've said yes. You care."

He picks up a paint brush from one of the workstations and walks away from me. He goes to the stairs that opens into a little loft space looking over the blacked in studio. I follow behind him up the stairs until I can barely stand up straight. I take off my shoes and move over to the futon he has that he said is for napping, when he can't think of anything to paint and doesn't want to go home.

"Close your eyes," he says.

I do as instructed. The wet tip of the paint brush chills my skin as he drags it slowly from the center of my forehead around the perimeter of my face.

He says, "I care about the work I do. I care about how people interact with what I do. I care about those who are learning more about what I do as it guides them into what they're supposed to be doing. Child or adult, I care about their experiences when they encounter me or my paintings. But I also have to make money. And I'm a man . . ."

"Ass, access, and opportunity, right?"

"You said it, not me."

The paint brush is on my lips. The damp bristles trace the perimeter of my mouth, before he changes the stroke to fill in the plush, and plump centers. He takes the brush away. Next I feel one of his fingers. The skin is smooth and hard, calloused over from his grips on his brushes, pencils, and other utensils he uses to create.

"What sense is the strongest right now?" he asks me.

"Touch," I say.

Next, I feel his lips on mine and the curve of his palm on my chin. His kiss starts slow. Mouth to mouth, lips to lips, he allows the time for every cell to connect and send a signal to my brain in response, before he continues his gentle march forward through the gateway of my face. Our kiss is gentle and unhurried. I taste the essential oils I drizzled into my hair on his lips. We tingle with the tea tree oil between us. Leaning into the back cushion of the futon, my hands find his face, his hair, the thick new growth at the root of his locs detangles as I force my fingers through it to reach his scalp. I massage his head as he massages the inside of my mouth with his tongue. I feel both his desire and his restraint as he puts a hand on the outside of my face and stills his moving mouth.

I pant as he retreats from me. I can hear my heart beat, feel the flush in my body from the rush of blood flow; I can still feel his tongue moving inside me as he painted his name on the inside of my cheeks. I open my eyes and I see his face. His boyish, unassuming face that is wise beyond it's appearance, and aged with wisdom beyond its youthfulness.

"Where did your senses go?" he asks.

"I don't know."

"Think about it."

"Touch," I say. "Everything went to touch."

He nods his head and drops his hand from the side of my face.

"I want you to paint me," I say. "Naked."

The look on his face morphs from surprise to appreciation. A smile creeps across the lips that I've kissed, and I see his dimple deepen.

"Why?" he asks.

"Because I want to see what you see, when you see me."

"But I haven't seen you naked."

"Now you will, and it will be for work."

"You know my work is a little more abstract than an exact replica."

"Then see me in the abstract and explain it to me."

He nods his head. "When?" he asks.

"Tomorrow," I say. "After the show."

"Okay."

"I'll come by here after I get off set."

"No," he says. "Your place. I want you to be relaxed, comfortable, and in your element. I will leave if it's not right."

"Okay. Meet me at my place at nine tomorrow night."

"Do I get to paint Naomi Jean, or Naomi Grace?"

"Both. We both live in this body. We both move in this world, even if only one of us is broadcast."

"Then, I'll paint Naomi Jean Grace," Kiyan says, leaning in toward me again.

His kiss is different this time. It is urgent and insistent with an expectation of what more can become. I follow his movements and close my eyes and surrender to my senses. I submit to the touch of him and then to the taste. I vacillate between the feel of his lips and tongue with mine and the sound it makes in the empty studio loft. I think about which sense is at work until he kisses the thoughts out of my head and brings the focus solely into the mouth on my body. His kiss leaves me floating on clouds, with birds singing in the trees. It Disneyfies my senses and makes me see happily ever after as a real possibility, and not just a cheesy ending to a certain kind of book or movie. His kiss consumes the self until we are just shapes and parts of two bodies becoming one.

I break.

"It's getting late," I say.

Suddenly shy, I stop where we could be going with an excuse. I swap out the ease and go with the flow comfort of Naomi Jean with the focused and determined structure of Naomi Grace.

"I'll see you tomorrow."

I stand up with my heels in hand and walk down the rickety wooden stairs. The sound of his canvas sneaker covered feet squeak as he follows behind me. At the bottom of the stairs I put my shoes back on. When I look up, his brow is wrinkled and the cleft in his chin is gone. The space where his dimple is supposed to be is smooth. I hold up my hand to his face and wait until he nods before I touch him. I smooth the lines of his forehead, his chin and his cheeks, until the man with the baby face is back.

"Why the look?" I ask.

"Because you're extending an invitation and running away at the same time," he says. "I don't get it."

"I'm not running away. You'll see me tomorrow."

"So why not stay?"

"Because it's late."

"But you want me to paint you? Naked?"

"Yes."

He shakes his head. "Okay."

"Thank you for inviting me to your class," I say. I kiss his lips and pull away quickly. "I'll see you tomorrow."

I walk out of the barn doors and through the common space, until I get to the warehouse door that will take me outside. Kiyan is beside me the whole time. Silent, but beside me. I know he wants to know why I'm leaving. Why I'm interrupting the moment when the timing seemed right and the progressive orchestration of the inevitable was organic and completely natural. Eventually I know I will have to tell him what is on my mind. It is what he pulls out of me, whether I want him to or not. Eventually he gets to the peeled back pieces of me. To the core of who I am and why I do what I do, and why I act the way I act no matter how dressed up, made up, and prettified for TV I am. He always gets to my roots, but now is not the time to be stripped to the stem.

"Thank you," I say again, dragging my hand across the chest of his T-shirt.

I walk down the stairs, cross the street, and crunch the gravel beneath my feet to the car. Inside, I see him still looking at me from the doorway. I see him standing with his face twisted, lines and wrinkles of age that are not normally there are forced into his visage, and chiseled into his features giving his normal, resting face a brooding quality. I drive away from the warehouse, away from the contemplating man, focused on the curiosities of me. I leave my old neighborhood headed toward the highway. I escape downtown for sprawl and suburbia, all the while focusing on my sensory memories I still feel. His lips, his tongue, and his teeth. The vocabulary he left on the inside of my cheeks. It does not go away as I brush my teeth or rinse my mouth. I still feel his pulse as I pad from room to room in my house until I am face-to-face with myself and my vision, and I say "thank you."

Eye to eye with myself and the headless groom in my periphery, I repeat my mantra from the mornings.

"I am loved. I am safe. I am protected. I am covered. I am his. He is mine. He is safe. He is protected. He is covered. He is loved. We are love."

I cross the room and dip my hand in the pot of water and cross myself. I look over at the faces of M.O.M. and my Bible, of what to expect in the single life and wonder:

Maybe it's time for a new devotion. A new Holy Grail.

I close the door on my manifested prayers and visions and head back into my room. In the bed, beneath the covers as my eyes close and my breath slows, as sleep takes over and I drift from memories to dreams, I remember my senses and I focus on one that was drowned out before. The scent of him.

12.

The Artist and The Muse

He smells like Irish Spring when I give him a hug after opening the door. His return squeeze is awkward because of everything in his hands. In one hand are rolls of paper and in the other, a few plastic grocery bags I assume are his painting materials.

"Hi," I say stepping back from the doorway.

"You're ready," he says, surveying me and the house as he comes in.

I've cleared the space for him. The coffee table is in the kitchen and the couch is covered with an old sheet that I don't mind getting dirty. My dining room table is pushed up against the wall and the six chairs are stacked on top of it. I spent the morning before work arranging the space so all I had to do when I came home was shower and wait, scrolling though the endless options on Netflix.

In my oversized, Ankara printed duster I watch him come in and take survey of the space lit only with candles. Tea candles line the countertops of the kitchen along with a few large gourmet, hand-dipped candles infused with my favorite essential oils. The smell of sage lingers in the air from my cleansing of the space to make it as intuitively sacred as his studio.

"Will this work?" I ask.

"Mmhmm," he answers, setting down his materials on the floor at the foot of the couch.

He pulls off his faded jean jacket to reveal his undefined arms in a wife beater. The tank top is tucked into the waistband of his loose-fitting, faded jeans that have splotches of yellow, white, and purple paint all over them. I watch him as he kneels on the floor and unrolls one of the white sheets of paper. He pulls two weights from one of the bags and sets one on each end to keep the paper from rolling back on itself. The sheet has to be at least six feet in length, more than enough room for me in my bare feet and tall hair.

"Come over here," he says standing.

I do as I'm told and walk into the center of the living room space like it belongs to him and not me. He grabs my chin and lifts my head to look at him. I see the boy. I see the man. The cleft chin, the dimple, the sobering gravitas in his eyes. His pensive face studies mine, I am sure looking to see if I will back pedal or change my mind. I know he is looking to see if I will run, make an excuse to escape, as he says I am wont to do, like I did last night.

"Close your eyes," he says.

I do. I can feel his body bend down in front of me. The plastic bag rustles before he stands up. I can feel him walk around me and then I feel it, a satin scarf, or do-rag covers my eyes and is tied around the back of my neck.

"What's this for?" I ask.

"I want you to anticipate without seeing what's coming next," he says.

He takes my hand and leads me onto the paper. It crunches beneath my feet. Slowly, he removes my robe and helps me lower my body down to the ground, until I'm lying on my back, my face to a ceiling I cannot see. I can't see myself or his expressions at what he's seeing, seeing me naked for the first time. I can't make an assessment of myself from his facial expressions observing me, and for that, I am surprisingly appreciative.

He says, "Tell me about your day."

"It was a normal day," I say. "I went to work, I did the news, I came home, and now you're here."

I listen as the bag rustles and I hear objects being set to the ground. I assume it's the paint plate, the paint itself, and his brushes. He takes his time setting up, leaving me time to feel what it's like to wait for something I cannot describe, for an experience I've never had. Naked and in anticipation, I feel as if I'm losing my virginity all over again.

He says, "Something must have happened at work, that requires more of a story."

"You want a story?" I ask.

"You're the news lady. Tell me a story."

"My friends want to meet you," I say.

"Oh really?"

"Yes."

Jennifer and Diedre made their request known in text messages I didn't read until this morning, in multiple trips to my office during the day, and before I walked out the door to come home after the show.

"So, we've decided we get to meet Mr. Man," Diedre said, shortly after I walked into my office this morning.

"So, you and Jennifer just decided what's going to happen in my life without my input."

"Yeah," Diedre said. "It will be a triple date. Jennifer and Octavius, me and Jacob, and you and Kiyan."

"Oh really?" I asked.

"Yes. You're coming. We've decided."

"Not tonight," I said. "I already have plans."

"Tell the fountain of Fontaine we say, 'Hey,'" Deidre sang walking out of my office.

I watched her as her long, low ponytail, sans colorful highlights, swung across her back, flirting with her butt. In a tan blazer, *Purple Rain* T-shirt, black tattered jeans, and patent leather flats, Diedre buoyantly walked back to the pod to tell

Jennifer she had delivered the message. A message with a plan I had not specifically confirmed.

"Spread your legs for me a little bit," Kiyan says.

"Really, Kiyan?"

"Get your mind out of the gutter and separate your ankles," he says.

I do what I'm told giving him the space to fit his knee between the base of my trunk.

"Are you ready?" he asks.

"I'm ready," I say.

I feel his arm move, brushing up against my calves and my inner thighs as he works. The paper crunches beneath him.

"Do you want me to meet your friends?" he asks from the outer sides of my body.

"I don't mind, but I'm not pressed."

"Is that your way of saying you can take me or leave me?"

"No," I say. "It's my way of telling you that I like what we have, and I have no desire to rush other people's opinions and perceptions into whatever this is."

"You mean you don't have a definition for what this is?" he asks.

"At this very moment, I will say I am your muse."

"And when this moment is over?"

"I'll define it when we get there."

"That's a way to live in the moment."

I don't respond. I let his statement be a period on that part of the conversation. I relax into the paper and what is happening around me. I can not see, but I feel the paint brush moving around on the outskirts of my body. I hear the strokes of the bristles and feel grazes from his hanging rope locs against my skin. I focus on the feel of his spirit, his essence around me until he is back at my feet on the outskirts of my body, squeezing bottles of color onto his plate.

"Are you ready?" he asks me again.

"Let's find out," I say.

Without warning, the tip of the brush touches my skin. He paints one nipple and then the other. Goosebumps rise on my skin and I immediately feel chilled as my body adjusts to the foreign wetness. He encircles my navel, and draws in the life line that has not darkened on my womb that has never carried a child. I resist the urge to shiver, quake or quiver. As quickly as the cold sensation is applied it is removed, and then he is back with another brush. This one is thicker, colder, and wetter than the last. I feel my nipples harden under his stroke, and moisture gather between my thighs. My breath becomes ragged as he paints my legs, my arms, my belly, and the fat of my chest in long strokes, as if with a rectangular house painting brush.

"Can you tell me what color I am?" I ask.

"You are you colored," he says. "Take a deep breath, I'm going to put this over you."

The second long sheet of paper is rolled out and laid over my painted body. I am wrapped in his medium, the muse covered by her creator, the ingenue depicted by her auteur. Like the shroud of Turin, I am pressed and molded into the top sheet by his hand. Even through the paper the feel of his hands squeezing, kneading, and massaging my body quickens my heartbeat. I am greedy and he is slow. I take the deep breath he suggested and lean into his touch. The paper is rough on my skin, but the closer it is to me, the closer I am to him. He pushes and squeeze until it seems like every ounce of paint has been transferred from my body to the top sheet. Only then does he remove it and lay it out beside me.

Standing behind me, through the top of my blindfold, I can only see part of his face. His forehead and his nose. He removes the satin and I open my eyes to his. I can only focus on what's in my sight before he redirects my sensory focus. He gets down on both knees and kisses my lips. Laying prostrate on the other end from me, he kisses me slowly. I taste the mint on his tongue, and I know he can taste the wine on mine. I savor the texture of his taste buds, lazing in the feel as warmth washes over my semi-damp skin.

He breaks from my mouth to kiss my forehead, then my nose, my mouth, and then back again, the tongue between my lips. He parts me and relishes the moment where we left off from the night before.

"Are we done?" I ask between breaths.

He says, "I have your outline and your color. I will finish the rest later."

His kiss covers me before I can ask or have answers to my questions. I move by instinct and reach my arms over my head. I grab the sides of his tank top and pull it toward me. It forces us to break our connection. When I have successfully pulled it off of his shoulders, I arch my back and extend my mouth up, but I am met by his navel and not his lips.

I kiss his stomach as he kisses mine. He kisses my skin covered in the quick drying acrylic paint. Between my breasts, in the middle of my belly, dipping his tongue into my innie, he takes his time traveling the length of me in full push-up position. His hovering over me is tantalizing. The heat from his body radiates to mine. I pull at him, but he doesn't come down. Anticipation builds like fire from the seat of my Svadhishthana, my sacral chakra. There is fire in my belly, moisture at the meeting of my thighs, and sweat beads gathering beneath my shaved pits. I arch to reach him, but he moves away, planting a kiss on each one of my toes, my ankles, then my shins as he makes his way back up. He kisses each of my thighs and my nipples, and my cheeks. I poke my finger into his dimple as he returns to home base, my lips. We break.

"Take off your clothes." I hear my own need in the low pant of my voice.

"Don't be impatient." He stands.

I've been patient enough.

He picks up the sheet of paper he pressed into me and pushes it to the side. "You're beautiful," he says.

"Thank you."

Kiyan walks to my feet, looking over me like I am the art and not the model, the finished product and not the raw materials. He stands staring over me. His eyes are what give him his age. He looks at me with sage intensity and I have to resist the urge to cover myself; to hide what he's already seen, to become ashamed of what he's already appreciated, to pretend like the sexual affectation is not there. I resist, relax into the floor, and never break his gaze.

See me. See all of me.

He drops to both knees and picks up one of my feet. He kneads and massages my metatarsal and arch before moving to my heels. My moan is illicit and involuntary. I feel his hands directly on my skin without the barrier of the paper or the brush. Sounds rise from within me and escape my lips, and I let them. I feel weightless, like I'm levitating. I suck the inside of my cheek as he continues inches away from my long-lost virginity. He is unhurried in his exploration. His hands pull and grip my legs, brushing a careless few fingers over my sex I know is intentional, but he pretends is accidental. He is testing me. Waiting to see if I will say stop, waiting to see if I will revoke consent, waiting to see if I become the "me too" who will end his career, even though this whole setup has been my idea.

I look at him with all the warmth I can muster and a slight nod to acknowledge that this is what I want. He is what I want.

You are what I want.

I wonder if I had not explicitly said yes, if he would have kept going or would he have been content to be friends who sometimes see, and only see, each other naked.

He lays down in front of me. I am the Sphinx and he is a Hebrew slave. I am Mecca and he is on the hajj. Prostrate before me, I see only the top of his thick hair, even though it's been tightened and retwisted. But sight is not what I need. I wait for feeling to takeover. His lips on my inner thighs, his hand cupping over the little, big me creates heat. He reaches me through the body paint and rolls his tongue though my anatomical waves. My built up and blindfolded anticipation explodes in tides. The warm moisture that had already gathered runs from a trickle to a stream, and I surf the first rolls of an orgasm, feeling heat color my cheeks, and making the top of my head tingle.

Kiyan doesn't stop. He catches my essence, lapping up my lunar pull, as his fingers work magic in the reflexes of my feet, the muscles of my calves, and eventually inside of me. He stirs until I am sticky and empty, writhing on my own ecstasy, spent from the deliverance from this last drought of my self-imposed celibacy. He does not release me from the power of his play until my body calms, aside from the shake in my leg.

I reach my hands for him, but he is not close. Instead, I just look at him with wonder as he stands ups and takes off the remainder of his clothes. He drops a cluster of condoms onto the ground, then his pants. Even though he has been unselfish his need is evident. Long, curved and pulsing, I am amazed at his restraint, his need to please rather than be pleased himself. I sit up on my elbows and he pulls me into him. I grab the barrier to protect us on my way into his lap. Together we open the package and unroll the latex onto his length. I wrap my legs around his waist, he lifts me until I'm astride him, and then releases my weight. His sharp intake of air puts a smile on my face.

He's wants this more than I do.

Ass, access, and opportunity.
The stars have finally aligned.

I remember snippets from our first date as I rock over him forward and backward, gently and with control. We are connected, skin to skin, body to body, chest to chest, face-to-face. I claim his mouth. I fill this orifice as he has filled me. I rock and we wave, rubbing and thumping our way through our own fantasy. The undulations we create stir me from the inside out. I feel the current swirling in a place I can't reach, with a mastered reflex I can't replicate. My arms around his neck, my head buried in his shoulder, I move with gentle ease back and forth and in circles, succumbing to the imprint he's laying inside me. Flushed with fever, I fit myself closer into his crevices and blink back the residue of tears forming in my eyes.

He is divine.

His hands find my hair and mine find his, massaging scalps, or brains into focus, we fill each other with the reckless abandon of passion increasing our speed and changing our positions. From his lap to my back to my belly, Kiyan fills me with the waters of his Fontaine fountain. Streaming into me is every lesson of the English language his surname was trained to give. With a stroke of another kind he brushes through my thighs, painting every color he came with on my insides until he has run dry.

All I feel is him. All I see is him. All I remember is him. He lays behind me, and I'm on my side in his arms. His hands are in my hair, pulling my locs away from one another.

"Why did you leave last night?" he asks.

"Because I wanted this," I say.

"And what is this?"

"I wanted this to be special. Different. So many times, we hurdle past third base, and fumble through fourth that the sex is forgettable, and a waste of a notch, if you're keeping score."

He laughs that sound that makes me want him more, before asking, "When did you know you wanted this?"

"When I watched you teach last night. It was intimate not risqué. Sacred instead of overtly sexual. I wanted that energy for myself."

"So, you were being selfish when you left?"

"Yes," I answer. "Would you have preferred that I had stayed?"

"I would have."

"You wanted this last night?"

"I did, but I realized I had opportunity but no access."

"And how do you feel now?"

"Sated."

"Good."

I lay in his arms, listening to his body, listening to our bodies, aware that I am covered in colors and have become an outward expression of his inner contemplation. I lay still, feeling my way through the strongest sense present between us. My body perseverates in the afterglow of his art. He is beside me, but I still feel him inside. I feel where he stretched and gaped my being into accepting him as he is, without pretense or consequence.

"Naomi."

"Yes, Kiyan."

"What do you want?" he asks.

"Right now?"

"Yes, right now?"

"I want to sex and eat my way through life without getting pregnant or fat," I say, throwing my leg backwards over his body.

He laughs as he catches my thigh with a grip that is stronger than what is evidenced in the sinewy limbs of his body. The sound of his satisfaction emboldens me as I reach for another condom. Completely sheathed, I put both hands behind me to hold his waist, mount him backwards and begin to move. Dancing life into his flaccid limb, the wood of his brush goes back to work on my painting. The fever returns, the swirl returns. I am flush, warm, wet, levitating, and covered in color. I infuse life into his art. Choirs resound in my ears, a glow from heaven alights a smile on my face, I move my outline on him as he works within me to create another masterpiece, and we feel divine.

13.

Do It for the 'Gram

I feel the light of day before I see it. It is bright against my eyes and orange inside of my lids. I open my eyes to the sunlight streaming in my bedroom windows and wonder how I got here. I blink the sleep away and look more toward the windows. I can see the blinds. My heavy, gray, black out curtains have been pushed back and the blinds opened to the light. I look down at my body and see I am still naked, but clean.

"I washed you," Kiyan says from the doorway of the en suite.

"When?" I croak out my first words of the morning. I clear my throat. "How long have you been up?"

"A few hours," he says. "I got restless and decided to paint since all my materials are here. You know you need your grass cut?"

"I know," I say. "If I can catch one of the crews when they're working at one of my neighbor's houses, I do. But sometimes it doesn't work out."

"Why don't you just hire a service?"

Because I don't want to. I don't sleep outside.

"I just haven't gotten around to it."

He nods. I look from him to myself. Him in the doorway and myself in the bed.

You still haven't explained how I'm in the bed and not on the floor downstairs where we finished.

"How did I get up here?" I ask.

"When I woke up you were shivering, but knocked out. I peeled the paint off of you that didn't transfer, brought you upstairs, and wiped you down with a warm wash cloth."

"I see you found the bedroom okay."

"I thought it was the other room by the steps, but it was locked."

I nod. I know he is waiting for me to explain why I have locked doors to rooms in my house when I'm the only one living here, but I don't. I sit up in the bed and pull the sheet closer toward me. For some reason I feel shy. Exposed. Even though he's already seen me. I look to the edge of the headboard, and surprisingly the Ankara printed robe I had on last night is hanging in the place where I normally keep it.

How did he know?

I grab it, push my arms through and wrap it around me before I let the sheet fall. I can feel him looking at me, his eyes wondering about the sudden modesty, seeing what he's seen, knowing what he knows; he's already been intimate with me in ways I could not predict. My face warms and I can feel my cheeks flush.

He brought me upstairs, washed the paint and himself off of me, and tucked me into my bed without me even waking up.

Damn.

What did I do to deserve this?

I resist the urge to grab my phone off of my nightstand and scroll. I leave myself present in the moment. He watches me as I decide what to do.

Do I do my morning routine like he's not here?

Do I invite him to see my sacred space since he's shown me his.

And I still have to go to work.

I pull the robe tighter around me and get out of the bed. I ignore his stalking eyes and go into my bathroom. I begin my routine out of habit and without a plan of what I will tell him, or what I will show him. I brush my teeth. I wash and moisturize my face. I fluff my locs. Kiyan watches from the doorway until I finish. I let my actions speak for me as I walk out of the room and into the hallway. I open the shutter doors of the linen closet and remove a key from a shelf. His eyes watch me from a respectful distance as I close the closet and walk to the locked door of the vision room. I unlock it, walk inside, and close it behind me.

He didn't follow.

With my ear to the door, I listen until I hear his feet on my steps. Once I know he is gone, that he is not on the outside listening in, I begin the second part of my routine. I greet myself and my vision, and give thanks. I affirm myself in the mirrors and to my M.O.M. before sitting on the yoga mat with my head against the wall, and my eyes closed. There is no stress present in my body. My muscles from my calves to my shoulders are loose, limber, and relaxed. The warmth that presented in my face returns to me in my belly. A swirl of excitement grows within me. A swirl I barely recognize. One I haven't felt since the early days of Aaron.

I've missed this.

I am overwhelmed by the satisfaction residing within me. Verklempt at my own contentment. Questioning my own life and choices before this moment.

Why would you deprive yourself of this?

Because you're scared?

Because you're still in recovery?

I shake away my thoughts and the impression of others that would steal this moment from me. I take a deep breath to recenter my focus and remain in my gratitude. When my deep inhales and exhales subside, I listen beyond my own ujjayi to the sounds coming from the first floor from the man who has made my home his studio.

I hear music. Jazz music. It reminds me of home. My lips spread across my face as the swirl in my belly gets bigger and I recognize what I've been without for years. Joy.

Kiyan from Chicago likes jazz.

*The Fountain of Fontaine has an old soul and a baby face.
What else does he like?*

I stand up in the middle of my vision room and look at myself in the full-length mirror. I feel lighter, even though nothing about me has physically changed; only the addition of an intriguing man who paints naked bodies for a living.

I open the door to my vision room and head downstairs. My first floor is a sonic landscape of horns and percussion instruments. My living room is his studio. Kiyan is on his knees in only his boxers, painting with both a brush and his hands. I can see the perimeter of my body has been cut out of one of the long sheets of paper and transposed on to the other sheet that contained all the colors extracted from my skin. I walk to the kitchen counter where the home speaker is blasting music, and turn it off.

"What do you think this is, *Love Jones*?" I ask.

He looks up at me and sees me smiling.

"A Sentimental Mood is not the only jazz song that exists," he says.

"Yeah, but most people don't know anything about Tank and the Bangas or Trombone Shorty."

"Tank I found through YouTube, but I went to Trombone Shorty's set when he came to jazz fest the last time he was here. It stuck. It's good music to paint by."

"And what are you painting?"

"What you asked me to."

He steps back from the layered sheets of paper to show me, me. I see my body and I see the colors he put on me. Brown and black are streaked with dark blues and purples. My face is incomplete, but my hair is crinkled and twisted, each strand of my sister locs defined, one from another. Around my curves he outlined me with red. I gaze at my unfinished form and notice the flecks of white painted into me as well. They contrast against the dark richness of my skin.

"It's nice," I say.

"I'll finish it later," he says.

"Are you working today?" I ask.

"Yeah. I have to go by the school for my class there, and then after that, it's my own stuff."

I nod. "I should get ready for work."

I turn the speaker back on and music blasts out of it. I sidle my way from the kitchen and dining area back to the steps. I am overcome by my own shyness. Not wanting to be this naked, this open, this vulnerable in front of him. I am happy and afraid, and I feel my modus operandi instinctually kick in. It is self-preservation. Self-protection. The inner censors that tell me, *run*.

I don't get far. He grabs my wrist with his paint wet hand and stops my ascent to the second floor. I don't pull away or shrug him off. My body does what it wishes. My mind at war with my heart. I follow where he leads me, to stand right in front of him. Face-to-face, and eye to eye, he kisses me and I inhale his morning breath as he takes in the mint of my toothpaste.

"Good morning," he says, breaking the kiss.

"Good morning."

"What time do you have to go in?"

"I try to get there by eleven-thirty."

"Then you have plenty of time," he says.

"I guess I do, since I woke up with the sun."

"Good."

His mouth finds mine again and I am overloaded by the touch from the tangles of his tongue. He walks me down off of the first step, around the painting and backwards to the sheeted couch. He lays me against the tattered covering, while he sets the brush he held on the discarded paper he cut the lines of my body from. He places his painted hand on my body beneath my robe, and with his free hand unties the loose knot I put in the duster. Paint is transferred from his hand to my stomach, both breasts, and my shoulders. He rubs the color onto my skin as if it is lotion.

My shower is going to get really dirty.

Paint covers my body from my collarbone down, until he covers me with himself. I feel the throbbing of his want against me and I wrap my legs around his back to bring him closer. He kisses the spots covered in paint, and kisses my lips depositing color, and erasing it with the swapped saliva of our mouths. His kiss is the salve I need to stir the swirl in my belly faster, pushing my thoughts farther from me.

The warmth returns. Modesty dissipates. Reluctance reverses. Joy triumphs.

I push his boxers off of his waist with my feet. He steps out of them and backs away from me. The warmth inside manifests at my thighs as I look up at his retreat to the kitchen, where another condom package sits beside the speaker.

I didn't even notice that there.

He returns to me quickly and enters me swiftly, pushing himself as deep as he can go until I am full with him. He moves slowly. Short, succinct strokes beat the inside of me into a frenzy. He gives a little. Retracts a little. Slows his stroke . . . a little, so that the normal color returns to my flushed features, the tingles over my body lessen, and I can open my eyes and look into his, and see his smirk at my reaction to his power.

"You're not funny," I say.

"I never said I was. I never said I was."

Kiyan grips my forearms and pulls me up into him. I am a willing rag doll. I throw my arms around his neck as I am suddenly lifted from the arm of the sofa where I laid. His fingers are firm, gripping the cheeks of my ass as he walks.

He walks and I move up and down, as he carries me across the living room and up the stairs to the second floor. I match my down drops to the plant of each foot on the step, until he reaches the top step and carries me down the hall to my bedroom.

We disconnect as he drops me on the center of the unmade bed. I bounce in the middle of the white sheets until his weight on the mattress steadies my flopping frame. My mind is mush as my instincts take over. His hands find me. My ankles, my knees, my thighs, the warmth of my insides dripping wet and waiting for him. He runs the palm of his four fingers and thumb up the apex of my pleasure, bathing them in me. I watch him as he brings that hand to his mouth and sucks his own fingers. I watch him as he tastes me in a non-traditional way, and I am hungry.

I sit up on my knees to push him down on the bed. I take over and take control of our congress of coitus. My knees surround his hips, my vagina is in his lap, and my ass is spread over his stiffness. He cannot move unless I want him to. He squirms beneath me, trying to rush his way back inside, but I make him wait. I make him want.

Two hands to his chest, I push him into the bed and then lower my unrestrained breasts onto his chest. We are enveloped by my robe. I kiss him. I taste the magical lips on his face and suckle them until they ripen in my jaw. We dance the dance of tongues until I have to pant for breath.

He squirms beneath me.

Ride it out.

"I want you to wait until it hurts," I whisper onto his mouth.

I kiss him again. He squirms more, trying to reach the source of wetness pouring out of me. I kiss his neck, his collarbone, the sternum of his chest, his navel where the trickle of hairs that lead to his pubis are curled on his skin. I slide down his legs until I am facing his offering. I blow the head of his lingam and watch the protruding vein on the side pulse.

"What do you want me to do?" I ask.

"Suck it. Sit on it. Suck and sit on it. Just do something."

The pleading in his voice is followed by an attack of his own hand. He grabs himself and begins to stroke toward his own nirvana.

"Nope," I say grabbing his hands.

I restrict his motion, his need to be in control of his own coming, and hold his hands at his sides. The grimace in his face excites me. The swirl within me is amplified. He loses his self-restraint as the glow returns to my face. I feel my cheeks radiate as he writhes. His pleasure pained expression tells me there is something more beneath his typically relaxed and unbothered persona. That inside of him lives a man that he's worked to suppress and evolve. In this moment of raw, unadulterated, unfiltered passion, his suppression techniques are not working, no longer applicable, and I am pleased.

I run my body back up his and give in to his need and my own. I take all of him in, relaxing my muscles around him. I ride slow in my robe, still making him wait, still making him deny himself, and do for me. His eyes are closed beneath me, and his mouth is fixed as if he's wincing from the sudden shock of being burned. He exhales a slow breath and moves his hips beneath mine. He rides out on what I give until my hands forget to grip his and he flips his wrist. Our fingers intertwine, he bucks his hips, and I am on my back. His hand presses me down into the bed. One leg on his shoulder, he drills in to me without restraint. He pounds and pulses, feeding his own beast. He pours out his energy, filling me with one thousand points of light until he dies one thousand deaths, is resurrected and crucified inside me, again.

He strokes past his selfish satisfaction until he feels my own pulsing around him, forcing him out of me with the fulfillment of our promise that placed pleasure over procreation. Even though he has been expelled, he is not done with me. Kiyan's painter trained, rough-hewn, calloused hands find me writhing and wet. He circles the epicenter of my energy with his fingers until I pour out another orgasm under his power. He taps my well until I am empty, and all that is left are the ricocheting dry heaves of lust, the aftershocks of pruriency.

On the bed we rest. Our nakedness is face up to the unmoving ceiling fan. Our breath is in time with the pace he kept, the beat we made together, until it slows and staggers.

I feel the warmth he created in me, the swirl he stirred, the feelings he awakened, and the forgotten emotions he aroused, and I am thankful.

Beep. Beep. Beep. Beep.

My alarm blares. Our morning moment is interrupted by what is supposed to be the start of my work day. I grab the phone from the track pad charger and dismiss the signal. Closing and opening apps, I scroll through emails, read through comments, and swipe from headline to headline, arming myself with information. I close the apps to open my podcast, when Kiyan takes the phone out of my hand.

"Give it back."

"I will, just hold on."

Kiyan swipes to the first screen of applications and opens the camera. I reach up my hand to block the lens, but he pushes me out of the way.

"What are you doing?" I ask.

"What does it look like I'm doing? I'm taking our picture."

"Our?"

"Yes," he says. "Don't you want to remember this moment."

"I thought that's what the painting was for."

"That's for me," he says.

"Oh, really. And this whole time I thought I could keep it."

"We'll see," he says. "Maybe you can work out something with the artist."

"Like lagniappe? I thought I already did."

"Nah, Baby, you've got to put in more work to get a free painting."

"Then I guess I'll settle for this picture."

"Oh, so you're one of those. You can appreciate, but you can't buy?"

"That was rude."

"Just an observation."

"As was mine."

"Are you mad?" he asks.

"Take the picture, Kiyan."

"You're cute when you pout," he says.

"Take the picture, Kiyan."

He closes the camera and opens Instagram. He looks at me to see if I will stop him. He is daring me. Testing me. I don't protest, though part of me wants to. I ignore the inner warning signs that say caution as he opens the function to take pictures right in the app, and frames it so that only our faces and the top of my robe is showing. He snaps the picture. I don't smile, I don't flinch. He is daring me, but I am daring myself.

"Filter or no filter?" he asks.

"You're the artist."

"No filter it is," he says.

I watch him as he types a caption on the picture. It says, "What mornings are made for." He does not tag himself. He looks at me before he clicks share. I don't stop him. The picture is sent into the world. Kiyan hands me back my phone and I put it down on the bed beside me. Muscles I didn't know I had been holding, relax. My mind races with the significance of the moment. I can't ask what he wants or what does this mean, because I've just been claimed for all my followers to see. I didn't stop him from posting or sharing, which means I want the same things.

Do I?

Do I want to be in a relationship, or do I want only slightly more than what Matt was offering? Kiyan offers dick on demand. That's good enough for now.

Then why'd you let him post that picture.

Why did I?

"I'm going to be late." I sit up and turn away from him trying to hide my complicit confusion.

"Get dressed. Do your thing."

I stand up from the bed and begin to pull the sheets. He helps me gather them together. I toss them into a pile near the door and then head into the bathroom. He gives me space to empty my bladder and get in the shower, before following suit. We are naked in another way. Intimate in another way. Steam rises between us and soap slides off of our bodies. I wash away the paint, my sweat, and hopefully with it, my returning hesitation. Remnants of his Irish Spring are washed down the drain, and I set the intention to send my lingering doubt and disturbia down with it. I lather him with a natural soap from my favorite apothecary as I try to find that swirl of fire in my belly. I wash him clean from his head to his feet, behind his ears, and massage his hands as I work to reawaken the contentment he set within me. He returns the favor and lathers me from my neck to my toes. We rinse.

I wonder what he's feeling. If he's just as confused and concerned, or content?

I say, "There are some extra towels in the closet in the hall."

"The one you took the key out of to unlock that door."

"Yes."

He looks at me before leaving the shower. He gives me the space to tell him what's behind door number one, but I don't. When he is gone, I turn the water off, drape myself from my towel hanging inside the shower, and get out. I ring out the tips of my locs as I approach the mirror, and repeat most of what I've already done: brush teeth, wash face, moisturize body, apply foundation.

He appears in my periphery as I halo twist my locs into the crown I wear to go to work. He watches me as my fingers weave through the strands. I wish I knew what he was thinking. What he was feeling. Did he have swirls of satisfaction or bubbles of apprehension? Where's his mind taking him.

"Do you do this every morning?" he asks.

"Do what?"

"Hide who you want to be behind who you're supposed to be."

"I'm not sure I know what you mean. I'm getting ready for work."

"And you're hiding who you are, or who you want to be, under that thing."

"It's a wig I wear for work."

"Why?"

"Because it's the standard. It's like what Paul Mooney said, when my hair is relaxed, white people relax. I'm on TV. I want the white people to relax, and most of all, not be in my inbox about something as petty as my hair."

"You get emails about that?"

"You'd be surprised the ownership and commentary people think they have a right to because they see you on the stupid box every day."

"I didn't know."

"We all have to conform and assimilate in some way," I say.

I take off my towel and walk into my closet. Pulling a dress from my rented rack, I walk it back into the bedroom where I pull underwear and a bra from my drawers, and get dressed. Under the watchful eye of Kiyan, who's still wrapped in a towel, I transform into my nine to five self. I feel my courage come back; the bravado I have because of who I am, because of what I do, and I am thankful for my ego. In the solid, royal blue dress, with strategic seaming for structure, I feel my power as a recognizable face replace the intense vulnerability that makes me shy beneath his gaze. I walk back and forth from the bedroom to my bathroom and closet, putting away my towel, grabbing shoes, putting on jewelry, and getting the items necessary for my wig. Each trip, each added item arms me with more of my usual projected confidence, until it is the only truth inside of me, and the indecision introduced by our connection becomes a murmuring afterthought in the recesses of my mind. Standing at the door, armed with my full self, I wait for him to catch up.

"C'mon," I say. "I'm done."

He stops in front of the door to my vision room that I didn't lock back and stares at it. He is curious. It would have been different if the door was closed and not locked. Last night when he put me in the bed, he may have peeked in, but walked away because he would have noticed there is no bed. Because the door was locked, he is curious. Because he saw me take out a hidden key to unlock it, he is curious. I walk down the stairs and leave him standing, staring at the closed door of my single life, and wait to see if he will invite himself in to where he has not already been welcomed. The renewed trust in myself begins to wane as I wait to see if he will test me, and put more than a chink in my armor.

He doesn't.

I exhale my relief as I wait until he meets me on the first floor. His bare feet pad down the carpet until he has caught up to me.

"Are you going to tell me what's in the room, or ever let me see inside?"

"That depends?" I say.

"On what?"

"Can I keep the painting."

"Is that how this goes? Naomi, gets everything she wants?"

"You have to give to get."

"We'll see," he says. "It's not even finished yet."

"Then there's your answer. We'll see. Get dressed."

I smirk as I watch him as he moves around the cleared out living room, collecting yesterday's clothes. Underwear, jeans, wife beater, jacket. He covers himself.

"What kind of room is it?" he asks, gathering his paint and brushes.

"It's my vision room."

"What kind of room is that?"

"Just what it sounds like."

"Okay," he nods.

He gathers the sheets with my abstract body and rolls them together.

"I'm ready," he says.

I walk to the back door and we step into the dark garage together.

"Do I still get to meet your friends?" Kiyan asks.

"You're going to have to, considering the picture you posted. I'm surprised my phone isn't exploding right now."

"Probably because it's still on do not disturb."

"Perhaps," I say. "This morning kind of through me off."

"In a good way, I hope."

"In a great way," I say.

And just like that my ego is gone, my bravado banished, my armor removed. Questions and concerns that I tried to push him away cloud my mind as I turn to face him, hoping the brightness in my voice was enough to clear any doubt from setting in on his ego. As self-assured as he is, he is still a man. He is still fragile. He is still human. He is still vulnerable, as I am vulnerable. We have become connected beyond the physical, outside of the realm of just sharing a bed, we have shared intimate and sacred spaces.

Almost shared.

I didn't open up in the same way.

Didn't bring him in my vision room.

Didn't let him see that side of me.

Because it's not meant for anybody else.

But you like him.

I do.

"So, I'll see you later?" He asks.

"Yes."

He comes to me and brushes his lips against mine, and then walks to his car. It is an older slate gray Jeep. The kind where the doors and top can be taken off in the summer. I watch him as he loads his materials into the truck and then walks around to the driver's side. When I don't see him is when I unlock my own car door. He backs out of my driveway, giving me space to come out of the garage. I follow him through my neighborhood, out of the subdivision and onto the highway. I skip the podcast and radio replay of the NPR show I was too busy to listen to. I drive into the city with the radio low, following behind the gray jeep of the man who saw me in the nude, and stirred me from the inside out, but still has not seen me stripped down to the bare bones version of myself, in the room where I face my inner thoughts and cannot lie to myself.

Why didn't you tell him?

The question lingers with me as I get off of 95 and drive toward the station.

Why did you hide it?

Because I don't want him to see the bride and groom and the mirror, and think that's the role I want him to play in my life. I want to get to know him without the pressure of expectation. Can we feel our way toward the future instead of trying to fix it and define it.

I argue with myself as I park. Indecision and doubt, loud. My swirl, my fire, my glow gone. Instead of letting Kiyan get at the root of my truth, I do the hard work myself. I walk into the newsroom and pass the producers.

Here we go.

I shake my head as I step into my office. Jennifer and Diedre are sitting in my chairs waiting for me. I close the door behind me. They pounce as soon as the lock clicks.

"So y'all are Instagram official now?" Diedre asks.

"It's one picture."

"It's not even the picture, it's the caption," Jennifer says. "What mornings are made for? I know y'all sexing now."

"Last time I checked I was grown. What's your point?"

"We want to meet him," Diedre says.

"And what if I don't want you to?"

"Get over yourself, Naomi," Jennifer says. "We want to meet the man that's got you smitten. Got you acting different."

"Whatever."

I set the bag with my wig and hair supplies on my desk, take my phone out of my purse, and plop down in my chair. I finally take my phone off of do not disturb. It populates with missed messages. Missed calls from my mother and my daddy. Thousands of likes and loves on the picture he posted. Hundreds of comments. Dozens of news notifications about stories I should be well versed in. Messages from Jennifer and Diedre in our group thread about the picture. And one from him.

I open it:

Take your time.
I'm not going anywhere.

My belly warms and I feel it spread to my cheeks. My swirl returns and I exhale my relief, basking in the glow of gratitude I worried might have faded for good.

He gets it.

I'm not hiding.

I'm just taking my time.

My vision room is special to me, like his private classes are to him.

I'm taking my time.

"So, are you coming out with us tonight or no?" Jennifer asks. "It's Friday, so you shouldn't have an excuse."

"Sure. Why not?"

"Bring him with you." It is a command. Not a request.

"We'll see."

"Where are we going?" Diedre asks.

"We can go to Black Sheep, or River and Post, or Hoptingers," I suggest.

"For someone who moved out of Riverside, you sure as hell like hanging out over there," Jennifer says.

"What can I say. It was my first home away from home. I'm a sucker for the nostalgic."

"Whatever," Jennifer says. "Just bring the boy."

"We'll see."

She gets up out of the chair and walks out of my office. Diedre stands up as well.

"I'm so happy for you," she says.

"Thank you."

She closes the door behind her and leaves me alone with my phone in my hand and my thoughts in my head. I turn in the chair leaving my back to the door, and open my messages and respond:

> Thank you.
> For understanding.
> For being patient.

The twinkling ellipses alight and his reply comes through immediately.

> You're welcome.
> What are you doing tonight?
> Painting you.
> You want to meet me for drinks with Jennifer and Diedre?
> Who?
> My coworkers.
> Friends.
> I told you they wanted to meet you.
> Only if you want me to.
> You can.
> I will be there.

Just tell me where.

K.

***

Inside of Black Sheep there is the familiar sound of workers welcoming their long-awaited weekend. Ties are off, skirts are hiked, liquor is overflowing. The five of us sit at a group of tables pushed together in the front of the restaurant, overlooking Five Points. I sit against the booth looking out over the street with a clear view of people as they enter and exit the trendy eatery. Diedre and Jacob, Jennifer and Octavius, talk amongst themselves as they all wait to meet the man who inserted himself into my life, and declared his level of care and affection with a post instead of in words.

I wait wondering whether I should have called this off. It feels like an ambush. A setup. A trap for both me and him. But it is too late. I see him walk in the front doors. His face is fresh, the hairline extra sharp with his locs pulled back off of his face into a low ponytail. The dimple is there and so is the cleft in his chin. I raise my hand and wave him over to where we are. In a graphic tee with abstract art on the front and black jeans, he strides toward us casually. I stand up to greet him.

"You look different," I say.

"So, do you."

He runs his hand through a handful of my hanging locs that I unraveled after the show. Standing next to him, I can still smell the lingering scent of the soap I used on him this morning. That, along with his deodorant and cologne alight my senses, and I remember how he smelled last night. How he smelled this morning. How we smelled together. I lean closer into him and he throws an arm around me.

"I missed you," I say.

My own admission surprises me. He hugs me tight, kisses my forehead, and then my lips.

"I'm here now."

"So, are you going to introduce him to the rest of us, or are you two just going to pretend that we, and everybody else in this restaurant, are not here?"

"Excuse me, Kiyan," I say. "That loud mouth woman down there is my soon to be ex-friend Jennifer."

"And I'm Diedre," Diedre says.

"The gatekeepers," Kiyan says.

"Yes," I say. "And this is Octavius and Jacob."

"Nice to meet you, man," Kiyan says to each one of them. "Have y'all ordered yet?"

"Just drinks," I say. "Here's yours."

I pick up the glass of Hennessy and hand it to him. He takes a sip and kisses me again. I can taste the liquor on his lips and the mint of his toothpaste.

"Have a seat," I say against his mouth. "Before we have to leave."

"Why is that?" he asks.

"You know why."

He laughs.

He laughs and I back away from him, back to my side of the table. My reaction to him in this moment is purely physical. He has stimulated my mind for months with conversation and questions, but in this moment, it is not what I want. With my hair down, my dress hiked, and liquor flowing in my system, I want to leave the restaurant to escape the trap I helped lay, and abscond to his studio, his apartment, my house, anywhere but here where we can be naked and alone.

"So y'all met on vacation, right?"

The question is from Jacob. He is tan, with dark brown hair, and the easy nature of a man at the top of the food chain. He is comfortable with Diedre's electric nature. Today she has thick box braids interwoven with pink hair, and gold and purple string. Ornaments dangle from her braids. He caresses her shoulder as he sips his beer and waits for Kiyan to answer.

"Yeah. We met on vacation."

"No, you met Diedre on vacation. Remember?" I correct. "You met me sliding through my inbox like 'Hey, big head."

"I was not sweating you," Kiyan says. "I just wanted to clarify that the fish I met on vacation was actually, factually the news lady who eviscerated Neighborhood Watch Wanda."

"That was pretty cold the way you talked about that lady," Octavius says.

"Duly noted," Jennifer says. "But we said, what we said."

"We?" I raise my eyebrows.

"You know Boyce said something to us about that segment after he talked to you, so it's we."

I nod my understanding that served both as my backup and a signal to Octavius to drop the subject. Where she is aggressive, he is passive. He is the yang to her yin.

Tall and thin, his small, round afro is picked out and full. It's militant enough to be greeted on the street with "Wassup, brotha," but corporate enough to not distract from his day job as an investment banker. His outward appearance matches hers, down to her standard twist out that has grown in size as the week has progressed.

"Y'all know that lady was wrong for calling the cops on those kids," I say. "I just said what everybody else was thinking."

"And that's why the segment was canceled," Jennifer says.

"Yet we've still been able to do the same kind of controversial watercooler stories that drive content, ratings, clicks, hits, and impressions. So, if anything Boyce only gave us a bigger platform to wreck shop with."

"Don't you think you're a little provocative though?" Jacob asks.

"As far as what?" I ask.

"As far as what you talk about on your show outside of the daily death, destruction, development, corruption, and politics."

"No, I don't," I say.

"I think it's a little provocative," Jacob says, bringing the bottle of beer to his lips. He takes a swig and then continues, "I mean, you went from Neighborhood Watch Wanda, to cancel culture. You've done microaggressions in the workplace, "me too" for Black people . . ."

"That was Diedre's idea," I say.

I watch Jacob cut his eyes at the woman he doesn't know as well as he thinks he does.

They're still dating each other's representatives, I think to myself.

". . . I still think it's pretty provocative," Jacob says.

"If I can't titillate the masses for three minutes out of an hour long show with a story they wouldn't normally see in their carefully curated Facebook feed or timeline, then what am I doing this for?" I ask.

"I like the segment," Kiyan says. "I think it's fun and smart."

"You're supposed to say that," Jacob retorts. "You're the boyfriend."

Is he my boyfriend?

Is that what this is, the coronation of the "b" word?"

"Even if I wasn't, I would still think the segment is fun and smart. It's no different than Bill Maher's "New Rules" or any of the monologues from the late-night comics."

"That's the operative word," Jacob says. "Comic. Naomi is not a comic. She's a journalist."

"And the best jokes are rooted in truth," Jennifer jumps in. "Can we stop talking about work now, and get to the real reason why we're here?"

"And what's that?" I ask, cutting my eyes at her.

"To get to know Kiyan," Jennifer says.

"You've got to be one special brother to get Naomi to change up her whole life," Diedre says.

"I have not changed my whole life."

"Might as well have," Jennifer says.

"I'm just happy," I say. "Damn. Can I be me?"

I bring my drink to my lips, stewing in the trap I voluntarily stepped in. The gotcha plan I laid for myself. I sip my Bourbon and hear Kiyan's own astute observations from this morning. *Do you do this every morning? Hide who you want to be behind who you're supposed to be.*

"I think whatever change you see in Naomi that you're attributing to me, started long before she met me."

Thank you.

I look at Kiyan until he sees my gratitude, grateful that he's taking this inquisition well.

"Well damn," Jennifer says. "Baby, how come you don't say sincere shit like that about me?" she asks Octavius.

"Don't put me on the spot," he says. "We're here to get to know your friend's boyfriend."

"So, Kiyan, what do you do, where are you from?" Diedre asks.

"I'm an artist," Kiyan answers. "A painter specifically. And I'm from Chicago."

"Did you leave because you were scared for your life?" Jacob asks.

"Contrary to the headlines and popular belief, Chicago is not the raging war zone it's made out to be."

"But it's called Chi-raq for a reason, isn't it?" Jacob asks.

"The city has issues with poverty, inequality, lack of opportunities, racism, and segregation, which creates a cesspool of a breeding ground for crime," Kiyan says.

"And those same issues are right here in Jacksonville," I say. "We're in the gun shaped state and every major area has a candidate for trigger city."

"Y'all tag team and back each other up like y'all been together forever," Jennifer says.

It's good to be with someone who takes the "us against the world" shit seriously.

I smile first at Jennifer, then at Kiyan. He is at ease at the table sitting across from me. Neither Jacob's ignorance, nor Jennifer's insistence has seemed to rattle him. He nurses his drink as I sip mine, and we wait for whatever is next to come our way. If this were a test, he would have passed with flying colors.

What do you mean would have? He's passed every test. Even the one's you haven't given yet.

"Kiyan, what do you paint?" Diedre asks.

"Bodies," he says.

"Why?" Jennifer asks.

"Because I think there's nothing more beautiful than the human form," Kiyan answers.

"Do you paint just women, or men too?" Diedre asks.

"Both," he says. "I'm attracted to the strong and the feminine, the masculine and the delicate."

"That's really evolved of you," Jennifer says. "Most dudes would probably only paint chicks with big titties and big asses and call it art."

"I'm a man. I like that too. But there's more to art than putting sex on canvas and hoping it sells."

"Where the hell did you get him from and where can I get me one?" Diedre asks.

I see Jacob's face wince at her unintentional rebuke. I look from his reddening face to her blank stare. She jumps closer to me, and I know Jennifer slapped her leg or kicked her beneath the table. I don't know if Diedre and Jacob have had the difficult conversations of what it means to be in an interracial relationship, but I know her outburst will lead to it. Her excited utterance over her preferred preference in a mate will inevitably take them through the wormhole of what it means for her to walk around in society as a white man and a black woman in a relationship, and not feel like she's selling out on her community, her people, her culture, and the sitcom created dream that there was a good Black man for each of us.

I should do a final segment on interracial dating and bring Jacob on as my expert.

I smirk to myself and sip my Bourbon, appreciative of the lull in the conversation and the ramp down of the third degree.

"Did you finish?" I ask Kiyan across the table.

"Finish what?" he asks.

"You know what I'm talking about," I say. "My painting."

"You mean, my painting."

"Whatever."

"No, I didn't finish yet."

"I thought you would have been so inspired, that you worked in a frenzy all day with lucent thoughts of our decadent morning."

"Y'all down there talking about something nasty," Diedre says.

"Mind your business," I say.

"But we're here to mind yours," Jennifer says.

"And you've been successful at it too," I say.

"Good," she says. "Kiyan, so you're from Chicago, right?"

"Yes."

"Did Naomi tell you we're going up there for a conference next month?"

"She made mention of it at least once," he says. "I offered to be her guide."

"You still can," Jennifer says. "You can show us around after the business is done on Friday. We don't leave until Sunday."

"You're all going?" Kiyan asks.

"Yup," Diedre says. "It'll be nice to get away."

I already hear the wistfulness in her voice affected by what she knows will be an argument between her and Jacob later on. She is running away from her foot-in-mouth comment with the longing of vacation. I imagine what their argument sounds like and wonder if he will bring up the fact that he asked her on their first date, if she had a problem "dating a squeaky clean white guy, who wants to get to know her, and not just like in a *Jungle Fever* sort of way."

That's how she said he described himself once they got back together after Cuba. I told her she should have let him go then.

"Anybody who says he wants to get to know you in not a *Jungle Fever* kind of way, is only there for the jungle fever," I said to her.

"No, he's not," she denied without proof.

"Yes, he is," Jennifer said.

"He's fetishizing you," I said. "But you know him better than I do. I hope I'm wrong."

I tried to end the conversation on the most positive note I could. I didn't want to be in her relationship, telling her what would and would not work, and I didn't want her in mine. Looking at her now, angry at herself for being honest, and making Jacob feel uncomfortable, I feel for her, knowing that she didn't have the foresight to see this coming; that even if she could make the interracial relationship work, Jacob was not the one.

She should have known he wasn't the one when he broke up with her over her wanting to have her own hypothetical house, without his or any other man's input or support.

Conservative ass.

He's only entertaining us.

He's with her for the experience, and now that he's had it and been made to feel bad about himself, he's going to dip. He'll probably ghost her.

I hope I'm wrong, but he looks like the type.

We are definitely doing this segment on the show.

I should come back out to get drinks with them more often.

I can get all kinds of content here.

"Now that you've met Kiyan, is there anything else you need to ask him, say to him, or try to get him to do for you?" I ask.

"If you're serious about being our guide in Chicago, I'll take you up on it," Jennifer says.

"Me too," Diedre says.

They look at him and wait for an answer. He doesn't give them one, but instead looks at me. I shrug my shoulders. My answer is noncommittal, and my facial reaction is nonplussed.

"If Naomi wants me there," Kiyan says. "Then I'll be there."

"It doesn't bother me none," I say.

"Then it's a date," Kiyan says. "Or dates, depending all on what you guys want to do."

"I just don't want to go broke," I say. "I have an easy enough time doing that here."

"I got you," Kiyan says.

"Then we'll see you next month during BJA?" Diedre asks.

"What's BJA?" Kiyan asks.

"Black Journalists of America," I say. "They hold a conference every year and we go."

"It's fun," Diedre says. "There's enough work-related mentorship and cultivation, along with ratchetry, that we get the best of both worlds."

"Then, to the BJA it is. I'm sure I can set up something for me to do so it's not just a basic trip home."

I look at him, and with my eyes, I again say "Thank you."

Maybe he is a keeper.

Part 3

Business Trip

"Girl, the world is just one big place waiting for us to go out and fuck up in it."

— "Iesha" (Regina King), *Poetic Justice*

14.

BJA
(Black Journalists of America)

The lobby of the Hyatt hotel at Chicago's McCormick Place Convention Center is overrun with every kind of journalist of color I can imagine, and even some I can't. The on air anchors and reporters and wannabe anchors and reporters are distinguishably noticeable from the hundreds of others who are checking in, finding friends, or grabbing drinks in the middle of the afternoon at the lobby bar. I fit in right with them. My wig is freshly washed, curled, flipped, and gripped to my head courtesy of Dominique, much to Kiyan's chagrin. He dropped me off at the airport two days ago, and just shook his head at me as I kissed him goodbye and rolled into the airport with my carry-on packed with the best of my rented wardrobe.

"So, are you going to be back to being you when I come up on Friday?" he asked.

"I'm always me," I said.

"You're different with your wig on then when you have your locs out."

"How so?"

"Different. More uptight. More serious. More following the rules. Not as expressive. Not as free."

"We can't all be free painters, living the life of a humble artist full of ideals and no priorities."

"And that's exactly what I mean. With your wig on, you're mean and rude and dismissive."

"This has nothing to do with my wig, and everything to do with your judgmental ass attitude. Always talking to me and about me, like I'm two separate people."

"Because you are."

"When are you going to be more of who you are, and less of who they want you to be?" I mocked.

"It's just a question."

"It's a dumb question. I am me. Wig on. Wig off. There is no Naomi Jean versus Naomi Grace. There's just Naomi. The anchor. The sister. The daughter. The girlfriend. You should know that by now."

"I just want you to be your authentic self, and you're jumping down my throat like it's bad for me to want the best for you."

"Because, Kiyan, you should know being my authentic self comes at a cost. There is a price for being authentic. It is a luxury I cannot afford. Instead of pushing me to live the life that you live why can't you support me as I become the best version of myself that I can whether you think it's authentically me or not."

"Okay, Naomi."

I got out of the car, pulled my bag from the backseat, and kissed him through the window, out of habit more than affection. I hoped the kiss would give me the butterflies I always felt whenever any parts of us connected. It didn't. No swirl. No heat. No fire. My belly was empty, my skin was normal, and my face held no glow. Only a mask over my true feelings because I did what was right and expected, instead of what was authentic to me in that moment. The same thing when I landed in Chicago and when I made it to the hotel with Jennifer and Diedre. Since the airport, we've had two days of texting short updates on our itineraries. No talking, no skyping, or gchatting, or FaceTiming, just short message after short message after short message. I didn't want to argue with him then. I still don't now. But I had so many questions and I still do now.

Why can't you just see both sides of me as me?

In the lobby I see both his point of view and mine. I see the inauthenticity of all of us who put our faces in front of the camera and pretend to be something that we're not. I can count the wigs, and the full weaves, from the girls who have just a few tracks. I'm aware of the false lashes and the layers of foundation we have all shellacked on our faces for the three days we present our best selves to current and future employers, in the name of keeping the doors open and opportunities, but a bridge away via a phone call, email, or message on LinkedIn. I can even tell how many of us in the room subscribe to the same rented line of clothes, or who have the same consultants who peddle their own line of dresses, suits, and skirts from newsroom to newsroom in the 207 television markets of the country. I see all of this in those of us who choose to be on air, and I hate the pang it leaves in the pit of my stomach.

Damn, he was right.

I want to call him and tell him, but I don't want to give him the satisfaction. Even amidst all that I, and the rest of the on air personas in here are not, we are still our most authentic selves.

We play the game and we play to win, and that is authenticity at its finest, but of course he doesn't get that.

I walk to the bar and grab a seat on one of the stools. It's still too early to drink, but it's what I need to take the edge off before the next session I plan to go to with Diedre and Jennifer. "Tokenism in Diverse Newsrooms" is the name of the panel discussion being held in one of the larger ballrooms instead of just a small conference room. The panel is being hosted by a selection from the handful of Black anchors from the major networks, both broadcast and cable. It is yet another opportunity to build a bridge into my future and manifest the vision that hangs from my wall in my room, curated for dreams with deadlines.

"Can I get you something?" the bartender asks me.

"Club soda, with a shot of vodka," I say.

He raises his eyebrow at me but walks off to make the odd request. I watch him as he works. Low fade, trimmed facial hair, slight paunch at his stomach not hidden by his black shirt, pants, or the pocketed apron tied around his waist. I watch him as he rinses the glass, fills it with the bubbly liquid, and wonder what his story is. Is this the life he thought he'd live as a bartender in his late thirties? I assume his age by the condition of his hands, and wonder the wisdom they've rung through. He sets the glass in front of me, and gets a shot glass and cleans it as well. He sets it in front of me and fills it with liquor.

"If you need anything else, let me know," he says. "The name's Kenneth."

"Thanks," I say. "Charge it to the room. 1123."

I wait until he's walked away to take my shot. I knock it back with one gulp. I wish I had a lime or lemon to take the edge off. I savor the burn as the liquid streams down my throat and settles in my belly.

"Look who's being a lush in the middle of a professional conference."

It is Diedre. I turn around to see her and Jennifer standing behind me. Even they are the best representations of themselves. Inauthentic as Kiyan would say. Diedre's normally multi-hued hair is completely the color that grows from her scalp, only it's braided up into a mohawk with silver cuffs and clasps that makes it a bejeweled creation along with the rest of her. Instead of jeans, a T-shirt and blazer, she wears a pink pencil skirt and navy blouse. Jennifer is the only unapologetically authentic one among us. Her twist out is big, perfectly curled and spiraled, her hoop earrings are round, and the buttons of her blouse are undone enough to show off the edges of her lace bra beneath it. She is sexy, and professional, and still down for the cause with her own brand of mantra band on her wrist that says "Stay Woke."

"I was waiting on you two," I say, picking up the virgin part of my drink.

"We got caught up in the other session," Jennifer says.

"What was it on?" I ask.

"How to innovate from behind the lens."

"And what did you learn?" I ask.

"That we drive the narrative, even if it's coming out of your mouth?" Diedre says.

"Basically, the same thing I figured out for myself in undergrad," Jennifer says. "It only counts to be a talking head if you've got real power behind it."

"And even then, you have to make sure your power is in deed, and not in name only," I say.

I didn't need a seminar to tell me that. It's the story of my life.

I suck down the club soda and then leave the empty glass on the bar.

"Are you ready?" I ask.

"After you?" Jennifer says.

I lead the way away from the bar into the bowels of the hotel, following the signs for the ballroom where the panel is being held.

"You know it's going to be packed in here if they're holding it in the ballroom instead of a conference room," Diedre says.

"That's because of who they have speaking on the panel," Jennifer says.

"I'm excited to meet Dawn," Diedre says. "The way y'all talk about her, I hope she lives up to the hype."

"You'll find out soon enough," I say.

"Did you see who else is on the panel?" Jennifer asks.

I know the question is for me, but I don't answer her ringing bell. We reach the doors of the ballroom just as they are closing. We show our conference ID badges to get in, and find three seats split between two rows in the back of the room. Diedre and Jennifer sit side by side in one row, and I sit behind them. I am grateful to be slightly distanced from them for the ninety-minute session.

I look around the room and see all the women who look like me, and our male counterparts who are low-faded, clean shaven, and suited and booted to the nth degree. In their own masculine way, the men who happen to stand in front of the camera, all have a prototype too. I see them, I see us, and then I see all those who are either behind the camera or in what they call "new media," where ascribing to a certain look doesn't matter, and authenticity is what drives content. They are bloggers, vloggers, influencers, and people who have deemed themselves social commentators by the very nature that they run to the Internet to insert themselves into cultural conversations.

We all sit together in the room to listen to the few who have reached the mountaintop of media, and decided to come back down to tell us whether what we see is even real or attainable. I look at Dawn Anthony seated amongst the panel of eight and I see how she fits in with us as well. Her hair is still in the same bob she's always worn with long bangs that fall in her eyes, no matter how much she adjusts or pushes them back. Her face is permanently trained to smile, even when her eyes don't, and she is angry. In light gray slacks and a gray pinstriped blouse, her licorice skin glows and her presence is commanding; exuding both the strength typified of men and the vulnerability singularly attributed to women.

"Dawn Anthony, same question," the moderator says. "Do you now or have you in the past experienced tokenism in the newsroom?"

The room is silent awaiting her answer, every one of us aware of her meteoric rise, thanks to one case she broke every detail of as it exploded from local, to national news.

She smiles wide without her teeth touching before she answers.

"I think in some way every one of us sitting up here is a token, just as everyone sitting out there is a token. There may be a number of us, and by us, I mean Black people, in a newsroom together, but it is very rare to find all of us on the same levels, doing the same jobs, or with the same equality of power. We are just like any other profession, only the nature of what we do gives us the platform to be seen and the visibility to be heard, versus someone working in a different kind of corporate structure."

The room applauds. I applaud. Jennifer and Diedre applaud. We give our accolades for her saying something we all already know. The moderator moves on with the next round of questions.

"She's pretty," Diedre turns around and whispers to me.

"Does it matter what she looks like?" I whisper back.

"It always matters, and you know it," Jennifer adds to our clandestine conversation.

"I guess."

"Everybody can't be on the butterscotch side of brown."

I roll my eyes.

"For her to be where she is and look like she looks says something," Diedre says. "She's a real-life *Being Mary Jane* and she's darker than Gabby."

"Please don't compare the two," I say.

I hear the scoff in Jennifer's voice without her even turning around to show her disgust.

"The finale wasn't that bad." Diedre nudges Jennifer's elbow. "She got the man, the baby, and anchor desk."

"I'm glad y'all found your shero," I say. "In real life and on TV."

"Why are you so pissy, lately?" Jennifer turns around again. "You've been in a mood since you got to Chicago."

"Kiyan and I had our first fight sitting in the car at the airport."

I sigh, as the fact I've been trying and failing to ignore now becomes the center of our conversation.

"Excuse me," the woman sitting beside me says to us. "Can you guys keep it down please. Some of us are trying to listen. Thanks."

I look at her in her purple dress, fresh jet-black wig with the baby hairs glued to her forehead, and long false eyelashes and resist the urge to tell her the panel is not worth her time. I resist the urge to rain on her parade because I can't get Kiyan's accusatory observation out of my head.

I should just apologize to him.

But you didn't do anything wrong.

But shouldn't I be the bigger man? The bigger woman?

I sigh to myself and let my indecision and confusion swirl in my belly, where excitement and anticipation at just the thought of him, used to.

"Your first fight in how many months y'all been dating?" Diedre whispers.

"Four."

"That's not bad. I just hope you recover."

I look at the woman beside me. Her face is attuned forward as she listens intently to the panel. I lean closer toward Jennifer and Diedre

"What's that supposed to mean?"

"When Jacob and I started fighting after your housewarming party we never stopped. It was always something. Whether it was my fault or his, it always led to a fight. I just couldn't deal."

"Thanks." I nod.

"You realize you didn't help any," Jennifer says.

They turn back around and leave me to my thoughts. I put my head in my hands, careful to touch lightly so I neither smudge my foundation or accidentally adjust my wig. I want to text Kiyan and tell him he's right and make up before he arrives tomorrow, but I don't.

Even if he's right, he's still wrong.

Wrong for making me feel like I have to choose between what I do and being with him.

Wrong for trying to make it seem like I'm fake.

He's the one living the fairytale.

He's the one in a fantasy.

And I'm supposed to apologize.

Doubt it.

I stew in my renewed anger and hear Diedre's voice. *I just hope you recover.* Her tone was without hope. She was more wistful than realistic, more placating than pragmatic. It does nothing to add to my uncertainty. My knuckles mash themselves into the palms of my hands needing something to do.

Hell, I hope we can recover too.

I roll my eyes at the back of her head and at the anchor who's steered the conversation.

He is mid-diatribe, ". . . I don't think of myself as a token. I think of myself as someone who has worked hard, and laid a path for the next Black male investigative journalist to walk through the doors that I opened. Someone is always going to be the first, but that doesn't deny the achievements of the second. Neil Armstrong wasn't a token because he walked the moon first, just like Buzz Aldrin won't be forgotten even though he came second."

"So, what are you doing personally to make sure there is someone behind you?" Dawn asks.

"I speak at schools, I mentor, and I lead by example."

"But have you walked someone through the doors in your department into a job you already do because they deserve the opportunity and you can't cover every story?" Dawn asks. "Because if you haven't, even though you and I are colleagues, you are as much a token as I am."

"This sounds personal," Jennifer whispers, turning around toward me.

"I'm not surprised," I murmur.

"If you guys aren't going to pay attention, why don't you leave?" The woman in purple says to us.

"My bad . . ., Rhonda," I say looking at her name tag.

I watch the conversation devolve into professional name calling and work shaming, under the guise of having a healthy debate on the serious issues facing our industry.

I knew I should have gone to the other seminar.

I open the conference app on my phone and click on the seminar taking place in one of the conference rooms. "Them vs. Us: The place of the Black story when every group is fighting for equal rights." The details say the seminar focuses on how to make stories about the Black experience still remain relevant in the midst of women's rights, gay rights, trans rights, and immigration rights headlines.

Maybe not. I don't even feel like being this deep.

"I'm going to go," I whisper to Diedre and Jennifer. "I'll be at the bar."

I exit my row not waiting for them to protest. I walk out of the ballroom doors not caring who sees me, not caring if I'm being rude to the panel, or the moderator, who are all donating their time in the name of enlightening us. I head back to the bar, back to the stool I vacated, and I wait for Kenneth to notice me.

"Another club soda with a shot of vodka?" he asks.

"No. Bourbon neat," I say.

"Coming up," he says.

I wait at the nearly empty bar. The chatter in the lobby area is at a minimum with most everyone else in town for the conference in a seminar session. I watch a few business travelers check-in and check out and wonder if Kiyan still wants to stay in the room I have for us, since we haven't been speaking.

"Here you go," Kenneth says, pushing the drink in front of me.

"Thank you," I say.

"So why are you back out here?" he asks

"Because the forum I went to was whack," I say.

"Aren't all conference seminars trash? It seems like people only come to conferences just to get away from work."

"Maybe, but this one is usually pretty fun."

"Doesn't seem like it from the look on your face."

"I'm good," I say. "Just a lot on my mind."

"Drink up. It won't help, but it may make you forget for a while."

"A bartender encouraging me to get drunk. Hmm."

"You're already in a hotel, and you already have a room. It's a win win. You forget your problems and I make money. Drunk people tip the best."

"Completely self-serving."

"Not completely," he says. "You're smiling."

I raise my drink in the air. "Thank you," I say.

He walks away and leaves me to sip my drink and sulk. I turn my back to the bar and drink facing the lobby. I watch the people coming and going and listen to the pianist keeping the ambiance for no one in particular. I hear Kiyan. I hear Diedre. I hear Dawn.

Why do you hide who you want to be behind who you're supposed to be?

So, are you going to be back to being you when I come up on Friday?

I just hope you recover.

So, what are you doing personally to make sure there is someone behind you?

I came behind her at the station, I wonder if she's leaving a door open for me at the network. It's been four years, might as well cash in on her Post-It note and find out if she's a friend or an enemy.

My relationship and my career. I sip my drink and play the wonder game with myself. I wonder when I became content with the status quo and stagnant with myself. I hear another voice. One belonging to my mother. Just a few weeks ago she asked me, "How long are you going to stay in Jacksonville."

"I don't know," I answered.

"You need a plan, Naomi."

"You didn't press me to have a plan when I was in New Orleans," I said.

"Because I thought you wanted to stay home, work, and have a family here."

"So, you assumed I didn't want anything better for myself, and so you didn't push me to go further?" I asked. "That sounds like the opposite of what you tell your clients."

"You're not my client. You're my daughter."

"That doesn't mean the advice you give me should be any different."

"You want me to treat you like a client, I can."

"No, I want you to treat me like a mother who actually gives a damn."

"First of all, you need to get the damn bass out of your voice and remember who you're talking to," she said. "Secondly, you've never seemed to want more for yourself. At least when you were at home it was okay for you to be average because you were still technically excelling over everyone else in the family, even if you didn't want more for yourself. You ran away because you were embarrassed, and now you're getting just as complacent somewhere where you have no roots."

"So, it's okay for me to be complacent if I'm with family?"

"At the end of the day, family is all that matters."

"Is that why we have such a shitty relationship?" I asked.

I hung up the phone on her before she could answer, but her words landed whether I wanted them to or not.

I can hang all the vision boards, inspirational quotes, and find solace in all the articles I want to, but nothing will change unless I make it different.

Maybe I just want to be average.

No you don't. You like attention too much for everything to end in market 44.

I sip the last of my drink as more and more people begin to trickle into the lobby and bar area. It isn't long before I see Jennifer and Diedre. They are walking and talking with Dawn. I wave my hand at them and set my empty glass on the bar. I know I'm in no mood to have a productive conversation about anything with vodka and bourbon sloshing in my system, but I stand up to try. I adjust the hem of my embroidered mesh dress and blink my eyes to clear the liquor from my visage.

"Hey, Naomi," Dawn says when she gets to me.

"Good to see you again," I say.

We don't shake hands and we don't hug. We stand face to face. We are peers in one respect and mentor-mentee in another.

"I saw you walk out early," Dawn says. "I guess talking about tokenism was something you've heard before."

"Everybody on this side of the camera knows it and is aware of it. What you said when I was in there is true."

"How's everything been in Jacksonville?"

"It's been good," I say.

"I see your segments going viral all the time now," she says. "Seems like you're getting ready to make a major move."

"All options are on the table."

I say what she's expecting me to say. Unmarried and over forty, Dawn is ambition personified, fuck whoever and whatever tries to get in her way. I see the sacrifices she's made for being her authentic self in her lack of attachments.

I can be average and happy, or above average and alone.

The thought comes to me and depresses me immediately. I want to leave the now crowded bar. I want to escape the room of look-a-likes, twins, and doppelgängers. I want to run away from the pretense and the pose of our profession that doesn't allow us to have both the career and the personal lives we choose. When we are on air, we belong not to ourselves, but to the people. Even behind the scenes there is an element of stifling and suffocating of voices because every day is a good day for a firing, when you speak out of company turn.

I am tired.

"I'm sorry," I say interrupting Dawn, Jennifer, and Diedre.

"I'm tired," I say. "I'm going to head back to the room."

"Are you coming back down for the dinner mixer?" Diedre asks.

"Text me," I say. "Maybe."

I walk away from Jennifer, Diedre, and Dawn toward the bay of elevators that will take me away from my peers, colleagues, and competition for the next job and the next position, to the eleventh floor. My head is swirling with everyone's voice but my own. My mother's dissatisfaction at my apparent lack of future and ambition. Dawn's quip on upward mobility. Diedre's lackluster hope for my relationship. Jennifer's loaded question and Kiyan's insistence that I be something I'm not completely. My head hurts with everybody else's thoughts, suggestions, and wants for me, that I can barely hear my own.

I stand in front of the elevator and I wait for it to ding. I wait for it to arrive and whisk me away. It gets to the floor smoothly and opens with a simple swish. I step inside, press eleven, and relax into the corner. My head against the wood paneling inside the vertical carriage gives me just enough support to quell my dizziness.

"Going up," the automated voice inside the box says.

I wait for the doors to close. They ding open again. I open my eyes and see a hand caught them before they closed. The body is revealed little by little. A long sleeve mint green shirt coves the arm. I see a shoulder and then a face. It is both who I expected and who I least expected in one breath. Dawn's colleague, the man she argued with on the panel, the reason Jennifer asked if I saw who else was speaking, implying he was the reason I was so pressed to go. I see the face of my ex and my head throbs, with everyone else's voice except my own.

He says, "I take it you didn't appreciate the conversation. Is that why you left early?"

I roll my eyes, even though it hurts, and try to resettle myself in the corner of the elevator.

"You're not talking to me now?" he asks.

"I haven't heard from you in four and a half years. Why should we all of a sudden be so chummy now?"

"You've changed," he says.

"I didn't realize I was supposed to stay the same."

"I didn't stop you to fight," he says. "Let me start over. Hi, Naomi."

He extends his hand toward me to shake as if we don't know each other. Like he's reading my name from my badge and not from his biblical knowledge of my body. I look from his hand to his face, and I feel the disgust creeping across my mug. In the moment I wish I could have mastered Dawn's permanent smile.

But then he wouldn't see how pissed you still are.

He retracts his hand and steps into the elevator. He pushes the door's close button but not a floor.

"Going up," the automated voice says again.

We lift.

"Hi, Naomi," he says again.

I wait. I seethe silently. I roll my eyes. I suck my teeth. I am pissed.

He's got a lot of fucking nerve.

"Long time no see, Aaron."

15.

Case of the Ex

It's been four years and eight months since the last time I've laid eyes on Aaron Moore. He left in October from New Orleans for his new life in Atlanta. We had goodbye sex but no closure, we said we'd keep in touch, but we didn't. I had my interview in Jacksonville a month later, and I moved away from the only city I've ever known to a new place in a new state, in the name of doing what I loved, but differently. I told myself it wasn't about Aaron and how he left me embarrassed in front of my family. I told myself that it had nothing to do with him proving my mother right and me wrong. I told myself that it had nothing to do with my unrequited love. That I didn't lie myself into believing he felt a certain way about me. That when I said, "I love you," and he said, "Mmhmm yeah, me too," he was saying the same thing.

Or maybe he was.

Maybe he only had room to love himself.

"It's good to see you again," Aaron says.

I don't respond. I don't want to respond.

What could be good about seeing me?

What do you want?

I ride until the elevator dings on the eleventh floor. I hear the doors open and I propel myself from my corner of the elevator toward the doors. The carpet is plush beneath my aching feet shoved into a pair of high heels. They sink into the thickly woven material and make no noise as I walk. Neither do his shoes. He is a few steps behind me; a respectable distance as if we were sneaking around and trying not to get caught.

"Naomi, talk to me."

"For what?"

"Because I came all this way to see you," Aaron says.

I shake my head. I don't believe him. I know he is lying. I don't even have to turn around to check his face and confirm my suspicions. I know a lie when I hear one.

Walking.

I keep walking to my room. To my door. To the door of my room where inside is one king sized bed overlooking a lake that might as well be an ocean, the open top football stadium, and skyscraper upon skyscraper upon skyscraper. I put my key in the door and wait for the light to turn green.

"I've missed you," Aaron says.

He closes the distance between us before I can slam the door in his face. He jams his foot in the doorway to continue his access to me. I push against it with all my weight, waiting to see him wince. I want to see him squirm with pain and I want him to leave; to go somewhere else with his half-truths and whole lies.

"Naomi. Stop."

"Stop what, Aaron?"

"I'm just trying to talk to you," he says.

"And you should get it by now that I don't want to talk to you. We don't have anything to say to each other."

"After all these years, you don't have anything to say to me?"

Go fuck yourself.

I shake my head and sigh at the arrogance in his voice. He has always been hubris over humility. Demanding people consider him a venerable journalist, one worthy of the gravitas he thought others ought to approach him with.

I have never been your groupie.

"Why would I have anything to say to you, Aaron?" I ask. "Didn't you say you came all this way to see me. Sounds like you're the one with something to say."

His face says that he does. I look at him, finally, and see up close what I have not seen in years. The face of the man I used to admire. He is the color of the inside of a biscuit with the butter already melted in. I see the man, who made me despise anything and anyone who remotely reminded me of him. His is the face that makes me scoff when I see it on television in the newsroom, the people who don't know him hanging on his every word, the women and the men charmed by his command of the camera. In his face I see what many will never; his nerves. His hazel eyes jump from one corner to the other. His skin takes on a slight red tint. It is not a full blush. I've only seen him completely flushed when he's exerting energy, pumping toward nirvana in the name of trying to satisfy himself, and maybe someone else. This look is different. It is a posture he doesn't take often. A side of himself that he doesn't show to many. The one and only time I saw it was when he told me he'd gotten a job at NNC. That he had lied to me about going on a day long assignment with the Parish Police and had instead, taken a morning flight to Atlanta and a late flight back for a daylong interview about his future in cable news. Only then, did I ever see his eyes shift and his skin tint.

Maybe he did care about me.

Not enough to stay or take you with him, as something more permanent than his girlfriend.

"Speak your piece or get away from my door," I say.

"Come with me," he says.

I sigh. Typical Aaron. Give a little. Take it all back. Show a little vulnerability. Take it all back.

I'm not doing this.

"I want to introduce you to some people at the network."

"I know enough. I know you and Dawn. I'm good."

"Just come with me."

"Goodnight, Aaron."

He moves his foot and I push the door closed behind him. I fold over the top lock and lean against the door with my body weight. My head spins in my lean. Dark and light liquor work against each other in my body.

"C'mon, Naomi," Aaron pleads. "Let me help you."

I don't need your help.

I've got a job.

"Goodnight, Aaron."

"If you change your mind, our mixer is in the lobby outside around the fire pits."

I don't know if he's walked away or not. I don't know if he's waiting. I kick off my shoes and slide to the floor in my rented dress, with my badge still around my neck and the convention satchel with my phone, pamphlets, business cards, and list of programs and activities, still hanging from my shoulder. We thud to the ground. In the silence of my room I can hear my head aching. My breath is slow, my heart is slow, my body is lethargic. I want to move, but I don't. I want to be alone, but I don't. I reach for my phone and open my messages. There is nothing new from him. Nothing from Kiyan from today. Nothing from Kiyan from yesterday. The last thing I said was that I made it, and he said, okay.

Is he even still coming.

I text:

Hey

I try to feel him out. It is a "What are you doing? Why are you not talking to me? I'm thinking about you," kind of message wrapped up in three letters.

He doesn't answer. He doesn't hear my ringing bell. There is no blinking ellipsis or even a read receipt to let me know he's read what I have to say. Beneath the message in light gray font is only the word delivered. My message is on his phone and that is all.

That should be enough.

It's not.

I close the messages and switch to the dialing screen. I dial the ten numbers I've memorized and wait for the rings. There are none. It goes straight to voicemail.

"Follow the lady's instructions and I might get back with you."

His greeting is unconventional, like him, like the job he has, like the life he lives. He doesn't have to be all business when telling people how to contact him. He doesn't have to put forth a good impression when he's not readily available to impress people in person or over the phone. I envy his freedom and I hate it at the same time. I hate his assessment of my life, of who I am, of what I do.

Why do you hide who you want to be behind who you're supposed to be?

So, are you going to be back to being you when I come up on Friday?

"I'm not hiding."

There is no one here to hear me; no one in front of me to argue and make my case. He did not answer. Neither text nor call. I switch from our traditional communication to the open lines that connected us in the beginning. I find his life online and scroll through his timeline to see where he's been and what he's been up to, since I've not been home. I only see one new photo. It is from the loft in his studio. The picture of a canvas on an easel. A red, blue, and black line run down the middle of whatever the painting is going to be. The caption says "Working on something new" with the emoji of paintbrushes beside it. The post says it is from an hour ago.

He's working which means his phone is not on.

I darken my screen and set it beside me. I try to find comfort in what I know to be true. I've seen him work. I've watched him as he's found his zone, his hum. The mentally creative space where he doesn't smell food cooking or hear me when I call his name. Lost inside of his own aura, he only answers the call of his bodily functions, and even that is put off until he has to race down the rickety stairs to the communal bathroom in the warehouse for creatives. I tell myself a story I can accept, reasoning I can buy, and push myself up from the floor.

It takes all the effort I can muster to move from the door into the inner part of the room to the bed. I take off my badge and my bag, pull my dress over my head, and strip out of my underwear. I take off the wig, the grip and my stocking cap, and leave the remnants of the day's wares—meant to make those with hiring power look at me—on the floor. In the bathroom, I confront my tipsy self in the mirror.

I see the lack of sleep in my face, the dark circles under my eyes barely masked with my fading concealer. Beyond the makeup, past the smile lines, the age beside my eyes, and the youthfulness in my body, I see what I am.

You're still in recovery from your last relationship.

Jennifer's words from Cuba haunt me months later as I stare at my singleness.

I just hope you recover.

Diedre's words from the seminar add to the sinking weight of my status wrapped around me.

One man who won't answer. Another who wants to makeup and pretend like we don't have a history and he has nothing to apologize for.

It could be worse. It could be no men.

I laugh at myself as my inner critic takes my side for once. I step in the shower and turn on the water. It goes from cold, to warm, to hot over my skin. My body regulates from goose pimples to being steamed in a matter of seconds. I put my face under the water and let the beat of the stream from the showerhead rinse my makeup. With my head under the water I feel the droplets work their way through my tightened and cornrowed locs. The oil I rubbed in my scalp is rinsed away with the water, and drips down my face and neck. The mixture of products burn my eyes and I can't help but cry. I cry to rinse away the makeup and oil clouding into my pupils. I cry because I want to. I cry because I need too.

One argument and I'm questioning everything.

I sigh to myself, lift my head, grab my soap and shower puff, and wash. I scrub my body and try not to see Kiyan's nakedness. I scrub my body and try not to see Aaron's nakedness.

And this is why Matt was convenient.

No feelings.

No emotions.

No regrets.

No wants other than our arrangement.

I didn't have to pretend I cared about him or his businesses, and he didn't have to pretend to care about me.

We got what we both needed and wanted, and kept it moving.

That's what I need.

Not a relationship.

Not companionship.

Not emotional support.

They're the ones who leave me with all the emotions to sort the shit out by myself.

That's not support.

That's baggage.

That's not what I need.

I get out of the shower and wrap one towel around my body, and the other around my head. I take the lotion with me to the bed. My phone is face up. The screen is alive with messages from Jennifer and Diedre.

Are you alright?
Are you coming back down?

I ignore their beacons and rub the moisturizer in my body. Back in the bathroom I reapply what I washed away. Sweet almond oil on my scalp, makeup on my face. I darken my eyes with black liner, and smoke out the lids with eye shadow. Red lips, gold body dust, I admire my nakedness as I get dressed. Black lace thong, no bra, I step into another rented dress with a black sleeveless bodice, and an off black skirt that sparkles with flecks of gold and silver. The straps of the so-called skater dress crisscross at the top of my back and leave the rest of my skin exposed. It is the dress I planned to wear for tomorrow's closing night party with Kiyan.

We may need to have a night in.

Dressed, I pick up my wig and wig grip from the floor and put them both back on my head. I adjust everything that adorns me in the mirror until I look the way I'm supposed to, showing more skin than I'm supposed to. I grab my key and leave my room headed toward where I've been invited.

The elevator takes me to the main lobby floor. There are people gathered in groups everywhere with drinks in their hands, top buttons and ties loosened, and hips sitting sideways to relieve pressure on ankles shoved in heels with no support. I tip past all of them in my red pumps until I am outside on a patio with fewer people gathered in groups. All of them are faces I know, personas I'm familiar with, journalists whose crafts I've studied, but they aren't the reason I have come.

I see him first. Same mint green shirt and light gray slacks he wore on the panel. He is back to being himself. There is no tint to his skin, no shifting of his eyes, no pleading in his voice. He is Aaron Moore the consummate, emotionless professional, who will sacrifice what means the most to him if it is for his own personal greater good, the betterment of himself. He is Thanos in human form on his own personal quest for power and influence, waiting to command and conquer. I walk in the opposite direction of where he entertains a group of suited men he could pass with, drinking from bottles, and laughing with their lower jaw moving up and down at esoteric ironies. I gravitate toward the pit of fire between two low slung outdoor love seats. The area is secluded and warm as the last of sun's rays begin to dip and fall behind the clouds.

"Would you like an appetizer, ma'am?" A waiter asks.

"Thank you," I say.

I take an empanada from his tray and pop it into my mouth. It further takes away the headiness from my imbibed drinks at the bar.

"I didn't expect to see you here."

"Why is that?" I ask, looking up to see Dawn.

"Jennifer and, what's the other girl's name? . . ."

"Diedre," I say.

"Yes. Diedre. They said you weren't feeling well, or had either already gone to the Telecom mixer."

"I barely go to station staff meetings, I for damn sure don't want to be in a mixer with the whole company."

"I understand," she says. "Mind if I sit down?"

I gesture toward the open seat across from me. Dawn, still in her slacks and blouse, sits so we both face the fire. We face each other. Between us is the awkward silence between two people who should have something to say to one another, but don't know where to begin. The fire crackles. The sun sets. I see the sky turn majestic colors of pink and purple. I don't look in her direction and I don't look in his. I focus on the orange flames erupting from the pit of black rocks, and rethink my choices.

You should have stayed in your room and ordered room service.
Waited for Kiyan to call back.
Made up before he got here.

"How long have you known Aaron?" Dawn asks.

The question catches me off guard. "Excuse me?"

"How long have you known Aaron?"

"What makes you think I know Aaron?"

"He came from New Orleans. You're from New Orleans."

"And?"

She sighs, "And he has your picture on his desk?"

Why the hell is my picture on his desk?

I nod. "What did Aaron tell you?"

"I didn't ask him," she says. "I asked you."

"Eight, almost nine years more or less."

"What do you mean more or less?"

"I haven't seen or spoken to him since I moved to Jacksonville. So, if those years count then almost nine years."

It is her turn to nod. I watch her process what I said and what I didn't say. Her pleasant face takes in and turns over the information as she prepares to ask a question that will make me talk. I know her tactics. I've watched them and incorporated some of them into my own interview style. She asks the surprising yet obvious question, the one the viewer wants to know, that the guest doesn't want to give up. The question that gives the guest pause, but makes them follow her into a wormhole, not knowing if there is an opening on the other end.

"I take it your relationship ended badly," she says.

I smile. Only across my mouth. No teeth. No joy in my eyes. "When it's time to move on, it's time to move on," I say.

"No one understands that more than me," Dawn says.

Her admission surprises me. The weight of her honesty. Her words sound laced with grief. I don't pry. I don't poke. I wait. It is something I've watched her do in many an interview. She finds comfort in the silence, the dead air, and then waits for the guest to fill it in, unbothered by the lack of noise, the muted sound of breath, unheard heartbeats and nothingness.

"Just know that when you move, you can't always go home. You can't always go back and pick up where you left off."

"Who says I want to?" I ask.

She smiles her real smile. The one that shows her own dimples at the tops of her cheeks. I know she realizes she's put herself in the susceptible position to share, because she began sharing. Dawn says, "I wasn't talking about you."

"Is there something you want to go back and pick up from where you left off?"

"There are a lot of things I wish I had done differently."

"Like what?"

"I'll say this," Dawn says. "When you reach the summit of Everest, it's better to look around and see the people who made the climb with you, than it is to look out and see the beauty of the world and have no one to share it with. Even if you go back to tell them, they'll never experience that moment you had with you."

I nod and smile into the flames, knowing her reflective words are a cautionary tale.

I don't know what Aaron told her or didn't tell her, but whatever he said, he's never told me.

I ask, "If you had the chance to do everything all over again, the same way, would you?"

"The bad part is, the answer to your question is probably yes. I know who I am. And a lot of people can't handle that. And I have to believe that's too bad for them."

"Even if you're lonely at the top?"

"At some point, someone will scale the mountain alone and we'll be there together."

Not if my picture is still on his desk.

"Are you willing to wait?" I ask.

"My choices are to wait, go back down, or find out if I can fly. Have a good evening."

Dawn stands up and walks away from me and the flames, leaving only her cryptic words.

Find out if I can fly.

What the hell does that mean?

"Is this seat taken?"

"Not anymore," I say.

Aaron sits down where Dawn left.

I say, "I guess I'm pretty popular these days."

"Wearing that dress, I think you are."

"Do you like it?" I ask with a sneer.

"Naomi, I wanted to introduce you to the head of my division. I can't do that if you're wearing that."

"Is that why you didn't speak to me when you saw me? I don't fit into your perfect world."

"Ugh," he sighs, wringing his hands. "I knew this was a bad idea. Same old Naomi."

"What the hell is that supposed to mean?" I ask.

"I thought you had changed," he says. "I thought that since you got your own show, you've covered a few viral stories that got you national press, that you would've changed by now. Would have grown up."

The fuck.

I swallow my anger. If we're going to finally argue the points we never made when we were together, then so be it.

"I've been grown since the day we met."

"You've been a legal adult, but you've hardly been grown. You've been childish since I met you."

"Says the man who was too scared to tell me he didn't love me, he didn't want me, and had to lie to leave the city."

"Because you smothered me, Naomi."

"I smothered you? How?"

"You were so content to go nowhere, to do nothing, that you planned a whole life for us that I didn't even want."

"You never said what you wanted."

His chest heaves with his own anger. I watch his face through the flames, and I wish he would fall in. I wish he could feel the heat of my wrath coursing my veins as I stare at his red tinting face, furrowed brow, and shifting eyes.

Fight or flight, Aaron. Fight or flight.

"I wanted you to be more of who I needed you to be, and less of who you are," he says.

Everybody wants me to be somebody else.

"Everybody wants me to be somebody else," I say. "Why isn't being me good enough for you?"

"I didn't say that, Naomi."

"You just did. You, my mother, even Kiyan."

"Who is Kiyan?"

The name sounds as weird in his mouth as it probably did to his ears. I look at him with smug satisfaction and lean back into the love seat. It is the best I've felt all day. I cross and recross my legs, stretch my arms out across the back of the cushions, and relax into the seat. It is not a question I plan to answer. It is not a question I have to answer. His analytical mind adds one and one and retrieves the answer on his own. I see the realization in his grimace. His jaw tightens and sets to one side, his eyes still their bouncing from left to right, the nostrils of his thin nose flare.

"I really did come here to see you," Aaron says.

"You always said coming to this conference was stupid. A waste of time. You don't need BJA because the real deals are done in rooms where there are few people."

"And I still believe that. But I know you come every year, whether you're looking for a job or not."

"There's other things to get out of this, besides just my next step up."

"You think too small."

"Insults will get you nowhere."

"I'm not insulting you, Naomi. I just want you to think outside the box. Instead of taking a next step up, how about jumping to the next level?"

"It's the same thing I just said."

"No, it's not," Aaron insists. "I don't want to see you take just the next step. I want to see you blast through the floors, scale the mountain, reach the peak."

Maybe he and Dawn are made for each other.

Or maybe they've worked together too long.

I shake my head and laugh to myself. He is the same Aaron I knew. Always wanting what he wants for everyone else around him, damn if they have their own wants. If Aaron wanted sushi, we had sushi. If Aaron wanted to listen to country music, we found the country bar. If Aaron wanted missionary, I laid on my back. His wants were all consuming and all encompassing, and mine were never addressed. He was the gift and I was supposed to be the happy recipient.

Fuck that.

I belong to me.

"Aaron," I say. "What I do is no longer your concern. You don't have to look out for me. You don't have to root for me. You don't have to come to conferences to see me, stalk me around hotels, or pretend you want to introduce me to your managers, and get mad when I show up as me, and not the Naomi you thought you saw on TV."

"Naomi . . ."

"When you had the chance for me to come with you, you didn't say a word. Take my picture off of your desk, stop living in the past, and I'll do the same. Goodnight."

"Naomi . . ."

I don't let him finish his sentence. I don't answer as he calls my name. I walk away from the flames burning in front of my ex, and head inside the hotel. I bypass the bar, click through the lobby, and wait at the elevator.

"Naomi, stop running away from me."

"Running away is what you did," I say. "I've decided to leave. There is a difference."

"What did you want from me, Naomi? To stay and pretend to be something I'm not with someone who wasn't ready?"

"You assume a lot of shit about me, Aaron. All you had to do was to tell me the truth. I'm a big girl. I can handle it."

The elevator opens and I step inside. So does he. I press eleven. He presses seventeen. Three others get on. Eight, ten and fifteen are pressed. The doors close. We are on the elevator, pushed back into the corner, our argument paused. Eight gets off. We stop at nine. Someone gets on and presses twenty-two. Ten. Eleven. I move toward the door to go to my room on my floor. He grabs the fingertips of my hand and holds me back. I glare at him. His eyes don't shift. His face doesn't tint. He waits for me to make the scene and make him out to be something different from what those in the elevator know his on air persona to be. I wrench my hand from his and step back into the corner. The doors close. Fifteen. Seventeen. The doors open. He steps out of the elevator. I don't move.

"You coming?" he asks.

I look from him to the man who got on at the ninth floor. I look from the pleading personality to the leery-eyed man waiting on me to make a decision. Suddenly self-conscious of the open access of my dress, I neither want to ride up on the elevator with him or get off with Aaron. I step off the elevator. The doors close.

"Thank you," he says.

I don't respond. I don't follow him as he turns down the hall to go to his room. I wait by the elevator and press down. It dings immediately. Aaron turns around.

"C'mon, Naomi," he says.

"I'm not running, I'm leaving," I say.

"Naomi, you came all the way up here with me for a reason. Let's finish our conversation."

"We don't have anything else to say to each other."

"I wasn't done talking."

"Aaron, you were done talking to me nearly five fucking years ago."

"That was a mistake."

"So, you've come down the mountain to right your wrongs, in hopes I'll go back up with you and marvel at the view?"

"Huh?"

"Nothing," I say.

The elevator beeps from being held too long. I move my hand from the doors and let them close. It descends to whoever has called for it next. I press the down button again. I show him I am serious about leaving. I am serious about being over his insults. I am serious about belonging to me.

I am serious.

The elevator arrives with a pronounced ding. He is closer to me than I am to leaving.

My left hand blocks the door while he pulls on my right. His grip is stronger than it was when he held on to my fingertips. He is intent and insistent. He is Aaron. Aaron who always advocates for his point of view. Aaron who always gets what he wants.

"C'mon, Naomi. I just want to talk."

The elevator sounds with the beep of being held too long. The alarm of my indecision forces me to decide if I should stay or go. My mind is racing. My thoughts are running.

Am I running?

What am I running from? Him?

I'm leaving.

No matter what.

I move my arm and let the elevator go. He pulls me toward him. I hit the button for down again. I am in his arms.

His fingers are on my naked back and I remember what it used to be like in the middle of summer, when there wasn't enough air conditioning to reduce the humidity of the swampy city we called home.

I ask, "Why is my picture on your desk?"

"I told you, I missed you."

"Bullshit."

"I'm telling the truth."

I roll my eyes.

He says, "Would I fly seven hundred and twenty miles for a conference I've never been to, for an organization I'm not apart of, for any other reason, then to see you?"

"Aaron, you spoke on a panel," I say. "One I'm sure you got paid for. And if you didn't get paid to speak, I'm sure you didn't fly here on your own dime, and that your room, meals, and Ubers will be comped as soon as you file your expense report when you get back. Tell me I'm lying."

"The only reason I asked to speak was so I'd have a reason to be here instead of just standing around, trying to find you in the crowd of everyone else."

He knew I would come to his panel with him and Dawn.

And I did.

So now what?

What does that say about me?

I might as well hear what he has to say.

I win the argument with myself and relent. His hands move from my back down to my waist before skimming my skirt. I swat at him. Both hands come to his chest.

"Say what you have to say, Aaron."

"I will. Come on."

He walks down the hallway and I follow until we reach the room in the corner. It is a suite inside, complete with a living area separate from the bedroom. I am thankful. I sit on the angular yellow sofa that reminds me of the one in my living room in color only. He closes the door, and I immediately notice the chill in the room. I cross my arms in front of me to keep from shivering.

"Are you cold?" he asks.

"I'm good. Talk."

"Damn, Naomi. I'm just trying to make sure you're comfortable."

"You don't have to worry about my comfort level. Say what you have to say so I can go."

If you didn't want to be here, you would have gotten on one of the elevators you let go. He's not that strong.

"Do you want anything to drink?" Aaron asks me, crossing over to the refrigerator. "There's bourbon but not the kind you like."

"I'm good," I say. "I won't be here that long."

"It's like that, huh?" Aaron asks, shutting the door of the mini-fridge.

I don't answer. I watch him cross the room and sit on the beige love seat. Aaron relaxes into the cushions of the armless couch, and then begins to unbutton his shirt. He gets it all the way undone and pulls it off, revealing his spotless arms in his plain white undershirt. Seeing this much of him, pure and unmarked, I begin to compare and contrast Kiyan against Aaron. Aaron against Kiyan. One naturally skinny and without thought to what his body looks like, the other pumped with sperm reducing protein shakes to bulk up and fill out a suit. Kiyan's tattoos give him character, while Aaron's unmarred arms make him blend in with the rest of the men in his age range climbing the corporate ladder. Aaron's hair cut is longer than a fade, long enough to create an ocean of waves that have been trained by years of forward brushing, and regular haircuts. The only meticulous grooming Kiyan completes is edging his hairline every week. He makes sure it is precise, whether his locs need a retwist or not. I look at one and see the other in my mind's eye, and get disgusted with myself.

Why am I even here?

"Why am I here, Aaron?" I ask aloud. "What do you want?"

"I miss you." He says again.

I scoff at him. His delivery of the three word sentence was flat and without emotion. He looked straight ahead at the door of the room rather than at me, when he said it.

Did he expect that he was going to swoop in and say some magic words to make my panties wet so that I'd fall for him, and we'd pick up where we left off, like these damn near five years didn't pass in silence?

He's out of his arrogant ass, self-entitled little mind.

"How can you miss someone you didn't want?"

"I never said I didn't want you, Naomi."

"Your dick might have, but you for damn sure didn't."

He squirms in his seat. It is visible that I touched a nerve. His eyes bounce, one knee shakes, he adjusts his hips to possibly alleviate pressure from his groin. Why men's genitals understand when they're being referred to, whether in a good way or a bad way, is beyond me.

I continue, "I mean, how can you want somebody you needed to be less of who they already were? You wanted me to be something I'm not, to fit in your little box of the kind of woman you're supposed to have on your arm."

"That's called consideration, when you're in a relationship, Naomi. You are a reflection of me, as I am a reflection of you."

"Is that why you didn't introduce me to anyone downstairs, because you don't like the reflection you see in me?"

He sighs. His leg shakes. His hips shift. He is affected and I don't know why. His body fidgets as if it's under it's own magical power; as if my voice is the hammer that creates the visible reflex in his body. Aaron stands up from his seat and crosses the room. He steps through the separating doors into the bedroom portion of the room, and lays his shirt atop the white duvet cover. Pacing, he walks from the bedroom to the door, to the love seat, and then to the kitchenette. There is nowhere for him to go and nowhere for him to run from the conversation he's forced me into having.

He says, "You're wearing the hell out of that dress and those shoes. I saw you when you entered the bar and stepped out on the patio."

"But you didn't speak."

"How could I, when the guys I wanted to introduce you to could only say when they saw you, how much they wanted to fuck you?"

"So, what, Aaron? Grow up! Lots of people may want to fuck me. That doesn't mean I'm going to let them."

"That's not the point," he says exasperated. "It's a business function. I told you I wanted to introduce you to some people, and you come downstairs looking like a high dollar hooker seeking a sugar daddy, and not a job?"

"You just called me a ho? Because of my dress? Fuck you, Aaron. Fuck you."

I stand up and walk to the door. He is steps away from me in the kitchenette. He is behind me. Hands on my shoulders, he turns me around and keeps me from leaving, again. Facing me his eyes are still, his hands move from my shoulders to my bare back, and then, respectfully, skim the rise of the skirt part of the dress, again. He is trying to touch my ass while still being polite. This time, I don't swat his hand.

"It's after five. I can wear whatever I feel when it's after five. Those are no longer business hours."

"You know good and well our business is twenty-four hours," Aaron says without the prior conviction.

"And in the twenty-four hours of the day, I'm not always buttoned up to my neck in business attire. I'm a girl. I like to have fun."

"You are all woman, and I remember what kind of fun you like to have."

His tone of voice is deeper than his normal speaking voice. It is deeper than the fake voice he uses on air with the precise diction and the rigid enunciation. This voice is the one I remember. The one he used when he was comfortable. The voice that adapted a Cajun quality from his years in the swamps and bayous, despite his Los Angeles upbringing. It is the voice of desire I hear in his throat, and it ripples everywhere in my body that is within proximity to his.

I need to leave.

I put my hand on the door handle and turn the lock. His fingers flirt with the hem of the skirt of my dress.

"Don't go," he says. "Please."

"Why am I staying?" I ask.

"Because I asked you to," he says.

Aaron presses his body against mine on the door. The turned lock clicks back into place as I release the handle. I feel his need throb against my thigh as the heat from the rest of his body pulls me in. His fingers ruffle the hem of my skirt. Playfully respectful, he is gravity and I am a star being pulled into his orbit, forced to follow the path that he has set, the course he has laid, the pattern he predetermined.

I fall into the line of my ellipse as his mouth covers mine. There is nothing awkward about the moment our lips reconnect. Plush skin against plush skin and our tongues dance the dance of valiant warriors, ready to fight to love. He is Shango and I am Oya. Our kiss rides out against the door, and initiates a wave of need within me.

My own body betrays my horrified thoughts as it pulses away from the door and into him. I reverberate from the stroke of his lips into his awaiting chest. His fingers move from fondling my skirt to pressing the runner toned skin of my inner thigh. His hand is near my heat, his mouth is on my mouth, and I can think of nothing else beyond my own needs. I am a carnivore deprived of meat and ready to feast.

His finger finds its way up my leg, around the thin shroud of material that passes for panties, and inside of me. It is not the meat I crave but it will do. He stirs my pot from the inside until I want to boil over onto him. He strums my pain with his finger until I know why the caged bird sings. I ride his middle digit on the edges of my ecstasy pulsing around him as if he is my own personal yoni egg, I use to strengthen my muscles, and expand my own expertise.

I pulse until he withdraws. I am empty. His hands are beneath my skirt, both palms lift my bare behind into the air. He carries me back to the yellow sofa where he sits down and sets me atop him. His belt buckle and button is a formality, and his zipper becomes a casualty of my hunger, my need. He is unleashed and rushed inside to feel the hole he left behind.

Full and fulfilled I lift my cheeks to adjust for length, width, and girth to allow all of him in. I lift and lower. I rise and fall. I bring my body to the tips of his sensation and let myself fall around him again. He is filling me with what I need, erasing what I don't want to remember, muting the voices that try to reason with me, and satisfying the heartbreak I resist to admit remains nearly five years after he left.

With hands on his shoulders I increase my pace. Up and down, up and down and around and around, I ride Aaron the way I remembered he likes, with vigor and without abandon. I let my body speak up for me. It tells him why it was wrong for him to leave. My stroke explains why he should accept me for me. My wetness floods him with reasons to regret his own selfish decisions.

I grip his shoulders and rub my hands down the length of his arms, until I feel his skin. It is smooth. I open my eyes. There are no raised abrasions in patterned ink. No tattoos. No Kiyan. Only Aaron. I stop moving.

It is only Aaron.

Smooth, baby-skinned, unmarked, unmarred, arrogant Aaron sits beneath me with his head back, his eyes closed, and his mouth open.

"C'mon, Baby, don't stop, I'm almost there."

I swing my legs off of him and stand. "This was a mistake."

My voice is croaked and feverish. I say words I don't fully understand, trying to readjust my soaking underwear and the dress in place. I am not steady on my feet. I stumble as I stagger to the door.

"Stop."

"Please."

"Don't go."

"Naomi."

"I'm sorry."

They are all words I hear but don't understand, as I open the door into the dimmed lighting of the hallway and close it on a mistake I consciously made. I leave as I should have left hours ago. I leave as I should have left him after the first wedding we attended together years ago. I leave him as he left me, hard up and hard pressed for answers that will never come.

I look down at the patterned carpet as I trudge to the bank of elevators. I am afraid to look up. I don't want to catch myself in any of the mirrors lining the hallway, used as tools of decorations. I don't want to see myself. I don't want to look at me and see the woman who rode her way to rhapsody in response to the years' long linger of insecurity in an unrequited love.

The elevator dings and opens to take me to my floor.

The doors close. I look up and see me in the reflective metal, and I do not recognize myself.

What would make you cheat?

Ass, access, and opportunity.

What would make you lie?

Judgement.

I deserve to be judged right now.

I replay my first date conversation with Kiyan as the elevator takes me from seventeen to eleven.

I don't want to lie.

I can't tell him the truth.

I still don't want to lie.

I don't even know if he's still coming tomorrow. He didn't answer the phone and he didn't text back.

He was painting.

Or maybe ass, access, and opportunity presented itself in someone else, and we're both trying to figure out how not to lie.

It's not like we've ever had the exclusive conversation. I don't even call him my boyfriend.

Because everyone else already does.

The doors open on the eleventh floor and I reason myself in and out of the truth as I walk to my room. My eyes watch the floor and my arms hug my body. I don't want to get another glimpse of me. Not another look. I am disgusted with me, infuriated with my own lack of self-control.

I should have canceled coming as soon as I saw he was announced on the panel. We didn't have to share space. Share a hotel. Nearly five years of distance, a good relationship, job security, and emotional stability, ruined for what?

"There she is."

I hear them before I see them.

Diedre and Jennifer stand outside my door.

"Ugh," I sigh to myself.

They are the last people I want to see. I want to see them less than I want to see my own reflection. Still in their gear from earlier in the day, they wait until I get closer. I keep my head down.

"Naomi, what's wrong?" Diedre asks.

"Nothing," I say.

"We came to check on you," Jennifer says. "You never responded to our messages."

"I got caught up," I say.

"Dawn said she saw you for a minute at her mixer, but then you disappeared," Jennifer says.

Either ask the question or shut the fuck up.

I temper my response as I unlock the door. "And now I've reappeared. I must be magic. I'm going to bed."

I close the door in their faces and cross the top hotel lock to bolt the door. I don't lean against it to linger in my fragrance of someone else. In the bathroom, I strip out of my clothes, shoes, and hair, and turn on the shower. Cold. Hot. Warm. My body adjusts. My thoughts race.

What would make you cheat?

Ass, access, and opportunity.

I guess my answer to that question would be dick on demand.

I don't laugh at my self-deprecating joke. I cleanse. Beneath the water I run my fingers up through each cornrow until my locs are loose and they hang in my face. Oil runs off of them, makeup off of me, and what remnants Aaron secreted inside me flow out of my body. I stand beneath the water and hear his voice.

What would make you lie?

Warmth floods my face, salts my lips, and stings my eyes.

I cry.

16.

4:44

The light and the noise awaken my senses before I fully comprehend what is happening. Red replaces the black on the inside of my eyelids, and buzzing sounds from somewhere beside me in the bed. I feel the vibrations and I hear the rings of my phone. I search for it with my hands to shut off the noise adding to my headache.

Dark liquor or light liquor. Always pick one.

The advice my daddy gave to me when I moved into the dorm for college, in the name of having the full experience instead of staying home, comes back to me. The only other thing he told me was to drink it how it comes. Straight out of the bottle. No juice, no chaser, no mixer.

I did one and not the other, and now I'm paying for it.

I should've had more empanadas to soak it up.

My hands find the phone and cease the noise of the alarm. Slowly, my eyes open one at a time. I see why my disheveled room is so bright. The curtains are wide open, the sun sparkles on the water which shines with an ebullient brilliance that is reflected off of the glass and steel skyscrapers and aimed directly into my open window. I blink to adjust to the intrusion of light. The phone dings again and again. I have messages, many missed messages. I ignore them until my body follows my eyes and begins to wake. I wiggle my toes, stretch my hips to my legs, and I feel what I have done.

"Fuck!"

I yell in the empty room, about the unfilled emptiness I feel that I filled, last night.

I should have never gone out after I came back the first time.

I give myself the advice I ignored the night before in the name of closure. The bastard word women invoke when they need to know what's been over is still dead. The bastard word I am invoking after confirming there is no future in the past.

There's no future in your future, either.

He doesn't have to know.

I scoff at myself. My deceit disgusts me as my phone dings in my hand. I look around the room. I see the embroidered mesh dress I wore all day yesterday; my badge and my conference bag on the floor. I get out of the bed and look for the other pile. It is by the door and in the bathroom. The black, lace thong, my backless dress with the sparkly flirty skirt, my wig and wig grip. I turn on the light and look in the mirror. Dark circles greet me, puffy cheeks say hello, my tearstained face says good morning.

You didn't need him.

You didn't want him.

And you slept with him anyway.

I know.

So, why did you do it?

I argue with myself as my phone dings in my hand.

I turn it over and I see missed calls from Kiyan and missed messages from Jennifer, Diedre, Kiyan and Aaron.

Aaron: I'm leaving today.

Kiyan: I'm on my way.
　　　I've landed.
　　　I'm here.
　　　Downstairs in the lobby.
　　　Take your time.

Why did you do it?

To know it was over.

Liar.

Because, I didn't know where me and Kiyan stood.

You knew he was painting.

I can't even come up with a good excuse, a good lie for myself.

You were drunk.

Not that damn drunk.

I dead my chance at absolution and accept my own suffering. I went to Aaron's room and I slept with him when I shouldn't have.

Because you wanted to.

The answer I've been avoiding enters my mind with the same decisiveness as the decision I made to get back on the elevator with Aaron. Something in me wanted to. Wanted him. Wanted closure.

Or reconciliation?

Closure.

"Closure," I say out loud to convince myself.

I switch screens and look at the clock, and then back at the messages.

He's been here damn near an hour.

I turn on the water and splash my face. I splash away my guilt stained tears and wash away the salt residue of my regret. I brush my teeth and look in the mirror again. I still see what I've tried to wash away. What I did. What I've done. What my insecurity needed. What Kiyan didn't, doesn't deserve.

Well, I'm a piece of shit.

I pick up the clothes off of the bathroom floor and from the hallway in front of the door. The distinct smell of sex, of combined bodies and exchanged bodily fluids emanates from the garments in my arms. I see the dried white secretions on my underwear from my misplaced excitement, and I feel the heat of tears forming, threatening to fall from my face. I want to cry all over again.

You did it, you know why, and now he's here.

Figure out what you're going to say and do before you go get him.

I ignore the instructions from my inner voice as I drop the dirty clothes in my arms on top of the pile by the bed.

Where are my shoes?

I search for my flip flops until I find them. Phone in my hand, key in the pocket of Kiyan's running pants that I stole, my locs loose around my face, I leave my room headed toward the lobby with no plan in place. Down the carpet, to the bay of elevators, I press buttons; I move in reverse of what I did last night; of what I shouldn't have done last night.

"Going down."

The emotionless and sterile voice of automation greets me as I'm whisked away to where my mistake began. I fidget with my phone. It dings in my hand. The messages are in the group chat from Diedre and Jennifer. I scroll through the thread that began last night. The messages they sent after they saw me, after I dismissed them, after I shut myself in to let them think what they wanted.

> Diedre: I hope you're okay.
>   Let us know if you need anything.
> Jennifer: Are you still doing conference stuff in the
>   morning since Kiyan is coming?
>   We're going to hit breakfast and then to
>   the keynote master class.
>   Let us know if you want us to save you a
>   seat.

I still have three unread messages by the time the elevator opens on the lobby floor. It is from Jennifer to me. Not in our group thread. Something she doesn't want Diedre to know.

<blockquote>
Jennifer: Dawn told us she saw you leave with
Aaron last night.
What did you do?
Is everything alright?
</blockquote>

She condemns and then she cares. It's like my mother and my daddy all rolled into one person.

I close my messages, darken the phone, and shove it in my pocket as I walk around the lobby.

You've got to be fucking kidding me.

I see him before he sees me. I see both of them at the same time. My mistake and my reality that I've ruined. They sit at separate tables, one in front of the other, in the hotel snack bar, where grab and go food is available. Aaron is with his suitcase, and Kiyan is with his. Light, muscular, and well groomed, dressed in tan slacks and a white polo, engrossed in his phone, sits with his back to his polar opposite, the dark brown man who is unkempt save for his hairline, thin and lanky, dressed in running pants that match mine, and a white T-shirt with the Chicago city flag fading from the material. In Kiyan's hands is a pencil he's using to draw in a small sketch book set on the table.

I approach without saying anything. I don't want to draw attention from either one, from hearing my voice.

This is going to be interesting.

Neither of them looks up until I pull back my chair. It scrapes across the tile flooring made to look like hardwood. Aaron's eyes alight and bounce, I see questions as he notices my hair, and then his face grimaces, as I force a smile at Kiyan that he gives back to me genuinely.

"I tried calling you last night," I say.

"I know," Kiyan says.

"Why didn't you answer?"

"I was working."

"I saw. Did you finish it?"

"It's just something I'm messing around with," he says. "How have you been? How's the conference going?"

"It's been good. A little predictable, but it's always good information."

"I see you took your hair down," Kiyan says, reaching toward my face.

He grabs a few strands of my locs and separates them with his fingers. His touch is gentle as it leaves my hair. His calloused fingers brush against my scrubbed face. I revel in the momentary touch and I'm flooded with guilt again, as I see Aaron loudly pull back his chair and ball his hands into fists. I close my eyes and turn my head into Kiyan's caressing hands and kiss his palm.

I can't lie to him.

Is it a lie if he never finds out the truth?

People don't tell this type of truth to help anyone. They do it to alleviate their own guilt.

I kiss his palm again and then pull back. I grab his hand and hold it across the table.

"I've missed you," I say.

"I wasn't sure if you would," Kiyan says. "You know me and my judgmental ass attitude."

I force a smile. I know he's testing me to see how I feel, to see how much he can press, how much he can push, how much he can challenge me like he normally does without making me angry. He is testing me, but trying to hold on to me, to keep me from leaving, from running, from swimming away like any other fish in the sea.

A phone rings. There is coughing in the background. "This is Aaron."

"I'll be right outside."

Kiyan turns around. He sees what I see. He sees my mistake in business casual making a production of leaving with his roll away suitcase.

"Yo, that's Aaron Moore," Kiyan says turning to me, and then back around to gawk at Aaron.

"Good morning," Aaron says, coming over to our table.

"Yo, you're Aaron Moore," Kiyan says to him.

"I am. And you are?"

"Kiyan English."

I watch my mistake and my reality shake hands and dap each other up. The only thing they don't do is come together for the mutual black man's hug. Too familiar for Kiyan, and too Black for Aaron.

You've got to be fucking kidding me.

I shrink in my chair and try to disappear like the Wicked Witch from the West, after water has been poured on her body. They continue. I hold Kiyan's hand, I glisten with nervous sweat under Aaron's gaze. They continue:

"Are you here for the conference?" Aaron asks him.

I hear the arrogance in his voice, the superiority in his tone, the scoffing disbelief in his pitch that says he already knows Kiyan is not one of us, that he could not possibly do what we do.

"Nah, man, I don't really do the news thing," Kiyan says. "I see your videos on social, but the only one I really watch is my girl here."

I smile genuinely as I look up at Aaron. I squeeze Kiyan's hand and hold back a laugh. It is the best I've felt in the hours since I left the room on the seventeenth floor. The smug man's pride is humbled, his ego broken, and his claims to me destroyed.

"Hey, Naomi," Aaron says. "I like your hair."

I should've known this shit was going to go left.

"You two know each other?" Kiyan asks.

"We used to work together for awhile in New Orleans before I moved on," Aaron says. "It was nice meeting you, Kiyan. Good seeing you again, Naomi."

Before I moved on.

I feel the punch straight in my gut. Where he was aiming. Where it landed. The diss intentional.

Asshole.

I watch Aaron walk away with my good feelings secured in his roll away. Again, he's left me with an emotional grenade ready to detonate all over my life. I want to run but I can't. I want to escape, but it will be my tell. I want to tell the truth, but he doesn't deserve to be hurt.

"You ready?" I ask Kiyan.

"You never told me you used to work with him," he says.

"I used to work with a lot of people," I say. "The business is small. Everybody knows somebody or somebody who knows somebody else."

I stand up from the table and grab Kiyan's roll away.

"I got it," he says.

I lead him away from the table and chairs where my mistake and my reality collided. We walk in the opposite direction of Aaron toward the elevators into the innards of the hotel. The bell dings before we even have a chance to press the button. We step into the empty lift and the doors close.

"So, what was this about you missing me?" Kiyan asks.

"Just what I said."

"Don't clam up now."

The elevator stops on the second floor and the doors open. Before us are a sea of people, men and women dressed in suits, and their finest dresses, skirts, and tops. I spot the anchors and reporters immediately. Wigs in place, weaves perfectly curled, hair bone straight, hairlines sharp, facial hair freshly shaven, we are a cult all on our own and we don't even know it. Today I'm not one of them. A handful get on the elevator in full chatter mode. Kiyan and I are pushed to the back corner of the elevator.

". . . I can't believe I forgot my badge in the room," says one woman searching through her convention tote.

"You should've known security was going to be tight with who they have coming to speak," says her friend with thick Marley twists.

"But still. We're all here for the same reason. They should just let us in," says another woman with an annoyed look.

"That's what I'm saying," the first one agrees.

"Now we're going to be late and have to sit in the overflow room," the annoyed woman says.

The women talk amongst themselves and my mind drifts, wondering exactly who they are. I make up my own story and assume the woman without the badge is a reporter by the youthfulness in her face, and her lack of preparation for the day's activities. The annoyed woman I believe is her friend, who may be in the same market as she, or in another, but has known her for a long time, at least since college. The reassuring woman with the Marley twists I give the job of being in the industry, but in an online or behind the scenes capacity based on her hairstyle.

My phone vibrates against my leg.

I pull it from my pocket and see the message in my group text.

Jennifer: Are you coming?

I respond.

No.
Kiyan is here.
I'll see y'all when I get back.

I darken my phone. It dings again. Another message. It is from Jennifer only. One word.

Really?

I don't answer. I don't even open the message to clear it from the home screen. I put my phone on airplane mode and turn off the WIFI, blue tooth, and roaming signals. I drop it back into my pocket as the elevator stops on the ninth floor. The chattering women get off and Kiyan and I are alone again.

He says, "Everybody looks alike."

"I noticed that too," I say.

"So maybe I'm not so judgmental after all."

"You're still judgmental because you didn't take the time to understand."

"And what do I need to understand, Naomi?" Kiyan asks as we step off the elevator on the eleventh floor.

I look up at his face and see his dimple as it rests. Another small indentation in his face; I see the cleft in his chin and the wonder in his eyes. I reach my hand and I smooth the bushiness of his eyebrows. He grabs my wrist and brings my hand to his mouth. He kisses my knuckles, intertwines his fingers with mine, and places them by our sides.

He asks, "What do I need to understand?"

"The only people really allowed to be themselves are white people," I say. "They make the rules, they rule the industries, they hire and fire."

"And you're okay with that?" he asks as we get to my room.

"I didn't say I was okay with that," I say as I unlock the door.

"You didn't say you weren't, either."

"Because it's not that simple, Kiyan. You're an artist. You have a level of freedom that will never be afforded to me in my industry. Name one on air Black person sporting sister locs on an anchor desk."

"The lady that's on MSNBC," Kiyan says.

"Melissa Harris Perry? She hasn't been on air since before Obama was reelected and we've got a whole new President in office now."

"Damn."

"And she didn't have sister locs. She had twists. And her show was only on the weekend, not every day."

"There's white ladies on the air with curly hair," he argues.

"The operative word is white, and beyond that, if it's a really good kink, they're probably Jewish."

"What does that have to do with anything?"

"The holocaust is memorialized as a warning to never let something so horrific happen again. Slavery is forgotten and anyone who brings it up is told to get over it and move on."

"So, what's your point?" Kiyan asks sitting on the bed.

"My point is that I'm never going to be given the same opportunities or benefits of doubt as afforded to my melanin deficient coworkers." I say, "Instead of giving me grief about how my hair looks, or how I look and what I do, try understanding the world in which I operate, and the industry that I'm in."

"But it seems like the industry that you're in doesn't love you, so why are you busting your ass to prove something to people who will never accept you as you are."

"This industry, this country may never accept me for who I am, but that doesn't mean I can't be better, faster, stronger, than any mediocre blonde Becky from Wyoming at what I do."

"So, you're okay with knowing you're twice as good and only getting half as much?"

"You get what you negotiate," I say, echoing Boyce's words to me.

"Then I hope you negotiate well."

"I'm learning," I say.

He opens his arms to me and I go to where he sits on the unmade bed. In his lap, he wraps his arms around me. I lay my loose locs against his loose locs and we sit. I kiss the side of his forehead to show him I appreciate his comfort. I am thankful for his understanding. I am grateful that he came despite our fight.

I don't deserve his compassion.

He doesn't deserve my deception.

The reality of my mistake intrudes on the moment and I want to run, but I can't. I want to put him out, but I don't. I want to pick a fight with him and make him mad at me so he leaves on his own, but I can't. I sit in his lap with his arms around me, my hair in his hair, my lips against his skin, and I suffer. I suffer in silence pretending I'm okay. I pretend I'm not wrong. I play the wonder game with myself and wonder how long I can lie. I wonder how long I can sit in judgement of myself and keep it inside. I wonder.

I wonder.

"You said something about missing me," Kiyan says.

"Mhmm," I purr against his skin.

"What's that about?"

"Just what it sounds like. You always think there's a double meaning to everything. I missed you."

"I just wanted to hear you say it again."

"Is that right?"

"I missed you too," he says, turning to look at me.

His brown eyes meet mine and I try not to see flashes of hazel. Forehead to forehead, nose to nose, lips to lips, he kisses me. I don't resist. I let the insistence of his kiss cover my indiscretions. He rolls me to my back and pushes me up the bed. I close my eyes and play pretend. I follow his lead and his tongue as I make myself believe I didn't do this with someone that should have been him.

With his weight on my body his mouth moves from my mouth to my neck. He kisses. He sucks. I suffer in my surrender to his wants. Objecting would be telling him I lied. To stop would be saying I didn't miss him. To oppose would raise questions about why I don't want him, why I don't want him to paint inside the lines of the canvas he's claimed.

Stop thinking and let your body respond.

I follow the best advice I've given myself in the last twelve hours and surrender to Kiyan's kiss. His hands lift my T-shirt to expose my unrestrained breasts. He pulls it off of me and then works on the pants that match his. They slide off my hips and I am completely naked. He joins me in nudity tossing his T-shirt and jumping out of his pants and boxers. He pulls a three pack of condoms out of his pants pocket and throws it on the bed.

"Really," I say. "In your pocket."

"I always want to be prepared."

I want to laugh, but I can't. My memory steals my levity. I remember hands on my thighs, fingers inside, and fitting until I was fulfilled on bare skin that I should have never felt. Here, now, I want Kiyan in the same way. I watch him as he works the condom on, and I don't tell him stop. I don't tell him to do what Aaron did to me because it will help make me feel less guilty. Less reckless. Less whorish. Less of feeling less.

Kiyan comes back to me and kisses me where he left off. My lips, my neck, my breasts, my navel. My body lifts to meet his lips and he obliges my request. I am the canvas, he is the artist, and his lips are his tools. He dampens my surface before trying to swallow me whole. The pressure of his suction makes me release rivers I dammed away from Aaron's dick. Kiyan frees me to flow and licks me continuously as I do. He is patient. Again, holding himself back until he is sure I am satisfied. His penchant, and proclivity to make sure I am writhing, dry heaving, and damn near on empty before he thinks about himself, is only one trait of his I admire.

I lay beneath him, my legs wrapped around the back of his head, burying his face as I shake with another blast and blow from my unplugged dams beguiled by his tongue. The torture of his tasting me rocks my body back and forth on the bed. I release his head and reach for him. I want him to fill the emptiness inside me. I pull him into position, slip the protection off with a slide of my hand, as he slides inside, and I feel the curve and the width of his dimensions.

His eyes are wide as he looks at me. I pull his face toward mine and cover his lips with kisses, to kiss away his surprise. My hands move from my face to his back, his back to his butt. I encourage his strokes to deepen; to stretch, gap, and gape my gift. I pull him into me. I want to show him how much he was missed, even if I'm just playing pretend.

Kiyan pushes his way through me until he is balls deep and we are nearly one. My hands find his arms and I run my fingers over his tattoos. I rub the raised ridges of the ink deposited on the skin of the tribal markings as I throw myself into him and squeeze as he pumps. He stops denying himself for me and becomes selfish. His strokes are a force and I take what he gives. I take what he gives. I take what he gives until what he gives is of himself and he collapses on to me. I am empty of me, and full of him.

I am good at playing pretend.

<h1 style="text-align:center">17.</h1>

<h1 style="text-align:center">Happenstance
Homecomings and
Unpleasant Surprises</h1>

I pretend I don't smell the sex from the bundle of dirty clothes already in my arms as I take them to the hotel closet and stuff them in one of the laundry bags. I pretend I don't see the dried stains on my thong, the evidence of my indiscretion. I push the lace thong down into the bag, along with the backless, black dress. I pull the laundry bag out of the closet and make my way around the room, picking up our discarded clothes.

He is in the bathroom with the door closed and the shower running. I take my time moving around the room, cleaning up, hiding my wrongs and masking my mistakes. Naked, I pad around the room trying to make less work for housekeeping. I set my dirty clothes bag down beside my roll away sitting beneath the window, then pull the sheets and ball them up on top of the bed.

I join him in the bathroom, in the shower, as he pours soap into the puff. He pushes me toward the water and steps behind me. He is back to being selfless. He gives me the heat of the water even though his body is already wet and being away from it will make him cold. I take the puff from him, lather it beneath the water and wash his body. I soap his shoulders and tattoos, his chest and his back, his waist, butt and his legs. I get between his toes and then work my way up over his knees and down the length of his lingam. I wash all of me away from him and push him into the water to rinse. I stand behind him in the cold washing my body, scrubbing my skin, punishing myself.

"What do you want to do today?" I ask him.

He spins beneath the water, shakes his wet locs, and then steps out.

He says, "I thought we could take a trip. Let you see some of the city."

"Like the magnificent mile?" I ask, stepping beneath the water.

"No, like the Southside," Kiyan says. "Where I grew up."

"Huh?"

He peeks his head back into the shower where I lean against the wall. He says, "I want to take you to meet my mom."

"Oh."

Shit.

He pulls the curtain back to give me privacy and I die one thousand deaths that have nothing to do with my orgasm or sex.

Could I be any worse?

"Is it close?" I ask, rinsing off beneath the shower.

"It's not far," he says.

"How are we getting there?"

"I thought we could take the bus."

I get out of the shower to see Kiyan with one towel around his waist and another around his hair. He spreads toothpaste on his toothbrush and rinses the rest of me down the drain. I step beside him and do the same. We cleanse, we groom, I dry his locs and pour oil onto the parts of his scalp.

He rubs the oil between his hands and massages my head. We make the hotel like my home or his apartment. We move in sync with each other moisturizing, clipping, primping, shaving until we are dressed. He in holey jeans and a graphic tee, me in black leggings and an oversized blouse. It is my only non-conference attire. What I planned to wear on the way home.

We leave the room and remove the do not disturb sign from the outside of the door. Down the hallway, back to the bank of elevators, all I can see are the footprints made before he arrived. Aaron outside of my door, my stride to the lobby mixer, my staggering walk after leaving the seventeenth floor. Outside of my room I am reminded of all the memories I made before he arrived. I stand apart from him and wait for the elevator. It dings and I jump. We get on alone and ride down. On the second floor a sea of my doppelgängers are in front of me. Some get on. Others wait. I close the gap between us as the doors close. I grab his hand. He lays his head down on mine. Our locs touch and I feel the warmth in his head add to mine.

"I think I may love you," he says as the doors open on the lobby.

I don't have time to look at him as we are forced out of the elevator and thrust amongst the throngs of people enjoying the last day of the conference. He grabs my hand and pulls me toward the doors that lead to outside. We bypass the cars and valets until we are on the street on King Drive, standing on the grounds of the massive hotel and convention center complex, waiting for a bus. My eyes want to take in the massive pillars, the freshly cut grass that looks like carpet, the perfectly shaped shrubs, and the glass encased architecture that makes up the campus, but all I hear is his voice.

I think I may love you.

"What do you mean, you think you may love me?" I ask as the red, black, and white bus pulls up in front of us.

He gets on in front of me, slides bills into the fare machine, and then leads me to the back of the bus. Up a platform and on the last row, we squeeze into corner seats surrounded by windows. The driver pulls off and I'm jolted back against my seat.

"Hold on to the handle of the seat in front of you if you start moving."

"Got it," I say. "Now answer my question."

"There's nothing to answer, Naomi. It's like what you always say. Just what I said. I think I may love you."

"Why just I think?" I ask. "Why don't you know?"

"Because I don't. I'm just telling you how I think I feel."

I nod my head and don't return the sentiment as the bus pulls off.

I have no integrity.

At least not in this relationship.

He doesn't deserve this.

I don't deserve him. Especially not his love.

You could at least say thank you for his love.

What good would that do if I'm not going to give it back?

He doesn't seem to pressed about it anyway.

Probably because he's still figuring out what he feels.

When he says I love you, then I'll say something back.

You still cheated.

I argue with myself and lose. I turn to Kiyan and see he's engrossed in his sketch book. It is balanced on his knee as he scratches lines into the white paper. I see curves and know the body belongs to a woman, and I wonder if it is me. I leave him alone in his work, his doodles that could become something else, and I look out the window. We have left the convention center campus and the scenery changes. I realize the hotel is on the outskirts of downtown, and the Southside of his city is closer than expected. We pass Dunbar High School, and a statue of what looks like Black men cut out of green stone and surrounded by eagles.

The scenery changes again as the streets widen and the north and southbound traffic is separated by large medians of green grass and trees. Each side of the street is lined with stone houses, that look old, and remind me of New York. I look out of the window as the bus moves quickly down the street, passing old homes, churches, schools, apartment high rises, a smattering of small neighborhood businesses and the occasional vacant lot. I watch out of the window not knowing what to expect. What I see surprises me, but again, I don't know what I expected.

You expected guns and drugs and shootings and bodies like New Jack City.

I see a sign on a post in the median that says Liberty Baptist Church in Chicago celebrating 100 years.

"There are a lot of churches on this block."

"The Southside is just like any other Black neighborhood in America, and King Drive just like any other MLK boulevard or street or road, or circle, or parkway in the country. There are churches. Every other block for every denomination under the sun."

"I see."

"Everything looks so nice."

"This is Bronzville," he says. "Keep looking, tourist."

Kiyan buries his head back in his sketch pad and I look back outside the window. The scenery changes again. Gone are the wide boulevard like streets with the grassy tree-lined median. As the numbers on the signs go up, the neighborly quality of the blocks decreases. Gone are the large stately homes, and in their place are more vacant lots, massive apartment buildings, and two and three flat homes. The schools are larger, like fortresses, more industrial, more warehouse like, less emphasis on form than there is on function. At Sixty-First Street I see the makings of any hood. Storefronts without signs, medical clinics in corner buildings that could easily house a liquor store. At Sixty-Third Street we pass under the train tracks and emerge into the periphery of a stereotypically Black neighborhood. Shopping plazas advertising cheap cell phones and fried fish are juxtaposed beside sets of apartments walled in by wrought iron fences.

We pass under a viaduct the numbers go up, a mini mart and an advertisement for abortion are what I see on the billboard, and I begin to notice a pattern. The corners of each block let me know that I am amongst my own kind, but the blocks themselves with the cut grass and the mostly well-kept grounds of homes and apartments let me know the people care. It reminds me of the neighborhoods in Jacksonville that are ordinary neighborhoods in the day with homes that are mostly well-kept, and the signs of poverty, of struggle, relegated to the corner hustles, convenient businesses, and midnight crime. I see more people on the street, the bus makes more stops, but it is unspectacularly ordinary, and yet this is the place I know the city gets its violent reputation from.

"Looks normal to me," I say.

"You can't believe everything you read," Kiyan says without looking up at me.

I know he brought me here on purpose. He may want me to meet his mother, but we are on the city bus intentionally.

He thinks I'm sheltered because I live in the suburbs.

One day he'll have to come home with me and see Nola beyond Bourbon Street.

That's if we last that long.

I have to tell him.

I sigh and sit back in my seat. Looking out the window at the changing face of the neighborhood on King Drive no longer interests me. I don't care to see the marquees of fast food chains that populate the blocks, or the shade tree mechanics and other signs of people barely keeping their heads above water. I'm no longer interested in the architectural changes of the homes and apartment buildings from Bronzville to this area without a name, on a street named after a King. The modest brick faced homes with obvious basements and extended porches, do nothing to move me from the heaviness in my chest.

I see why he always asks me to repeat myself.
Words matter.
He said it at breakfast, and I thought he was being dramatic. *Words matter.*

We get off the bus at Eighty-Seventh Street and stand at the stop in front of a federal credit union. I see homes and a gas station. The two lane traffic is steady and the buses passing are frequent. We get on another city bus, Kiyan pays and he directs me to the middle where we stand amongst the afternoon riders. There is a group of teens sitting in the back of the bus talking loudly, and showing each other whatever they're watching or messaging about on their phones.

"How much further do we have to go?" I ask.

"Why, are you uncomfortable?"

"No." I say. "I'm just asking a question."

"Not too far," he says. "We'll get off on Stoney and walk the rest of the way."

"And exactly how far are we walking?" I ask.

"Just a few blocks. Relax."

"It's hard to relax when I have to hold on for my life on these little handles."

"It could be worse," he says. "You could have nothing to hold on to."

I shrug my shoulders and tighten my grip as the bus lurches forward breezing by a street called Cottage Grove, where discount stores are a plenty from Rainbow to Target. The streets are narrower, the traffic more congested, and the energy of the people seems to be more intense. More urgent. They are living in insistence of having life and not on or in purpose. We pass an AM radio station and a light brown brick building with a purple sign that just says The Rink on the marquee. I see Payday Loan places, more liquor stores, grocery stores, subdivision type single story homes, and fast food restaurants, before we get to a massive intersection.

"This is our stop," Kiyan says, moving toward the accordion doors, even though he didn't signal the stop.

We get off at the corner with Walgreens on one side of us and Maxine's Clothing and Shoes on the other.

"C'mon," Kiyan says, grabbing my hand.

He puts me on the inside of him so I walk closest to Maxine's store front. He is possessive in the way he holds me, and I don't know if it's because I look foreign, or he's afraid for both of us. We pass a beauty supply store, beauty shops, a braid shop, and Thomas's Restaurant before turning down East End. Tucked behind the small businesses on the main thoroughfare of 87th Street is a quaint and quiet neighborhood of brick faced houses, cut grass, and cars parallel parked perfectly in front of each home.

On Ninetieth Street, three homes from the corner, Kiyan walks up the four steps of a home with red brick, and red and white awning, and rings the doorbell. The blinds are drawn in the three panel picture window, but I hear movement inside of the house. The large wooden door with an oval decoration in the center is pulled back and I am face-to-face with a medium sized brown woman with a thick long braid running down the middle of her head to her back.

"What are you doing here?"

Her voice is a shrieking cry, both excited and pissed off about being surprised.

"Hey, Ma," Kiyan says.

"And who the hell is this. I know you didn't bring company to my house and you don't even tell me that your narrow ass is in town."

"Hello, Ms. English," I say.

"Uh-uh, Baby," his mother says. "My name is Fontaine. I kept my own damn name."

"Well okay," I say putting on a smile. "Ms. Fontaine, my name is Naomi."

"That's a pretty name."

"Ma, are you going to let us in, or are you gon' make us stand out on the porch and talk to you through the door, like we the Jehovah's Witness."

"That's what happens when you come home unannounced and don't have your key."

"Because I'm not trying to get shot."

"You damn right. Your daddy gun around here somewhere."

"Ma, the door."

"Hold on, boy, don't rush me. I gotta go find my key."

Ms. Fontaine walks away from the storm door decorated with rectangles running in a two column pattern.

I say, "Your mom is funny."

"Oh, she's just getting started," he says.

"Anything I need to prepare myself for?" I ask.

"Not that I can think of."

"C'mon in here," Ms. Fontaine says, coming back to the door.

She puts the key in two separate locks and turns them loose before she can push the door open and welcome us in. We are immediately in the living room and I'm confronted by gray leather couches shiny from polish, but worn from dents made by years of behinds resting on the cushions. The walls are filled with family pictures. Ms. Fontaine and Mr. English are on the wall along with pictures of Kiyan, whom I recognize as a child. I smell food but I'm not sure what it is, and I am overwhelmed by emotion.

This is the first time I've been in a parent's house other than my mother's in a long time.

I never even met Aaron's parents.

Ugh.

Why can't I get him out of my mind?

Everything always comes back to him.

I know I'm holding the inside of my jaw between my teeth as Ms. Fontaine directs us to sit down on the sofa, beneath the pictures facing an upright baby grand piano.

"Do you play, Ms. Fontaine?" I ask, nodding toward the instrument.

"Naw. This is Dennis's piano. He tried to teach Kiyan how to play, but as I'm sure you've realized, the only thing this boy here care about is his damn pictures."

"I'm an artist, Ma," Kiyan says defending himself.

"And you'd be a more talented artist if you learned another art form," Ms. Fontaine says.

The words of her critique are harsh, but her tone is kind and loving. I can tell she was a strict mother. A no-nonsense mother. A mother who raised and indulged her children, and did not feel that one was mutually exclusive of the other. I look at her and see two dimples where Kiyan only received one. The indentations add a sweetness to her face she was probably never able to hide no matter how angry she became at her son. In a navy blue blouse with Peter Pan collar, dark tan slacks, and pink fuzzy house shoes, Ms. Fontaine is dressed for the day, whether she decides to go somewhere or not.

I like looking at her and seeing pieces of her son. I want to turn around and look at the picture of Dennis English, Kiyan's father, mounted on the wall but I don't. I imagine he is where Kiyan gets the cleft in his chin and the melodious sound of his laughter. I sit back against the couch and try to relax my excited nerves. My senses work overtime to dull my own knowledge of myself, in an effort to take in what I'm being offered about the man sitting beside me. I work to keep my face straight, pleasant, permanently smiling like the anchor I didn't study enough when I worked with her.

Maybe this is my mountaintop and Kiyan is the one who came with me to enjoy the view.

Then what is Aaron?

The guide I left along the way for one who would show me better.

So that you could be trash to him.

I berate myself as I comfort myself in the cushions, wanting to shrink from sight once again. I feel naked and exposed, as if they can see Aaron's handprints on my body beneath my clothes. Did Kiyan feel the indentations where Aaron's fingers pressed into my thigh, did he notice a space he had not touched with his length, that was explored by someone else manually, when he was inside. I feel like they can see the imprints of Aaron's lips left on my neck, and I try not to squirm. I try not to crumble under the gaze of a mother assessing the woman her son has brought home. A woman he says he thinks he might love.

I shouldn't be here.

Again, I want to run. I want to escape. I want to swim away to a space that is less claustrophobic than the living room. I want to bolt for the door, run down the steps, out to the street and back to the bus stop, to find my way downtown to the convention center complex, where the hallway walls hold the moans of my mistake with one man, and my attempt to make up with another.

This is wrong.

He doesn't deserve this.

And I don't deserve him, or to meet his mother.

From her perch on the piano stool, Ms. Fontaine says, "Kiyan's never brought a girl home before. He must really like you. I thought one day he was going to come out and say he was gay."

"Really, Ma?" Kiyan asks.

"Really, Kiyan. You're over thirty and the last girl I met was that lil' fast tail thing you was dating in high school. And you only took her to prom. I didn't hear hide nor hair about her before or after that weekend. I thought she was a pity date."

"Maybe I don't want to bring just anybody home, because they're not fit to meet you."

"Or you're afraid," I say, bringing myself to joke when nothing I feel is in jest.

"Ain't that the truth," Ms. Fontaine says laughing and slapping her leg. "Like I said, he must really like you, Naomi. The boy might even be in love, because he's *never* brought a girl home."

Why did she have to say that?

Kiyan laughs beside me, but it is not his usual musical sound and I can tell he didn't want his mother to find him out.

Maybe he told me because he knew she would tell him how he felt about me.

She is his mirror of truth and I'm lying to both of them.

I hear her voice and nothing else.

He must really like you.

Her words back up his verbalized thoughts. I feel exposed for the wrong reasons, though no one knows my secret.

I'm lying to both of them.

The truth crucifies me where I sit with my arms stretched against the couch. I die one thousand more deaths and it's still not enough to release me from my misery.

Part 4

The Aftermath

"On that independent shit.
Trade it all for a husband and some kids."
— "I Wonder," Kanye West

18.

We Should All be Feminists

Miserably. That's how I feel watching the package as it ends. My stomach is turning as it has been all day. As it has been all week. As it has insistently become less and less stable no matter the delicate foods I try to eat. Lettuce and it rumbles, crackers and it rumbles, broth and it rumbles. I am weak and hungry and in need of food that sustains, but the thought of anything beyond chicken broth from a bouillon cube, makes me want to hurl.

The mic clicks.

"Next on Naomi Tonight.

Should Cultural Appropriation be Criminal.

When we come back, we look at the obvious instances of style, and culture biting, and talk to sociology professor, Doctor Gayle C. Waters from the University of North Florida, about whether major companies should pay reparations for their theft of soul."

The mic clicks.

"You would wait until Boyce is out of town to do this story," Jennifer says in my ear.

"It's not like he can't see the segment from the NewsOn App, or watch it back from his DVR on his phone," I say.

"John, how much time is left in this break?" I ask.

"Two-fifteen," he says.

I hop down from my swiveling chair at the anchor desk and run on the tips of the toes of my shoes from the set, through the newsroom, and to the ladies' room. I enter the darkened dressing room and keep running until I'm in the empty bathroom. Bursting through the swinging doors of the middle stall, I hurl bile and the lining of my stomach into the toilet. The disgusting green acidic liquid flows out of my mouth, and drips down my chin into the porcelain bowl. I hold on to it and the cool chrome handle. The damp dankness of the toilet cools my body, despite the sweat beads on my forehead.

"Thirty seconds."

Diedre is in my ear. I flush the toilet and walk out of the stall to the sink. I wash my hands with the foaming soap, rinse, and then cup my hand to fill them with water. Swishing the city tap around my mouth, I rinse away the taste from my empty stomach. I rinse away evidence I tossed up the nothingness that was in me. Grabbing, rough hewn, paper towels from the automatic dispenser, I wipe my mouth and my brow as I run-walk back to the set.

I sit in the chair as John begins his countdown. Doctor Waters is already sitting beside me.

I wish I had some mints.

I wave at her with my hand as the open rolls.

The mic clicks.

"Welcome back to Naomi Tonight.

Doctor Gayle C. Waters is joining us from UNF to talk about whether cultural appropriation should be criminal.

Good evening."

"Good evening," Doctor Waters says.

I say, "Cultural appropriation is in the spotlight and this time it's over a Swahili phrase made globally popular by a 1994 children's movie. But the fight over who has rights to use "Hakuna Matata" is just scratching the surface of cultural appropriation."

The mic clicks and my voice-over package plays. On the screen flash images of Al Jolson's Jazz Singer beside the Nicholas Brothers, Bill Robinson, and Stepin' Fetchit. Elvis beside Chuck Berry. Madonna and Dorothy Dandridge and Lena Horne. The music shifts and changes as the video in the package goes through a time lapse to present day, and the viewer sees Azelia Banks beside Iggy Azalea, Bruno Mars beside Michael Jackson, celebrities from the Met Gala beside priests and nuns, models walking a runway in an elastic string bikini beside women on the beach in Brazil in similarly fashioned wares, and scenes from The Lion King—the cartoon, and the live action trailer—beside images from Africa. The package ends with the side by side of a lion roaring. One of a lion in the wild taken from a documentary, and the other of Simba.

"Doctor Waters," I say, "these instances of cultural appropriation have been happening for centuries. The question is, in some instances should they be criminalized?"

"I think criminalization is a bit harsh. As the famous teacher has taught us, 'What has been will be again, what has been done will be done again; there is nothing new under the sun.'"

"And what teacher is that?" I ask.

"Ecclesiastes," Doctor Waters says.

She says, "All of us in some way are stealing what we do, the way we act, the words we say, how we dress, and even the way we worship from a culture that may not have innately belonged to us . . ."

I try to listen as Doctor Waters talks, but I can't focus. I see her in parts. Her mouth moves, her hands gesticulate, the pitch of her voice rises and falls, the arch of her eyebrows rise and fall, the lines of her face crease, wrinkle and smooth out, depending on her point. I see her in the bits of her body, and I am more drawn to look at her shape than her face. I focus in on the apparent smoothness at her belly and I can tell she's wearing a body shaper. Nothing about her is small, but she is pulled, snatched, and tucked into her fitted black pants suit with wide-legged trousers, and a jacket that skims the curve of her obliques, and flares away from her behind. Hers is the shape of a woman who has birthed babies and lived long enough to see them grow. I look at her body and I wonder what sacrifices she made. I see the emptiness of her ring finger and I wonder if she did it all alone, or if she just doesn't like to wear jewelry. I don't give her a life of my own conjuring because I have too many questions about what she's presenting in herself in front of me, and none of what she's talking about.

"Thirty seconds," Diedre says.

"Are you going to ask another question, or are you going to let her keep going like it's her show?"

The question is from Jennifer. I smile with my mouth instead of rolling my eyes, since I'm still on camera.

"Doctor Waters," I say interrupting. "If cultural appropriation is not criminal and we all acknowledge that it happens, then what can we do as people to preserve the arbiters of culture and appreciate their contributions, without being accused of biting, when perhaps we were inspired?"

"There are two things we can do," Doctor Water says. "We can pay tribute to wherever our culturally appropriated inspiration came from and we can also learn the history behind what we are attracted to."

"But most importantly pay tribute," I say. "Thank you, Doctor Waters, for joining us. I'm Naomi Grace, thank you for watching "Naomi Tonight," on Nine News Now, Linden and Hillary will be back for Nine News Now at Eleven."

The mic clicks and I slump over onto the glass desk.

"Are you alright?" Doctor Waters asks.

"I've been better," I say.

"I can tell," she says. "Your eyes are really glassy, and your skin is looking sallow."

"Just a stomach bug," I say. "Let me walk you to the door."

I sit up in the chair and then step down. I wobble and grab for the desk to regain my balance.

"Wooh, I'm worse off than I thought."

"I can find my way out," Doctor Waters says.

"I don't mind walking you. I feel bad enough I wasn't able to greet you when you came in."

Doctor Waters nods as I take the lead in escorting her through the newsroom, down the hallway, and toward the lobby where she can exit to go into the parking lot. I keep a pace that is a step ahead of hers until we reach the wooden door to the empty lobby. It takes all my strength to push against it. I lean against its sturdiness until she passes through.

"Thank you for coming," I say.

"The pleasure was all mine."

I smile.

She smiles.

I don't move. She has exited the sliding lobby doors and I'm still leaning against the wooden door I opened for her.

You should've let her leave on her own instead of trying to prove something to somebody who doesn't know you.

I don't listen to my inner critic long. The urgency of my rumbling stomach lurches me away from the door, down the hallway and back into the bathroom. Through the dressing room, the door, the stall, I empty. There is nothing left in me. What stares back at me from the toilet is clear liquid and balls of yellow mucus. I hold the handle and the bowl. Cool. Damp. Dank. The cold bacteria filled condensation on my hands is the only thing that settles the flips of my belly. I dry heave what's not there until the rest of my body calms in response. Only then do I yank the handle.

Only when I have nothing left to give do I straighten my back, smooth my dress and, make my way over to the sink. I look in the mirror as I wash my hands. My eyes are tired, my skin is sallow, despite my makeup; most of which has been washed off from the rinsing of my mouth, and the drying of my face with the brown paper towels.

In the outer dressing room, I turn on the lights. The makeup lights around the long mirror flicker and then illuminate, forcing my eyes to squint as they adjust to the brightness. In these mirrors I look at my body. In a navy blue wrap dress I bought from Target, I look at myself and see nothing different. My weight is more or less the same. The sit of my breasts and behind are perky, but not overly plump. I don't see what I think I should. I don't see what I think is there.

Because you don't know.

I would know.

I turn off the lights and stride back into the newsroom, and head for my office instead of the set. John is waiting for me.

"You need something?" I ask, closing the door behind me.

"We need to record the promos for tomorrow," he says in a gentle voice.

"Shit, I forgot."

"I figured," Johns says.

"Have Jennifer or Diedre email me the scripts and I will voice them at home and email in my track."

"Okay," John says standing up.

He waits by the door looking at me. In his alabaster face with tints of pink, I see concern forming in his light brown eyes. He has never been a talkative man for the years I've worked with him. He's always given direction, manned the cameras, and maintained the studio. The most we've ever spoken, was over the course of his wife's pregnancy. Now in my office I see words running on the inside of his mind, wanting to spill out of his mouth, but he doesn't say anything.

"Anything else?" I ask.

"Your microphone," John says.

"Oh," I say. "I'm so used to having this thing on, I completely forgot about it."

I unstrap the battery pack from my calf brace and remove the clip of the mic from the neckline of my dress. The cord scrapes down my chest and stomach as I pull it loose from my body. The slight friction sends another dry heave from my stomach and I am forced over to grip the desk.

"Here," I screech as I suck the emptiness of my belly back down. "Take it."

"I'll tell Diedre to get you some water."

I nod my head and wave behind me. Using my hands, I inch my way around my desk to my chair and collapse. The seat receives me, and I recline as much as I can against the mesh back. The seat spins on its own under my weight, and my head and stomach whirls with it.

This is not happening.

This is not happening.

This is not happening.

"Naomi, are you alright?" Diedre asks, knocking on my door.

I want to spin around to face her, but I don't. I am afraid of what my face looks like. I am afraid my body will betray me. I am afraid.

"I'm good," I say. "Just leave the water on my desk. I told John I will voice the promos from home and email my track into promotions later."

"Okay."

"Have Jennifer email me the scripts."

"Okay."

Diedre leaves my office after setting the water on my desk and I'm grateful. I'm grateful she came to check on me instead of Jennifer. I'm grateful her lack of knowledge of the business, of life, and her unsharpened journalistic intuition didn't send her down a road of twenty-one questions to poke and prod me until she got a response from me. That is what Jennifer would have done. That is what Jennifer is going to do. I am unprepared and afraid of the coming inquisition. It will be Jennifer Carrollton versus Naomi Grace. Jennifer for the people, for truth, for her own warped sense of justice against my preservation of privacy.

I want to shake my head, but I don't.

Don't make any sudden movements.

It's too many people in the newsroom who can see you through this fish bowl.

I listen to my own internal, protective compass, and use my feet to turn me around. Step by step I work my way around until I can hold on to the edge of my desk and turn myself straight. A plastic cup of water from the break room is facing me, along with the eyes of Jennifer, Diedre, Linden, Hillary, and the eleven o'clock producer.

I half smile as I pick up the water. I ingest it in slow sips, watching them, watching me. I know their looks are both a mix of concern and wonder.

What's wrong with Naomi?

Is she okay?

Why'd she run through the newsroom in the middle of her show?

You know she barely made it back to the set for the last segment?

Is she okay?

I know the dialogue going on about me. I sip my water and wait to see if any of them will come ask me to my face. Not that I want to answer. Diedre's gotten all the answers she will get out of me. It's only on Jennifer.

We're going to do this at some point.

I sigh to myself as I lean back against the chair. The water is gone, and my stomach is only somewhat settled.

How long before I throw up water is the real question.
I need to leave so I don't do that here.

I want to get up, but my body begs for rest. I listen. Closing my eyes, resting my head against the back of the chair, I listen to my heart rate slowing and my steady breath, and try to invite peace into my body and the air around me. With my eyes closed I pretend I'm in my vision room and not in my office. I pretend the four walls around me are solid and not glass, and that the energy in the space is one I've curated for my own well-being. I relax against my chair and pretend the six eyes of my M.O.M. are watching over me. Two teen moms and a first lady who's opened up about the game of chance of her own fertility. I imagine their all-knowing faces and I hear their voices as one, saying, "And this too shall pass."

And this too shall pass.
Whatever it is.

I open my eyes to my nosy coworkers and see they are no longer looking at me, at least from what I can tell. I stand up slowly and walk over to the mirror. Sitting on the edge of my desk facing myself, I take off my wig and work my fingers through my locs. I leave the hair hat on the Styrofoam mannequin wig head I bought, and hand toss my locs until they all fall into place.

It's now or never.

Pushing my body off of my desk, I grab my purse from where it hangs on my coat stand, hit the lights and leave my office. My purse is my shield as I walk through the newsroom. I take the perimeter, walking the outskirts, avoiding the inner empty desks, avoiding Diedre, avoiding Jennifer.

"Goodnight," I say as I pass by their general area.

"Where are you going?" Jennifer asks.

"Home." I pull the rectangular purse across my body and cover my belly.

"I was going to ask if you wanted to go out with us," Jennifer says, motioning between herself and Diedre.

Not really.

"I'm tired. I don't want to hang out down here, and then still have to go home later."

"What if we go somewhere south?"

"I still have to stop before I get home."

"C'mon, Naomi," Diedre says. "You probably just need to eat."

Hardly.

"I have a salad at home."

"That's not real food," Diedre says.

I look at them and know they are unwilling to take "no" for an answer. Diedre, with her fantasy hair in shades of blue, green, and purple, is insistent in her plead, and Jennifer waits for me to give in. Her lengthening twist out is perfectly framed around her face where a new pair of thin, rimmed glasses, sit on her nose. She stares me down through them, daring me to make a wrong move, give a wrong answer, so she can swoop down on me and pick me apart like prey.

"Kiyan is coming over," I say, trying another excuse.

"Doesn't he have a key?" Jennifer asks. "Tell him you'll be home later."

"He doesn't have a key."

"You can still tell him to come later," Diedre says.

Ugh.

"I'll hang out for a little bit," I say. "Where are we going?"

"Moxie," Jennifer says.

I nod and resume my walk. I hear their, "wait for us," behind me but I keep walking. I don't want to go. I'm not drinking. I text Kiyan in the car to come later, and then pull out of the lot into the late evening traffic.

The drive to the Southside, to Town Center is a blur. My windows are up, the radio is off, and the only sound keeping me going is the timing of my breath and my heartbeat. I grasp for the edges of serenity I found in my office as I navigate the congestion at the massive outdoor mall until I find a parking space near the door of the trendy, local restaurant. Reclining my driver's seat, the peace of my stillness returns to me. Heartbeat and breath. They are the only things I hear.

Laying down in the car I close my eyes and wait to see what my mind conjures up. It is Ms. Fontaine. Kiyan's mother. I see her face as it was during my one visit in her home. She, like all parents meeting the significant other of a child, grilled me in her own motherly way. Where are you from? What do you do? Where did you meet? What do you want? Do you want to get married? Do you want to have children? What's important to you? Who are your parents? How are they doing?

Ms. Fontaine asked me question after question until she felt like she knew me. I answered them all as I honestly as I could. The ones I didn't know the answers to, I pretended I did.

Do you want to get married?

Do you want to have children?

I hear her voice and the questions of my own that I didn't answer in the moment.

Marriage and children. Why are those the parameters under which I must live my life? Why are those goals of marriage and family weighed just as equally as goals of career advancement and generational wealth?

Because all some people know is family.

Family holds you down when money can't.

I see Jennifer and Diedre bopping toward my car. I beat them out before they get to me and join them to cross the parking lot and enter the restaurant.

"Good evening and welcome to Moxie," the hostess says.

"Hey," Jennifer and Diedre say.

I say, "Hi. If it's not too much trouble, can we sit upstairs?"

"Sure," she says. "Go on up."

We take the wooden and steel stairs to the second floor that opens onto a patio and outdoor bar area. I grip the banister as I walk, trying to keep a normal pace, and not show that I'm struggling. I exert effort and energy I don't have, to avoid having a conversation I don't want to engage in.

"Let's grab a booth," Diedre says at the top of the stairs.

We walk even further into the upstairs area and take a booth beneath a window. I sit on one side and Diedre and Jennifer take the other. One's face is bright and the other is hawkish. I sit up straight against the thick cushion, even though I want to lay my head against the wall.

Why do I do the things people want me to do, instead of what I want to do?

I question myself and my motivations. It is my own version of the assessment both Kiyan and Aaron made of me. For one, I was not enough of who he needed me to be, the kind of woman he thought he ought to be with. For the other, I am not enough of who he thinks I want to be, the kind of woman he ought to be with. I write both of them off as selfish for summing me up in terms of what they need and what they want in their lives.

That's what people do.

They want you to fit into their lives without concern of how that affects you, or how they fit into your own life.

"Good evening ladies, my name is Gwen; I'll be your server for tonight. Can I start you off with anything?"

"I'll have the 'Comethru,'" Jennifer says without looking at the drink menu.

"Same," Diedre says.

"And for you?" Gwen asks me.

"Club soda," I say. "With lemon."

"I'll get your drinks started for you."

Gwen walks away from the table without question. She leaves me with the wondering eyes of Jennifer and Diedre. My drink choice, a non-alcoholic beverage, my behavior from earlier, and my reluctance to come out gives them more queries for my eventual interrogation.

"What?" I ask.

"What's going on with you?" Diedre asks.

"Nothing," I say. "I told you I was tired earlier. I don't need to be tired and tipsy."

Jennifer nods. "Are you sure it's just you being tired?"

"Pretty much," I say. "I keep late nights and early mornings."

I try to smile to bring some levity to the conversation before it goes left, but I don't have it in me to fake. I don't have anything in me. Literally nothing. It's all been washed down a drain to be turned into city punch that will eventually come out of my faucet.

"Is your stomach okay?" Diedre asks. "We heard you throwing up in the bathroom."

"You heard that?" I ask.

"Everybody in the control room and on the floor heard you puking your guts," Jennifer says. "You didn't turn your mic off."

"I didn't really have time, now did I?"

"So, what's going on with you, Naomi?" Jennifer asks.

"I don't know," I say. "My stomach's been upset today. It's either a stomach flu, some random bug, or . . . I don't know. It'll pass."

Jennifer nods.

Diedre says, "You better tell Kiyan he's playing nurse tonight."

I see Jennifer roll her eyes. I say, "I'll tell him. All I have the energy for is to lay down."

"Mmhmm," Jennifer says.

"What's with the look and the faces? You've been looking at me sideways since the show ended."

"What are you talking about?"

"The fish bowl works both ways."

"I guess it does." Jennifer says.

Here we go.

"Say what you have to say," I say loudly, exerting what energy I have.

"I don't have to say anything. You know you're not sick. At least not the type that'll pass in a day or two kind of way."

"How do you know she's not sick?" Diedre asks.

"Because she's not," Jennifer says. "Look at her. Most people who vomit for their life don't look all radiant when they finish. She got back on set glowing."

"It's called makeup," I say.

"Ain't that much makeup in the world," Jennifer says. "She knows why she's sick."

"I don't know, shit," I say. "And when and if I do, I won't be telling you."

"Who will you tell?" Jennifer asks. "Kiyan or Aaron."

"Huh?" Diedre asks.

Another ringing bell I don't answer. Jennifer's known me longer than Diedre. She befriended me first. Got close to me first. She was in Kelly's shadow and I was in Dawn's. The associate producer and the reporter, both of us waiting in the wings for a turn in the spotlight. Dawn left, took Kelly with her, and suddenly we got our chance. By then I had already told her all of my business, confided in her about my background, first professionally and then personally. She did the same with me. She knows my secrets and I know hers. Only now she has found her way inside my emotional graveyard and she is rooting around and digging for bones.

She stares me down, talking to me and accusing me with her eyes. I keep my face blank and wait. I wait for Gwen to come back with our drinks. I wait for Diedre to figure out what Jennifer's alluding to. I wait for the Earth to swallow me whole. I wait for whatever is to come next, without the energy, or even the will to fight back.

"I feel like y'all are having a whole 'nother conversation without me," Diedre says.

"Because we are," I say.

"About what?" Diedre asks.

"About the fact Naomi cheated on Kiyan with Aaron at the conference, and now she's pregnant," Jennifer says.

"Well, damn," Diedre says. "I guess it's true what they say. Cheater's never win."

"That's fucked up," I say.

"But it's true," Jennifer says.

"You don't know whether it's true or not," I snap. "All you have are a bunch of assumptions and no proof or evidence."

"I know if we go to the CVS and get a pregnancy test, once you pee on the stick, that will be all the evidence you need."

"But guess what? I'm not peeing on shit."

"Why did you cheat on Kiyan?" Diedre asks.

"Do I need a reason?" I ask. "It happened."

"But why? I thought you really liked Kiyan. And he seems to really like you. He even took you to meet his mom."

"I met his mom after it had already happened."

"It shouldn't have ever happened," Jennifer says.

"Thank you, Mrs. Morality," I say. "Next time I get ready to fuck somebody, I'll make sure I find you first to get your approval."

"Don't snap at me because of your dirt," Jennifer says.

"But didn't Kiyan come the next day of the conference after you saw Aaron?" Diedre asks.

"He did," I say.

"Ooh, Naomi . . ." Diedre says.

I watch her big eyes bounce back and forth as she puts together what Jennifer figured out the night I saw them standing outside my room, banging on my door, waiting for me to emerge. She connects the dots between my backless dress, my barefoot walk of shame down the hallway, Jennifer's comment that Dawn saw me at her mixer, and my rush inside my room slamming the door in their faces. She puts it all together and looks at me with a mix of horror and empathy.

"Why?" Diedre ekes out.

"Because shit happens," I say. "By the time I realized what I was doing, I was already doing it. I stopped. I left. Aaron didn't come, but it happened."

"He didn't have to come for you to get pregnant. That pre-cum shit is potent, too," Jennifer says.

"And then you saw Kiyan the next day?" Diedre asks the question we all already know the answer to.

"Yup," Jennifer says. "And she did him too."

"Don't jump down my throat like men haven't been doing this shit for years," I say. "Dudes will fuck three chicks in the same day and go home to a wife, like they haven't been out in the street doing everybody dirty."

"Not all men," Diedre says.

"We're not even talking about all men," Jennifer says. "We're talking about you and what you did and what you didn't do, and what you clearly didn't use."

"Are you enjoying this?" I ask. "You've been waiting to have this conversation for what . . . two months now?"

"I haven't been waiting to have shit," Jennifer says. "You're the one out here raw-dogging two men within twenty-four hours, like dicks are always clean and diseases don't exist."

"You sound like you were there. I didn't know I had a cuckold in the room."

"I didn't have to be there to know that's what happened if you're pregnant, and don't know who the daddy is."

"But Naomi, why weren't you on birth control?" Diedre asks.

"Because before Kiyan, I wasn't having regular sex. Run-ins with Matt were condom only rendezvous," I say. "And it's been like that with Kiyan . . ."

"Until now," Jennifer snickers. "And now you're pregnant by one of two men you slept with in less than twenty-four hours."

"First of all, we don't know that I'm pregnant. Secondly, who the father is doesn't matter, because if I am pregnant, I'm not keeping it."

"So, you're not going to even tell them they could have a seed before terminating it?" Diedre asks.

"Right now, it's not a seed. I don't know what it is."

"It's a life."

"Ugh. Please don't tell me you're one of those."

"One of what? Someone who believes in the sanctity of life. Someone who believes little babies should have a chance no matter the circumstances."

"No matter the circumstances?" Jennifer questions. "What about rape, incest, the life of the mother, birth defects . . . hell, choice?"

"There can be exceptions, but at this point, we all know Naomi made her choice," Diedre says. "There's nothing wrong with her or her baby—that we know of—she's just being selfish."

They talk about me like I'm not even at the table.

"Oh, so now I'm selfish because I'm choosing early not to have a whole baby, and make a mistake out of their entire life. That shit is selfish to you?"

I've barely even thought about my next steps. My next moves. My next phone call. Yet here we are getting into a deep argument about philosophical and moral differences that won't be assuaged over dinner and drinks. My head pounds as Diedre and Jennifer continue to the conversation without me. Their words bounce off of me, forgoing comprehension, and instead, hover above me in disparate snippets as I focus on the spreading pain around my temples.

"I'm just saying, Naomi's stable enough to have a baby and raise it well," Diedre argues. She doesn't need to have an abortion."

"Is that what you people believe?" Jennifer asks. "That this is about need."

"What else is it about if it's not a necessity?"

"It's about autonomy over one's own body. It's about access and equal rights. It's about the separation of all the shit the founding fathers said was supposed to be separated. The Constitution is three pages for a reason. Those old racist bastards in their profound wisdom knew the government didn't need to be getting into shit that didn't have shit to do with them."

"All I'm saying is, Naomi doesn't have to abort. Even if she doesn't keep the baby, she could give it up for adoption. There are hundreds, thousands of families I'm sure that are trying to have kids and can't. And you just want to scrape yours away."

"Umm, last time I checked, there are dozens of kids in the system that aren't being adopted because most families don't want little brown babies and all the drama they bring by the fact of their existence."

"It still doesn't give her the right to delete the baby without even consulting the father."

"It's not their concern," I say, rejoining the conversation. "I know Aaron doesn't care and Kiyan doesn't need to know. We're not there yet."

I think I may love you.

Kiyan's one and only admission comes back to me as soon as I tell the lie that we are less than what we are. I ignore the sentiment he's said once and only once, and revel in the fact that I finally have the last word. For now, at least. In this victory I can focus on my headache, and not their argument that's been hashed and rehashed since before they were born.

Neither Jennifer nor Diedre say anything to me in reponse. I am grateful. I don't want their cosigns or their criticisms. I don't want support or censure dating back to 1973. I just want to go home and get in my bed.

I should tell Kiyan not to come.

But that might start an argument and I'm not in the mood for that either.

"Did you tell your mom?" Diedre asks.

"Why would I do that?"

"Because she could help you. At least talk and think through it with you."

"She's never done that for me in my whole life, I don't know why you think she would start now."

"Here you are, ladies," Gwen says, approaching our table with our drinks. We watch her set each liquid spilling glass on the table in stony silence. She says, "Can I get some appetizers started for you?"

"None for me," I say. "I'm not staying."

Gwen looks from me to Jennifer and Diedre.

"Give us a sec," Diedre says.

Ever the diplomat. Ever acquiescent, except apparently when it comes to the subject of abortion, Diedre interrupts the tense mood of our trio with her lightness. Gwen walks away from the table and I envy her. I stand up.

"Naomi, don't go," Diedre says, grabbing for my hand across the table.

"Why should I stay?"

"So we can talk this out," Jennifer says.

"Now y'all want to talk to me?" I grab my purse. "There's nothing to talk about. There's no Kumbaya, come to Jesus way out of this, and I don't even know what this is."

"Are you going to tell Kiyan?" Jennifer asks.

"Tell him what?"

"Anything?"

"Why would I do that?"

"Because he deserves to know."

"Why? Why does he deserve to know? What does he deserve to know?"

"Everything."

"We're not even there yet."

I think I may love you.

I continue, "We're dating. I like him. He likes me. We've never had a conversation about exclusivity, or what we're doing."

"Who does that over thirty?" Jennifer asks. "If you're grown and you're going out and not seeing anybody else, then you're together and that's your person. You don't need a big production and conversation."

"That's you," I say. "I like grand gestures and expensive overtures."

"That's why you're in this situation now," Jennifer says.

"And that's why I'm leaving."

"Naomi," Diedre whines, "Please consider the alternatives."

"For what? I should be happy I still have choices. The heartbeat bill didn't pass here, but with the way shit looks in Georgia and Alabama, I don't know how long Florida can hold out."

"So are you just going to drag your feet until you figure out what you want to do, and kill the baby after it's already been born?"

"The fuck?"

"Like the laws passed in Virginia and New York."

"You need to read more," Jennifer says.

"I read," Diedre says.

"Not reputable newspapers or websites you don't. Hell, try reading the bill before you start spouting hyperbolic talking points."

Diedre rolls her eyes. "Then enlighten me."

"I mean, you can't just get a third-trimester abortion because you want one. A doctor must still certify that you're facing death to do it."

"This isn't helping!" I yell before Diedre can begin her retort.

I lower my eyes and shake my head at the floor. I'm the one who might be pregnant and they're arguing over what won't even be their responsibility. If I'm pregnant and keep the baby, they won't be the ones helping me to pay for it. If I'm pregnant and don't keep the baby, they won't be the ones feeling what I feel because of what I did, if I even feel anything.

I can't feel no more guilt and regret than I do right now.
Can I?

"Like I said. I'm leaving. This isn't helping."

"Naomi," Diedre whines my name again.

"Naomi nothing," I say. "Talking to you won't help. Talking to my mom won't help. And telling Kiyan does nothing but relieve my guilt and make him feel like I ain't shit."

Because you ain't shit.

I walk away from the table berating myself, stomach rumbling, head banging, and thoughts spinning, trying to imagine what I could have never planned or predicted. I cross the parking lot beneath the black sky, get in my car and just breathe.

If I am pregnant, I'm not keeping it.

My own words come back to me. I said it just to get them off my back, but it came out of me with a conviction I didn't know I had, about something I don't even know is real.

I remember Tarren. Her late night confession that she'd always wanted a child. The longing in her voice when she said it, the happiness on her face at her baby shower, and in the videos she posts on the station website about her journey and the new babies, are palpable. I drive away from Town Center knowing I don't have that longing.

I don't think I've ever wanted kids.

What about Aaron?

I wanted Aaron.

I would have had children for Aaron.

In the traffic on I-95, I drive, thinking back to the relationship that was supposed to produce marriage and maybe a reluctant baby. The relationship that provided for me what my immediate family didn't, and what my extended family couldn't. Aaron was understanding and simplicity, until I proved to be for him complications and stagnation; a wrench thrown in his dreams, a full stop on his goals. He left to climb Everest and forced me to summit a mountain on my own.

Who is this?

My mother's name alights on the navigation screen as the phone rings through the car interface.

Speak of the devil and she will call.

"Hello," I say.

"Hey, what are you doing?" She asks.

"I'm driving?"

"Driving where? Shouldn't you be home by now?"

"I stopped with some friends after the show. Now I'm going home. Did you need something?"

"Why do you think I need something from you every time I call?"

"I didn't say that. But you called for a reason."

"I haven't talked to you in weeks, Naomi. I called to see how you're doing."

"I'm good," I say, letting my defenses down.

"You don't sound good."

I don't need you to doctor therapist me.

"But I am. I'm tired, and I've got a little stomach bug, but I'll be fine."

"Are you sure you're not pregnant?"

"Why is everybody assuming I'm pregnant?"

It is only after my exasperation that I hear my mother's laughter. It subsides quickly after she realizes what I've said. Silence descends between the line of our communication. Her gums smack before she speaks.

She says, "What do you mean everybody is assuming you're pregnant?"

"Nothing," I say.

"It must be something. I was just joking with you."

"Me too."

"Naomi, what's going on?"

"Nothing," I told you. "I'm tired and I don't feel good. I'll be alright."

"Naomi, are your pregnant?"

It is a legitimate question. Her voice goes higher in the end. I wish I could see her face. I wish I could see if her concern was genuine or baiting; if she's using her gentle therapist voice with me to get me to reveal something I don't want her to know, so she can judge me later. It's what she does. It's what she's always done. With my brother and I, she would lure us in with her voice, get us to trust that she was a friend and not just our mother, and once we told her whatever it was we were holding back, she beat us for it, either with her words or with a belt. Her job as a therapist was and is purely occupational, not applied to her daily life outside of her office.

She operates well in silence. In her profession, it makes her clients uncomfortable until they have no choice but to state the reason they're on her couch. At home it made us want to retreat, because we knew her silences meant something, and we never wanted to find out. Now, I'm neither under her roof or on her couch, and the silence is still getting to me. She waits for an answer and she will respond in kind, but my answer is the crux of the course of the rest of the conversation.

"I don't know," I answer honestly.

"Then maybe you should find out," she says.

Her suggestion is solemn, but I'm still unsure of her motives. I say, "And what if I am?"

"Then you're pregnant, Naomi. You're in a relationship. You're grown. And I want grand-babies."

Her chuckle is both freeing and constricting at the same time. I am free from her criticism about being irresponsible, technically single, and pregnant, and yet I'm constrained by her admission that she wants grandchildren when I don't know that I want a child.

"We'll see," I say. "I gotta go. I just got home."

"That don't mean you gotta get off the phone," she says.

"No, but Kiyan is coming over and I want to have some peace before he gets here."

"Then maybe you should tell him to stay home and you'll have all the peace you need."

"Goodbye."

She chuckles. "If he stayed home more often, you probably wouldn't think you were pregnant either."

It's the last thing I hear before I hang up the phone. Her words cut, even when masked in laughter. Her words always cut. Even when she's genuinely concerned or caring, she always goes back to who she is, instead of maintaining the front of who she's trained herself to be.

I turn off the car, close the garage and go inside my empty town house. I move in the dark, dropping my purse beside my sofa, and taking the stairs to the second floor. I bypass my vision room and head straight to my own. In my closet I take off my shoes, unwrap my dress, and lay on the floor beside my rack of rented clothes that barely fit. One hand on my belly, one hand on my chest, I feel softness and tenderness. The early signs of pregnancy; hardening breasts, and loosening abs.

Fuck.

In the darkness, I stare at the ceiling I can't see. My mind rolls around all the things I never knew until I had to learn them for myself, all the tests I had to take in life before I ever learned the lesson. Now I face another. One that can only be confirmed by a test.

I've never even thought about kids. Tarren's babies are cute, but it doesn't give me womb fever like everybody else. They're just cute babies. I can't even see myself with a kid. Especially not if it's Aaron's. Kiyan would be a better dad. He's more patient. More understanding.

But he's not that damn understanding.

Ugh. One mistake and it won't go away, not unless I make it go away.

He deserves to know.

Jennifer's words come back to me as I get up off the floor. I leave my closet, my bathroom, my bedroom, to answer another call, another beckon, another person ready to take up some of my time, my space, my energy. The doorbell rings again when I'm on the stairs, and again as I approach the front door. I turn the lock and open it as Kiyan presses the bell for a fifth time.

"I was coming," I say.

"You were taking too long," he says. "Why is it so dark in here?"

"Because I didn't turn on the lights?"

"What's wrong with you? You on your period or something?"

If only you knew. "I'm good. Just tired. It's been a long day."

"Then why didn't you come straight home instead of going out with Jennifer and Diedre."

I shrug my shoulders, not wanting to make an excuse and not wanting to rehash the conversation.

"Look," he says.

He is standing in the kitchen when the lights come on. He holds a painted canvas in his hands over his face. The background is yellow and the picture itself is the head and body of a naked woman, her back to the audience, her head stretched to one side touching her shoulder, tiny sister locs hang down her back and away from her face. I'm looking at myself captured the way I stretch my neck in the morning, before I get out of bed. It is me in the abstract. I've been painted in an assortment of colors. The red, blue, and black lines that I saw in the picture he posted are before me in real life, in the expanse of my back.

"It's beautiful," I say.

He pulls the canvas down and I can see his face. He is smiling and I see the boy man that thinks he's in love, and I feel sick. I rewrap the dress I didn't fully take off and hold my hands in fists in front of my stomach. I resist the urge to wretch or pound on the side of my head as I look at his pride in my appreciation.

He says, "I thought you could use some more art on your walls."

"Where do you think I should put it?" I ask.

"You can put it on that wall going up the stairs," he says pointing.

"What do you call it?" I ask.

"Naomi Tonight," he says.

"Stop playing."

"I'm not playing," he says.

"Then you've got to call it something else. Give it a fancy name like the other one."

The first painting of me he did is framed above my bed. Its name is literal but sounds better. "Naked a Noire."

"Okay, what about "Night and Joy?" Kiyan suggests.

"I like that."

"Good."

"Was that the real name the whole time?"

His sheepish grin starts in the corner of his mouth and creeps across his face. I shake my head and start upstairs. My dress falls away from by body and blows behind me like an open robe. I hear him set the painting against the wall beneath the stairs, the light turns off, and I hear his feet behind me. He follows me in the darkness into my bedroom.

"Are you alright?" he asks.

"I'm tired and I don't feel well," I say.

I throw pillows off of the bed, pull the covers back and get in. I am being ungrateful and unappreciative. When I thought he was mad he was painting. When I thought he was ghosting me, he was channeling whatever he felt into a representation of me. When I was with Aaron, reliving the past to remember we have no present or future, Kiyan was using the tools of his love language to express himself with acrylic on canvas. I lay down and curl myself in a ball, wanting him to touch me, but knowing I don't deserve it. Knowing he doesn't deserve this. Jennifer and Diedre's words ring true.

"Come here," he says, laying down beside me.

His arms are around me before I can stop him. His cheek is against my cheek before I can protest. His loose, thick locs mesh with my tiny strands before I can say no.

"You need to rest," he says against my skin.

I nod my head yes and relax in his arms, as his rough fingers hold on to my softening stomach. He pinches my weight appreciatively and I brace myself against him. I wait for my body to react negatively and send me rushing in the bathroom to regurgitate my spit, until he wonders why I'm sick and becomes a tenor in the chorus to ask the question, "Are you pregnant?"

My stomach doesn't flip. Bile doesn't rise in my mouth. My body is settled. I settle. Into his arms I settle myself as he caresses my stomach and lays in my hair. I close my eyes, but my mind doesn't sleep. It races with thoughts, snippets of conversation, bits of information, line after line of texts, messages, inferences, and assumptions until it too settles on one:

> *If this is true, I hope he's the daddy.*

19.

The Truth Shall Set You Free

My stomach rumbles and I am awake. It flips again and I launch out of Kiyan's arms, out of the bed, and run into the bathroom. I slide to the floor as I lift the seat and wretch into the toilet. More bile spews out of my mouth. The sips of water Diedre got me, the sips of club soda from Moxie, and spit; all that was left in me comes out. I hold the cool porcelain, feel the condensation on my skin, and my body bubbles with air and forces my head into the open ass sink. There is nothing more left. Nothing left but the only explanation for the man who stands in the doorway watching me. I see his feet in his patient stance. Flushing the toilet, I set the toilet seat back down and slide across the floor until my back is against the wall. The wrap dress I slept in is open. My stomach rises and falls, and I see a pudge trying to work its way up and over my underwear. The same with my bra. The fatty tissue spills from the cup nearly revealing my nipple. I look at my body and try to imagine myself bigger than I am, with life, and I can't. I can't see into a future I never fathomed that would force itself to become apart of my life.

"What's going on here?" Kiyan asks.

"I told you last night I didn't feel well."

"This looks like more than not feeling well," he says.

I can't do this right now.

"Help me up, please," I say reaching my hand out to him.

He comes over to me and pulls me to my feet. I mumble my thanks as I shuffle by him and turn on the faucet. I busy myself rinsing my mouth and brushing my teeth, knowing the sound of the running water will drown out the conversation, or at the very least, limit my ability to answer.

"Good morning," I say when I'm done.

I don't give him a chance to give the greeting back. I leave out of the bathroom and bedroom, walk down the hall and go into my vision room. I lock the door behind me and lean against it. Face-to-face with M.O.M., I wonder how they felt the first time they suspected they were pregnant. I wonder how they felt the moment their suspicions were confirmed. Their smiling faces look back at me with secrets only spoken of in books, and talks held by those whose job it is to discuss the world. I see them. I turn around and look at myself in the mirror and see the imprint of my body. I see the painting Kiyan gifted me. The painting he created after our first argument, before he said his sentiments of how he felt about me out loud, after I let my petty anger, and my frustration at his less than enthusiastic acceptance for me ruin my mood, and leave me vulnerable and wanting something neither he nor Aaron could give me.

I look at me and hang my head in disgust at my own visage, resentful of the fact I'm not even living up to my own vision. The three boards hang behind me with the manifested promises of what I thought I was working toward, of what I thought I wanted my life to be. In the mirror, my face and my body tell a different story. One I can accept or change, no matter the consequences of the rejection from the man on the other side of the door, or the one hundreds of miles away.

I turn the handle of the door and leave the room of outdated dreams and head back to the bedroom. Kiyan is sitting in his boxers on the bed bench I stuck beneath the window. The fluffy and furry decorative pillows are on the floor at his feet. In his hands is a pencil and his sketch book. The same one I first saw on the bus in Chicago.

"What are you doing?" I ask.

"Sketching," he says. "This light is too good to waste."

"Come here," I say.

"You good?" he asks.

"I'm fine. Come here."

Kiyan sets the sketch book and pencil on the bench, gets up and trudges toward me. I grab his hand and pull him behind me. We walk the hallway. He starts down the stairs, but I don't let him go.

"Wait, I want to show you something."

I open the door to the vision room, pull him inside and close the door. I stand beside my altar as I watch his eyes look around the room he's never been in. In the nearly six months we've been dating, he's only asked about the room once. He's been content to let me go at my own pace to show him all of me, as long as I was authentic while doing so. This is another step.

This is manipulative.

You're setting him up to break him down.

"What's all this?" Kiyan asks.

"This is my vision room."

"I see, but I don't know what I'm looking at."

I step beside him and take his hand as I give him a guided tour around the room. The vision boards, M.O.M., the essay, and the altar. We end back at the mirror, staring at ourselves looking at each other.

"This is nice," he says.

"Thank you. I guess."

"Why do you seem hesitant?"

"Because I wasn't really expecting commentary. You're the only person who's ever been in here."

"Thank you for sharing it with me."

"What were you drawing?" I ask as we walk back to the bedroom.

"You hugged over the toilet," he says.

"Stick to painting, sweetie, comedy is not your thing."

"I was drawing you. The way you look when you sleep."

"You woke up after me," I say.

"But you went to sleep before me."

"Let me see."

"It's not done," he says.

He takes a protective stance in front of the bed bench where his sketch books sits. I sit on the bed. The sun is just above the horizon.

I need to start getting ready, but nothing in me wants to go to work.

"Let me see," I insist.

"I'll let you see something else that's done."

He grabs the sketchbook and gets in the bed beside me. He opens to a page toward the front of the book, and I see myself staring back. It is me on the bus looking out the window in full black and white. There is texture and depth in his pencil from the shading, contour, and highlights.

"This is beautiful," I say.

"Why, because you're the one in it?"

"No. It's a beautiful picture whether this was me or somebody else."

"Thank you," he says.

"Do you do this with every girl you date, paint and draw pictures of them, or am I the only one?"

"Would you believe me if I said you were the only one?"

"Would you have believed me if I said I was a virgin when we met? No?" I ask watching his eyes. "Okay then."

"You're my muse," he says.

"For now."

"Maybe longer," he says.

I change the subject. "What do you call this one?"

"Why does it have to have a name?"

"I thought that's what artists do; name their works when they finish with them."

"Sometimes I do and sometimes I don't. These sketches are just for me."

"Okay. So, what would you call it if you had to give it a name?" I ask.

"Riding with Love," he says without hesitation.

No. No. No. No. No. No.

"Excuse me?" I say.

"You heard me the first time," he says.

Fuck.

"You think you love me?"

"I know I do now," he says.

Shit. He can't love me. He won't love me after this.

He doesn't have to know.

Yes he does.

I sigh.

"That wasn't the response I was expecting," he says.

I sigh again, close the picture, and hand him back the sketchbook. Sitting on the bed in my uncomfortable bra and panties, and my dress from last night's show, I am consumed with guilt. My guilt is an extra appendage that hangs from my body, grody, gross, and grotesque. It is not vanquished by his love or healed by his emotions. My guilt grows and grows whether from his goodness or my own desperation, because of what I did.

I sigh. I say, "You can't love me, Kiyan."

"Why not?" he asks.

I turn to him and his look kills me, more than his words. His hairline, the dimple, the cleft, the locs, the warm eyes, and easy smile, all pick at me. I am Prometheus and his words, his kindness, his gestures, all combine to create the eagle feeding on the seat of my emotions. Again, I wait in the space of my own silence to be swallowed whole inside the Earth, but neither the floors inside, the foundation outside, or the crust of the Earth open to receive me. Sitting beside him in the bed there is nowhere for me to go, nowhere for me to run, nowhere for me to hide. I can only bow my head, bring my hands to my face, and let my locs shroud the rest of me.

It doesn't stop him. His fingers maneuver through my hair to my cheek to my chin. He lifts my head to face him. I blink back guilty tears.

He says, "Why can't I love you, Naomi?"

"Because I don't deserve it, Kiyan. You're too nice to me. Too good."

"And you don't think you deserve that because?"

"I just don't," I say.

"Naomi, stop. Don't open a door and then close it. What's wrong?"

I sigh.

I may be pregnant.

The words come easy enough in my mind, but they do not come out of my mouth.

"What's wrong, Naomi?"

His persistence is the reason we're together. His persistence is why I feel guilty. He is genuine and caring and persistent enough to get what he wants, even if it feels like he's just being patient. His persistence makes me want to tell him the truth. But I know he is persistent and patient because he cares, because he loves, and that all of that will go out of the window when he sees the authentically fucked up me.

"What's wrong, Naomi?" Kiyan asks again.

I sigh, blow air through my nose and sigh again. I open my mouth, but nothing comes out.

Just rip the band-aid off. You can't control him. You can only control you.

My lack of self-control is what got me into this situation in the first place.

Keeping it to yourself won't get you out.

It will if I keep from making it an issue.

He deserves to know.

Diedre's words come back to me and I'm overwhelmed with guilt, regret, and indecision.

"What's wrong, Naomi?"

"I think I might be pregnant," I blurt.

"Whoa," Kiyan says. "How long have you been hugging the toilet in the morning?"

"The last week and a half."

I see the pause in his face as I begin to admit the truth I've been hoping, wishing, and praying wasn't true. The truth I've wanted to be a stomach bug. A virus. The flu. Anything but permanent as evidenced by all the new additions to my medicine cabinet. Theraflu, NyQuil, DayQuil, Sudafed, and a Z-pak. Everything but a pregnancy test.

"Were you going to tell me at all?"

"I don't know," I say. "I didn't know if you needed to know."

"That's fucked up," Kiyan says.

"That's not the fucked up part," I mumble.

"Excuse me."

I feel his weight shift as he stands up from the bed. I watch him as he sits on the bed bench. He doesn't lean back on the sliver of wall between the windows. He sits up straight and waits for what's next. He braces himself for the unknown. He's waiting for my sucker punch and still doesn't see it coming. I hang my head. I don't want to see his face, his reaction, or his impression.

"Naomi, what's going on?"

"If I am pregnant there's a chance the baby may not be yours."

"Wow," Kiyan says. "You open doors to drop bombs. What do you mean the baby may not be mine?"

"Ass, access and opportunity," I say.

"What the fuck, Naomi. Who? I've been with you damn near everyday since we've been together."

I don't say anything. I let him process our relationship out loud until he gets to the dates that we weren't. The dates I wasn't here. The day we fought. The day he didn't answer his phone. The night I stalked him on the Internet because I thought he was angry.

He says, "The only time we weren't together is those two days you went up to Chicago for the conference before I got there . . ."

I am rigid against my pillows. Back as straight as an arrow as he pieces together my infidelity puzzle.

". . . Did you sleep with somebody up there?"

I resist breaking his gaze. His eyes flutter rapidly until they narrow on my face.

". . . Who?" He asks through gritted teeth. ". . . I let you meet my mom while we were there," he says more to himself than to me.

I watch as the news of my duplicity moves eight inches from his head to his heart, and I feel my own heart shatter under his gaze. His typical cool nonchalance disintegrates. The last of my lingering butterflies fly away. The swirl is gone. It is dead. My belly is empty. My mouth still tastes like bile. And I feel the color leave my face as I wait for him to figure out what he doesn't know. What I still have to tell him. I am ashen.

". . . Who, Naomi?"

His voice is a roar. It is the loudest I've ever heard him. His anger is visceral. If it were visible, his body would be steaming; cartoonish. His seething has contorted his face so that the dimple disappears, and the cleft in his chin becomes a visible question mark.

"Who, Naomi?"

"Does it matter?"

"Don't do that. Don't do that now. You opened the door, you walked in it, you dropped the bomb, go ahead and let that shit explode."

"Aaron," I say shaking my head.

"Who the fuck is Aaron?"

I don't answer. I let him do the work of putting it all together. I have no more secrets left to hide or tell. My slate is clean, my conscious free, my heart heavy, and my butterfly less belly, burdened. My freedom has constraints and my truth consequences.

"You mean the jumpy, light skinned nigga from NNC?"

I don't answer. I can't answer him. His expressions vacillate between rage and sorrow. I see the pain split down the middle of his face and continue through the rest of his body. He is torn in two and I am the cause. I turn my head as warmth wells in my eyes. I have no right to cry. No right to be sad. I am remorseful, but most of all watching his heart break, I am ashamed.

"Naomi!" Kiyan snaps.

"Yes," I eke.

"Are you talking about the guy that was leaving when I got there?"

"Yes."

"The one you used to work with?"

"Yes."

"So, you had me all in his face, knowing you fucked him before I got there, and you're just now telling me this two fucking months later, because you think you might be pregnant?"

I don't answer. I can't answer. I have no defense. My tears aren't for him. They're for me.

This is why people lie in the first place. This is why people don't tell the truth. The truth neither sets you free, nor relieves your guilt. The truth only brings other people in your shit so they can roll around in it with you. Now we're both hurt.

"We've only not used protection that one time in the hotel room, when you took the condom off . . ." His voice is an octave higher than normal and cracking at its peaks. "I guess you were covering your tracks."

"It wasn't like that," I say.

"It wasn't?" Kiyan asks. "Then tell me what it is then, because that's what it sounds like to me."

"I called you. You weren't answering. I texted you, you didn't answer."

"So, it's my fault you fell on another nigga's dick because I was unavailable. Grow up."

"I am grown."

"Then act like it. You did this because you felt like it. Don't make your shit my fault."

"I'm not making anything your fault." Even to my ears my defense is weak. All ego and no receipts. "We got into it before I left because you're always pushing me to be this way or that way, when I'm just out here trying to be me. If I look like my job, I'm not being authentic enough. If I have on my wig, I'm being fake. You're doing the same shit Aaron used to do to me, but in reverse. The two of you are just alike. You only want what you want. You only care about yourselves, and you want me to fit into it on your terms and not on mine."

"I don't have anything to do with him. I thought I was helping you discover yourself."

"I'm not a child. I'm not lost."

"You're right. You're not a child. You're not lost. You just don't know what you want to do, or where you want to be in life. You glorify chicks that're single and struggling, and look up to women who have no duplicates. Their success can't be replicated. But you don't get that yet. Instead of staying in your own lane, you're out here trying to be like everybody else."

"I see how quickly your love goes. Don't worry about it. If I am pregnant, I'm not keeping it. We can dead this right where it is."

"Are you fucking kidding me, right now? Naomi, how are you just going to make a choice and not even consult me? If you're pregnant and that's my baby, I have rights."

"It's my body. My choice."

"I have rights, Naomi."

"Not to my womb you don't. Besides, why would you want somebody to give birth to your child who you think is lost, and not going anywhere with their life. Why would you want somebody like that to have your baby?"

"Because it's my baby. You may be fucked up, but the baby didn't do anything."

"Well, we don't even know if I'm pregnant. So, don't worry about whose baby it is."

"I can't believe you're doing this," Kiyan says.

"I haven't done anything yet."

I see his face ball up, words held at the tip of his tongue, and I expect the worst. My attitude is irrational. It is fight to keep him from fleeing. As long as he fights with me, as long as he argues back, as long as we are in the middle of my shit together, I still have a chance. I wait, expectantly, to see the next level of his rage. All I get is a sigh.

"This shit is for the birds," he says grabbing his sketchbook and pencil.

He gathers his clothes and walks out of the room. I hear his feet as they go down the hall. I follow. Down the stairs I watch him as he pulls on his jeans and a T-shirt. He picks up his keys from a counter in the kitchen, and that is the last I see of him. The back of his head, his rope locs swinging on his neck and against his T-shirt, and then the door slams.

The sound is finite and definitive. The swan song of our relationship.

I come down the last two stairs to the living room. I stand where he stood. I turn around and see it still there. "Night and Joy." The painting he did of me when I was with Aaron.

My stomach rumbles.

My stomach flips.

Bile rises.

I let it go on the floor, in the space he left early in the morning without joy or solace, comfort or contentment.

My belly is devoid of all the good he ever imparted, all the emotions he ever stirred, and all the love I rejected with my recklessness.

The truth gets you nothing.

20.

The Break-Up

It's been three weeks. Three weeks since I've last seen or heard from Kiyan. Three weeks since I've told him the truth. Three weeks since I told him about Aaron. Three weeks since I told him I might be pregnant. Three weeks since my life turned into an episode of "Who's the Daddy" on *Maury*. The only change is there is no longer a might, no longer a maybe, no longer a shred of doubt. There is a baby growing inside me that I do not want, and I still don't know what to do about it.

Every time my phone buzzes or dings it is never who I want it to be. Every time I open apps to dial his number, search his handle, send him a long message of my diarrhea of the heart, I don't. I stop myself. I want his love, but I don't deserve it. I want his affection, but have ruined it, ruined him for me. I've broken his trust, bartered his love for something less than lust, acted on my own insecurities, and driven away the one thing, the one person who might have been made for me.

All the mirrors in my house and I don't even bother to look. I disgust myself. I want to do nothing, but in my condition, it is not an option. I only have two, and what at once seemed so simple, so decisive, so easy to get back to the business of being me, is now anything and everything but.

It is the reason I haven't called Aaron to tell him the news. His life is his life. My life is my life, and Kiyan's life belongs to Kiyan. The three of us have nothing to do with each other, especially not if I don't plan to keep this baby. But I haven't made any moves that say I don't, that my body is all mine, and belongs to no one else, not even an inhabitant with one half of my DNA. I've done nothing but go to the doctor to have the pregnancy test confirmed, and picked up a bottle of pre-natal vitamins. That, and lay on my couch with my phone in my hand, scrolling through timelines and feeds of, for, and about, the people I am no longer connected to; typing expansive diatribes and never hitting send.

The feed for TheRealAaronMoore is clip after clip of his own news stories. Scrolling through his timeline makes the point I learned in J-school so much clearer: "No one will advocate, market, or work harder for you than yourself." I know Aaron has an agent, but his feed shows the fifteen percent collection he takes from every check is free money; his agent's role is ancillary at best. The timeline for FountainofFontaine is much different. Almost all of the pictures of me have been erased. The only one that remains is the beginning of the work of "Night and Joy." The canvas with the red, black, and blue lines running down the middle. The picture is not of me, but I know what it became, and by foolish choice, and silly reasoning, I choose to believe he left it up for a reason. I deny the reason is because he's doing what everyone else is doing on social media, that he, just like Aaron is promoting himself and his work as a means to a better future. I believe the lingering image of the canvas that became me at night, and in joy, is a testament to how he still feels about me, that despite his anger he still cares, he still loves, and that this too shall pass.

He's posted two new pictures as well. A canvas on an easel painted in all blacks and grays with the caption: #grief. The latest photo on his feed is a flyer for an event tonight. It's been posted in the last twenty minutes with the caption: this may not be a bad idea.

The thought of running into him makes me sit up on the couch. The thought of seeing him, of knowing he will be somewhere I can get to and I don't have to be invited or let in, provokes me. Off of my couch, up the stairs, and in my bedroom, I strip off clothes and leave them where they land. My upstairs is as disheveled as downstairs. Clothes are all over the room and my bed is not made. Downstairs, "Night and Joy" still leans against the wall, take out containers are stuffed in the garbage can, and socks and blankets line the floor in front of the couch, so that when I come home, all I have to do to get comfortable is lay down, and everything that aids in that comfort is on the floor at my fingertips. The only rooms that are halfway decent are my closet, because I'm not paying for damaged rented clothes, and my vision room, which I haven't been in since Kiyan left.

So much for new year, new you.

Standing in the mirror, the bright makeup lights don't allow me to lie to myself. My skin may be glowing but it's still dry, ashy, and tearstained. My locs are thick and lumpy. The new growth is long, and I haven't seen Dominique to tighten the strands. My breasts are heavy, and even though no one can really tell I know my belly is bigger. It is loose and untamed. I look nothing like I look on TV.

This is the real me, and no one is here to see it.

I turn on the water in the face bowl and turn it off again. I need a shower. Turning around, I get into the shower and turn on the water. It falls on me cold, warming gradually. I stand under it until it is too hot on my scalp. My locs are soaked and heavy, and my changing body is drenched. I pick up the soap bar and shower puff and lather my body. I work between the creases and folds and remember Kiyan's kiss. I remember when he would take a shower with me, how he would stand behind me until I was done, and make me get out so I wouldn't get cold. I soap my body twice and remember his. His body was unspectacular by most accounts. Thin and sinewy, no evidence of running, jumping, lifting, biking or swimming, but it was still beautiful. What he lacked in physical presence, he made up for in power and personality. The boyish face that made him easy to talk to, the dimpled cheek, the cleft in his chin. I remember him as I wash me. The hairline I used to wipe my finger across, the locs he let me tug on to feel their thickness and softness. I put the bar of black soap to my scalp and wash between my parts until suds rise from my head and drip down my hair. It is a habit I picked up from Kiyan.

He said during one weekend wash day, "Why do you buy all those different products for your hair, and all those same ingredients are in the soap and stuff you buy from Aunty Peaches?"

"I don't know," I said.

"Just take your soap and lather your hair. It works just like shampoo."

"Is that what you do?" I asked.

"Yeah," he said. "Soap is soap."

"All soap is not made equal. You use Irish Spring. I don't even see how you think it's okay to put that in your hair."

"Don't worry about me," he said. "You're the one spending a small fortune on all these products that do the same thing for your body and your hair."

Since then I've used every product for everything. Soap, oil and shea butter applied to both my hair and my body. I wash in memory of Kiyan, I rinse with the hope of seeing him. Stepping out of the shower, I look in the mirror again and I almost see the woman I used to be. Only now, my uncertainties are replaced by sadness, and my insecurities, sorrow.

You can't go see him weak.

I'm not weak.

But you look like it.

In my closet I can't see myself. I can't provoke thoughts that will talk me out of my half-baked plan. I pull the African print wrap dress I wore to Lexington's wedding from the rack, and the blue pumps with the gold spiked heels. Walking back and forth from the closet to my bedroom, I pull my look together, only stopping in the mirror for moisturizer and makeup. I get dressed without looking at myself in glass. I see me in pieces, in parts: legs, toes, arms, fingers. Only after I'm dressed, and my face is based, do I stand in front of my leaning mirror to apply eyeliner and mascara. I'm enhanced but I'm me.

I wonder if he'll think this is authentic enough.

I see where the dress is tighter around me than before. The truth squeezes my body as I walk away from my image in the mirror. I leave the towel that I wrapped around my body on my bed and remove the one I wrapped around my locs. In the bathroom I keep my back to the mirror as I lean my head backward over the face bowl, and apply oil to my damp locs. It runs down my scalp, the excess into the sink until I rub everything in with my hands. I smell like tea tree and orange, and I wonder if he will like it as I head downstairs.

I move and try not to think, I act and do and try not to let my mind linger, wander, or wonder. There is no more wonder in my wonder game. I find no more joy in imagining other people's highs and lows, when I barely want to live through my own.

In the car, on the road driving in silence, the scenery changes as I traverse from suburbia to city, from highly-developed sprawl to underdeveloped and neglected. It is a metaphor for my life. I began the year excited, moving, going places, in celebration. I moved. I started a new chapter in my life. A homeowner. I added a stamp to my passport. I met a man. Now, three-quarters of the way through, and I am weary. The course of my life, the distance between my celebration and my failure makes my head hurt, and my belly flip with more than just the flutters of new life growing inside of me. I'm in recovery. I'm in survival mode and I'm not sure if I'm the fittest. I have been forced into metamorphosis. Transformation has been thrust upon me, and I'm driving to crawl back into the cocoon, to return to the nest, or the den; the safe place I created away from the ways of the world, away from the mess I've made.

I park behind the French restaurant on Park Street in Avondale beside several other cars. I see Kiyan's Jeep and I feel the flips of nerves in my stomach. The evening is still warm and I'm beginning to sweat beneath my arms and between my legs in the dress. I slow my walk to the front doors to bring down my adrenaline. The blast of air conditioning when I walk in also helps. The restaurant is closed for the private event, I'm not on the list for. It is already well underway with men and women facing each other at tables covered in white table cloths, a tea candle flickering between them. Instrumental R&B music plays in the background. The smooth, honeyed vocals of a 90s singer have been removed from the track, but the beat is recognizable and conjures up memories of blue water and a rocking boat. My head bobs instinctively as I search the room for an opening to join the rotation. I don't see the hostess and I'm thankful. I don't know what the protocol is for when a match doesn't work, when an alignment falls out of line, and the two people pieces come back to the same well to cast lines for other fish.

I search the room with my eyes as I wait. Everyone's representative is on full display. Haircuts and hairdos are fresh, manicures pop, skin shines, and teeth are whitened. At each table I see lots of smiling and nodding between the engineered couples that may not walk out together, let alone submit a matching name that says they want to learn more about one of the twenty dates they had in a night. I search the rustic room with dark hardwood floors and exposed beams until I see the back of the head I'm looking for. His locs are pulled into a tight man bun, and a white collar peeks over the edge of his black jacket.

I watch the woman he's with. She's darker than me, thinner than me, with a head of hair that she probably didn't grow herself. The thin spaghetti straps of her dress leave her arms and chest exposed. Her neck is void of any jewelry and I don't see the movement of any earrings. All of his attention is forced to choose from looking between her chest to looking at her face. His head bobbles up and down, and I know his eyes are dancing between the offering.

Ass, access, and opportunity.

She is offering him what he wants without giving him what he needs: emotional support, safety and security. She is feeding his one physical need with no access point to the other. I see her and I want to laugh. I want to laugh at everyone in the room. Everyone who is trying. Everyone who is pretending. Everyone who is longing. Everyone who is in need. But I am among them and I know I am just as needy. Maybe even more so because I am pretending that I am not.

The bell rings.

I walk to where they sit. Kiyan gets up as do all the other men in the room. I follow their eyes as they all move one place to the left. I catch his shoulder before he sits in front of another Brown Betty with her breasts in her throat. He turns his head one way and then the other.

"Hi," I say.

Recognition alights in his eyes. It is followed by grief and then anger. His jaw tightens, the dimple disappears, I can tell he is clenching his teeth.

"Why are you here?" he asks.

I say, "I thought we could talk?"

"We don't have shit to say to each other," Kiyan says.

"And you don't have shit to say to the other women in here, either, so you might as well talk to me."

"Go home, Naomi."

"I'm not."

"Naomi, you're making a scene."

"That was my intention. Just like you are wearing that suit."

"I thought I'd try something different."

"I thought you were all about being authentic."

"Somebody told me we can't all afford to live life full of ideals and no priorities. I'm getting my priorities straight," he says, walking toward the table where the woman with the wild hair and spilling over titties awaits.

"Then I should be one of your priorities," I say before he sits down.

"Excuse me," I hear him say to the woman.

He closes the distance between us in two steps and stands directly in front of me. His body nearly blocks mine. We are face-to-face, eye to eye, and nose to nose, though I am slightly taller than him because of my heels, it still feels like he's looking down on me. His face flushes and I want to touch his cheek. I want to touch him, just to feel his energy, even if he is angry. I need it.

He seethes as he says, "Naomi, you were one of my priorities. You ruined that. Not me."

"I'm still pregnant."

"You made it very clear that doesn't have shit to do with me. Go home. Figure it out. Make your appointment. Do whatever the fuck you feel like and leave me out of it."

He stalks away from me and sits at the table.

"I'm sorry," he says to the woman.

She says, "Seems like a lot of drama."

"It's not. Just somebody I used to know."

My mind says I'm walking away, but my feet take me to their table. Their eyes look at me and I hear my own voice saying, "Ma'am, I'm sure you're a real nice lady, but I'm pregnant and he's the father. I need to talk to him. Thanks."

I feel my butt bump against hers as I sit down before she can fully stand. I stare at her. My eyes say, "don't test me." I see her evaluating whether I'm worth fighting. Whether Kiyan is worth fighting for. I stare until she backs down. A little.

"I'll be right over there," the woman leans down and says to Kiyan. Her stance is one for a whisper, but her voice is above the volume of the room. She brushes her breasts against his neck, before standing upright and sauntering less than three feet behind his chair. I watch her as she posts up in her tall heels, and short bodycon skirt that rises up her muscular thighs. She smirks at me.

Not today, Bitch.

I bring my focus back to Kiyan. The flame of the candle between us flickers in his eyes and adds to his quietly controlled rage.

"What are you doing?" he asks.

"We're talking," I say.

"We don't have anything to talk about, Naomi. You made that clear. You don't give a shit about me, or the baby you say you're carrying."

"It's yours Kiyan."

"You don't know that."

"You're right, I don't know that . . ."

". . . So, stop making shit up because it suits you. This is not the news."

"I don't lie at work."

"But you sure as hell lie in real life, so it doesn't matter what you do at work."

"We're not here to talk about my job."

"And I'm not here to talk to you."

"Then why are you here, Kiyan? Huh? Why are you here? More ass, access, and opportunity, right. SENT gives you all the opportunity you need to run through and smash girls who will accept a halfway decent man, with a bit of common sense, and a touch of act right."

"Hold on. Hold the fuck up. I'm not the pick-me chick who got insecure after one argument and ran into the arms of my ex, and lied about it for two months. If you're going to air dirty laundry, air it all, Baby, because your shit stank."

"And I'm here to try to make it right."

"Naomi, there is nothing you can do to make this right. There is no more us. There is no this. It's you over there, and me over here. Live your life and I'll live mine."

"And living your life means you're doing this meet your mate in five minutes or less, shit? Isn't that what you called it?"

"It doesn't matter where I go or what I do to meet my mate. It for damn sure ain't you, so you shouldn't give two, three, or four fucks about what I do."

"Kiyan, I'm trying. I was scared."

"Bullshit."

"Kiyan . . ."

"What, Naomi? It's been three weeks. It took you three weeks, twenty-one days, and what . . . two hours to realize that I'm out. I'm gone. I'm done."

"So, you put that post up on purpose, so I would come here so you could embarrass me?"

"Embarrass you? I can't embarrass you no more than you had me standing in front of a man you happily fucked, kissing me in my mouth, and him smirking because he did the same thing the night before."

"You don't know what I did with Aaron."

"Cut the crap. I know y'all didn't go to church and hold hands."

"So, this *is* about embarrassing me?"

"Get over yourself. Everything is not about you."

"Apparently it is, if you removed all your pictures of me and are painting a piece called grief."

"What I do is no longer your concern," Kiyan says.

It is the first time his venom has subsided, and his wrath has weakened. He is tired. I see the sleeplessness in his face. His anger is a mask for his hurt. His lashing out, a facade for other ways of processing pain. I reach across the table and our fingers touch. A flutter ignites in my belly. One touch, even in anger, and I am alive again. It is slight, it is subtle, it is a start.

He jerks away from me. "Go home, Naomi."

"I have a doctor's appointment next week," I say. "If you want to know if the baby is yours you can come, and we can do it then."

"Go with your first plan. Have it scraped and forget my name. I'll block you on Instagram so you don't feel compelled to find your way into my life."

I watch him as he pulls his phone out of his pocket. He swipes on the screen and makes a series of taps, but I can't tell what they are. He doesn't look at me. If he's deleting me from his life this will be the last time I am supposed to see him. I won't be invited to his private classes; I won't receive any more paintings dedicated to me as gifts. I watch him erase me and I'm subsumed by emptiness. In the noisy room, filled with dozens of conversations, for dozens of chances to engage the single, ethnic, and not taken, I hear silence as I watch myself be deleted from his data and then removed from his contacts. Our stars no longer align. My access has been revoked and my opportunities rescinded, all because I mistakenly, drunkenly, chose to find a piece of ass, my dick on demand, somewhere else.

I am a fool and I don't want to own it.

I am pregnant and I don't want it.

I am in love and I can't deny it.

"Go home, Naomi."

"Goodbye, Kiyan," I say, standing up from the table.

"Take care. Be safe. Enjoy."

His formal pleasantries hit me harder than if he wouldn't have said anything at all. He dismissed me with niceties, never looking at me, not making any more eye contact. He's cut me off and I have no choice but to accept it. All the words I want to say in return are rendered moot and still I stay. Still I stay, standing beside his shoulder, staring at the still smirking, brown boobalicious Betty, her patience paying off, as she wins at waiting for her own opportunity for some dick on demand.

I say, "If you want to come, the appointment is at Baptist South on the third floor at nine-thirty on Wednesday."

"I'm busy," he says, still swiping and tapping on his phone.

"I'm just letting you know," I says as I walk away.

I leave him with his eyes focused on the game on the phone in his hands. I bump the waiting woman on purpose as I walk toward the doors and leave Restaurant Orsay. I don't turn around to see if she scurried back to the table to pick up where they left off, or if she's following me outside because I pushed her on purpose.

There is nothing I care about. Nothing I want. Nothing I'm looking forward to. I am numb, and empty, and all I hear is Kiyan.

Take care. Be safe. Enjoy.

Screaming, yelling, cussing, and fussing, I can take. Anger I can handle. Rage I can manage. It is the subtle emotion that eats at me. In the end the patient stranger who waited for his fish has released me back to the ocean that I'm no longer used to, no longer accustomed to navigating, and terrified to swim around in. I am free, and unattached, and longing to be taken captive by Kiyan. To be claimed once again, to be loved in return, despite not displaying the same.

I guess I'll be in recovery from this relationship for a long time too.

My thoughts vacillate between Kiyan's warring words the whole ride home.

Have it scraped and forget my name.
She's just somebody I used to know.

His easy dismissal of me stings. His lack of concern for the child I'm carrying burns. It was the one thing I thought he would want to hold on to. The one thing I thought would bring him back to me. I am left alone to act, and do as I wish, on my own. My own words, a self-fulfilling prophecy.

I'm not keeping it.

I try to count how many times I've spoken lack into my life. I try to count how many times I've said something before I knew how I would feel. I try to count how many times I decided on an outcome before first choosing to go through a life changing experience.

Do I even want my life to change?

Do I want my life to change here?

Do I want my life to change alone?

I mull over the questions my doctor told me to ask myself before our next appointment. Before I make my final decision.

"Ms. Grace, if you're serious about termination there is still time, but I must warn you that with this being your first pregnancy at thirty-four, anything after this makes you high risk."

The warning gave me pause. The warning put me on the couch; scrolling, eating, crying, and whining. The doctor's warning, three weeks ago, after Kiyan left, changed my outlook and adjusted my perspective. I was certain of one thing and then became confused, my decision was no longer definitive, and my future course of action still an unknown.

You could always have the baby and send him a picture after it's born and let him know.

That's too much commitment.

I can't give the baby back if he doesn't come around.

My own thoughts disgust me. I have become a woman I never wanted to be. Needy, clingy, unable to make a decision for my own life. I am beholden to a man who doesn't want me, and the idea of a baby who will need me to fix us.

Just start over.

All the way over.

From the beginning.

"That's always a choice," I say out loud as I park my car in the garage. "Start over. New job. New city. New life. New Naomi."

New baby.

Inside I return to where I like to lay. In the dark, on the couch, the sign above my head saying "Yaaaasssss" to everything my body is saying "no" to. I unwrap my dress, pull the blanket over my exposed body, and look toward the black TV screen and the stairs.

I see his loc'd bun, his thin body tucked into a tailored suit, and I remember the glimmer of excitement he had at seeing me before he remembered he was mad. I see the dimple before it disappeared and the cleft that widened when he wanted to smile. I hear his voice.

I'm not the "pick me" chick who got insecure in one argument and ran into the arms of my ex.

And I'm still asking for him to pick me.

The same way I did with Aaron.

My mother would say I need to start picking myself.

Anything after this makes you high risk.

My mind swims with his voice, my mom's voice, the doctor's voice, all in place of my own. I don't have anything to say and I'm delaying taking responsibility for what to do next. All I can do is lay on the couch with one hand on my chest and the other on my belly. I press into one for tenderness and the other for flutters. I feel nothing. It is what I longed to feel after Aaron. It is what I will long to feel now, after Kiyan. It is what I am unsure I should be feeling, knowing my womb is not empty though rapid growth hasn't yet begun.

"Ugh."

I close my eyes and open them again. Staring out into the spaces I've bought and paid for, curated and created, my mind filled with every thought and no decision. I am without action in the darkness. My eyes bounce around the room recognizing everything, landing on where I know the painting lays. I lay there in the dark staring at "Night and Joy," feeling every shade and undertone of the black and gray streaks of grief.

21.

Bills, Babies, and Boyfriends

The sky is overcast and gray as I pull up to the single story, single family home. I park in the driveway and cut my engine. It's been almost six months since I've seen Tarren, and nearly four since she's had her babies. Twin girls who spent the first weeks of their life in the NICU at Wolfson Children's Hospital until they were strong enough to come home. I've watched Tarren's journey from reporter, to pregnant, to single mother of twins every week in her vlog series on the station website. She's been open and honest about her journey, and protective of her children at the same time. I have only seen the babies' feet, hands, and the tops of their curly heads in the videos Tarren has posted. Her reason, she chose a public life, they did not. Now I will meet them face-to-face.

I pull the gift I picked out from the hospital gift shop from the backseat and check to make sure there are no tags still on the onesies or balloons I bought. Those will go to her girls, while the bottles of wine are for her. Slamming the door with my foot, I walk up the curved pathway to the front door and ring the bell.

"Coming," I hear Tarren yell from inside.

I should have moved in here.

I look up and down Tarren's block and see signs of upper middle class life all around. The well-manicured lawns, the walkers, the joggers, the mothers pushing strollers, the people who look like me few and far between. The neighborhood, similar to my own, gives me a sense of pride and a sense of shame; survivors remorse. The lives Tarren and I live are unremarkable. We are not special, and yet we live in neighborhoods that when bad things happen, the first soundbite in the package is, "Stuff like that doesn't happen here." We have bought our way into high society, where unlocked doors are an everyday privilege, crime is unconscionable, and white flight is real.

"Hey old friend," Tarren says brightly, opening her blue wooden front door.

"Long time, no see," I say.

I lean in to her for a hug and I can smell milk emanating from her pores. She is soft and squeezable and back down to her old size all at once. Her face is bright, devoid of all makeup, a little tired, but joy is across her countenance.

This is what happiness looks like.

"You look amazing," I say.

"Girl, these babies sucked that weight clean off, and took my booty with them," Tarren laughs. "C'mon in and get out the heat. They got me around here looking like a pre-pubescent boy."

"Those jugs don't look like nobody's boy," I say stepping into the cool house.

"That's because they're full of milk. After they eat they'll deflate like the rest of me."

"You still working with a lot," I say. "Those hips don't lie."

"They better not the way they had me pushing them out. You know they tried to come out two at once. The doctor had to hold one back to deliver the other, and then deliver the second."

I smile as Tarren chatters about her babies. She walks through the foyer to the open space set up as both a dining room and family room. Two baby swings occupy the living room floor. I set the tall-bagged bottles of wine on the granite island in the kitchen and join Tarren in the living room with the gift for the girls.

"This is for them, and that is for you," I say, nodding toward the bottles.

"Ooh, Naomi, you're an angel," Tarren coos.

"I thought you might need something to sip on in the evening time, once you put them down."

"Chile, you ain't never lied."

"Okay, so tell me who am I looking at," I say.

"On the right is Madison, and on the left is Kennedy. They should be waking up from their nap in a little bit, because their milk just dropped."

"Wait, you know when they're going to wake up to eat before they wake up and cry?"

"They're breastfed. When the milk comes down, I've got five, maybe ten minutes, before they wake up with an attitude."

Wow.

As if on cue the swinging babies begin to kick against their covers waking up little by little. I watch as their sock covered toes push the blankets that cover them away. Their tiny hands push against the air, and their eyes blink rapidly. The last thing to follow is the sound of their cries. The whines start off simple enough as their eyes bounce from me to Tarren. She lifts Madison first and attaches her to one breast, and then does the same with Kennedy.

Whoa. This is a lot.

"Shit just got really real, huh?" Tarren asks, reading my face.

"You can say that again."

"Yeah, I've stopped even trying to put on a bra. I spent more time trying to pull the cups up and down to adjust to their latch, that I just said F it. If these boobs are going to sag because of my girls, then they're going to sag."

"You're not worried about what your next boyfriend is going to say?"

"Naomi, look at me," Tarren commands.

I do as I'm told, and I look at her from head to toe. Her sandy brown hair is pulled into a messy bun atop of her head. It's still thick in the middle, but her edges are all gone. She wears a milk stained peach colored T-shirt, and purple yoga pants. Madison and Kennedy nurse in her arms with their faces covered by the hem of her raised T-shirt.

"Whoever, the next boyfriend is who comes my way, is getting a package deal. I come with attachments now; and whoever he is, if he's out there, is going to have to be okay with that, because right now, they come first. As you can see, they come before me."

"So, how's it been? Are you ready to come back to work?"

"I'll answer the second part of your question first. No. I'm not ready to come back to work. Nothing in me wants to go out on the street and cover murders, political corruption, or city development. My agent is working on trying to make my role as an online mom blogger permanent, since I've been gone so long. But I make too much money to justify it."

"You could start your own thing," I say. "You already have the following."

"I could. I can. I might. Waiting to see how things play out with Boyce. It'd be much easier for him to add me to the web team and let me keep working from home. I even told him I'd consult for him and train the next crop of investigative reporters. I know Lexington wants to do that. You could do it too."

"I don't know," I say.

"Why not?"

"Because, I don't know if I'm staying or going. Don't know what I want to do or where I want to do it."

"You sound restless."

"I guess, I am. I don't know. I felt so sure of myself at the beginning of the year. Moving into my house felt like New Year's Day all over again. It was a fresh start in the middle of March. Now it's like . . . I don't know . . . I can't even describe it."

"Naomi, that's the way life is. You have good days and bad days. Hell, good years and bad years."

"I just wish I knew how to better prepare for it."

"We all do. Nobody ever tells you as a kid, an adolescent, a teenager, all the reasons why we should want to wait to grow up. They just say don't get grown too fast.

Ooh, ooh. C'mon, baby. Let's get you burped. Naomi, can you get their burping cloth for me. I think I left it on my bed earlier. It's right through that door."

I get up from the couch and walk through the open door into Tarren's master bedroom. It is beautiful. Black artwork and high definition photos from her maternity shoot hang from the walls. Her bed is made, showing off a silver paisley duvet cover and matching decorative pillows that go with the silver headboard and dark gray cushioned back. Two night stands, a dresser and mirror, chest of drawers, and vanity with stool are all in their places in the room. I pick up the burping cloths from the edge of the bed and walk back out into the living room.

"Your home is beautiful," I say looking around the room.

"Thank you," Tarren says. "If you hadn't come over I don't think I would have cleaned or showered, so I have you to thank for looking and living halfway decent today."

"Glad I could be your motivation."

She continues, "I knew this was going to be hard. I knew it was going to be harder than I ever imagined. But this is on a whole different level."

I watch Tarren put Madison back in her swing, and then pull Kennedy from her breast to burp her as well. Her movements are fluid and natural. Her arms move as if they've always held and burped babies. She doesn't flinch, she doesn't squirm or jumble them. She is strong and attentive, and I wonder if I will be this natural if I continue with my own pregnancy. I watch her with awe and feel flutters in my belly.

"Do you want to have a sonogram done to see the fetus?"

"Sure?"

I went to my appointment alone. I saw my baby alone. I got the sonogram and shoved it in my purse. I knew the doctor called it a fetus so I wouldn't get any attachments to the word baby. He referred to what's growing inside me with the technical, clinical term, of unripened DNA, just in case I decided to go through with having that DNA removed from me. But now, looking at Tarren, and her fully formed babies, I see what my end result could be, and I wonder if I can do it too. I wonder if I can mother like Tarren. I wonder if I can give my life over to someone, something so helpless. I wonder if I'm made to be a mom, too, no matter the circumstances that get me there.

"Naomi, if you want to hold them you can," Tarren says. "Wash your hands first."

"Alright," I say.

I get up from the thick red sofa and trek back to the kitchen. I wash my hands in the sink behind the island while watching Tarren.

She is so in her element; it wouldn't matter if I was here or not.

She flips switches on the baby swings and twinkling music comes on as they rock by themselves.

"There you go, my babies," she coos. "That should keep you occupied for a little while. We'll do tummy time when Ms. Naomi leaves, because I know you don't like it. No you don't. No you don't."

I laugh listening to Tarren baby talk the twins as I come back into the living room.

"What?" she says.

"Nothing," I say. "It's just you. I'm so used to hearing you so serious, it's funny watching you with them."

"Kids will change your life," Tarren says.

"Has it been a change for the better?" I ask.

"I don't regret it. Whether it's a change for the better, I don't know. We're only four months into this thing. I've got another seventeen years and eight months to find out."

"Okay, which one is easier?" I ask.

"Pick up Kennedy," Tarren suggests. "Madison is funny-acting."

I reach for baby Kennedy and she stretches her arms as I pick her up.

"Support her head now," Tarren advises.

"Yes, Mama T," I say.

Cradling my arms, I sit back in the sofa with Kennedy pressed against my chest and looking up at me. Her big eyes explore my face. The face that doesn't belong to her mother. I explore hers in return. Her tiny round nose and thin eyebrows; she has tiny white heads of baby acne and thick, curly sandy brown hair. I pinch her toes and she kicks. I squeeze her belly and she squirms with her own baby coo.

"She is precious, Tarren. They both are."

"Thank you. So, tell me what's going on with you. This is my first real adult conversation outside of my parents, and they only come to see them."

"Nothing much," I say. "Just living life day to day, trying to figure it out."

"Are you still dating that guy I saw all over your timeline."

I wince. "Not anymore."

"Aww, Naomi, I'm sorry. If you don't mind my asking, what happened? You two seemed very happy together."

Where do I even start.

I adjust Kennedy in my arms and cradle her in the opposite direction. Holding her feels natural. It feels like armor against my own emotions as I think about the sonogram in my purse, and how it came to be. A baby with a father, but the mother doesn't know who. I look down at Kennedy and then to Madison in the swing, and realize that they, too, are babies with unknown fathers, and yet with Tarren, they are still family.

"Let's just say I did some irresponsible, irrational, emotional shit, and we broke up because of it."

"I'm sorry to hear that," Tarren swoons. "You guys looked so good together."

"It was good until it wasn't," I say.

"You don't have to explain anymore to me. I know how that goes. Somebody in the relationship usually self-destructs and it's usually unintentional."

"Why do you think that is?"

"Chile, if I had the answer to that question, I'd be somewhere raising these babies on my own private island."

I laugh. I hear the joke in Tarren's wistful sentiment, but also the truth born out of her own pain. Her life has been one of lessons learned after the tests, as has mine, as has my mother's, as will be Madison and Kennedy's. I pull Kennedy away from my body and set her back in the swing. I stretch my arms.

I wonder if my baby will be this easy.

"Do you wish someone else was here to help?" I ask Tarren.

"You mean, like a dad or a husband?" She asks.

"Yeah."

"I can't lie and act like it wouldn't be nice, but I also couldn't wait around forever, either, to find the right guy, and get married and have a baby with because my body said, 'Boo, you're overdue,' feel me?"

"I feel you."

"I didn't want to rush in a relationship just to have kids, because then I would know I was probably lowering my standard, lowering the bar, and settling."

"Do you think all women settle when they get married?"

"I don't know. I can't speak for all women. I can only tell you my truth. My last relationship was cool, but it wasn't going anywhere. We were comfortable, but we weren't that serious or committed. There were things about him that I didn't like, and I'm sure there were things about me he couldn't stand. We tolerated each other because it was easy. He had his own house, I had mine. When we got mad, we could each go to our own place."

"Sounds like an agreement, a contract, more than anything else."

"It wasn't that basic. We had good conversation and good sex, but there was no fire. We're better off as friends. Though I'm not sure if we're friends. I haven't heard from him since I told him I was pregnant."

"Ha."

"It's no love lost. People will be in your life, or they won't be in your life. If they choose to bounce out, let them."

I nod my head.

I guess that applies to Aaron and Kiyan.

"Where's your bathroom?" I ask.

"Right down that hall," Tarren points to a space between the living and dining room.

I get up from the sofa, walk around the babies, and head down the hall into the bathroom. Two baby tubs are side by side in the white bathtub. They're filled with rattles, pacifiers, teething rings, and sponge letters. I smile closing the door, seeing the two sides of Tarren's life. Her bedroom that still looks like it is her womanly oasis, and her hall bathroom that has been taken over by her new life.

Sitting on the toilet I look at my stomach, wishing I could see what is looking back at me. I empty my active bladder and just sit, my mind drifting off to wonder what I will do if I have my own baby.

Tarren is so prepared for this, it's not even funny.

Her house is laid out, her parents come by to help.

She's at the top of the food chain when it comes to pay. I think she makes more than me. She was made for this.

I flush, wipe, and wash my hands, still unsure of what to do next. I look at myself in the mirror, in my oversized multi-colored striped blouse and tattered jeans, and try to imagine myself with a big belly and no bra; with a baby on my shoulder and no man.

Why would I want to put myself through doing it on my own when I don't have to?

Tarren's doing it.

Because Tarren wanted to. I'm not sure I want to. I'm not even sure about what I want to do tomorrow.

"So how come you're not at work today, Miss Thang," Tarren asks me as I step back into the living room.

"I had a doctor's appointment this afternoon and I just asked for the whole day off, instead of trying to go in, leave, and come back."

"Got it. Is everything alright with you?"

"Everything is fine and in working order," I say, sitting back on the sofa.

"Uh oh," Tarren says. "Sounds like you've got something serious on your mind."

I'm pregnant.

"It's nothing really. My doctor is just starting to have the talk with me, about, you know, having babies before it's too late."

"They started that when I was your age too."

"I just don't know if I'm ready," I say.

"No one is ever ready, Naomi. I've wanted these babies forever, and sometimes I wonder, when they're screaming, and crying, and pissing, and shitting at the same damn time, if I am a fool for doing this to myself."

"And what did you come up with?"

"I might be, but I wouldn't have it any other way."

"But don't you feel like you're giving up on your life for them?"

"We all make sacrifices for somebody. You're either making a sacrifice for your husband, your kids, or your family. No one walks through this life alone and autonomous, without being beholden to somebody, if they've got any amount of love in their life."

"True. No matter how far I am away from my parents, they still call to check up on me if I don't call them first."

"And I will do the same for my girls when they get out of my house. If there's not someone you're willing to put before you, then you should probably reevaluate your relationships."

I nod my head and look down at the twins. Their eyes are focused on the mobile's hanging in front of their faces. Every now and then they swat at the dangling toys, kick their feet, and stretch their legs.

They are beautiful, and scary, and beautiful all at the same time.

"Do you want children, Naomi?" Tarren asks me.

"I don't know," I answer. "I never really thought about it. Jennifer and Diedre and I, we talk about this all the time."

"And?"

"And I still don't know if I want to travel down the road of trying to have it all. I mean, is it even all worth it?"

"You will never know until you try."

It's a life.

Diedre's voice crashes into my thoughts. Her unpopular position that ignited the argument between us over what was supposed to be a relaxed night of dinner, drinks, and ki-kiing.

Naomi's stable enough to have a baby and raise it well.

Naomi doesn't have to abort. Even if she doesn't keep the baby, she could give it up for adoption.

According to Diedre I have options. Choices. I can choose to go after it all. To try to have it all. Or I can pick me and be . . . selfish.

She called me selfish.

There's nothing wrong with her or her baby—that we know of —she's just being selfish.

So what if I am. If more people thought of themselves, there wouldn't be so many fucked up kids who grow up into fucked up adults.

"Sooooo . . ." Tarren drags out the word to snap me out of my own thoughts.

"It sounds like trial by fire."

"It is, but that's the only way to do life. There is no blueprint, no guidebook. Everybody is just doing the best they can. Even the people who lose their minds and kill their kids, all probably thought they were doing the best they could until they couldn't do it anymore."

"That's dark and morbid."

"That's the truth," Tarren says. "You know it and I know it. We see the worst of the world on a daily basis. There are some fucked up people in this world, and we know for some people, life is fucked up for them from the beginning."

Exactly.

"Tarren, the babies are listening."

"They're going to hear a lot worse the older they get. I'm not hiding anything from them."

"So you will be their guidebook and blueprint that your parents didn't give you?"

"If I can, I will be. They won't know, what they won't know, because some things you can only experience. Like I can tell you about pregnancy, and labor and child birth, but I can't really tell you about motherhood because I'm still going through it."

"That's probably why our parents couldn't tell us nothing about what they were going through, because they were or are, still going through it," I say.

"Perhaps. Or maybe they don't want you to know because they want to spare you the pain of life until you have to experience it for yourself, probably hoping you never know their kind of pain."

I nod my head.

The pain of life.

"That could be different for so many people," I say. "What you consider a pain may be easy for me. And what I think is too much, or Lexington thinks is too much, or whoever, may be a cakewalk for you."

"How does that song go, life's a bitch and then you die? That's pretty much the way it is."

"And things will never be the same," I sing, finishing a lyric to a completely different song.

"Exactly," Tarren says.

"Well, I guess I better figure my shit out sooner than later."

"What's the rush? You're single, sexy, and free," she says.

Hmm. Single, sexy, and free.

I wish that were true.

"I wish that was true," I say.

"What do you mean?" Tarren asks.

I sigh. I turn my head and dig into my purse for the glossy paper with the black and white picture of the inside of my body.

"I'm pregnant," I say, handing her the sonogram.

"What!" Tarren shrieks, taking the picture from me.

Madison begins to cry at the loud noise. Kennedy follows behind her sister. Tarren reaches for Madison and I reach for Kennedy. I cradle her back in my arms and stare down into her eyes. She settles quickly, nestling against my chest. I watch Tarren as she pulls up her shirt and latches Madison back to her breast.

"When in doubt, put a boob in her mouth?" I ask.

"It works for men and babies." Tarren laughs. "Now what do you mean you're pregnant?"

"Just what I said. I'm pregnant."

"I thought you and the boyfriend broke up."

"We did."

"Because you're pregnant?" Tarren asks.

"Something like that."

"Naomi, what happened?"

I have to tell the truth to somebody.

"I fucked up at BJA," I say.

"What happened?"

"Kiyan, that's his name, and I got into it before I left about something stupid. While I was there, I ran into my ex. And then, I ran into my ex."

"Naomi . . ."

"And then Kiyan came to visit the next day, because he's from Chicago, and I ran into him too."

"Shiiiiiiitttttttt," Tarren exaggerates, handing me back the sonogram.

"Tell me about it," I say, stuffing the picture in my purse.

"Have you told your ex you're pregnant?"

"No, ma'am. I wasn't going to tell Kiyan. I was going to have an abortion and go about my life like nothing ever happened. Then he said he loved me, and I couldn't lie to him anymore. I couldn't lie to him or to myself, anymore."

"Guilt will do that to you. I've had my share of fuck ups and mistakes."

I sigh as we commiserate. I rock Kennedy and see Kiyan. How he looked at me the last time I saw him at the SENT event.

Take care. Be safe. Enjoy.

His words have haunted me for the last week; keeping me up at night, waking me when I finally get to sleep. All I hear is his voice saying goodbye. All I see is the Brown Betty with the big hair and bigger boobs, sliding in the booth across from him, ready to make Kiyan her mate in five minutes or less. I replay the scene over and over and over again, as if I didn't live it, as if I were not apart of it.

Make your appointment. Do whatever the fuck you want to do and leave me out of it.

"Naomi, what do you want to do?"

"I don't know. I thought I did, and now I don't. Diedre's on my ass about keeping it. I went to my appointment today and heard the heartbeat and had that damn sonogram done, and now looking at you and Kennedy and Madison . . . I just don't know."

"Don't do that, Naomi. Don't let somebody who's barely grown guilt you into a permanent decision they will never have a part in. Don't look at my life and think it has to be yours. We each have to walk our own path."

"I know that. I just don't know where my path should be."

"Wherever you want it to be," Tarren says. "Nobody can make this decision but you. I can tell you why I did what I did, and your mom can explain to you her choices, or whoever you go to, to confide in, but at the end of the day, it comes down to what you want. If you want it all, then, Naomi, go out there and get it."

"That sounds a whole helluva lot easier said than done."

"It absolutely is," Tarren says. "But does that mean you can't do it? No!"

"Have it all, or die trying."

"We're all gonna go someday," Tarren says. "Might as well go out having tried to do everything you thought you wanted to in this life."

I nod my head and look down at Kennedy who's settled in my arms. I place her back in the swing and flip the switches until the music starts twinkling and the swing begins to rock on its own.

"I just don't know if I'm ready for this," I say. "You . . . you were made for this."

"I'm glad you think so," Tarren says as she puts Madison on her shoulder. "But I'm not. Girl, I looked at the cost of daycare around here and mama's going to need to take a job dancing for dollars the way these prices are set up."

"Exactly what I mean. I'm still making sure I can take care of myself. Make the mortgage, the lights, and eat. I don't have cable, just the jailbroken firestick, and if my Internet goes up, I may start mooching WIFI from my neighbors."

"Naomi, you'll figure it out. You won't have a choice if you have your baby."

"And if I don't?"

"Then that's your decision and I won't like you any less. I can't tell you what's right for you. Only what was right for me."

I sigh, feeling no more sorted than I did when I arrived from the doctor's office. I stand up from the sofa and stretch my arms into the air.

I guess I'll tell everyone what I decide when I decide.

"I'mma let you get back to enjoying your babies," I say.

"Okay," Tarren says setting Madison back down into her swing. "Let me walk you to the door."

I walk between the rocking and swinging babies to the front of the house and unlock the door. I feel Tarren's heat behind me. I turn around and lean into her open arms. She squeezes me against her body, and I resist the urge to cry. Her hand moves up and down my back and then steadies against me.

"You'll figure it out," she says to me. "We all do."

"Thank you," I say.

"And congratulations," she says.

For what?

"Thanks." I let her go.

I cross the threshold and take the winding path from the front door to my car in the driveway. It is hot from sitting in the sun. Heat blasts on my face and mixes with the warmth of my salty soul water, trickling down my skin. I start the ignition and the air dries my falling tears as I drive out of the neighborhood toward my own home, full of indecision. Tarren's voice is loud in my head:

We all sacrifice for somebody.
The question is, who am I willing to sacrifice for?

22.

insecure

The old gospel hymns are loud in the room as I dismantle my vision. The framed essay from *The Atlantic* is down, the printed paper with the thousands of words are thrown into the trash, and the frames themselves tucked into the storage closet on the first floor. M.O.M. has been removed and lays against the wall. Their pictures will go on the first floor. Instead of Jesus, Doctor King, and Obama, I will have Maya, Oprah, and Michelle.

I remove the three framed vision boards from my wall and take the mirrors off of each one. Those I will donate, along with the long mirror hung from the back door of the room. I take everything downstairs. The frames go into the closet, M.O.M. in the living room, and the mirrors and poster boards with my outdated vision, in the garage. Balling up each poster board, I crush the magazine cutouts, and affirmative words until they are the size of a volleyball, and toss them into the dumpster for recycling.

This is somebody's vision but it's no longer mine.
I don't know if it's ever been mine.

With the vision boards discarded, I open the back door of my car and put the mirrors inside. It may be the end of the summer, but this is my spring cleaning. Inside, I take down my "Yaaasss" sign above my sofa. That, too, will be stored in closet with all the other relics of my former incarnation. In its place, I will put M.O.M. They can watch over the house, who comes in, and who goes out, from the wall. I set their pictures on the couch and lean them against the wall to remind myself to eventually hang them.

I pass "Night and Joy" as I go back up the stairs. It's hung high up the wall leading to the second floor. The only time I can see the full painting of myself is if I'm going up or down the stairs. Naked a Noire is still mounted above my bed in my room. I leave the memories of Kiyan, the memories we created together, because they are too beautiful to toss. The paintings are abstract enough that few will ever realize they are looking at representations of me.

He brought only goodness into my home and for that, I will leave his spirit here even as I try to forget our last conversation.

Conversations.

Back in the vision room I look around the emptiness.

I need to find a place for my altar.

The song on the speaker I brought from downstairs, changes. The organ chords dirge and whine as the song with few words and mostly moans, begins to play. Walking over to the desk I pick up the framed Post-It note Dawn left me. Know yourself. Know your enemies. I take the paper out of the frame and run my finger over the raised ink. I feel the ridges of her cursive as I lean against the back wall and slide down to the floor on my yoga mat.

I think I am my own worst enemy.

That will have to change.

I lean my head against the wall and let the sound of the music fill the nearly empty space around me. The vibrations raise the hairs on my arms and my legs, and sweep across my soft, flat belly. The music plays uninterrupted from text messages, notifications, and phone calls. It plays while everyone else connected to me, attached to me, remains on mute. I do not want their intrusions into my life. I do not want their advice or their shame. I do not want suggestions of help. To Kiyan and Aaron, my message was purely informational:

I'm pregnant.

I'm keeping it.

Send a hair sample if you want to know if it's yours.

To my parents, I told them I'm pregnant. For the rest of the world, I posted the sonogram of my full womb and disabled the comments. I did not do it for commentary. I do not want well wishes or congratulations. Not even Tarren's, to which I already said thanks. I posted the picture because it's a reality I must face. I am pregnant, no matter how much I don't want to be, no matter the dubious circumstances under which my child may come into this world. I posted the picture to begin my own journey of clarity, which must start with the truth.

"I am pregnant," I say out loud in the empty room.

I set the Post-It note to the side and pull the folded sheet of sonogram pictures from my back pocket.

I look at each black and white photograph. The grainy detail of the inside of my uterus. The large head with what looks like a serene face. The outline of an arm, the roundness of a belly, what will eventually turn into a foot, and the lifeline from me to it, growing the both of us.

"You are in there," I say to the string of photos in my hands.

Pushing myself up off of the ground I walk to the altar. I touch the water and the oil and bless myself. Folding one of the photos back and forth, I make a crease and tear one off. I set it on top of the Bible and put the others back in my pocket.

I leave the blinds open for the sunlight to continue to stream in and close the door behind me. I see the top of "Night and Joy" and smile.

The lock clicks and I release the handle from the door. One hand on my belly, the other on the banister, I walk away from the room of dreams, aware of my new reality.

I say, "This is your room now, Baby."

Coming
August 2020

Beyond
Bourbon Street

1.

Mardi Gras — 12 Weeks

"This is the type of shit I hate," Graigh says walking through the open french doors into the Bourbon Street hotel.

"And what's that?" Joy asks, dancing a two step behind her into the cool interior.

"All of this." Graigh waves her hand at the revelry. "The tourists, this ingratiating show for people who don't even get it."

"Graigh, it's Mardi Gras." Joy rolls her eyes. "All of this is for tourists. What's there to get? It's a party."

"Yeah, I guess." Graigh lags behind, letting Joy lead the way toward the bank of elevators that will take them to her floor.

Joy dances the entire way. Her body twists and shakes in time to the multitude of brass bands passing the hotel door celebrating the PG debauchery of Fat Tuesday in the daytime. Graigh watches her friend watching herself in the reflective metal of the elevator doors. Her hands shake rhythms into the ringlets of her long Indian temple curls. Her unrestrained A cups test the seams of her yellow tank top to see if they'll hold or let them spill out for the occasion. Her booty bounces up and down then sways into a rhythmic shake. Joy is the personification of carefree. Her light twerk denotes adulting in the daytime; belying the secrets yet to come when the sun goes down, and her husband returns to their room.

The elevator dings mid-shake. Joy continues her shimmy moving the rhythm from her ass to her shoulders. She steps onto the elevator inviting fellow guests to dance with her. An older beet red burned couple sidle up next to her toasted peanut butter arms and join her shimmy as they head into the chaos of the Mardi Gras parades.

"Graigh, what's wrong?" Joy asks half-heartedly, once the elevator doors close. Her bounce continues in the elevator thanks to the music piped in from the street.

"Nothing," Graigh answers, wrapping her arms across her belly.

"I know what it is," Joy says booty dancing in front of Graigh. "You're mad you can't drink."

"Oh really."

"Yeah. No one told you to get pregnant before carnival in the first place. Afterwards sure, but before? Who does that? You know you want a daiquiri."

"You have all the answers don't you?" Graigh says, stepping off the elevator onto the third floor.

"Of course I do." Joy walks the plush carpeted hall to her hotel door throwing her words behind her. "I mean you can't be mad at the tourists for enjoying the delectable offerings of the Big Easy. That would mean you're mad at me. I'm a tourist, and I'm your best friend, which means you can't possibly be mad at me. That's against the bestie code."

"What are we twelve?"

Joy ignores Graigh's flippant taunt and slips the room key out of the tight fitted back pocket of her cutoff denim shorts and inserts it into the door. The lock clicks and she sashays into the room letting her hips emphasize the long and short notes of the trumpets, trombones, and drums rocking the room walls from outside. The music moves Joy through the door, past the king sized bed, to the french doors leading to the balcony. Music blares from the street below. The plumage from colorful floats pass proudly carrying krewes along the route of the twenty-four hour party.

"I have to pee," Graigh yells to Joy on the balcony.

"Ok," Joy yells behind her. "Hey, Mista, throw me some beads."

A thick rope of colorful beads clatter on the wrought iron balcony railing. The clinking sound is muted by the resounding hush of the closed bathroom door.

Graigh unbuttons her jeans and eases them over her thighs. The rough hewn fabric stutters before following her fingers guidance to slouch around her ankles. She sits on the white hotel commode and exhales the tap water from her faucet. Looking at her almost flat belly she exhales again. Another kidney processed stream from the bottle of water she drank earlier whizzes into the pipe. She sits and drips dry, trying and failing to forget the uncomfortable truth. She is pregnant; twelve weeks pregnant with what she knows is not her first baby.

Toilet paper disintegrates against skin. She shivers as fingers brush against her super sensitive sex. Jumping makes the jeans comply over her legs and butt. They remain unbuttoned and barely zipped, a comfort for her mini pooch. She flushes the toilet and steps up to the immaculate bowl sink set in a granite counter. Her eyes avoid the large rectangular mirror hanging above.

Soap in hand, water running, Graigh scrubs her soiled fingers against the friction made suds. Her eyes nearly avoid contact with the mirror. Nearly, but curiosity wins. A raised brow. A lifted lid. One pupil gazes back at itself trying not to acknowledge the rest of the brown skinned face: the other tired eye, the narrow nose flaring just a bit around the outer nostrils preparing to spread with impending weight gain, bow shaped lips that refuse to disappear into a straight line no matter the height of her anger, razor sharp cheek bones cutting angles into her face, the one wrinkle line in her forehead with a small white head near her hairline, and the wispy hairs of her edges raising up from their shellacked gel prison to frizz in the humidity and heat with the rest of her fluffed, spiral curls. Thirty-eight and pregnant. Graigh shakes the excess water from her hands, rubs them dry on her pants, and succumbs to her reflection. It is the first time she has seen her unobscured self in weeks.

She glares at her belly from the raised hem of her blue tee. The thin pointed tips of three previously formed stretch mark lines peek from the band of her panties above the loosened waist of her jeans. The only physical evidence of what tried to grow. What tried to live. What tried to be born. What was stolen from her. Bushy eyebrows frown in the mirror. Graigh drops her shirt and turns away from herself. She walks through the cramped room with the oversized bed toward the brashy music beckoning from the balcony.

Joy sits in a high-backed iron chair, eyes closed, head bobbing to the music. Graigh silently takes the seat beside her and tries to imitate Joy's serene pose. Lids close over brown eyes, long lashes rest on the top of the thin skin covering her bony cheeks. Music encircles her, girding around her, putting a slight bop in her head and a tap in her feet. It is the exhale she's been waiting on all day. The one that alluded her in the bathroom as she sat with her thoughts trying to forget.

"And you're telling me you don't love this. You're a liar," Joy accuses, staring at her friend.

One eye opens with a menacing look but Graigh decides against her feeling to fight.

"It's not that I hate Mardi Gras. I love Mardi Gras. I think I just hate what Mardi Gras means in this city to people who aren't from here. It's just like everything else that people fly by here for; Essence Fest, Satchmo Fest, the Bayou Classic, Jazz Fest. It's an excuse to escape, celebrate the facade of good, and forget that there's still pain. Everybody wants to laugh, and joke, eat, sing and dance away their pain at the expense of someone else. I'm that someone else. The people that live here every day are the someone else."

"So you hate everything that your city is known for because tourists like me enjoy it?"

"Since you put yourself into the equation tell me how many times you've come to visit me in the last ten years? Twice. My wedding and now. Every time we talk it's 'Girl, I gotta come down there for Essence Fest. Girl, I gotta come down there for the Classic. Girl, I'm trying to be lit for Mardi Gras.' It's never 'Graigh I just want to check on you.'"

"Graigh, we are both married, with careers, and families. So yes I want to come see my bestie and get drunk and have a good time. That's not a crime. It's adulting. Besides you only come to see me when you're running from something. If it's not about drama then you don't even think about crossing ten to Tallahassee. So how about you stop trying to kill my vibe with your bitching and tell me what's really wrong with you."

"Well, let me tell you what else I hate first."

"What's that?"

"I love my home, but I hate the shucking and jiving. The trying to be trendy on TV. *Benjamin Button* was beautiful and *Treme* was necessary but *K-Ville* and *NCIS: New Orleans* seem to be over reaches. Performing for the sake of performing. People are only interested because of Katrina and that bitch is old, dead, and gone. Other people live here besides Brad Pitt, Wendell Pierce, and Wynton Marsalis. Jazz, food, and Hollywood's perception don't define us."

"What about *Queen Sugar*?" Joy asks.

"I'll have Ralph Angel's bail money ready anytime he needs it," Graigh says. "He is yummy. A whole meal."

"That's what I thought," Joy smirks.

"Don't judge me."

"But I am. So what does define you? Hating everything you just listed, with the exception of *Queen Sugar*, is like hating cheesesteaks and you're from Philly, or Harold's, Deep Dish, and Garret's popcorn in Chicago, or cayenne, chickory coffee, and beignets right here."

"Beignets make me nauseous."

"So is this a pregnancy rant or is this something you've been holding in for awhile?"

"It's not the hormones. People think because they know Bourbon street, been to one of Emeril's restaurants, and went on a ghost tour for Marie Leveau they know me. That they know us. Just because you can cook Food

Network's version of cajun cuisine and texted money to the Red Cross after you saw *When the Levees Broke* doesn't mean you fucking know me," Graigh yells above the parade music.

"Who does?" Joy whispers.

"Hell if I know," Graigh whimpers. "I feel like I don't even know myself."

Tears cascade down her face as her quiet mulling drones to uneasy silence punctuated by symbols, and snare drums from the high school band marching in shiny polyester down the litter dirty street. Teenaged girls twirl batons and shake overly developed body parts. They strut in white boots and blue and glitter gold briefs past the hotel balcony to the next tourist stop along the parade route. Graigh watches the show below and blows a dejected sigh deeper than the attachment of life growing in her womb yet to protrude from her belly.

"Graigh, you are more than twerking and a second line," Joy says, offering her hand across the black iron table. "You are more than bounce music, Master P, Cash Money and Big Freedia. But when people have watched five seasons of *Treme* and all the other shit that shoots down here we believe we have a connection that makes us want to come down here, shake our ass, drink ourselves silly, and see the reality behind the mystery and the magic. We want to get to know you. *I* want to get to know you. In your element and not just the drama you bring to my doorstep."

Graigh accepts Joy's hand without acknowledging her own shortcomings as a friend. The gesture is their apology. The exchange of energy admits what they will never say in words. The touch clears the air for the truth.

Breaking the embrace, Graigh stands in time to see plumes of feathers pass by the hotel on the parade route. The masked Mardi Gras Indians bounce step and buck jump their way down the street following behind high schools; keeping traditions alive for the drunken foreign assembly who will never care to learn their roots.

"So are you going to tell me what's really wrong with you?" Joy asks, leaning over the balcony beside Graigh.

"I'm pregnant," Graigh says, looking blankly into the yet to dissipate crowd below.

"You are; twelve weeks pregnant. I know you've got your appointment tomorrow afternoon. I wished I'd known you were going to get knocked up when I bought these tickets. I'd have sent the Tonys home and stayed to go with you."

"I know."

"So how do you feel?"

"I'm scared shitless."

"And your baby daddy?"

"Who knows."

2.

"Halvert," the nurse calls from the doorway into the waiting room. "Elaine Halvert," she calls putting extra emphasis on the "T."

"Call me, Graigh. I go by my middle name," Graigh says, approaching the nurse.

"And it's Hal-Verr," Bombei says exaggerating the roll of his "R" as he stands with Graigh.

"Oh, I'm sorry, Dad. I just need mom right now," the nurse says, blocking Bombei's path. "We'll come get you when she goes back to see the doctor."

"Alright," Bombei says.

"I'll be fine," Graigh says behind the nurse.

The door shuts behind them and Graigh follows the nurse in lavender scrubs. Fabric swallows the legs and arms of the waif woman holding the clipboard. She leads the way to her cubicle motioning for Graigh to set her purse down on the cloth covered chair cushion beside the cluttered laminate desk.

"Take this in the bathroom there and give me a sample," the nurse says with a yawn. "Use these too."

Graigh takes the plastic cup and the packs of sanitary moist towelettes from the nurse's cold clammy hands to the sterile bathroom just behind the three rows of cubicles. Five other women in varying stages of pregnancy sit or stand around the other nurses in the office making documented small talk about the past month, or weeks, or days of their pregnancy. Graigh lingers in the bathroom doorway watching the women; some of the bigger ones stand with hands on their protruding belly, while others, apparently in the beginning of their birth journey, sit with their hands on clenched quads.

"Is there a problem, Mrs. Halvert?" the nurse says from her desk.

"No, I'm just catching my breath.

The bathroom door closes soundlessly. Graigh turns the small metal doorknob lock and leans against the white-gray door. Her eyes avoid the basic mirror hung above the sink. Against the door she breathes. Hands beneath her shirt, over the skin of her own belly, she pushes, prods and pokes at her pooch waiting for a flutter that doesn't come. A sigh emanates through her gut but expels like a normal breath. She pushes the sides of her work pants, already unzipped and unbuttoned over her hips to her ankles. The breathable wide leg fabric pools at her feet covering her pointed toe, red ballet flats.

Graigh fills the sample cup and sets it on a distressed, white-wood side table. She flushes, readjusts her clothes and washes her hands. When she is done, she carefully picks up her sample, walks slowly to the door and lets herself out into nurses' bullpen.

"Just set it on the mat, over there, under your doctor's name."

The nurse's abrupt instruction startles Graigh. She meets the woman's steely brown eyes that seem to stare through her and the door to the inside of the bathroom. Breaking the gaze, Graigh tips to the counter sharing the back wall with the bathroom and places her sample on the marked up puppy pad under her doctor's name. She is the only sample under her physician's name. Clicking heels mark Graigh's long strides and her return to her seated nurse. Lavender fabric is collapsed where the woman's belly should rest. The material folds in on itself, never meeting the bigger body that should be there.

"How are you doing?" the nurse asks loudly, undoing the velcro strap to take Graigh's blood pressure.

"I'm doing."

"You can answer better than that. Make a fist for me."

"I'm tired."

The nurse squeezes the pump to inflate the blood pressure band. Her eyes hawkishly watch the needle of the gauge. Graigh works to calm her rising anxiety from the standard test. She concentrates on her breath, making them even, slow, and and as deep as possible without coughing for air.

"Ninety over sixty-two. That's good. Have you taken any medication besides your prenatal vitamins since you were last here?" the nurse asks, picking up her clipboard.

"No."

"Have you noticed any changes in your body. Spotting, cramping, dizziness."

"No."

"Do you have any concerns you want to address with the doctor when you see her?"

"No."

The nurse finishes scribbling on the clipped chart and stands. Graigh does the same.

"Go on out to the waiting room and grab your husband. I'll come around from the other side and take you both to the exam room."

Flat heels click down the linoleum past the bay of nurses to the door from whence she came. Bombei stands as she enters the room. The uneven mix of mothers and the handful of fathers barely adjust their eyes as she glides around squared chairs and end tables to where he stands.

"Everything alright?" Bombei asks.

The long hairs of his full beard tickle her skin as he whispers against her forehead. His soft lips leave a kiss as he pulls her close. She doesn't answer his question, only nods her head affirmatively, that for now she is alright.

"Come on back," the nurse's voice calls from a door adjacent to the check in counter.

Bombei takes Graigh's hand and pulls her gently behind him toward the nurse. They follow her into the office's inner sanctum, around the corners of the maze like halls, until they reach an open door to an exam room.

"Come on in. Mom we want you to take off everything from the waist down. Dad you can sit here," the nurse gestures to a dusty, cracked leather stool by the room's large window. "When you're finished drape this across your waist. The doctor will be with you shortly."

Graigh waits until the wispy nurse closes the door tightly behind her before she slides her black slacks and lace panties down her body. The sable tunic top covers her behind in the cool air conditioned room.

"Can you hold these for me, please?" Graigh asks with an outstretched arm toward Bombei.

He takes her hastily folded pants and underwear and sets them in his lap while she hops up on the exam table. Her butt jiggles with the bounce. A tremor of feeling ripples from a dimple down the sculpted and toned sides of her hamstrings and calves. Sitting on the exam table, Graigh pulls the ends of her shirt up from under her butt and drapes the excess fabric around her hips. She pulls the paper covering the nurse handed her apart, gently peeling each corner until it is prostrate and laid against her legs. She does not look at Bombei. Her eyes filled with with warring emotions over her belly avoid his gaze. She finds his feet perched on the bottom rungs of the stool he placed directly in front of her as if he wanted to conduct the exam himself.

Silence settles uncomfortably around them. The tick of the small round wall clock is loud above the unspoken thoughts of husband and wife. The typical traffic noise of Canal street is nearly muted beneath them. It only asserts itself in the chortling rumble of a semi truck headed back to the highway. The rays of the February sun stream through the large window at Bombei's back, immediately radiating heat on his body. Small bubbles arise on his skin and slide to his jean belted waistband beneath his thin, gray knit shirt.

The heat from the sun will be his excuse for the same sweat bubbles forming on his forehead and beneath his armpits, though he knows the latter began the moment Graigh disappeared with the nurse. His unanswered question lingers. The answer necessary to salve his own nervous energy.

"It's Doctor Marcella," a lilting voice accompanies a knock. "Are we ready."

"Come in," Graigh calls hoarsely from the exam table.

She looks up from Bombei's feet for the first time as the doorknob turns. The doctor's white coat flutters as she steps inside the exam room, and swirls around her brown slacked legs as she presses the door closed with one hand. The loosened ends of her salt and pepper pin curls bounce around the crisply starched collar of her beige striped blouse folded on the outside of her lab coat.

"How are you guys doing today?" she asks, pushing the rolling stool between Graigh's clenched knees and Bombei's prayerful pose.

"Fine," Graigh mumbles.

"Put your feet in the stirrups, lay back, slide down, and open your knees. Any changes since I saw you last month? Any butterfly flutters?"

"Nothing. Not that I can tell," Graigh says, crooking one elbow over her head and placing a protective hand over her stomach beneath her shirt."

"That's normal. It's still early. You're only twelve weeks. Give me a deep breath. Okay a little pressure," Doctor Marcella says, inserting a lubed finger into Graigh's vagina to check her cervix.

"Release the breath."

Graigh exhales as Doctor Marcella removes her digit. She rolls to the hulking trash can and discards the white latex gloves. Standing she scrubs her hands wrist to fingertips over and over under the water from the sink and then dries her hands on rough brown paper towels.

"Now, we're going to get that baby's heartbeat and do an ultrasound to see how it's doing in there," Doctor Marcella says, turning around to face Graigh and Bombei. "Any ideas on what you're having yet. Boy or Girl."

"No," Graigh answers.

"Just healthy," Bombei says, lowering his praying hands from his mouth to speak.

"Well, you'll find out soon enough. This is going to be a little cold."

Doctor Marcella squeezes the ultrasound activator gel on Graigh's tummy pooch and moves the heart monitor wand around in the goop. Left to right, up and down, from her navel to her knickers, and hip to hip Doctor Marcella searches with a stern face, and keen ears until the steady drone of what sounds like "wow wow wow" emerges from Graigh's uterus into the room for the gathered trio to hear.

Graigh and Bombei exhale the breaths they'd been holding since they arrived at the patient tower of University Medical Center. Their audible relief tells more about how they'd really been feeling than any one word answer to contrived questions ever could.

"The heartbeat is strong. Let's take a look and see how your baby is doing in there."

Doctor Marcella turns on the monitor to the ultrasound machine. The dark screen comes alive in shades of black, white, and gray. Warm, world rough knuckles skim Graigh's belly, gliding the wand through the gel as the makings of a baby manifest on the screen.

Graigh stares at the large pronounced head and the oval body. A head, nose, mouth, torso and the makings of feet lay serenely on her uterine wall waiting for more genetic information to stretch and grow before birth.

"It's really there?"

The words escape her mouth breathily. They interrupt Bombei's prayer. His hands drop to his sides and feet touch the ground as he sits on the edge of his stool.

"That's my boy," Bombei says with a smile slowly piercing through his closed mouth.

"Or girl," Doctor Marcella says with a smile of her own.

"Just healthy," Graigh says, sliding her fingertips through the gel of her belly to where the wand lays projecting the image on the screen.

"It doesn't look like a graham cracker anymore."

"They grow fast," Doctor Marcella says. "In utero and in life. You two should cherish these moments."

Graigh presses gently along the places that seem to match up with the sonogram image feeling for her baby's head and body.

"Your baby is healthy. We just want to make sure you are as well," Doctor Marcella says, rolling away from Graigh. "How's your breathing?"

"Okay, if I'm moving slow," she answers, still looking at the screen feeling for where her baby is supposed to be.

"And if you're moving faster than slow?" Doctor Marcella asks, handing Graigh a damp and warm white towel. "Use this to wipe off the gel when you're ready."

"If I'm moving faster than slow my breaths are shorter, more measured, but not quite gasping," Graigh answers. She stares into the monitor, eyes fixed on the image of her baby, serenely sleeping waiting on God's first breath of life.

"I take it then you don't do much exercise."

"I walk," Graigh says turning her head. "We walk the neighborhoods. The ninth, Lakeview, the East, St. Charles Street, the Quarter, Treme."

"How is her breath when she's walking, Dad?"

"It's fine," Graigh answers, wiping the gel and losing the image of her baby.

"I asked Mr. Halvert."

"She does alright," Bombei answers. "If we walk longer than thirty minutes though, she talks to me less than usual. That let's me know she needs to slow down. But we're alright."

"I suggest both of you do some meditation and work on deep breathing. Or swimming. Try to increase your lung capacity. Especially you mom. You're going to need it for labor if you're planning for a natural birth. Yoga could help too."

"I guess," Graigh shrugs. "What would you like me to do with this?" she asks, holding the dirty towel away from her body.

Doctor Marcella takes the towel by the corner and drops it on the sink counter.

"We'll see you guys back in a month. That's when you'll find out if it's a boy or a girl; if you like. I'll leave your chart here. Take it to reception and they'll make your next appointment. Take care of yourselves. Both of you. Especially you mom. You gotta carry that baby."

The doctor leaves as briskly as she came in. Her coat flutters behind her, walking shoes squeak on the linoleum as she travels down the labyrinthian hall to the next room where another patient waits.

"Feel better now?" Bombei asks, standing from his stool and handing Graigh her clothes.

"I never said I was upset."

"No, you didn't. And neither did I."

"So why are you asking if I feel better?"

"Because I can tell you do compared to when we first arrived."

"I could say the same about you."

Graigh pulls the ends of her tunic over her unbuttoned and partially zipped pants. Clothes in place she snatches the chart from the counter, opens the room door and marches out. Bombei catches the closing door with his hand and follows behind his stalking wife to check out.

"We'll see you back here in four weeks," an older lady with a nasally voice and green-veined hands says as she hands Graigh an appointment card.

She shoves the card into her pants pocket and flings the door open on the waiting area. Out one door and opening another Graigh is face to face with her reedy nurse.

"Everything go well with Doctor Marcella?" she asks, seemingly more out of polite policy than actual concern.

"Yes. Nothing to worry about."

"That's good to here," the nurse says with cloying warmth. "See y'all again soon," she drawls.

The nurse waves with an Wednesday Addams smile. It is the only brightness to the woman with sunken eyes and cheeks in a uniform two sizes too big even if it is probably an extra small.

"Thank you," Bombei says. "We'll see you next month."

He pushes the main door to the office open and waits for Graigh to pass through. She huffs by him, briskly walking down the hall and to the emergency exit door, opting instead for stairs than to wait for the elevator. Bombei too descends the steps in the dank, dust filled, musty stairwell until he reaches the ground floor where Graigh waits beneath fluorescent lighting just outside the doorway, hand on her belly, coughing, and catching her breath.

3.

"What's wrong?" Bombei asks, turning the music down on the car stereo.

"That's the third time you've asked me that and we haven't even left the parking lot," Graigh answers, looking out the window.

"The first two times I asked you didn't answer me."

"Nothing is wrong with me. We had a good appointment. I'm just tired."

"Ok, Graigh," Bombei sighs. "Take a nap. We'll be home in a little bit."

He gives her the room to think, and clear space in her mind for whatever thoughts are taking over. He's known this woman for nearly fourteen years, his wife for twelve going on thirteen, is moody and mercurial. She falls in and out of fits of gray just as her name suggests. Keenly aware she's in them, she chooses to brood, instead of talk, to retreat into herself, instead of opening up to the possibility that there are people who care enough about her to listen or help.

Bombei turns out of the parking lot of the massive University Medical Center complex and heads down Canal Street toward Claiborne. The sparsely leaved trees in front of the glass faced building cast shadows across the car in the late afternoon sun. At Claiborne Bombei waits at the light to turn left. A half full street car passes by them at the viaduct. Left over Mardi Gras revelers hang out of the windows of the electric train. Ropes of beads visible around their necks, and styrofoam cups filled with unfrozen drinks tells of a party still going despite the new season of lent. In the deeply Catholic city the site of the spring breakers, the sunburned and spritely aged hanging on to their youth, distinguish a marked difference from the folks on foot with black ashes crossed on their foreheads.

At the green light Bombei turns left on Claiborne opting for the scenic route home instead of the highway. He turns the radio back up. WWOZ. The city's lone jazz station. He catches the middle of a brass band song, one he doesn't know off hand. He nods his head to the steady beat of the music, fingers working to keep time and tap the unfamiliar beat on top of the steering wheel.

The music plays as he leaves Canal Street, the gateway to the city's downtown, toward the Treme. Fingers tap as the track changes to Louis Armstrong's "What a Wonderful World." Satchmo's husky voice fills the sedan scratching through Graigh's armor as she harmonizes an alto hum with the legendary trumpeter. Looking out the window she watches the immediate and dramatic change of scenery from new, modern construction to historic, old, and rundown. The streets narrow. The roads get more bumpy; the potholes more deeply felt. The grass wild and unkempt takes over strips of concrete paths meant to be sidewalks, and spills over the curb into the street. At Robertson and Louisa Bombei speeds past the cemetery. The high walled fortress looks more like a prison than a resting place. It is the only oddity, but what has always been, in the neighborhood that appears recovered. The exact opposite of what they passed a block over when they were headed to the hospital. There cars congregated in a grassy field where a garage will never house the parked vehicles beside the shotgun home the drivers either came to visit or live.

Small boxy air conditioners hung outside of the green trimmed windows of a white paneled house. The paint dingy and peeling needed several coats just to sparkle, juxtaposed against a vacant purple home with the windows boarded up on the neighboring corner. A brick faced church, with a well manicured lawn behind a wrought iron fence, and another old white paneled building that was probably a corner store made up the four corners a block away. The latter also had white paint, dingy, peeling, faded and cracked covered in large graffiti, grass and vines. The corner is post-Katrina personified. Some moved home, some moved home and recovered what was possible and rebuilt what was necessary and some, many didn't come home at all. It is New Orleans. One block of beauty, one block of normalcy, one block of poverty but every block of pride.

Bombei crosses the Industrial Canal slowing on the rickety bridge over the murky water that claimed hundreds of homes. He sees Graigh cross herself as he drives over the bridge. A habit she's had since he's known her. When they first began dating he asked her about the cross.

"Why do you always do that?" he chuckled in jest. "Praying the water doesn't come alive and swallow you whole?"

He thought the joke would break more of her ice, but he was met with a thicker berg than he guessed. She stared at him blankly, wide set eyes sliced to slits, lips parted but no smile forming.

"I pray for the souls who were swept away in the water without warning, for the families who survived but lost everything, and for God to forgive the city engineers, realtors and everybody else who thought it was a good idea to cut a canal and sell folks land on the other side of it, below the sea, because railroad tracks were no longer enough."

He didn't respond to her impassioned diatribe. No head nod of agreement, no apology for his insensitivity. He let her words sit heavy between them, storing them away to be analyzed another day; to use as a catalyst to pick her apart when she was willing. But in fourteen years she has never been willing. She is an open book with most of her pages stuck together.

The lower ninth ward greets them on the other side of the bridge. A community of it's own design where the waves are friendly, the food is good, and the poor Black charity case remains wanted for the crime of purporting stereotypes to desperate journalists without a second source of confirmation. They stop at the light at Claiborne and Caffin Avenue. The campus of Dr. King Charter School beside them. The red gated school where their child will inevitably attend from pre-k to twelfth grade buzzes with activity. Parent pick-up, members of the marching band playing random notes ahead of practice, and teens on corners talking trash to each other and into their phones. The sounds of youthful voices lift into the air and rustle through the thick foliage of old trees shrouding the school in shade. This so-called beacon of hope, that was here before, negates the neighborhood's unearned narrative. It's existence challenges the argument that to live and be black in the ninth, is to be ignorant and poor.

Bombei races past the new fire station and makes a left three blocks later onto Charbonnet. A house painted seafoam green and surrounded by a red fence sits on the corner blazing in the sun. It is the unofficial welcome mat to the block where empty spaces wait for their owners to come home. He pulls beside Graigh's old white pickup truck in the carport of their two story home. It's the sentry among their neighbors. The addition built on top of the original shotgun that was later squared off for more modern comforts.

"We're home," Bombei whispers above the stillness in the air.

Graigh groans awake, stretching her arms as high as they will go in the cars interior. Her jaw drops low into an elongated yawn as she arches her back and rolls her head on her neck bringing life into her stiff joints.

"I need a nap," she proclaims from the passenger seat.

"Go inside and lay down then. I've got to go back to work."

"Ok," Graigh says, reaching for the door handle.

"Wait, let me help you out."

Bombei jumps out of the running car and runs to Graigh's side. She stands in the space of the open car door.

Eyes alight, her lips smirked, hands reversed on her hips, with her thumbs in the dimples of her back.

"I'm pregnant. Not handicapped. You can close the door."

It slams shut as she steps high on to the butter and beige tiled porch; restored to look like the original her grandmother picked out before she was ever an itch in her unknown daddy's pants. Graigh unlocks the white iron storm door and the heavy wooden door behind it. Still air greets her face at the threshold. Bombei stands close behind, the breath from his mouth curls circles of heat around her neck as she steps into the formal living room.

It is now as it was before the storm. White. White sofa, white love seat, white walls, mahogany and glass end tables and coffee table. Large rectangular mirrors sparkle in glittering, crystal frames. It is the room of reckoning. The room to sit in your Sunday clothes and take pictures on Christmas, Mother's Day, and Easter. It is the room of tribute and honor, a love letter to her grandmother that she wanted everyone to feel welcome in.

From the living room she passes into the dining room. The room that once shared space with an everyday family room is now home to a wood slab sanded down by Bombei's hand, and stained coffee black by her. It is one of the many projects they completed together, building projects that helped them build their relationship as they restored what she lost. The table set for twelve is empty save for a centerpiece of fresh fruit. It leads into the chef's kitchen. Where there was once a wall for a bedroom the space is now completely open. A wide butcher block island marks the separation point between the kitchen and dining room, with four black, leather backed bar stools on either side. The kitchen, back splashed in dove gray subway tiles, sparkles in the natural light from the French doors that break up the back wall of gray quartz countertops. The polished stainless steel appliances gleam in the rays. The rarely used recessed lights lining the ceiling remain as unnecessary as the rectangular tiered chandelier.

Graigh takes the stairs in the middle of the kitchen to the second floor. The stairs she demanded take the place of what used to be the home's only bathroom. Bombei fought her on the design. He wanted to keep the three piece washroom. The bathroom he suggested be designated for guests. He thought the rounded, spiral staircase was a bit much for the modest home even with the second floor addition; especially for the neighborhood. Graigh, was flippant in her compromise. "I got it, and I'm going to flaunt it." The construction of a half bath forced her to square off the stair case, but she got her way in the end because the transition from floor to floor still happened in the heart of the home.

Graigh is snuggled beneath a royal blue fleece blanket when Bombei gets to the loft at the top of the stairs. Her eyes are closed but he knows she's not asleep.

"I gotta get my horn so I can meet the kids at practice," he says.

"What are you practicing for, Mardi Gras was yesterday?" Graigh asks without opening her eyes.

"St. Joseph's Day," Bombei says, passing Graigh into their master bedroom.

He picks up his trumpet case and walks back into the loft. Graigh lays uncomfortably on her side, trying to get used to the position she will be forced to sleep in once her belly gets big. Normally a stomach sleeper, her legs are adjusted for the new position. One foot sits atop her leg, knee in the air making a perfect triangle. She lays posed, pretending, with the blanket up to her nose, bearding around her ears, her attempt to avoid conversation.

"What's wrong?"

"Why do you keep asking me that?"

"Because I haven't seen you like this in a long time?"

"Seen me like what? How am I today?"

"Just different. Quiet. Distant. Guarded."

"I don't know why you think that. We had a good appointment. We're through the first trimester. The baby is healthy. I'm healthy. We're working. The house is done. What could be wrong with me?"

Her question bothers him. Maybe because it's not a question at all. It is a statement, rhetorical, a period at the end instead of a question mark. It is her tone that tells him to leave. The upspeak. The inflection. She's baiting him, goading him into a disagreement he will regret. When she is angry her eyes smile and her words cut. Her tone is her warning, her dare.

"I don't know what could be wrong with you," he begins. "I know you're different. Ever since you found out you were pregnant, you've been different. You won't let me in, you won't let me help, you won't let me know how to get into you, or how to help you."

"Bombei, we've been together almost eleven years. If you don't know that by now, I don't know what else I can do to help you."

"Don't shut me out, Graigh, and make it like I'm the incompetent one. I know your past is rushing back at you. I can see it in that glazed, glass look you have."

"What are you talking…"

"You don't want to talk to me about it. Fine. But you need to talk to somebody. Especially before my baby gets here."

"Is that a threat?"

"It's not a threat. I would never threaten you, Graigh. It's a suggestion."

"One you've made repeatedly."

"Exactly. The record is broken, the stick is a twig, and the horse is dead. Talk to somebody. I haven't seen you this way since we met."

Bombei doesn't wait for her to respond. Trumpet case in hand he jogs down the stairs leaving Graigh behind in the same awkward position she argued from; closed eyes, knee in the air, blankets tucked around her frame. Disconnected.

He marches out of the kitchen, through the rustic dining room and to the door, avoiding the mirrors begging him to look at himself, to see the irritation, the frustration, and the defeat in his win. He had the last word, but he was no closer to what he wanted.

On the porch he descends the singular step to the paved walk way carved between two uneven loaves of St. Augustine grass. The grass is nothing like it was when he first saw it, when he first saw her. Standing in the spot where they met, the lawn lush and sumptuous, manicured and vibrant, he laments the marriage that has transformed into everything his home is not; unrefined, at the precipice of ruin and resurrection.

He crosses the grass to the carport, rounds the still running car, and gets in on the driver's side. The jazz instrumental blares as he backs into the pebble rough street. He turns the corner heading back toward the red gated school at the corner of Caffin Avenue. He drives toward his students leaving his past behind. Leaving behind the spot where he stopped when he first came home after the storm. The spot where she stood. The spot where they met about fourteen years ago.

Acknowledgements

Where do I begin? Ooh, Chile, who knows. I need to make this quick because my munchkin is standing beside me waiting for me to finish so I can read him a bedtime story. So here goes . . .

I really don't remember writing this book. Is that weird? It's the truth. *Adulting* was conceived in my head somewhere around March 2018, but I didn't exactly sit down to write the thing until November of 2018. The reason being, *The Appeal of Ebony Jones* and *Love Never Fails*, were written and then had to be released first. That being said, by the time I sat down to write the story that creeped up on me, ya gurl was tired. But me and the Lord got through it in about four or six weeks. I can't remember. The end of 2018 is a blur.

But anywho, my first shoutout as always goes out to my Lord and Savior, Jesus Christ. I feel like every word on every page is God-breathed, because after writing and editing it four times, I still don't remember actually, factually writing this myself, and before you even get the thought in your head, "No, I didn't pay a ghostwriter."

I'd also like to thank my awesome editing team, Roy and Arvita Glenn. You guys push me further and further on each project, and make me think more deeply and differently about my characters to really bring them to life.

Jasmine Williams thank you for lending your modeling services to bring Naomi to life. Theadford A. Christian, thank you for capturing the beautiful images of Jasmine, and Gisette Gomeze AKA GG, of Zodiac Studios you always give me the dopest covers. You've been with me since the beginning and we've got a lot more to do, and a lot further to go. Get ready.

Now to you dear reader, thank you so very much for buying and supporting this book, an independent author and publisher, and most of all a Black business. Without you, these books and all the others would just be sitting in a box collecting dust. So, thank you.

If you've read my other novels, then you'll recognize that *Adulting* plays in both the worlds of *Four Women/The Appeal of Ebony Jones* and *Love Never Fails*. I first introduced you to Naomi in *The Appeal*, you got another peak of her in *Love*, and now both Mosiah and Dawn have made an appearance in *Adulting*. If all of this is foreign to you, and you want to know how everyone else is connected, then I think you've got some reading to do.

For real, thank you for buying, supporting, and reading this work, and trust there's more to come.

Peace, Blessings, Abundance & Prosperity,
— Nikesha Elise Williams.

About the Author

Nikesha Elise Williams is an Emmy award winning news producer and author. She was born and raised in Chicago, Illinois, and attended The Florida State University where she graduated with a B.S. in Communication: Mass Media Studies and Honors English Creative Writing. Nikesha's debut novel, *Four Women*, was awarded the 2018 Florida Authors and Publishers Association President's Award in the category of Adult Contemporary/Literary Fiction. *Four Women*, was also recognized by the National Association of Black Journalists as an Outstanding Literary Work. Nikesha lives in Jacksonville, Florida, but you can always find her online at www.newwrites.com, Facebook.com/NikeshaElise or @Nikesha_Elise on Twitter and Instagram.